DISTANCE

WILL RYAN

For my friend, Shanks
I hope you enjoy it.
Forgive the mistakes -
Will Ryan

ISBN: 1490950974
ISBN-13: 9781490950976

DEDICATION

For anyone who has loved another a great distance away

CONTENTS

ACKNOWLEDGMENTS

I wish to thank my wife, Sumi, for her tolerance of the long periods of time I spent writing the book and ignoring everything else. The same thanks extends to Julia and Erin.

I also wish to thank Ms. Deborah Galloway for her invaluable assistance, encouragement and many suggestions.

Chapter One – A Day at the Opera

Kate Porter Hobson, named mid-ship for her distant ancestor (the admirable Admiral Porter), cocked her head and smiled a smirky little smile as Lt. Commander Pennington "Penn" Fuller, United States Navy, her *arranged* date, approached. He needed some loosening up. He was subdued, stiff and somber, upright and straight-backed in his blackish blue and gold uniform with its stripes and ribbons. No slouch in *his* stride. But he was handsome as well. The uniform was made of expensive stuff, well-tailored and immaculate, the gold stripes shimmering, the contrasting white of his hat and shirt iridescent in the afternoon sun, the ribbons in perfect rows adding a gaudy splash of martial color. All very military, very Navy, very serious.

As he drew closer she could see something else in him, though. His eyes, dark and lively, belied his military mettle. They were cheerful, charming, even a bit mischievous, conveying and promising a humor and irony that softened the superficial rigor of rank and command. At first glance put off by his military bearing, she was now glad he'd worn the uniform. The dress blues would do nicely for the opera, especially this afternoon's *Madame Butterfly*. He looked good in them, an officer for a recruiting poster or magazine cover. She took his arm and spoke to his cocky eyes with her own cocky grin.

“I like the uniform. It suits you, Penn, but they’ll think you’re part of the cast”

“Not if they hear me sing.”

Kate was an old friend, if “friend” was truly the word. They knew each other only in passing, met very briefly at weddings and funerals, spoke a few words, and knew a bit of each other’s reputations, but there was never more than a few minutes between them at any time. They were related in some obscure way, through attenuated tendrils of both marriage and blood, cousins removed so many times that any relationship at all was merely theoretical and impossible to calculate. He hadn’t seen her in years, and she’d grown and matured, just as he had. He was now a young Lieutenant Commander, who, at least to his colleagues and contemporaries, exuded authority and competence, who earned every stripe on his sleeve and every bauble and ribbon on his chest. She was a very pretty and accomplished woman, lithe, not overly tall, with naturally thick, wavy, auburn hair, a dark auburn – no highlights or augmentation there, her shining eyes a deep grayish blue, the color of a mountain lake just before the winter freeze.

Kate’s skin, a northern European skin, was creamy and seemed delicate, but her face was clear and smooth, with a small mouth and dimpled grin. She wore little makeup and subdued lipstick that enlivened but didn’t dominate her pale face. Her gown was simple, unadorned black. It suited her well and complimented the black-blue of the Commander’s uniform. No glitz for Kate. A single string of pearls and a pearl bracelet were her only accessories. Her teeth were natural, too, unbleached and very good but not exactly perfect. Her eyes were just a little skewed, not noticeable unless you, like Lt. Commander Fuller, were a person whose life and duty inculcated the habit of meticulous attention to detail. She was graceful, too, a dozen years of ballet training at Metropolitan Ballet Theatre left her with a tight, lithe body, balanced and poised. In all, the Commander thought her about as naturally beautiful as one could want, and he liked that, liked being with her.

Some unmarried men can meet a woman and imagine themselves at home with her, lying together, raising children, building a family, being with each other for life. At one time Penn Fuller was like that. He was a sailor who sometimes longed for a wife and children, a family that could tolerate absences and take pride and pleasure in the work he did. Unfortunately, like most men, when he had what he wanted, it was never what he dreamed it would be. At sea he longed for home and hearth. On land he longed for the sea, the life of movement, satisfying work, roving, and port towns.

Fuller, you see, was a sailor who actually sailed. He spent long stretches at sea. At least he sailed until he went to ground in Iraq and his troubles began. Until recently, his was a life of movement with no real grounding anywhere. The ship was home and life for weeks at a time, and ports of call were places to see but not to live, some more exotic than others, some dingy, some colorful and fun. He met some young women, but relationships were casual and light.

He thought he found a way to balance home with sea duty during his stint at the U.S. Naval Base, Rota, Spain. Rota was his home port for 18 months while he served as a line officer on the *Decatur*, a missile ship that cruised the Mediterranean. He was with Pilar on and off for over a year, and for a while it seemed to work but in the end Pilar wanted someone who would be with her and not be called to sea for two months or more at a time leaving her alone and waiting at home. They parted amicably, with a kiss, but internally he carried the wound of her rejection for a while, put away all photos of her and gave away any small gifts she had given him.

He subsequently had other girlfriends but he was no philanderer, even while on cruise at some other port of call. He was faithful with whomever he connected at that moment. It was just that the connections didn't last and his real home was the Navy, especially the Navy at sea, not a cottage or flat, no matter how charming. Sometimes at sea, however, he would delude himself with the wispy, gossamer dream of a comforting home, stability, children, a fireplace, and permanent attachment to a mate who understood everything, tolerated everything and took joy in just having him. Rationally, he doubted such a thing would ever occur. The dream was nice, though.

He was happy enough with that imperfect life, until Iraq and the assignment to Annapolis that followed. Iraq changed everything. It left him scarred, hurt, and scrambling to keep himself whole and focused.

He knew Kate already, or thought he did. Kate was a woman attached to home and would want a man who would stand beside her, provide well, be home for dinner every night and be there as she raised the children. At least, that was his impression, fair or not. Even if he wanted to, he couldn't make that kind of commitment, not now, when he was struggling to keep contained, controlled and together.

She was certainly beautiful and intelligent, and would make a charming colleague or friend. He could see that and he liked being with her, but even if he was whole emotionally and physically, there were other issues. Kate lacked the simmering sensuousness, the passion and proud independence he liked in women. She would never be an easy, casual catch; loving her would be a very serious matter, a lifetime commitment to anchored domesticity that he could never reconcile with his career. Besides, there were too many people too close to each of them. Their relationship, if any developed, would be the subject of interest and gossip for a raft of relatives in both of their extensive and complicated families. If he wanted her, he'd have to marry her, then endure a life of misunderstanding, unwanted advice, intrusion and prodding from well-meaning but annoying people. This all ran through his mind in a more or less cohesive manner, and may seem selfish or crude, but at least for now it was just the way he was.

Penn Fuller, despite his ambivalence to land-locked

domesticity, was neither selfish nor crude. He could be very generous with his money, although not foolish with it, and with his time. Naturally brusque and short-tempered, he didn't suffer fools but long ago he learned to curb his reactions and as an adolescent, with some work, trained himself to be patient, unflappable and tolerant until it was his habit, his style, his personality. He was a man, too, who prided himself on his refinement, if that doesn't seem too pretentious, too egoistical, too stiff. He tried to be good and restrained in spoken language, in heart, in the performance of his duties, in his relations with his fellow officers and with the sailors he led. He was proud of this and pride ruled his heart. Even the greatest provocation wouldn't jar a curse or obscenity from him, although he generously tolerated the rude language of others. As a result he was self-controlled, calm, cheerful and optimistic, even a bit self-deprecating and superficially humble.

People, men and women both, liked Penn and trusted him. He cherished the conceit that culture and refinement would make him a better person. So, he always read good books, classics and modern literature works that were substantial, thoughtful, penetrating. Thanks to his time in Rota, he could read Spanish well and indulged himself in the literature of Spain and Latin America, even the poetry. He read the Germans, Russians and others in translation and, with some effort and the help of a dictionary, some French works in French as well.

He'd been to ground now for over two-and-one-half years, teaching at the Naval Academy, and was finishing his Ph.D. work at Emory University in Naval History. At the Academy, he compiled a book on Naval ground and river operations in Iraq which was published by the Navy and generally well-received. In its more popular form, it was even selected as an alternate choice by the Military Book Club. In its academic form, with copious footnotes, extended notes and annotations, it was an original scholarly contribution to the history of the Iraq War, and formed the body of his doctoral thesis. His intellectual pretentions, therefore, were well supported with real if limited scholarship, and he was proud of that.

What was he doing this bright fall day with Kate on his arm, at the opera? The date was arranged in some obscure way by his mother, Meredith Julie Hawthorne Fuller-Chilton, known as "Julie" to her friends. She knew he would be in Atlanta and sent him the tickets. His mother sent the tickets, but he was sure the match wasn't her idea. *No, not mother, she never did that kind of thing*. She must be acting as the instrument of someone else's machinations. He suspected, with good cause, that the genius of this match-making was higher up in the family, both geographically and in terms of age and stature. After all, Kate's father was Admiral Hobson, a military behemoth, next in line for Chief of Naval Operations. Lt. Commander Penn Fuller in the fullness of his career being matched with her was no coincidence.

This wasn't the first time he'd been put into contact with the daughter of someone influential in command or government. Six months earlier, he was invited to a golf and cocktail event at his uncle's and there was paired with Alice MacFey, the pretty, square-shouldered, athletic daughter of Congressman MacFey, who was himself a retired Rear Admiral and chairman of the Congressional Naval Forces Subcommittee. Penn was never much of a golfer. He used borrowed clubs that day and the damage done to his shoulder in Iraq had left him a bit stiff and could be painful. It showed in his swing, which was worse than usual. On the other hand, Alice's game was impeccable, much better than his, but she won gracefully, joking and having fun.

Before Alice, there was Mary O'Neill, another Admiral's daughter, whom he was asked to escort to a Navy wedding. None of these were bad dates in any respect. The women were all intelligent, witty and gracious. He liked all of them, but not enough to call them back, to make a real date, to court any one of them.

What he liked and wanted was someone earthier, a Pilar or

Lucia who is easy, uncomplicated and passionate, who is sexy, could cook or at least enjoy good cooking, would make love hungrily and with abandon but respect his space and leave him alone when he needed to study or concentrate on his work. He had one girl, Judy Connor, in Annapolis, who was close to that, or promised to be. She was a bright, happy blond in her late 20s, a graduate student at Maryland, almost perfect for him, but the possibility of that liaison was spoiled by a JAG Lieutenant, a Princeton man, Pete Moresby. Pete also taught at the Academy, at least temporarily, and he shared an interest with Penn in the early Navy and the evolution of Naval tradition. He also played piano well, was never without a joke, had a dimpled chin and the whitest teeth Penn had ever seen on a New England Yankee. Penn made the mistake of introducing Judy to the young JAG Lieutenant and lost her forever.

Judy was a dim and fading memory, however. Now he was at the opera with Kate Hobson, and he would make the best of it. Besides, even if Kate turned out to be shallow and obnoxious, Penn could still enjoy himself. He was no stranger to the opera and he liked it.

Penn learned to like opera when he was stationed at the Brindisi Naval Base in Italy. Lucia, his Brindisi consort whom he found on the rebound from Pilar, a sometime singer herself, was mad about opera and kept prodding him to take her to a performance. He liked music, but it wasn't at the center of his life, as it was with Lucia, and with his own voice impossibly flat and best left unsung, he knew little about opera or singing in general. Who does? When he listened to music he preferred orchestral work, concertos and symphonies, or virtuoso performances. He liked a little jazz and Bossa Nova for variety, some other Latin music as well. Pop and rock alternately bored and annoyed him.

Lucia persisted, however, and finally all her urging and pleading worked. She managed to drag him to a local performance of *La Sonnambula*, Bellini's bit of grand opera fluff. He went along grimly, expecting to be bored comatose but was surprised to find it sensuous and exciting, and that he liked it. That night was followed by other operas in town and in the surrounding area. They were all 19th Century Italian works, fun and dramatic, if not always logical. It was the music and singing that mattered, not whether the plot or characters were either plausible or even sensible. Penn lost Lucia when he was sent to Iraq. She found another officer, a Lieutenant Commander named Marco Benedetti, and moved in with him the day Penn left.

After Brindisi there was Iraq, combat, chaos, pain, recuperation and repatriation. Assignment to the Naval Academy followed. The current phase of his life and career began.

All this ran through his mind as he and Kate milled with others in the theatre lobby. He bought glasses – plastic cups, actually – of white wine for Kate and himself, and Kate, discovering two of her friends, introduced them, Geoff someone and his fiancée Jennifer someone else. They conversed briefly.

"In the Navy, huh?" Long, tall Geoff wore a tightly-knotted knit argyle tie that seemed to be stapled to his Adam's apple. It bobbed up and down as he spoke. It was distracting.

"Yes"

"What brings you to Atlanta?"

"I'm meeting with my dissertation committee at Emory"

Blank looks

"I'm reporting on my dissertation. I'm trying to complete my doctorate."

"I thought you were in the Navy"

"I teach at Annapolis"

"Oh. Never been there. Heard it's some town," said Geoff unconvincingly. Geoff, in truth, had only the vaguest idea where Annapolis is. He thought it was somewhere in Virginia or Maryland, maybe Delaware. Geography wasn't his strong point. A child of the internet and GPS, he probably couldn't have found it on a map.

They smiled and fidgeted with their drinks. For a flash Penn wished he was holding a glass of Scotch rather than white wine.

Mercifully, the lights blinked on and off warning the performance would start in a few minutes.

"Well, good luck on your doctorals"

"Yes, thank you"

Geoff started to turn toward the Mezzanine, but wheeled back around, deftly pulling a card case from his breast pocket.

"By the way I'm with Southern Mutual Bank, if you're ever interested in a mortgage, let me know."

A card was offered.

"Thanks. I will."

The card, printed on glossy stock, was bright blue. There was a picture of a wizard conjuring up money with the caption, in elaborate script, "SOMU, Where Lending Magic Happens."

Penn took the card and put it in his pocket. It was later destroyed by the dry cleaner.

They had exceptionally good seats (an easy $35 each) in a suburban theater hardly 4 years old, comfortable, well ventilated, engineered with acoustics that would carry a whisper from the stage to the last row. The singers were unknown, at least to Penn, but the orchestra was well-led, the sets and costumes perfect and the singing – if not star class – still angelic in its own way. From Pinkerton's first tour of his house in Scene 1 to the tragic and lovely aria *Un Bel di* and the final grim denouement, the acting struck the right balance between stage pathos and reality, every note was made beautifully, every inflection and accent precise throughout the opera.

The Diva, Hye Young Rhee, was Korean, beautiful, well-trained in Korea, at Curtis and at Rome's Accademia Nazionale di

Santa Cecilia. For a singer capable of taking on the difficult role of Cio-Cio San, she was young and thin, although not too thin, and her voice was rich with a warm vibrato that underscored the pathetic irony and deep pathos of the role. Her Pinkerton, Emmanuel Goldstein, was a strapping, muscular young graduate of Julliard with a rich, warm voice. He looked every inch a Navy officer and wore the uniform respectfully and well. Suzuki was sung by a very young Japanese woman, Yoshiko Fujiyama, who trained in Japan and at Curtis in Philadelphia, concurrently earning an arts degree from the University of Pennsylvania. She had a fine, clear voice, perhaps not quite mature but time would add the right touch of darkness to the color of her sound. Her timing, pronunciation, and acting were superb. She was pretty as well, with a heart-shaped face, a compact body, graceful moves and just the right emotive skill.

Yoshiko had a strong stage presence, too. Although she played a character confined to the shadowy world of servants in a drama that focuses so much on the two main actors, she drew your attention effortlessly when she was on stage, or at least Penn's attention. It was hard for Penn to concentrate on the others when Yoshiko was on the set. She sang so well, seemed so beautiful, was so engagingly pathetic, and had such delightfully round hips.

Penn had done his research on the opera. He knew the first Japanese Diva to perform *Butterfly* in America was Tamaki Miura, who sang the role around the world for three decades, starting in the 1910s. She was good and audiences loved her. There is even a statue honoring her in Glover Garden, Nagasaki, the city where the opera is set. Since Ms. Miura's last performance in the United States, only three or four Japanese Divas have appeared as *Butterfly*, despite thousands of performances. Perhaps even now, with a little more effort Yoshiko could go to that height. Certainly, in a few years, if she kept at it, if her voice matured just a bit, she could be an iconic *Butterfly.* Of course, *Butterfly* wouldn't be her only role, but it was so difficult to sing and such a popular opera that to be accomplished in that role would assure exposure, employment, the gradual rise to international stardom and a variety of roles from the canon of opera as well as ample opportunity for recitals and recording.

The opera ended, of course, with poor Butterfly expiring in a paroxysm of song and music, and a flood of sorrow, pity, and red stage blood. Kate softly shed a tear. There was a standing ovation. Flowers. Penn was moved, but found himself more interested in pretty Yoshiko Fujiyama than Kate, and wondered if there was any way he could contrive to meet her. His own fickleness astounded him. He usually put aside everyone else when he was with a date. The impulse passed, although not without a struggle, and disciplined sailor that he was, he steered his mental ship back to its proper destination.

"Did you like it?" she sniffed.

"I don't know if 'like' is adequate," he said. "The performance, everything, was extraordinary, beyond words." Ms. Fujiyama flashed in his mind again.

"I saw it at the Met last year. Patricia Racette sang Butterfly. It was a marvelous performance, but this was marvelous, too."

"Patricia Racette?" he shook his head, acknowledging his ignorance. "I'm not an opera buff, but I learned to love the art in Italy. I'm trying to cultivate my knowledge of it."

"You're a funny guy," she said, "I was warned you were the sailor's sailor, all salt and strength, brave and fearless on land and sea. I expected tattoos and a can of spinach. Instead I get an opera lover who's working on his Ph.D."

"Every man has his foibles and follies," he said.

"Oh, and yours is opera?"

"No," he said, as he opened the car door, "My folly," he winked "is beautiful women," which was the truth.

He smiled. She blushed. The first time in years. She liked him, really liked him, and that surprised her because she had been resigned to find him dull, coarse, and superficial. Instead, he seemed sensitive, very polite, and quiet but not boring because he seemed to enjoy her and where they were and what they did, and that simple pleasure in her company spoke more to her than wit or babble or jokes.

She followed him to the Park Tavern, where they dined on salad and large hanger steaks washed down with *Three Philosophers Beer*. She told him about her career at the CDC, about attending Georgia Tech and Emory and her dreams.

"I know it sounds corny, a cliché, but I want to make some sort of difference if I can. You can do that in Public Health. I'm still an apprentice, I know, learning things, but one day I'll be able to take on projects, perhaps here and maybe, if I can, overseas in Africa or Asia. Public Health is one, you know, around the world. One. What happens in a village in Africa, or in a town in the Cambodian countryside can affect us, all of us."

"I never really thought much about it, but of course you're right."

"There has been so much going on in the past few years with global ramifications– SARS, Ebola breakouts, Bird Flu, H1N5, H7N9, even HIV… You know how many people die in the United States every year from regular flu?" she said.

"I have no idea" The Hs and Ns, he knew, designated flu strains. Other than that he knew little or nothing.

"40,000. Could you image the public outrage if, say, 40,000 people died of accident or food poisoning?" She didn't wait for an answer. "It would be tremendous."

He was quiet. They both were for a few minutes, but it wasn't uncomfortable, just a short break.

"I suppose you feel that way about your profession, too."

He thought for a moment before answering.

"The Navy is my home in a way. I enlisted at 17 – my parents were furious – but I was able to apply to Annapolis the next year and with extraordinary luck was accepted from the fleet. The Navy's been my career, my income, my home for 16 years. I know ships but less of shore operations. The service has let me attend universities and I'm about to earn my doctorate. The dissertation committee accepted my thesis with the provision that I make some minor revisions of form, not content, so I'm very close to completing it. But it's more than that…

A pause. She was about to say something when he went on.

"Many officers, perhaps most, and many other service members, are romantics at heart. The military is a career, of course, and they pay you, but for us, some more than others, it's not just a job, the feeling goes deeper. I'll sometimes hear young soldiers and sailors talk of their patriotism, but it's even more than that. Under it all, again for some of us, is a feeling of service to mankind, of being the shield and defender not only of the U.S., but of man's dream of freedom, the protectors of liberty, the rescuers from evil and tyranny, the shield of civilization and hope. Now that sounds corny, I know."

"It doesn't sound corny to me." Her eyes seemed to water a bit, whether from emotion or steam from the grill he couldn't tell, "You're an idealist."

Another pause. He grinned, breaking the tension.

"I'm a sailor man. I'll fight to the finish if I gets me spinach."

She laughed. "Have a tattoo?"

"Not one I show to nice girls." He winked.

The rest of the evening was fluff. Family gossip of sorts. Kate described her family. He described his. They talked a little of college and of Europe, comparing notes of the museums they'd visited and the towns they'd seen. He was never overtly flirtatious or risqué, but the few hints of something closer than friendship he seemed to offer were all the more attractive for their subtlety. After dinner, they went for a long walk in Piedmont Park. The sun was setting, but it wasn't entirely dark yet. The evening was cool and the grass green and fresh. By the time they returned to their cars, it was dark, but still bright under a gibbous moon and a sky filled with stars. He walked her to her car, took her hands in both of his and kissed them warmly. She wished he would hold her and kiss her on the lips, but he didn't and instead she smiled, thanked him, and left him with the promise that they'd do it again sometime. She had to get away quickly. She was falling for him.

****

Chapter Two – Kate

One would think that a woman like Kate, whose father was an Admiral, would know that military men, especially officers of the Navy, could be cultured, or at least respect culture, and be gentle as well as hard and professional. A man like Penn should not be a surprise to her. But Kate was no service brat. Her parents divorced when she was just eight years old, and her mother remarried little more than a year later. Her mother's new husband was a banker, or at least a man who worked in the bank's bureaucracy, much like an obscure bishop toils in the secret halls of the Vatican. Over the years as his career blossomed, he became a very wealthy banker.

Charles "Chip" Collins, Kate's step-father, wasn't an overly affectionate man, at least not demonstrably so, but he was unfailingly kind to Kate. He could afford to be. From a career of using other people's money to gamble on derivatives, from bundling mortgages, and from credit default swaps and other schemes and swindles just this side of the law, he earned a large salary, huge bonuses and other emoluments that enabled him without any effort or strain whatsoever to give Kate and her mother all they needed or wanted. He profited even from the bankruptcy of his old bank with a lavish separation package. The week the old bank collapsed, his separation bonus intact while the shareholders were left with little or nothing, he settled into a new, lucrative position at the bank that absorbed the residue of physical assets and toxic bonds left in the carcass of the now defunct bank.

"Chip" sent Kate to the very best schools, including Georgia Tech and Emory (although she could have gone to Harvard or Yale – she had the grades and test scores – or even Oxford – the cost was all pocket change to him), allowed her summer travel in Europe and Asia, her junior abroad in Paris at the Sorbonne, and gave her an allowance so generous that any tradesman would have gladly taken it as salary. She was no spendthrift, however. She husbanded her money, saving and investing what she didn't spend. Chip also encouraged her to pursue whatever career she desired; he figured she would marry well anyway and her real career would be wifing a rich husband. She handled all of this well. Instead of degenerating into a spoiled, self-centered lump, she took pleasure in studying and learning, was curious about the world and how it worked, liked studying languages and peoples, and used her gifts well. She majored in Public Policy at GA Tech, planning on law school after graduation. A summer internship at the CDC, however, diverted her interest and instead of Law School, she spent a year at Emory earning a Master's in Public Health, with her eye on a career at the CDC.

Right now, she wanted only to continue as she was, working as a civil servant at the CDC, giving her time and energy to tasks that were mostly beneath her intellect but vital to the agency's mission. She saved almost all the money she made. She lived at home, where she had her own apartment on the far wing of their large, mansion-like house in Buckhead. She was free to come as go as she pleased, or to entertain anyone privately at any time. She drove a spotless powder blue BMW convertible given to her by her step-father for her 25th birthday, dated any number of good men none of whom she ever loved to any degree, not enough to marry or even to date steadily or to sleep with, and was generally happy.

The date with Penn she accepted as a kind of duty. Her mother, Allyson, asked her to go. Allyson was a force of her own. She was intelligent and direct but she was also a strikingly beautiful woman, even more beautiful in her late 40s (actually 51) than she'd been in her 20s, her body fuller, her face mature but lovely with bright blue eyes, thick auburn hair with a touch of artificial red highlights, a high forehead, smooth pink skin, her mouth a cupid's bow, her hips delightfully round, her breasts ample and her legs long and famous.

Not all of this was natural, but the artificial enhancements, bought at some expense by her doting husband, Chip, were well done. No toxic assets there.

Allyson knew Penn's Mother, Julie Chilton (Or Fuller-Chilton. She hyphenated her name after the tragic death of her first husband, Penn's father, and her marriage to Roger Chilton.) more by reputation than by any personal contact, although they had met and conversed once or twice. Their husbands were much closer. The two men were business associates who sometimes golfed together when either was in the other's neighborhood. As husbands and wives, they had been to dinner together a few rare times, expensive dinners in glittering restaurants in New York paid-for by the magic of expense accounts. The boys chatted business. The girls listened and went to the powder room together to fix their makeup. It was as close to friendship as the two women ever got.

The call from Julie was, therefore, a surprise. In the absence of some special event, like the rare business dinner, the usual form of communication between their families was a corporate Christmas card with a sterile "Season's Greetings" that contained a Xeroxed family newsletter.

"Julie! What a surprise."

"Allyson, it's been so long since we had a chat."

Pleasantries passed from one to another. Everyone is well, thank you. Things are great. We're still here, in Buckhead, in Vermont, in wherever. Yes, he recovered. No, our old dog, Banner, died last year. He was 14. My mother is doing well, thank you. Chip sends his regards, so does Roger.

"Look, the reason I'm calling, my son, Penn, is going to be in Atlanta for a week. He's meeting with his dissertation committee at Emory – he's finishing his Ph.D., you know, and I've gotten him a special little gift. While he was in Italy…"

"He was in Italy? What was he doing in Italy?"

"He's in the Navy, you know."

"Oh, that's right, he graduated from Annapolis, didn't he?"

"Yes, yes. Anyway, while he was stationed in Italy he started attending the opera and became quite a fan."

"I didn't know"

"Well, I found out the Atlanta Opera is doing "Madame Butterfly" this weekend and I was able to get him two tickets. I thought it might be fun if he and Kate got together and went."

"You mean like a date?" She was cautious. The odor of matchmaking clung to the proposal.

"Well, really, just an afternoon – it's the Sunday Matinee performance. They could meet at the Theatre. He's staying somewhere near it, I think. And I'm sure it's not far from where you live, is it?"

"Huh… I'll check with Kate. If she's available I'm sure she'll want to go." This was said without conviction. Kate's social life was a mystery to Allyson. She knew that Kate must have one, but Kate either never confided in her, or never had anything to confide. She knew her daughter occasionally went out, but with whom and where were not known to her, and really were of little concern to her. Kate was too level-headed to be a concern to anyone.

Kate was available. This was duly conveyed back to Julie, who told Penn, who then called Kate and arranged to meet her at the ill-named Cobb Energy Center, with its well-designed theater, the venue for the National Lyric Opera, a traveling company reputed to be quite good, visiting Atlanta for a few days. Through this circuitous route, Kate and Penn came together.

It would appear, at least on the surface, as if Julie arranged everything. Julie, however, was prodded to do it by Harriet, Great Aunt (or as she preferred, "Grand Aunt") Harriet, of Waterbury, Vermont, reigning family matriarch. Harriet seemed to be in contact with everyone, and generally was. Penn, however, was her special project. He chose a career in the Navy, the last of his line to do so, and she eagerly followed his career from the moment of his matriculation at the Naval Academy. She was a Navy wife and widow who knew the service intimately and all who drove it -- Admirals, Navy Secretaries, even presidents. She shared in the whispered secrets, rumors and gossip with Navy wives and women all her adult life, and her tendrils and associations spread virtually throughout the world, or at least to those parts of the world the Navy went.

Harriett's late husband, Marion Butler, 20 years her senior, was a Captain slated for promotion to Rear Admiral when he died in an accident during the Inchon Landing in Korea in 1950. An observation plane's engine failed and it crashed into the bridge of his ship killing him, the quartermaster and the first officer. The pilot survived uninjured. Since Marion Butler was already selected for the rank, he was posthumously decorated with the Navy Cross and Purple Heart, promoted and buried a Rear Admiral. His grave is in Arlington, with a space reserved at his side for his wife. President Truman sent the Rear Admiral's silver two-star pins to Harriet with a personal note attached, and Harriet had them set in a broach with diamonds and rubies, a broach she always wore, less to remind herself of Marion than to let others know she was an Admiral's widow.

Harriet's father was Navy as well, as was her brother and her uncle, and then there was the great uncle, Vice Admiral Pennington, whose long service to the country culminated with his death in Japan after the war, another accidental death, another aircraft. The Navy line went back further than that, however. She could trace Naval officers in the family back virtually to the days of Commodores Barry and Truxtun. Penningtons, Porters, Fullers, Butlers, McElreaths, Ryans, O'Neills, Petersons – all ancestors who were Navy and who held rank from Lieutenant and Master Commandant to Captain, Commodore and Admiral.

Penn Fuller was now the only one in the family carrying on the Navy tradition, and she wanted to put him on the road to a star and a flag, to see him advance in rank as rapidly as possible before she died. He was still single, not a handicap during the first decade of his career, but he needed now to marry and to marry well. Hence the hunt for suitable brides, women that would bring to Penn influence and to Harriet hope. Kate Hobson was a prize, better even than the Congressman's daughter. Congressmen were always diddling someone, getting into trouble and losing seats. They might be helpful for a while but they weren't reliable in the long run. Kate's father would be the next Chief of Naval Operations. There was no question of that. Harriet's sources were impeccable and the projection of his promotion was made with absolute certainty. That was the kind of patron Penn needed. Without a four-star behind him, he'd probably rise to Captain then be pushed into retirement in his twenty-eighth year of service. No, she wanted him poised for two stars at least, perhaps three. He didn't have the political connections to become CNO, but he could come close, and if he came close well… sometimes luck and position, or war, does everything for you.

In contrast, Allyson, Kate's mother, was a practical woman. She grew up in a house run by tight-fisted New England Yankees and was brought up to be a realist, a person who could calculate the bottom line and see the potential or lack of potential in any endeavor. Her days in prep school at the Abingdon Lyceum, a Quaker academy, were marked by activities in the Student UN, the Economics Club, the Math Club and on the Hockey Field. She was part of the school academic team who cruised to victory on a TV student quiz show, GPA (Great Potential Americans). She had her pick of colleges and universities to attend, and she picked Amherst because it offered her a full scholarship including room and board. There, she eschewed the arts classes and majored in Economics. It wasn't enough for her, however, and she spent her summers at the

University of Massachusetts studying accounting, finance and quantitative business solutions. UMass changed her life.

At UMass she met Will Hobson, who was pursuing his MBA, cramming courses in a fervid attempt to earn the degree in 12 months. He was athletic, not terribly tall, but some inches taller than Allyson, who was 5'5" – add two inches for heels -- and he was strong, mature, immensely confident, a natural leader, a good friend, a person others looked up to. He was invariably cheerful, too, and had a way of reducing complex issues to simple ideas and simple choices that was both charming and powerful. He noticed her in class (in truth he had trouble keeping his eyes off her). He was angling for a way to get closer to her when he found her one evening sitting in an empty classroom stymied by a problem in business quant. It was a complex problem in simultaneous quadratic equations that called for a solution using differential equations. His undergraduate major at the University of Michigan was math and this was his meat. He took her through the problem in a manner that was so clear and logical it made the process and solution seem obvious. If her professor, with his Ph.D. from Columbia, had the skill of this student, she would never have had a problem.

Will was a Navy Lieutenant on active duty assigned to the university for a year to earn a Master's in Business. The Navy wanted more officers whose training included management and business solutions. His career was already on a fast track. He could make brilliant presentations, had a capacity for seeing through even the knottiest problems, and unlike some very capable people was able to use his gifts in a way that didn't alienate his peers or annoy his superiors. Everyone liked him. He could bring you through an issue, show the solution or at least point out the alternatives and their negative and positive sides, and make you feel that you had done it. That's a rare talent and a precious gift in a technology-driven world. He was infinitely patient as well and if one explanation didn't work, he'd try another until understanding began to dawn and the person he was instructing finally got it.

Practical Allyson practically fell for him that afternoon. She began to seek him out. She registered for courses he was taking and sat next to him. By the time he earned his MBA they were engaged. They were married six months later in a grand Navy ceremony – white uniforms, a sword arch, all the traditional display that makes those weddings special. The first few years together were very good, there was novelty of the baby and the newness of Navy life. That passed, however, and she soon found herself bored with the sideshow of being an officer's wife, even an officer as exciting as Will.

As the years went on, she grew more and more dissatisfied. The long separations while he was at sea or on some foreign detail, she living in the shadow of his career with little to do on her own, the limitations of Navy pay and the general tackiness, even shabbiness of military bases got to her. Will could see none of this. He was a zealot. The Navy to him was a calling, a religion, a home, a family, an icon of something pure and stellar. He wanted most of all to be part of this great thing that was so powerful and had such a magnificent mission. She wanted a career, to be free to grow and develop on her own, and to participate in her husband's career, too. There was none of this in her life as his wife. His career did blossom. He was promoted, and promoted again, put on the fast track to Captain, and everyone knew he'd make Admiral. She just didn't care. After eight years, she wanted out, and she left. Kate came with her. No tears. No tantrums. No arguments.

Will, always polite and eager, gave her space and let her go. He was hurt, of course, deeply hurt and confused by her defection, but he was a gentleman and kind, and he would not turn his shattered marriage into a noxious pile of accusations, fights, anger and jealousy. His real love was the Navy, after all, and the Navy wouldn't leave him. Less than two years later, he found his consolation in San Diego from a Marine officer's widow, Lourdes, a very pretty woman who bore him both a son and a daughter, and who reveled in her role as a Navy wife.

After leaving Will, Allyson, whose looks and figure had actually improved with age, found a job with First People's National, a bank headquartered in Braintree, Mass. First People's merged with Southern Mutual and the headquarters then moved to Atlanta. She moved with the bank – they paid for everything – and was promoted to assistant loan officer. Working for a living was not exactly the thing she wanted, however. Being an acolyte in a bureaucracy was dry, stultifying. Ahead of her were years of toiling at a desk, following rules, and hoping she'd catch someone's eye or have the luck of being in the right place at the right time. It ate time, broadened her buttocks, and stifled other ambitions she had. Besides, she didn't make enough money to live well, give Kate all that she wanted to give her, even with child support, and save any money. The more she thought about it, the more she thought she needed a man, the right man. *That* could be the fastest way out of her situation. She was still attractive now, but she was getting older and she knew if she didn't find the right catch soon, she might never find him. So, she watched her figure and avidly looked for a husband who could provide all those things yet wasn't a corporate zealot who'd prove to be another Will Hobson. The last thing she wanted was a husband who would put her back into the same sort of suffocating relationship she'd fled a year before.

That's when Chip Collins came on the scene. Divorced, but without children and miraculously unencumbered with any alimony payments -- "Bitch of a wife ran off with a CPA. Best thing that ever happened to me." – Good-natured, smooth, generous Chip picked her out from the mass of employees his first day at SOMU, as Southern Mutual was called. A few days later he took her and members of her team to lunch, which the company paid-for, ostensibly to get to know the people but really aimed at knowing her. He made sure he sat next to her, feigned interest in everything she had to say, and made an excuse to take her to lunch the following week. Then it was dinner. Then a show and dinner. More dinner. A fun date at the driving range – Allyson could play golf but seldom did. Dinner. Grappling in the car. The line was drawn. Kisses, but nothing further. Love and lust. The desperation of a man who, like Edward VIII, *must have this woman*. Proposal. Quick. Quick. Justice of the Peace. No party; no reception. Marriage. A week in Vegas. Bliss. The courting over in two months, start to finish. No fuss. Happiness forever.

Their marriage proved to be strong, permanent and everything she wanted. She had money, and more of it as time went on, investments to manage, time to pursue her interests, an indulgent, faithful husband ("Why eat boloney on the side when I have steak at home?"), a gorgeous home, stability, social standing and wealth. She sat on the boards of Atlanta Opera and Atlanta Ballet, dabbled in interior design and investment theory, wrote articles for various publications, was featured herself in articles in *Atlanta Magazine*, was Chairperson of Buckhead Republicans, organized the annual Heart Association Ball, and had any number of other interests. Chip had a wife who through some miracle of development and some surgical augmentation, grew more beautiful and shapely over the years, was ambitious and intelligent, able to climb socially seemingly without effort or push, a woman of charm he could wear proudly on his arm at any occasion, who was a past mistress at small talk and an asset at dealing with clients. It was a merger made in heaven. Or somewhere. They were happy together, had a happy, if terribly oversized home, very substantial bank accounts domestically, money hidden abroad beyond the reach of the IRS and millions in investments. Icing on the cake, they were proud of a daughter who was responsible, well-educated, sober and herself happy. The gods doted on them. They would have bored the hell out of Tolstoy.

Kate's relationship with her natural father, or "biological" father in the clinical lexicon of today's often disjointed families, Admiral Will Hobson, was warm but sparse. She saw him during semi-annual week-long visits to his home, although those had grown rare since she'd graduated from college and formed her own life. He did come to Atlanta on occasion. It is America's airlines hub and he often passed through. When he did, if there was any way he could, he stayed for a day and made time for her. His permanent station now was in the Pentagon, in Arlington, Virginia, where he was consumed with work and meetings. He testified on the Hill, knew personally Congressmen and Senators from both parties, and was one of the Navy's greatest advocates. He still loved her and took the time to write her regularly, though. Hardly a week went by without a long e-mail from him. He remembered her birthdays and holidays, and attended her graduations, where he did look splendid in his whites and braid. She, in turn, was invited to his "pinning on' ceremony, when he was promoted Rear Admiral, and about a year later a second ceremony when he was made Vice Admiral. At the latter occasion she was introduced to the Secretary of the Navy, and Joe Biden made a surprise visit to congratulate Will, so she met the Vice President as well.

Will's wife, Lourdes, was always gracious and kind, and seemed truly to like her, as she might since Kate was friendly, even sweet. When Kate visited, she was a compliant guest, easy to please. She always brought Lourdes a present and something for Peter and Mary, her children. Best of all, she made no financial demands on Will, and that greatly pleased Lourdes. Nevertheless, Lourdes, who was always a bit insecure, was anxious and even a little jealous when this precious vestige of Will's first marriage was with them, and relieved when she left. She never revealed any of this and seemed utterly serene and balanced on the surface, but the anxiety and jealousy were there, eating at her. She told herself these fears were silly, that Will was utterly devoted to her, but still those fears lingered just beneath the surface, malevolent, like a hungry shark cruising for prey.

Following his last promotion, Will was assigned to Central Command (CENTCOM) in Florida, then to Iraq for several months, followed by 6 months in Afghanistan. He returned from there and was placed on the Navy Staff in the Pentagon where he worked with both Navy Command and the Joint Chiefs. He was one of those rare and indispensable officers who can Command a ship or ground troops, yet have the personality and salesmanship to work with people at all levels, bring them together and to advocate successfully. Civilian presidential appointees felt comfortable in his presence. Congressmen and Senators, with their enormous egos, found he had just the right balance of respect and professionalism, a man who could be trusted, honest and respectful but also engaging and persuasive. He could have left the Navy any time for a very lucrative position with a defense contractor or a consulting firm but Allyson's assessment of him was right. He was a zealot. He would leave only when he had to and was ready to, and that time had not yet come.

Lourdes adored him and loved their life, but the worm in the rose was her two children. They were growing into unappreciative brats. When their father was gone, which he was most of the time, they were, at least to her, lazy, disinterested in school and difficult to control. She had little hope they would amount to very much and that saddened her. She didn't know her own children very well, however. John was attending a difficult high school run by Jesuits and he felt an almost inexorable pull to join the priesthood, an impulse that frightened him. Mary was not particularly popular in her school and thought she was a disappointment to her parents and a failure. Had Lourdes propped them up a bit instead of fretting about them, things would have improved, but parents and their children often don't understand each other until long after the damage is done.

****

Chapter Three – Sage Advice

Allyson knocked gently on the door to Kate's suite. This was foreign territory to her. She never wandered into that part of the house, although she did see Kate virtually every day, usually in the main kitchen, the entertainment room or the library, but of course they never discussed Kate's dates or social life. Allyson thought her daughter mature, practical, and well-grounded, and saw no reason to intrude on her privacy. Today, however, she was a bit concerned. After setting up Kate with Penn Fuller, she did an internet search for him, curious to see what he looked-like. She found pictures of him easily enough. He was athletic and handsome or at least not ugly, and that troubled her. God, what if Kate fell in love with him? Suffused with matchmaker's remorse she made the journey to Kate's door intent on talking about this.

"Mother! I was just making some tea, come on in. Would you like some?"

"That's OK, Katie. I don't want any. I just want to talk for a minute."

"Oh," said Kate, smiling, "This sounds serious. Are we bankrupt? Has the FBI finally come for dad Collins?"

"Not yet." She smiled. A short pause. "It's about Penn Fuller."

"Did he die or something?"

"He's fine, or at least I think he's fine. I haven't actually spoken with him."

"What about him?"

"I'm sorry about sticking you with him. Were I to be asked again, I wouldn't agree to set you up with him. I'm sure the date was boring. He has a reputation, you know, for being stiff and military and …"

"Not at all. He was polite, and gentle, and actually kind of deep and interesting. Thoroughly charming. It was the best date I've had in a long time. He could also be funny. I liked him very much."

Allyson's heart sank. Christ, the bastard was a charmer.

"I know. He's probably a real charmer. Your father was charming, too, when I first met him."

Kate reddened. Neither her mother nor her father ever talked about their marriage or their divorce. Allyson's sudden mention of it made her feel queasy and nervous, as if they stood in the Holy Temple of Family Troubles naked, blaspheming. She looked away and busied herself with her tea.

"He loves the Navy, doesn't he?" said Allyson.

"Yes. He was very demonstrative about it."

"That was your father, too, a zealot. The Navy is his life. Wife, children, home family are all secondary acquisitions. The Navy is his life, serving the country is the reason for his existence. I was his wife but being married to him was a life in the shadows, pulled out only now and then to attend an official function, a decoration to hang on his arm. That's good for some women. They like it, but I don't think this is what *you* want, is it?"

Kate sighed. "I don't think he's quite like father," she said.

"Oh? How's that?"

"Father's love of the Navy is spiked with ambition, He wants to be on top. It drives him; he's told me as much. I don't get that feeling from Penn. He loves the Navy for its mission but doesn't seem terribly ambitious. I got the impression he'd be content with teaching at Annapolis for the rest of his career, perhaps for the rest of his life."

Allyson thought for a moment before she answered Kate.

"I won't talk about this again, Kate, but, please listen and consider what I have to say. I loved your father, but life with him was vapid, boring, tacky and low compared to what I have now. It took time, but I was suffocating in my role as Navy wife. It killed my love for him and I had to flee. Chip's work in banking is also vital to the happiness of the world. His work allows people and businesses to get loans, live in houses and realize their dreams, and it rewards us with everything we have and gives us the leisure and resources -- meaning money -- to pursue our own interests. I thank my lucky stars that I met Chip and I wouldn't trade him for all the zealots in the world, no matter how charming or handsome they might be. .."

She paused, and put her arm around her daughter's shoulders.

"Look," said Allyson softly, "It's your decision, Kate. You're a fully grown woman and I would never interfere, but whatever you do, keep your eyes open. The charm fades quickly. The last thing you want is to wind up married with children and miserable, your husband away for years, and you living in dowdy military housing with one toilet and lousy ventilation in some God-forsaken Naval base in Crapburg somewhere."

Kate nodded. Allyson kissed her on the forehead and left. Kate sat on her arm chair, curled her legs under her and sipped her green tea. Yes, her mother was right. *God, was he nice, though.* She closed her eyes and thought of him holding her hands and kissing them, of him kissing her lips. Her mother may be right, but it's so easy for your heart to betray your head. She still wanted him. Badly.

Penn, meanwhile, returned to the University Inn at Emory, where he was staying, ran on the treadmill in the fitness center for 45 minutes, lifted weights to exercise his damaged shoulder and arm, listened to CNN for almost the whole time and mentally went over the notes he'd taken at his last meeting with his Dissertation Committee. He had a list of about 100 changes they requested, mostly small changes in format, punctuation or grammar. There were a few notes they wanted to be added and a few points they wanted clarified, but he had the sources he needed on his laptop – thank God for e-books – and he felt that if he simply put in the time, incorporated all the changes and did a final proof he could have it back to them by Monday afternoon or Tuesday, and have his degree in hand, or at least be passed for the degree by Friday. He went back to his room determined to keep pushing until he'd finished.

The Ph.D. was important to him, not only for the decoration it added to his name, but for the security it bought in his teaching position. The one thing the world did not need were more history professors. He was ensconced in a job for now because he was an Academy man and because he'd returned from overseas blooded and decorated, or at least the Navy thought so. His medals represented distinctions with which he never felt comfortable, however. Internally, he thought that what he did wasn't worth the fuss made over it, but he accepted the accolades because they were offered freely and they would help him gain the peace, security and promotions he wanted. The Ph.D. would ensure it.

Was he a hero? If he were asked, he'd call himself an accidental hero, a person who reacted rather than attacked. His responses had been so quick, and the experience so blurred that it was difficult for him to accept the notion that he'd done anything brave. To be really brave, there has to be some sort of premeditation to the act. There was none that day, just running and acting.

Pondering the justice of his decorations would just distract him from the task at hand, so he prepared for work. He showered quickly, pulled on his jeans and a t-shirt, and sat down to his laptop to make – he hoped – the final revision to his thesis. He was into the task about an hour when the phone rang. It was after 11 PM. Who the devil would call?

"Penn? Penn? It's me, mom"

"Mom? Is something wrong. It's after 11."

"I know. I know sweetie, but I figured you'd still be up and I was hoping I could catch you."

"That's OK, Mom. I'm glad you called. I wanted to thank you for the tickets."

"That's great! How did it go?"

"The opera was staged beautifully. The Diva was a Korean girl, er.., woman, Hey Young Rhee, and Suzuki was sung by the prettiest Japanese girl. I forgot her name…"

"That's great. And the theater was OK?"

"Wonderful venue for opera. Great acoustics and you gave us great seats."

"The date. How was the date?"

"You mean Kate?"

"Yes, yes, of course I mean Kate."

"She's very pretty and very nice. I liked her."

"Do you think there's something there? Will you see her again?"

"I don't know, Mom. That depends on her. Why all the questions? You never asked about my love life before."

"Yes I did. Remember when you dated Doris McMillian?"

"That was my Senior Prom in High School."

"Well, OK, but since Kate's parents are old friends, I just wanted to know if everything went well."

"It went great. Kate looked beautiful and we got along very well. I'll ask her out again, but right now I want to concentrate on finishing my thesis and getting my Ph.D.., so I may not see her again for a month or so. If she still wants to go out with me."

"Sure. You do what you have to. But, if you'd have to sum it up, you'd say it went well."

"It was super. Kate's a beautiful woman, intelligent and interesting, and the opera was done extremely well. I couldn't have asked for a better afternoon and evening."

"Oh, that's wonderful."

"Say 'hello' to Roger for me, will you? Tell him I'm working on my swing. Someday I'll break 100 and make him proud."

"Love you, Penn."

"Love you, too, mom."

In Vermont, Grand Aunt Harriett, one of the last of the old family Yankees, the doyenne of the family, sat by her telephone eagerly awaiting the report from Julie. She had instructed Julie to call her, no matter how late and let her know what happened on that date. As she waited for the call she couldn't help thinking about what might come of this. Both Penn and Kate were young, although not children, and in this day and age, with instant hook-ups and other activity that she found both shocking and interesting, even fascinating, anything could have happened.

One always assumes the old are prudish and strict, as if passion and sex had been invented by the young and were alien and disgusting to the old. As if the morals and mores of all the old were formed in an age when intimate things were only whispered and hinted-at. As if all old people came from a time when modesty, purity, virginity, abstinence and celibacy were the normal practice and people who did anything else, especially girls and woman, were aberrant, salacious, wanton whores. As if, in short, the old had never been young or even middle-aged.

Harriett, however old (no Spring chicken, that's for sure), was no prude. She was 87, a young 87, but up there and not particularly happy about it; she much preferred being 47 or 57 or 27, for that matter. Her marriage, although brief and abruptly ended when Admiral Marion Butler died on the bridge of his ship, had been intense, passionate, exhausting, fulfilling, sexy, romantic, lovely, sweet.

After Marion's death, there were others, affairs always pursued with discretion, and always, of course, with unmarried men, except for Patrick S., who was just separated and Ivan R., who was simply delicious, and one or two others, the exceptions proving the rule, whatever *that* means. The last of the affairs happened when she was in her seventies. He was an old lover who returned to her after his wife died, and for a man of his age he was unusually fit, strong and vigorous. He could make love half the night (She suspected this had something to do with the pharmaceuticals he took, but anything that worked was fine with her.), and she enjoyed him enormously. He still loved her, still saw her as young and beautiful, or so he said, and wanted to marry her. She refused and grew tired of his pleas and entireties and possessiveness (He was remarkably jealous of any man who looked at her.). After a time, she broke it off and broke his heart. He died a month later and she mourned for him grievously.

In her imagination, an imagination driven by the intensity of her own experiences, she saw Penn and Kate meeting, liking each other, and, intensely affected by the opera, the two of them intertwining spiritually and -- she hoped – physically, catapulted into the heights of passion by the emotional tsunami generated by the romance, the tragedy, the *intense pathos* of the story. (*Ah*, she thought, *I should write that down*, but she didn't.)

Butterfly, after all, always brought Harriett to tears, and it was at a performance of *Butterfly* that she fell in love, for a time, with sweet Michael. They went together to New York to see it. This was in the days before Lincoln Center, at the old Met. Like teenagers in love at the Bijou matinee, they leaned into each other and held hands while Renata Scotto sang the role so plaintively and so passionately. Their date was scrupulously arranged so that no one would ever cast aspersions on either of them. They even booked into separate hotels. All that discretion was forgotten, though, after *Un Bel di*, after the final curtain call. They took a cab to the Plaza, had a late dinner and champagne, and fled to her room, where they lived like Adam and Eve for two days before returning home, searing Central Park West with the heat of their passion, or so she liked to think. The power of Puccini was incalculable. Something similar happened when she went with William I-forget-who to see *La Boheme*.

"Ah, the memories!" she thought, "Why does one grow old? How much better it would be if you could just live to be, say 50, no, 40, and stay there without aging for a few decades then die suddenly." She still longed for her lovers, for love itself.

"Braaaap!" the phone rang. She picked it up immediately.

No "hello" at all. She knew who it was. "How did it go?"

"They seem to like each other very much. He said she was beautiful and intelligent and he would see her again."

"You don't know if they… you know, did anything?"

"Aunt Harriett, please! Even if they had Penn wouldn't tell me. I'm his mother and he's, if anything, a gentlemen."

"Gentleman still have sex. Lots of it, whenever they can. That's why they're gentle, not frustrated and mean. Anyway, it's probably better that Penn and Kate didn't. If she holds out on him, it'll stimulate his interest and get him to start pursuing her. Playing hard to get is a girl's best ploy, as long as she doesn't overplay it. Look, you heard his voice. How did he sound? Enthusiastic?"

"Penn isn't very demonstrative. I don't think he'd say 'ouch' if you his foot with a hammer. What he said about Kate was high praise from him. He obviously liked her, but he wasn't sure she liked him."

"What do you mean?"

"I asked him if he would take her out again. He said that depends on her."

"Of course it depends on her. I don't read anything into that except, perhaps, he's trying to lower his own expectations in case she turns him down. He likes her; that's the important thing. He likes her a lot. She'll fall for him and roll on her back soon enough. Hell, I would."

"Harriett!"

"Well, I would, if I were Kate, that's all. What's the bottom line on this?"

"In all. I think it went very well."

"We'll see. Thanks for calling. Goodbye"

Julie started to say "goodbye" but heard the phone click. Well, she'd done her duty. The rest was up to Penn.

Harriett, meanwhile, slipped into bed, but not before pinning on the broach she always wore with Marion's two stars in it. For luck, she kissed it first. "Marion, old man, if you're out there, somewhere, give me some help," She fell asleep before she finished the prayer.

As Harriett drifted off to sleep, In County Sligo, Ireland, in a small village with the interesting name of Ballintogher, an Irish wake was dying with a whimper, not a bang. The mourners had either passed out or gone home to sleep. The hours passed, the dawn came a rosy gray, the sun a smear in a sky that matched the gray mood of the town. Later that morning as the skies cleared, 300 people arrived for the funeral, much more than the entire population of the town.

Patrick O'Mara, the aviator and hero of the United States, was being laid to rest. He lived through 3 wars, braved innumerable dangers for his adopted land, and retired with the noble rank of Lieutenant Colonel from the greatest Army in the world. The President and the American Ambassador sent their condolences. For service in his last war, in Vietnam, he was awarded the Congressional Medal of Honor, America's highest award for valor. It hung in a glass case over his mantle. An American military contingent arrived from their station in England, and the Irish Army as well as the entire town council deposed themselves for the funeral, too. The coffin, draped with the flags of the United States and Ireland was carried on the shoulders of his grand-nephew, a hearty bull of a Sergeant-Major in the Irish Army reserves, two stout soldiers from his Regiment and three of the American soldiers. There were seven pipers, four drummers, flutes, piccolos and two honor guards. He was put to rest on an unusually sunny day in a shaded plot that overlooked a glen used for grazing race horses. O'Mara loved the horses so.

Patrick O'Mara emigrated to the United States at a bad time, during the Depression. He settled in Philadelphia because that was where the ship dropped him. Despite the shortage of work, he was a lucky fellow, a stout lad with sandy hair and a ready grin who won over gang basses and foreman, and always found work. He was a smart lad, too, and took classes at night, finally getting his citizenship and passing his high school diploma, quite an accomplishment for a country boy with no resources save his hands and his brains. He took classes at Temple University. It was a Baptist school then, but it was nearly free and there was no prejudice against Catholics. He even applied to the Drexel Institute of Technology. He would have begun at Drexel and perhaps become an engineer, which is what he wanted, if the war hadn't started.

On December 8, 1941, he enlisted in the Army. He stood half the night at the recruiting station to get in. The Noncommissioned Officer in Charge, Master Sergeant Connor O'Ryan, born in County Sligo, was told to look out for skilled mechanics and smart lads, to select them for special testing. He saw the name of a Sligo lad, pulled O'Mara out of the pile, and sent him to the testing station, where he did well and was singled out as officer potential. He was asked what he'd like to do in the Army. One word: "fly." He passed the physical and within a week he was a pilot cadet in training at Randolph Field, just outside San Antonio, Texas. He went from there to nearby Brooks Field for advanced training. Flight training took 9 months to complete. That done, two weeks leave and he was ordered to Roosevelt Field in New York, where he'd await further orders.

It didn't take long. He was assigned to the 8th Air Force and ordered to ferry a plane across the Atlantic to England, to a place called Grafton Underwood, Northamptonshire. The Plane was a B-

17. His co-pilot, Mike Burns, was Irish-American, and it was Mike's idea to christen the plane "Luck O'the Irish." The nose art featured a tastefully nude curvaceous red-haired colleen garbed only in a Kelly Green Tam O'Shanter (the artist was a Scott) who floated through the clouds dropping bombs.

Whatever magic was in the name, it helped bring them through. O'Mara and Burns flew 25 missions. The plane was hit a few times but the damage was always repairable. Most of the damage done to their crew was from too much drink, venereal disease, and bad hangovers, although once they lost a navigator and the tail gunner was replaced three times. Their 25 missions done, O'Mara and Burns were slated to go home and dearly wanted to before their luck ran out, but both had a horrid stubborn streak and neither would back down from a dare or a bet. Burns laid down the challenge over several drafts of warm English Ale, slurring out the words, *O'Mara, I'm going for another 25. If you don't volunteer for 25 more you ain't got a hair on your ass.* Who could resist such provocation? They did 25 more missions, by some miracle their luck held, and both of them returned to the U.S. unscathed, where they trained new pilots for the German meat grinder. Their survival was unusual, even a bit miraculous. Fully 1/3 of the airman in the 8th Air Force died on those bombing runs long before they made 25 missions. By the end of the war O'Mara was a squadron commander, a Lieutenant Colonel weighed down with awards and decorations.

Their plane, which stayed behind, continued to stay lucky. It lasted through the war, afterward was sent home to a bone yard, was acquired by a junk collector who used it as an advertising gimmick, was bought by another collector and partially refurbished, was sold for more that its original value new, and is now the centerpiece of a private museum in California owned by a retired dot-com multimillionaire, whose father was a WWII pilot and who carefully and lovingly restored the nose art to its original brilliance. The artist who did the restoration, however, changed the face a bit to resemble the millionaire's wife, Moira O'Connor of Kildare. The rest of the image suited her well and needed no modification.

O'Mara left the Army Air Corps after World War II to return to college under the GI Bill, but rejoined the Army during the Korean War. They took him back, but by this time the Air Force ran the bombers and fighters and the Army was relegated to small aircraft, observation planes, helicopters and a few larger freight vehicles. He went back into service as a Chief Warrant Officer, but retained his reserve commission and had the same pay and privileges as a Lieutenant Colonel. Later in the war, after flying over 90 missions, he was restored to the active rank of Lieutenant Colonel. He both trained pilots and flew observer planes. He wanted to be with MacArthur's forces at the vanguard of the attack and the Navy was short of pilots so he volunteered to fly as an Army pilot assigned to the Navy.

He was with the fleet as they approached Inchon Harbor, and catapulted off a Navy ship with orders to look for any enemy troop movement. It was late at night, but he might be able to see headlights or other flashes of light. He saw almost nothing until virtually at the end of his tether, incurred enemy fire, and with fuel running low, returned to the fleet. He was supposed to land on the water (the pane had pontoons) but as he flew over the incoming ships, his engine sputtered and died. The instrument panel, which was damaged, incorrectly indicated there was still fuel in the tank, but he couldn't get the plane restarted, so he pointed it away from the fleet (or so he thought) and bailed out. He had to jump. The pane's glide path was too sharp to allow for a pontoon landing, which would have been suicide anyway since he couldn't see the water at night and had to rely on unreliable instruments. The unmanned plane glided in a sharp decline towards the water, but the wind started to blow and about one hundred feet up the plane turned ninety degrees right into the line of ships. It smashed through the bridge of one ship, the *Sioux*, and killed its Captain, its First Officer and its Quartermaster.

O'Mara was the pilot who killed the beloved husband of Penn's Grand Aunt Harriet. He was rescued less than an hour after hitting the water.

There was an official hearing but it was a formality. His service record was so sterling he was exonerated and even recommended for an Air Medal, which was duly awarded. He returned to service and continued flying observation and rescue missions for the rest of the war.

After Korea he remained in service, training new pilots, and when Vietnam heated-up he served there as well – three tours. During his second tour, he put his observation plane, a flimsy Piper Cub, down on a dusty patch of road in the middle of a firefight, grabbed a rifle, and found a cowering infantry platoon that had lost an officer and its First Sergeant. He literally kicked them into fighting, booting men in the rear and roaring at them. Shouting ancient curses and invocations in Irish and Gaelic, he led them in an attack that routed a regular North Vietnamese company. He called down airstrikes almost on his own head. As the enemy retreated still shooting, although wounded himself in thigh and shoulder, under fire he hoisted a broken and bleeding Lieutenant onto his back, and carried him to his plane. He then limped back, and still under fire carried another wounded man to the plane, was wounded himself one more time in the calf, but still got the plane into the air and flew to a base Camp, saving their lives. All this took about 90 minutes. He was awarded the Congressional Medal of Honor, and was later honored by the Irish government as well for life saving as well as for valor.

He met and married a Vietnamese woman, Mai Nguyen, in 1968, retired from the service in 1972 and ran a pilot's school in Florida until his second retirement in 1986. His wife, 10 years his junior, started suffering heart problems in 1987 and died suddenly two years later. Grief-stricken and feeling old, he returned to his native town to die and there met one more woman, Mary Chin, widow of the owner of *China Tasty Delight* restaurant. Mary looked like Mai, had Mai's sense of humor and Mai's capacity for love. He courted her, they married in St. Teresa's R.C. Church, and were quite happy. He discovered he had a talent for telling tales, and began to tell folks about his adventures in the wars. It was therapeutic, for the memory of those days was inexorably sad and fearsome, and he was sometimes troubled with nightmares. He would invite everyone to his house, Mary would pour drinks and he would talk for hours about the men he knew and the things they did. There was little embellishment. None was needed. When he died, there wasn't a dry eye in the town or in the surrounding area. His tearful widow was honored with multiple flags and a surviving wife's pension.

Grand Aunt Harriett respected people of courage. Had Harriett known of his death, she would have sent a sympathy card.

****

Chapter Four – Hai Ba Trung

Penn Fuller's Ph.D. was awarded through e-mail. He was notified by the Dean and the head of his dissertation committee, and was told to come to the school to receive his sheepskin and, of course, to pay the final graduation fee. He even had a choice of diplomas to order, framed or not, on vellum or fine paper, etc. He splurged, went for the Vellum and, given a choice of Latin or English, took the fine Latin script. It was framed, boxed, and kept at the registrar's office for him until he picked it up a few days later. He was ahead of schedule. He planned to have it by Friday, and received it Thursday afternoon.

The process of receiving the degree was simple enough to be utterly antiseptic. He could have waited until graduation ceremonies, rented the regalia of the Doctor of History with its dark blue trim, puffed sleeves, medieval soft hat, and black robes, and marched in line for the handshake on stage, for the hugs of doting relatives but no, that wasn't for him. He was beyond that, and he wanted just to return to work at the Academy. The award of the degree should have left him elated and satisfied with the distinction he'd achieved, but there was no elation and little satisfaction. If anything, he felt deflated. He climbed the mountain, struggled along the way, worked hard and in the end there was nothing to see. He felt a twinge in his shoulder – the physical therapist warned him that twinges and aches might be felt for a very long time, so he took this in stride – massaged it a bit, and wondered what to do with the rest of the day. God, it had been a long and twisty road to this point in his life.

Like his famous great-grandfather, the Vice Admiral, when he was 17 Penn left home and joined the Navy, not for any good reason, but merely to get away, do something, to rise from adolescence to adulthood quickly. He chose the Navy because he thought it offered endless travel and adventure. His parents, both Yalies (His mother was Vassar with a Master of Fine Arts from Yale.), were bitterly disappointed, but he wore them down. They signed the papers and let him enlist at 17 anyway. Penn had gone to good schools and done well. He wasn't brilliant, but he was sharp, kept in the top 15-20% of his class, took challenging courses and certainly seemed destined for more than swabbing decks and chipping paint. He told the Navy recruiter he wanted to be a real deep-water sailor. The recruiter was happy to accommodate him. Once he was at sea doing duty that was tedious and dirty, he realized his mistake. There was no way out. He had enlisted for four years, and he was too moral, too ethical and too stubborn to go back on his word. He would serve every minute of it.

Ten months after enlisting, he got his break. He was serving in the North Atlantic on a Destroyer when one of the Yeoman was medically evacuated with a burst appendix and peritonitis. A second Yeoman was suffering from pathological seasickness and had to be removed as well. The Captain jokingly asked the Boson if he had any men on the crew who were Ivy League material, since he needed a top-rate Yeoman. The Boson, who was as good a judge of men as anyone in the service, and who hated to see a man underused, offered up Seaman Fuller. Penn Fuller took to the new job with enthusiasm. He was blessed with an immunity to seasickness, and actually enjoyed the thrill of North Atlantic storms and miserable weather. Perversely, for a fellow with his effete background, he seemed to love the Navy. He never griped, served long hours, and took on all the tasks he was given with gusto. The officers liked him; his fellow sailors thought him a bit odd, but found him to be square, honest, true and generous, and they liked him as well. The Captain, whose broken marriage had put him out of touch with his own son, soon adopted him, at least in spirit.

Six months after becoming Yeoman Fuller, the Captain sent a Petty Officer to him with a package of papers.

"Captain orders you to fill out these here papers, and mail them in," he was told, the man thrusting an envelope toward Fuller. Penn opened it carefully and withdrew the sheaf of papers. Inside the envelope was an application to Annapolis with all the attendant forms.

"Chief, this is an application to the Academy. I don't think I have a prayer of getting in."

"The Captain orders you to fill out the forms and send them in on time."

Captains are like God on Navy ships. Penn followed the orders, and followed them well, preparing the applications sharply, all typed correctly.

So, again following his great-grandfather, he applied to Annapolis from the fleet. The Captain and several officers endorsed the application, and everyone was rooting for him. The Naval Academy, however, rejected him and he resigned himself to serving out his enlistment as well as he could. Then, shortly before the Annapolis class for that year was to assemble, he received notice that a vacancy had occurred and he was the next on the list. He found out much later there wasn't one vacancy; there were six vacancies. Four accepted applicants had been arrested, one DUI, two friends caught smoking marijuana, and another for lascivious assault. Another two applicants had been given late admission to the Air Force Academy and quit their place at Annapolis. He was number five on the waiting list. He was in.

From the day he was accepted, the officers aboard the Destroyer began prepping him. He was schooled and drilled in the Annapolis traditions, told repeatedly what to expect in the first few months of his Plebe year, and warned not to make an issue of his former enlisted service because there were upperclassmen who'd use it a lever to harass him.

"You don't want them callin' you Popeye, and ordering you to get your spinach"

"Yeah, and the last thing you need is some shithead

upperclassman getting the idea that you think you're better because you've actually been to sea. You'll never get rid of the jerk until he's bilged or he graduates."

He took the advice to heart, and learned all he could from the ship's officers in the month or so before he had to report to the Academy. The final advice – show up in civilian clothes. Don't make yourself a target. Let them issue all your uniforms. Don't bring tailored uniforms with you; it'll mark you right away.

At the academy, he sailed through his Plebe year, was elected platoon leader, selected Political Science as his major, and concentrated on his academics. He pushed to finish in the top 10% of his class and graduate with distinction. His one mistake – or, if you will, challenge – was electing Japanese after 2 years of Spanish. It took concentration and energy to wade through the grammar and a tolerance for tedious, repetitive work to learn some of the ideographs. His enlisted service taught him to endure tediousness, and his pride kept him going. In all, he much preferred calculus, but he got through 2 years of Japanese, learned a bit of conversation and could read some basic Kanji. He also finished in the top 8% of his class, no mean feat at the Naval Academy. The caption on his *Lucky Bag* photo read "A Scholar, but a Sailor to the Core." As fate would have it, his first real assignment was to a ship out of Rota, Spain, where he practiced his Spanish and forgot much of the Japanese.

Graduation, a beautiful day in May, brought his parents and his two widowed aunts, Elizabeth and Harriett. The two aunts were rumored to be related to Katherine Hepburn, although how close the relationship no one knew. In their youth they were Katherine Hepburn types, attractive, athletic, long-limbed New England women, sharp tongued and assertive. Age had mellowed Elizabeth, but had honed Harriett.

Months earlier, Penn had been sent a photo of the two aunts taken by his parents at the 100th birthday of yet another distant relative. His Academy roommate, Steve Tran, Vietnamese-

American, saw the photo, laughed, and called them the *Hai Ba Trung*.

"The what?"

"The *Hai Ba Trung*. You're the Political Scientist and you've never heard of them?"

"No. What were they, Vietnamese witches?"

"They were heroes, Shit-for-brains. "Hai" means two, "Ba" means Misses or Madams and "Trung" was their family name. The "Two Ladies Trung" would be the way you'd say it in English, since they were the wives of Mandarins. The legend goes that in the year 39 A.D. the Chinese governor of Chiao Chi decided to frighten some of the Vietnamese landlords by assassinating one of them. The man who was assassinated was the husband of Trung Trac. She was well educated, strong-minded and being the daughter of a general, well versed in the military arts. She called upon her sister, Trung Nhi, and together they organized an army with the help of the other neighboring Vietnamese lords. They attacked the Chinese and forced them out. The Trung sisters captured 65 cities and were made Queens. It didn't last. The Chinese returned with a huge army and retook what they'd given up in Vietnam. The Trung sisters, rather than be captured, drowned themselves in the Hat-Giang River. The Chinese annals tell the story differently, of course. They make the Trungs out to be female war lords, rebels and bandits."

"You learn that at your father's knee?"

"My father is a helicopter pilot. I learned the importance of balancing rotor blades from him... Last year, I took an on-line course in Vietnamese culture as an elective. Anyway, those two aunts of yours look the type."

"I'll take that as a compliment."

"I'm not sure if I just complimented your aunts or denigrated the memory of the Trung sisters."

"Both, I'm sure."

Penn's parents seemed bemused by the whole graduation event. It wasn't much like it had been at Yale's graduation, but then there is only one Yale.

At the graduation ceremony, Penn's step-father, dressed immaculately in a double-breasted dark blue blazer, a rep tie striped in Yale blue and gray, button-down shirt and gray banker's slacks, smiling, shaking his head as if in total incomprehension of the event, took his son's hand, shook it warmly and said

"Congratulations, Penn, you did well. I don't mind admitting that we had our misgivings when you enlisted in the Navy, but you've managed to – he groped for words and found only 'do well' – *do well*."

His adventure in paternal pride seemed to end too abruptly, but he wasn't sure where he should go with this. Penn, after all, was his step-son. He had acquired a one-year-old step-child when he married Meredith, Penn's mother. In truth, Harald, his one child with Meredith, was more like a chip off the old block, off *both* the old blocks, than Penn. Harald had just finished his Freshman Year at Grant Prep, was already an officer in the school's student Republican Club and a member of the high school chapter of the Young Americans for Freedom. His greatest ambition was to go to Yale and buck for admission to Skull and Bones, just as the Bushes of Kennebunkport (whom Penn's family had known long before they went Texas, got into politics and became so damn famous) had done. Groping for something to say, Penn's step-father said the first thing that came into his mind.

"Now what? Have you thought about graduate school? Law school? Harvard, maybe? I hear you certainly have the grades."

Penn smiled in a remarkable mimicry of unrestrained joy. He was an honorable soul but not completely beyond a capacity for polite deception, especially where his parents were concerned.

"I'm committed to the service for the next five years. I'll see what evolves as my career progresses. Graduate school, even Harvard, is not beyond question." He was gently lying. He really wanted to go to sea, earn his stripes and advance.

Penn's mother's current married name was Meredith Julie Hawthorne Chilton, sometimes hyphenated as Fuller-Chilton. Everyone had always called her "Julie." She reserved the right to hyphenate because Fuller, as everyone knew, was a Mayflower name and she was sure that if she could just find the right sources, there would be a Mayflower medal of which she could boast in her dead husband's family. Her father's family, the Symingtons, bragged a connection of some sort to the famous writer, Nathaniel Hawthorne, and wanted it never to be forgotten. Her one sibling, a brother, bore Hawthorne as a first name.

So, she was at one time Meredith Julie Hawthorne Fuller, nee Symington. She was widowed early in her first marriage when her husband, Penn's father, Jack Fuller, a bright, handsome man with a taste for adventure, died young in a ballooning accident. The balloon he was piloting tore open and he fell some 500 feet into the Winooski River, where he drowned, although injuries from his fall would probably have killed him anyway.

At Penn's Annapolis graduation, which occurred on a hot, bright day, Julie wore a large, floppy hat, a subdued print dress that hung well on her lithe figure, and a string of natural pearls. From a distance, lightly freckled with bright blue eyes, she looked much younger than her 44 years. Close up she was still beautiful, if a bit too reserved.

"Five years?" said Julie , whispering for effect, "Do you have to stay on duty all that time?"

"Yes, Mom. I'm in the Navy for a while."

Julie stood back a bit, looked at her son, and for the first time saw him as a man of his own, not an artifact of her life that confused and disappointed her. There wasn't a wrinkle in his clothes and he filled out the formal, white uniform well. *He looks like an actor auditioning for a part in a movie,* she thought, *He's found his dream.* She smiled, happy for him, and kissed him on the cheek. The Naval Academy wasn't Yale, but it was up there. He would never make the life connections he would have made at Yale, but he would have a good life, if not a rich one. The thought satisfied her.

"Well, at least we've done our bit in the Gulf and sat on those damn Arabs. You won't have to worry about that," said his step-father, whom Penn called "dad Chilton."

He held out his hand.

"Congratulations, Penn," said step-dad Chilton, "You did well and you're going to do well."

They shook hands as if closing a real estate deal, which was the only way dad Chilton knew to shake hands. A hug was unmanly, déclassé, and out of the question.

Aunt Harriett (actually *Grand Aunt* Harriett) surprised him. Aunt Elizabeth, who was with her, just beamed and uttered something that sounded like congratulations and good luck, but Harriett, the widow of a Rear Admiral, lithe and sharp, in tweed skirt, bone blouse and blue jacket, the jeweled brooch with her deceased husband's two stars decorating her lapel, strode up, straight backed and strong, shook his hand with both of hers, then took him by the shoulders and kissed him on each cheek, like De Gaulle honoring an old resistance fighter.

"You've got the drive, Ensign; keep it up. We need another Admiral in the family. You know what the next step is, don't ya?" Her speech was educated New England, and, as everyone said, she sounded like Katherine Hepburn, a young Kat Hepburn whose voice was still strong and didn't quaver. She squinted her eyes and stared at him, but didn't wait for an answer.

"Marry well, and your career will blossom!"

"But, Aunt, a sailor has a girl in every port."

He tried to say the old cliché with charm, but even his charm had his limits.

She shook her head, put her arm on his shoulder and leaned close to him.

"Never stops them from marrying, Ensign. Lots of men like both pie and cake." she said with a sardonic smile and a wink, "Even known a few myself."

What she meant by this last remark was anyone's guess. Harriet wasn't known for her subtlety. She leaned even closer. Their noses were almost touching.

"Who's the little girl you took to the Ring Dance? Is she special to you?"

"Marie was special enough to take to the dance, but we're just friends, Auntie. She's my roommate's younger sister, just a kid, really. Steve, my roommate, asked me to take her, since I have no steady girlfriend (*or any girlfriend at all at this point*, he thought), and she was thrilled. She's a very nice girl, graduated High School valedictorian. "

"She looked kind of Oriental or Latin," said Harriet.

"She's Vietnamese-American, born in the shadow of the capitol, in Washington, D.C."

"You serious about this Chinese girl? I know she's pretty…" Harriet didn't finish the thought, at least not out loud.

"She's Vietnamese and she's way out of my class, Auntie. Her father runs a company that maintains and leases helicopters and does quite well. She plans to be a doctor, and I see no reason why she couldn't be. She's beautiful, but she's also brilliant. The night of the dance we talked physics and math. Her hobby is solving integral equations, and we talked for a long time about an improved computer program she was writing to take care of some of the more tedious trial and error calculations. Right now she's trying to prove some of the unproven results of Ramanujan."

Harriet had long ago earned her own degree in Math from Vassar, so she knew exactly what Penn was saying. Her eyes lit up at the memory of solving integrals, at the tantalizing mention of Ramanujan.

Penn continued "She'll wind up marrying a Thoracic Surgeon or some other medico who earns a cool million a year, and together they'll live in a minimansion on a golf course. Me, I'll drive ships. I hope."

Harriet poked him in the chest.

"Why didn't you ask Pattie, then?" Pattie was Patricia Iris North, a girl Penn had known practically all his life, the daughter of one of his father's associates, supposedly related to a friend of his mother's through marriage in some obscure way. Her image flashed in his mind. She was tall, with a good figure and a pleasant face, but she was a Preppy, a finishing school product who spoke in whispers and smiles as if she were confiding secrets, always ready to make a small joke about anything, but unable to carry on any real conversation. She was the kind of girl Penn liked only in 15 minute increments. After the first 15 minutes there was nothing to talk with her about. The thought of spending an entire evening with her was excruciating. He smiled winningly to cover the anguish of the thought.

Harriet went on. "I'm a Navy widow born to an old Navy family. There isn't a sea war this country has fought since the Revolution that hasn't had one of my own people, or my mother's, the Throxtons, in the thick of it. You ever need help with anything, give me a call. There isn't a thing about the service I don't know and I can't help you with. I have plenty of contacts, can get you good assignments if your career officers can't. Remember me, Penn, and take my advice, marry the right type of woman. Katie Fitz (Catherine Fitzhugh), your Great Grandmother, was well-connected and helped make your Great Grandfather an Admiral despite himself, in an age when it was damn hard to make rank. A good wife can help you along, too."

She locked eyes with him, then winked, patted his shoulder and let him go, confident she'd given him a lot to consider, but not at all confident that he'd take it to heart.

Penn's graduation was well over a decade ago but he was sure Harriett was the one who was ultimately behind all the match-making that occurred in the past year. The old woman had a strong personality but it would take more than just personality to get his mother to act as her surrogate. She must have some kind of hold over Julie but what it was he didn't know and care to know. Being sent on a date every six months or so was hardly a hardship or an intrusion, and if he really wanted to stop it, he could try to find a ship or an overseas assignment. It wouldn't be difficult to do once he had a totally clean bill of health. The girls he dated through this unsubscribed service, however, were fun and attractive, especially Kate Hobson. He might even have more time for them now that he'd gotten his Ph.D. Besides, his work at the Academy was not nearly finished. He had begun collecting information on his Great-grandfather, Vice Admiral Pennington, and planned to write a book about him.

Admiral Pennington was an enigmatic figure. There are reams of information available in the archives of the Department of the Navy on Navy Admirals and officers of lower rank, but when Penn began scanning the microfiche and the computer records little came to the surface. It was frustrating. The complete service record of some obscure Lieutenant could be found, but little on a man who had served in both great 20th Century wars in positions of influence.

Lost, he had turned to one of the older historians at the Academy, a retired Captain, Matthew Blake, for advice.

"I'm not surprised. Records were sometimes destroyed, lost or misfiled. You could spend a decade going through this stuff just to discover that someone had put everything under the wrong name or water damage and mice had gotten to a paper file and rather than clean off the mouse poop and photograph it, it was just thrown away. We're a lot more careful and scientific about records preservation these days."

"You think it's hopeless?"

"No. Just difficult, and it may take time. You have found some things, haven't you?"

"A few."

"If correspondence is involved, look at all the people copied on it, check their records, too. Check the biographies of associates and superiors. You know the drill. You're good at research."

"I've been doing all that."

"There may be some living witnesses. Have you thought about that?"

"I'm looking for them."

"How about family? More than one family has kept buckets of documents not knowing what to do with them."

As he drove back from Emory, he thought about his mentor's words, and an idea sprang to mind. Harriett. If Auntie Harriett was so concerned for his career, she might be helpful in unearthing some of the facts about his Great-Grandfather's life and career. She was eccentric and bossy, but she was also smart and knowing. At last telling, he was sure his mother said that Harriett was 87. That would make her, what? Twenty in 1945. Admiral Pennington had died at the end of '47, so she was 23 when he died. She might have known him, or known people who knew him very well. He'd call her.

"Harriett" she snapped. She didn't like the phone to ring when she wasn't expecting a call. Damn nuisance sometimes. Aside from that, unexpected phone calls were almost always about someone who had died, although so many people she'd known were already dead that font of depressing news was down to the barest trickle. Hell, now the children of the dead ones were dying.

"Hello, Auntie, it's me, Penn," he said.

"Julie didn't die, did she?"

"No, she's doing well."

"How about that husband of hers, whatshisname, Chilton?"

"No," he's fine.

"Well… Don't keep in suspense, did someone die?"

"I'm sure someone died today, Auntie, but no one we know."

She chuckled. "You're a Yankee at heart, Penn, with that fine touch of Yankee sarcasm in your speech. I was afraid you'd lost your grit somewhere. You were much too smooth the last time we talked."

"I save it for you, Auntie."

"What do you want? I don't have any money."

"And would I call you about money when Chilton is loaded?"

"If you didn't want him to know you would. Didn't get a girl pregnant did you?"

"It wouldn't matter. I never tell them my real name."

"Ok. I give up. No one's died. No one's born. You don't want money and I know you don't want a date, so what is it?"

"I need your help. I'm trying to research the Admiral's career and I'm running into dead ends. There's little in the archives about him and I'm wondering if the family has any documents or records, or files. You knew him, didn't you?"

Harriet paused.

Penn waited a minute, then concerned that the call was dropped asked "Are you still there, Autie?"

"I'm thinking, not dead. Wait a minute."

Twenty seconds passed.

"I sure as hell knew him. I talked to him, played cards with him, went on walks with him, loved him. He was a generous, good man, although, like everyone I suppose, he had his downside."

"What about documents or records?"

"There might be some. There's a house we own in the outskirts of Stowe, near the Little River. Some old trunks and assorted crap in the attic. I'll send you the key, if you'll promise to pay me a visit."

"Auntie, I wouldn't miss a visit with you for the world."

"Now you're lyin' but, hell, it's better than the truth."

The key arrived at his Annapolis address in an ordinary envelop with no note. He made arrangements to travel north on his own time with his own money.

****

Chapter Five – Letters, Harriet, and Elizabeth

The attic was musty, but the light from the two overhead bulbs was adequate. With some effort, he pulled an old trunk from under the sloping roof into the light. It was locked but the key was in it. He opened it carefully, with an historian's respect for old things, making sure he didn't damage the hinges or contents. What he saw wasn't promising. Some blankets and old clothes. He carefully removed them and placed them on a clean sheet of wrapping paper. He dug deeper. Beneath the moth-balled blankets and sheets was an ancient copy of *the Bluejacket's Manual*, and beneath that equally ancient copies of textbooks used at the Naval Academy. Penn Fuller turned every page of the *Manual*, looking for notes or concealed papers, but found nothing.

He put the *Manual* aside and gently lifted *Principles of Hydrography*, hoping to find some note or annotation made by his Great-Grandfather. He opened the cover gently, careful not to crack the old leather binding, and found a prize. Sandwiched between the cover and flyleaf was a well-preserved photo, one he'd never seen. Five officers, in dress whites, obviously celebrating something, their arms around each other's shoulders, broad smiles. Two missing their hats. White Naval uniforms haven't changed too much since the 19th century, but the hats, smaller in diameter than today's navy, with smaller brims, betrayed the age of the picture. The young, handsome men captured the moment the photo was taken were now all gone, of course, dust to dust. The memory of the moment was lost, except in that photo, which was only a captured instant. On the back of photo he found "1889 and up from Hades. We're O & G now!" O & G – Officers and gentlemen. The handwriting was precise, an engineer's or architect's hand. Penmanship and precise writing were more prized in the age before typewriters and computers. Officers of that day were expected to write clearly in straight lines.

All five of the men in the photo were Ensigns. He recognized his great-grandfather among them, the Ensign on the far right, well-built, in perfect proportions, neither very tall nor short, square-jawed, an image from a recruiting poster. *Looks old for an Ensign,* he thought, but that was a different era. Everyone seemed to look older then. He didn't expect to see any resemblance to himself and didn’t see any, but there was something in the man's stance, in his build, in the smile, something that was intimately familiar, a bit like looking at an old photo of yourself. The black and white image added to the illusion, because his great-grandfather’s brown hair and dark blue eyes were made dark, like his own black hair and dark brown eyes. He knew the true look of his great grandfather: light brown hair, which stayed mostly brown, even in old age, pink complexion, eyes gray-blue like steel ingots. The Admiral’s portrait hung in the Academy library and he’d stared at it often in his days as a cadet, then as a teacher and researcher. This imagined resemblance was a stupid notion, he thought, a coincidence, a trick of light and shadow, and, of course, of the uniform. His great-grandfather died childless save for an adopted son. That adopted son was Penn Fuller’s natural grandfather, so there could be no resemblance, except by chance, or by Penn’s own conceit. Even the adoption had its limitations. The Admiral’s adopted boy, renamed Asher Pennington Fuller, kept his last name, because, it was thought, he descended from the Mayflower Fullers, a pedigree, if ever proven, even more substantial than a Pennington.

Lt. Commander Penn Fuller, Ph.D. as of two weeks ago, was now an Assistant Professor at the Naval Academy. The promotion from adjunct to assistant was a welcome surprise. He was a Navy officer, so it brought no added pay, but there was a bit of prestige attached to it. The promotion also promised that if his health did force him into early retirement, he could remain at the Academy as a professor and be on tenure track. As he told his aunt, he was officially researching his second book, a book on the career of his own Great-grandfather. Although Penn was curious about his ancestor and was frustrated with the results of his research on the Admiral, by a happy coincidence a book on Admiral Pennington had been suggested independently by the Department Chairman, Captain Southerland who was curious about the Admiral himself. If anyone was a candidate for such a book, it was Penn with his penchant for scholarship, his naval experience and his family connection to the Admiral.

Vice Admiral Pennington, although a prominent and influential officer, seemed to have left behind very little documentation of his activities. The Admiral spent a good part of his career in the shadowy world of Naval intelligence, acting as an advisor to the CNO and the Secretary. His final assignment was to MacArthur's staff, at the General's request, just before the Japanese surrender. His influence must have been considerable because his name often appeared in cryptic but tantalizing notes and memos passed about the President's cabinet and the Navy Secretary's office. Penn had seen one of these himself while rummaging among boxes stored with declassified documents. In 1940, a long report, stamped TOP SECRET, on the state of the Japanese military was prepared for Secretary Knox by military intelligence. The upshot of the report was that the Japanese, for various economic and practical reasons, couldn't pursue an all-out war with the U.S. and its Allies for more than three months, six at most. Knox had checked marked each paragraph, but had written on the face page. *What does AP have to say about it?* Beneath Knox's comment, in a different hand, *Malarkey -- AP.* "AP" was Admiral Pennington. Knox had check-marked that, as well.

Penn knew the basic facts. Admiral Pennington, or, more precisely, Vice Admiral Pennington, Penn Fuller's great-grandfather, was almost seventy-nine years old when he died. The old Admiral was killed in an aircraft accident in Japan in 1947. After thirty-seven years of active service through 2 wars and after sailoring in almost every sea or ocean on earth, he retired with the permanent rank of Rear Admiral in 1920. He stayed on in government, however, as a consultant to the Secretary of the Navy, with the awkward title, "Special Assistant for Strategy and Modernization." His actual work in the Naval Department was concerned with Far Eastern intelligence and quite secretive. Now, of course, that work has all been unclassified, but finding records of it was not easy. The Admiral was recalled to military service just before WWII because of his extensive knowledge of the Pacific Rim, especially Japan, Japanese culture and the Japanese military. He also spoke passable Japanese, read the language somewhat, and understood much more of it than he spoke. As a young Lieutenant before the turn of the 20th century, he even trained for several years with the Japanese land and naval forces.

He stayed on active duty with the forces of occupation in Japan after 1945, a Vice Admiral, consultant to and confidant of MacArthur. He was vigorous, strong and clear-headed, and looked younger than his years. The Japanese liked and respected him. They respected age, which they confused with wisdom, and were charmed by his knowledge of their history and language.

He died because Bell Aircraft's quality assurance failed, or rather its subcontractors failed Bell. In the heat of wartime production, the company hurriedly bolted together a B-29 eventually delivered to Japan and used by the occupation forces. The Admiral died in that plane, one of the last to roll off the assembly line in Marietta, Georgia. He was on a flight from Osaka to Tokyo. The plane's landing gear collapsed as it touched down at Tokyo military field. That was the first failure. He would have survived that, but Bell had been shipped a set of pork-chop fittings that were not properly heat-treated. The subcontractor was being pressed to make deliveries and the foreman thought *what the hell, the war's almost over anyway.* When the Government's Quality Assurance official wasn't looking, he slipped the untreated fittings into shipment. The pork chop fittings are brackets that hold the sides of the plane to its bottom. When the landing gear failed, if the fittings had been properly heat-treated, the plane would have slid on its belly and eventually stopped. Passengers, crew and cargo probably would have emerged unscathed. Instead, the fittings split and shattered, the fuselage disintegrated, the wings collapsed, and the wing tanks ruptured and exploded. That, at least, was the finding in the official investigation of the crash. No one was ever blamed, fined or jailed.

As the Admiral's will requested, his burned body was buried with full honors in a tomb in Yokohama, Japan, in a coffin overlaid with American and Japanese flags. There, by express wish of the Emperor, he is perpetually mourned and prayed-for by Shinto priests. Funny fate for a Yankee from Lexington, Mass, whose ancestors had been among the first Englishmen to settle in the Massachusetts Bay Colony.

The picture of the five Ensigns must have lain between the pages of the book for a century. It was well preserved, not at all faded or cracked, and reasonably sharp. The sharpness of the image could be electronically enhanced. He photographed it then slipped it into a preservationist's envelope and put that in turn into a hard plastic casing. Although he was wearing thin lint-free gloves, he was nevertheless careful to touch only the edges of the old photo. He flipped through the remaining yearbooks looking for notes. Nothing. No inscriptions, no notes. With nothing to personalize then the books meant little to him and, besides, he had gone through the archives at the Academy a month before. He found his Great-grandfather's class of 1889, read through the entries. There was nothing much on the young man in them, nothing you could look to that would provide an inkling of the kind of officer he would become. The photo with the four classmates inferred more, that he was athletic, well-liked and made good friends. He'd find out their names later, when he review the microfiche or the computer files of the old books.

Penn was surprised to find the Admiral graduated among the

top five of the thirty-four graduates in his class. The graduates at the very top often didn't make careers of the Navy, but left it for lucrative jobs elsewhere, but not John Pennington. He went into the Academy with a lifetime commitment to the service. The family liked to brag that the Admiral ran away, joined the Navy, and like a true bred Yankee rose from the ranks. They boasted that he passed the Annapolis exam and was admitted that year as the only Plebe in his class who came from the fleet. As Penn himself knew, coming from the fleet was no handicap. It gave him an edge. By the time he started at the Academy he already had time at sea, knew ships and men, and had developed a keen sense of his own destiny. As a very young man, the Admiral learned to emulate the type of leader who gave orders and was obeyed by men not out of fear or duty but because he knew his craft, made sound decisions, and men liked and trusted him. As his career evolved, he was the perfect line officer who loved sea craft and sailing. He had other talents, though, and because of his other talents, was destined to spend more time at Naval Headquarters than at sea.

Penn was respectful of the things he touched, careful not to damage a thing, and careful regarding their placement. After clearing the trunk, checking for a false bottom or sides and looking for a secret compartment, none of which he found, he put the contents he didn't remove back in as he found them, sheets and blankets on top, and replaced the wooden tray that sat above them. The trunk was well made of white oak, lined with cedar, still fragrant with the smell of cedar. The lid curved upward, in an s-curve that flowed into a hyperbolic dome. In the dome of the lid were three built-in compartments with their own hinged lids. He opened one and found nothing. The compartment on the far right, however, contained a small stack of letters, as did the middle one. The letters were addressed to John Pennington, % Marbright, and Fuller, 221 First Street, Boston, Mass., USA. The handwriting was calligraphic, too pretty to be anyone's natural hand. The return address was

Hiroshima, Japan. Penn thought for a minute about the propriety of reading any of the letters -- he was a deeply ethical and moral man -- but decided that correspondence a century old could not betray secrets or harm anyone. He carefully opened an envelope and unfolded what appeared to be expensive and beautiful paper. The letter began "My Dearest John" and there the English stopped; the rest was in Japanese.

He knew some spoken Japanese, but he'd forgotten most of the basic ideographs he'd learned, and besides, this scrip wasn't Kanji, it was old, calligraphic, quite beautiful but to him virtually uninterpretable. There were a few ideographs he thought he could read - "child.," "good," "mother," "buy and sell" (business), "tree," he picked them out, but discerned no coherent meaning. He put the letter in a special envelope, opened no other letters, but collected them all, carefully sealing all 47 of them in individual acid-free bags, numbering and dating the bags, and labeling them with the place found. He then closed the trunk, perhaps for another century.

There was little else in the attic – a broken fan, ancient rat traps, a stack of worn women's shoes, a broken mirror with an elaborate carved frame, horribly ugly to his eyes, nothing more. He even walked the floor, testing for loose boards, but found none.

Harriet asked him to come to her in uniform. He knew she would. He had his best uniform cleaned and pressed, inspected all the ribbons and stripes to make sure everything was perfect, selected a new tie and shirt, and despite the fact that many officers now wore patent leather, he hated it, and donned real leather shoes polished to a high shine.

He called on her precisely at seven. She lived in a well-maintained Victorian house with a large enclosed porch that wrapped around three sides. It was November and chilly, the sun had set and the stars carpeted the clear Vermont night. The air was fresh and sweet with the smell of pine and oak and on her quiet street nothing stirred. No cars, no people walking, no stray dogs or cats, even the squirrels were hunkered down for the night.

He rang the bell.

"Open the door and let yourself, Penn," called Harriet.

"How do you know it's me?"

"Well, it could be a rapist, but either way I win," she said in her clipped Yankee accent.

He opened the door and entered the living room. Harriet always hated small rooms, and over the years had walls removed and the ground floor opened up. It wasn't exactly "open concept" since the large kitchen was still sealed off, but it was open enough. The living room flowed into the dining room to form an L-shape that made the house seem airy and light. The furniture was modern, the fireplace, with variegated glass tiles and a carved red-veined marble mantle, was pristine because she'd had it rebuilt to run on gas. The floors were of dark, rich rosewood, and the high plaster ceilings were accented with eight inch, rough cut cedar beams. The house smelled of cedar and pine and fresh air. Harriet sat ensconced on a large, soft, leather armchair the color of a Morocco-bound book, her legs crossed, blue pumps on, a drink in her hand. She was dressed in a pale blue that reflected the blue of her eyes. Her dress buttoned at the neck and her shoulders were covered, but she looked better than almost any woman at age 87, better than some at age 60.

"You're shameless," he said.

"Rather shameless than a feminist. You know what I don't like about feminists?

"No. Tell me."

"They've no sense of humor, no concept of irony. It's the same with any goddamn ideologue. Give me H.L. Menken, who no one reads any more, or Mark Twain, or Shaw, or even Huxley. They could see through the veneer of pretention and respectability, laugh at hypocrisy and cherish their own venial sins. Even their mortal ones… Want a drink?"

"Think I can handle it?"

He took a step forward.

"Stand there for a moment. I want to look at you." There was a pause. "Jesus in Heaven, you look like him."

"Who?"

"The Admiral, who else?

"I've seen his portrait. His eyes, hair, everything is different."

"I don't mean that. Ever hear of a Chinese poet, Li Po?"

"I never read him."

"He tells the story of a great Master of the Horse who was sent by the Emperor to find a beautiful horse for his new wife."

"The Horse Master, a very old man, disappeared for three months and returned at last to say he found the most beautiful horse he had seen in the course of his long life. It was a white mare now being kept by a farmer who lived near a certain town – I don't remember the name of the town. He could be found because his farm was the first one as you left the main road and followed the path to the village. Soldiers were sent with bags of money to purchase the horse, for the Emperor would pay a fair price for such a beautiful animal. Within a day, the soldiers returned without the horse. When the Horse Master demanded to know why, they said, 'We found no white mare, sir. The only horse the farmer had was dappled gray and brown, with a long, dark mane and tale.' 'Are you blind? That is the horse,' said Li Po, 'bring him.' 'But master he looks nothing like the horse you described,' they said. 'Yes, yes, but you're only looking at his skin. I see through that to the muscle and sinew and brain. The color means nothing.' They retrieved the horse and she did prove to be a very fine horse, loved by the Empress, a horse who gave birth to fine horses and thus served the dynasty for centuries."

"And I'm the horse?"

"You have a quick mind, don't you?"

"How am I like the Admiral?"

"You're his size. His build. You walk like him, hold your head like him, have his temperament, even have his interests. In this light you're him with darker hair."

"We weren't related."

"Oh, Penn, what does that mean? One doesn't know all his relations and sometimes very weak relations reveal remarkable similarities. There's a book on the shelf over there about MacArthur. Find the photo of Arthur MacArthur and see who he reminds you of."

It was Manchester's *American Caesar*. Penn retrieved the book and opened it. The photo of Arthur MacArthur was with the collection of images in the center.

"If I didn't know any better I'd say this was a photo of Teddy Roosevelt in uniform," said Penn

"MacArthur was a distant cousin of Roosevelt. See what I mean about relations?"

"There's a point to this, isn't there?"

She smiled. "Yes, there's a point."

"And?"

"You're destined for a star, three of four stars. Play your cards right and you'll be CNO, or something damn close to it one day."

"Auntie…"

"Don't 'Auntie' me, Lieutenant Commander. You've got the intelligence, the guts and the qualities to make it to the very top. I doubt I'll live long enough to see you get there, but I want to see you on the way."

"I was awarded my Ph.D., you know."

"Yes. Congratulations…" she said without enthusiasm. She paused and sipped at her drink. It appeared to be a Margarita. "Think about teaching school after you've retired if you're not too busy sitting on corporate boards or advising presidents. I know you're an idealist, Penn. So was the Admiral. Work for your ideals. Try to put yourself in a place where your influence can make those ideals a reality. You need power to do that and rank. You'll have neither as a professor, even an Academy professor. "

There was more than a little truth in what she said.

"What do you want me to do, Auntie? I'm stuck where I am until the Medical Board releases me for unrestricted duty."

"Piss on the Medical Board! They'll release you. Hell, they've released one-eyed, on-legged, on-armed jacks, haven't they?"

"It all depends on the needs of the Service. You know that, Aunt Harriett."

"They need you. Don't worry. The Medical Board is your least concern. What you need now is the right wife."

He smiled. So that's what this was all about. "Have anyone in mind?"

"Hell, yes. Ever hear of Katie Hobson?" Another pull at her drink.

"I went out with her a few weeks ago."

"What did you think?" She cocked her head to the side, like some predators do when sizing up their prey.

"I liked her."

"That's all? You liked her?"

"Let's see, she's pretty, has a tight body. Is graceful, intelligent and fun to be with. She speaks French and Spanish, has graduated from Georgia Tech and Emory, and has a job in Public Health at the CDC in Atlanta. Her parents are rich. Very rich judging by the size of their house in Buckhead, Atlanta's poshest neighborhood. Her biological father will probably be the next Chief of Naval Operations."

"You've been to her house?"

"I looked it up on Google."

"Yes," said Harriett, pulling at her drink again, "So did I. Got the address from Julie."

Penn finally took a seat on the beige leather sofa. It was inexpressibly soft and comfortable.

"Go, get yourself a drink. There's a pitcher of Margarita on the sideboard, pour yourself one and refresh mine."

Penn ventured into the dining room. The dining room set was contemporary, a large, oiled zebra wood table, with matching chairs and sideboard. The top of the sideboard was protected with a thick sheet of clear tempered glass The Margarita pitcher sat on the sideboard's glass next to a bottle of Bacardi Rum, and in the center of the sideboard was a large bronze statuette, almost a meter high, of a ballerina en point in arabesque. The ballerina was nude, an anatomically perfect nude, save for her ballet shoes. She looked like Harriett at age 20. The Margarita in the pitcher had a touch of alcohol, but not much. The rum was there to let the visitor spike it higher. Penn didn't add any rum. He wanted a clear head. But his throat was dry, the drink was cold and refreshing, and he practically gulped it down.

"That wasn't you in toe shoes, was it Auntie?"

She grinned.

"You'd never guess who it was."

"I have no idea, but she has your smile."

"She should. That was my mother. She earned her way through Brown modeling for a salacious old bastard in Providence whose hobby was crafting nude statuettes. Brown started admitting women in 1891, long before Harvard or Yale. Had they known about her, they probably would have reverted to misogynism and gone celibate again."

"The sculptor was heck of a craftsman. Have I heard of him?"

“Ambrose Graft.”

“Auntie, that statuette belongs in a museum. I’ve seen his work alongside Singer Sergeant at the Metropolitan. Heck, he’s in the Louvre”

“Yeah, the French would like him, and Sergeant had trouble keeping his pants on, too. They belong together, he and Sergeant, the Viagra twins, brothers of the one-eyed snake.” She laughed. “Don’t make artists like that anymore. Momma told me that old buzzard Graft – he was damn near seventy when she was nineteen -- would leave love notes in her locker and proposed marriage to her once a week. Liked to put his hands on her when she was modeling; she had to fight him off several times. Didn’t stop her from posing for him.”

“What did the family think about it?”

“She told them she had an art scholarship. Well, she did in a way. They never asked what an art scholarship had to do with her studies in geology, which is what she got her degree in. They were Yankees, and they didn’t ask any questions because she got the education for free. Since you like it, I’m leaving it to you. You can donate it to the Met if you want. As for me, I don’t want those goddamn New Yorkers to have a thing I leave behind.”

There was a pause. He went for a refill. She declined, and he took another long look at the statuette. It was gorgeous. She was gorgeous.

“I want you to court Kate. She’s perfect for you.”

“Auntie, I may ask her out again but I’m still far from courting her or anyone.”

“I know you’re not gay, Penn. Is there someone else?”

Everyone else, he thought. He wasn’t ready to settle with anyone yet.

“No, there’s no one else.”

"Holding out for something better?"

"No. I doubt if I could do much better than Kate, but that's judging her by only one evening."

"Then go to it, Penn. This is the opportunity of a lifetime."

"Auntie…."

"Alright, I hoped it wouldn't come to this, but since we talked on the phone, I called Seth Williams the other day – local lock smith – and we plan to open some boxes and trunks that are in the garage. You were looking for documents. I know there's paper there -- letters, reports, orders and photos going back to the 1890s, not a very big pile, but more than you have now. All from the Admiral." She paused.

Penn sat bolt upright. "And… Aunt Harriett?"

"They're yours if…."

"If what, Auntie?"

"If you just give Kate a chance. Ask her out. Open your mind and heart to her. Don't think of your career or advancement, just think of her as a woman and try honestly to like her and to let yourself love her."

"That's blackmail."

"No, it's not. It's bribery. Get your accusations and sins straight or you'll never go to heaven."

Penn sighed. Harriett was a rock. He knew that. She'd let the house burn down rather than admit she was wrong to the firemen.

"Ok, but here's the deal. I'll call her and ask her out. If she'll see me…"

"Don't act coy. If she's met you, she's already nuts about you."

"If she'll see me, I'll give us an honest chance. She may like me. She may not. I may or may not like her. After the first date I get free access to everything you have. If I like her enough, if I love her, I'll ask her to marry me, but that may not come for a while. Are we agreed?"

"Will you call her tonight?"

"As soon as I leave here."

"Agreed." She stuck out her hand.

He rose, shook her hand once, raised it to his lips with both his hands and kissed it.

"You're still my favorite, Aunt Harriett."

She closed her eyes and seemed to glow.

"You are so damn much like him. He could charm a Robin out of its worm. Come back tomorrow at 10 AM sharp. Seth'll be here. Wear your old clothes. It's dank and dirty in there."

"What if I cheat and don't call her?"

"You won't. You're an officer and a real gentleman."

****

Chapter Six -- Ballintogher

In Ballintogher, County Sligo, Ireland, Mary Chin-O'Mara collected her late husband's, Patrick O'Mara's, papers, and in an effort to do something, anything, to keep the death of poor Patrick off her mind, began reading, sorting and filing them. Her grandfather was born in Ireland but was one generation removed from a clan of clerks who resided in Peking (as it was known in her youth and which she still called it), or some other dynastic capital for hundreds of years serving in the court of one emperor or another. He taught her to be neat and methodical in all things, to keep accurate records and to back them with duplicate and triplicate copies. Sorting documents in logical groupings, filing them and indexing the files came naturally to her and was a soothing and gentle exercise.

She sighed deeply. There had been so many deaths in recent years. First her husband, then her brother and now Patrick.

Joey Chin, her first husband, a marriage arranged by her parents although she dearly loved him at the end, left her little more than a few small debts, a break-even business that demanded endless work, and a house that needed repair. Mark, her older brother, who was her best friend and protector as a child and who always loved her, left her two million dollars in cash and gold deposits. The rest of his businesses, whose assets and goodwill were worth 50 times the fortune he left to Mary, went to his children, save for a few odd deposits that went to various charities and to an Abby of Benedictine Monks that promised to pray for his soul for eternity, even if he went straight to heaven and didn't need it. Patrick O'Mara left her five hundred thousand in cash, and property in Destin, Florida, worth over two million and growing rapidly in value. She also received a widow's pension of some $70,000 per year from the United States Army. She was sixty nine years old, in good health, rich beyond any level she had ever dreamed, but lonely and depressed. Patrick's death was a great blow.

Her late brother, Mark, emigrated to the United States when he was still a teenager, saved his money and built a substantial business in restauranting. From his first venture, *Chang's Palace*, to a string of "*Chang's Forbidden Palaces*" in the Northeastern U.S., to a contract with an international hotel chain, to his later branching work in high-end buffets, catering and wedding planning and entertaining, everything he touched made money. He was featured in magazine articles, had his picture taken with every president from Kennedy through Obama, appeared on televised cooking shows, published a dozen books and was the pride of the Chang clan.

Her late husband, Joseph "Joey" Chin was a different sort. He was hard-working, loyal, kind, and honest, and he loved her. She repaid him with disappointment by birthing three smart, pretty girls and not a single boy. He loved his girls anyway, treated them well, got them matched with good husbands – two in America, both in San Francisco, and one in Canada – but he struggled to keep his restaurant in Ballintogher above water all his life.

She missed Joey, but Patrick displaced him in her feelings and even in her memories. Joey was so busy with the restaurant, he had little time for family. After the first daughter was born, he didn't even show up at the hospital for the next two, except to take his wife and the baby home. He wasn't a cold man, just a man who struggled and never quite succeeded. His daughters loved him but he was more of a stranger to them than a father. The one thing they learned from him was to find work that would let you have a life and a family, or to marry rich. They were pretty girls and they managed to do both.

She missed her brother, but she hadn't seen him in decades and his passing was an abstraction, like the passing of stranger. There was no funeral to attend. In a final act of retribution for all the fish and other sea life he'd cooked and served, by his will he was cremated and his ashes were mixed with cement by a company who managed such things. Their chaplain, in shorts and an Hawaiian shirt, said a prayer and they dropped his lump of concrete into an artificial reef made of similarly cemented remains, a veritable underwater necropolis in the Caribbean. A Catholic priest stood by to sprinkle holy water and give the occasion some solemnity with a Pater Noster and a special blessing. The Archbishop sent a card as well, and had a High Mass said for him. The reef was thriving and teaming with sea life, and he had added his stone to the monument. His spirit, if he had one, was delighted. His death saddened her but the blow was immeasurably softened by the fortune she inherited.

Patrick O'Mara brought her love, for this marriage of her later years was a true love match. He also brought her security and undivided attention for the first time in her life. He was thoughtful and kind, loved children, horses, dogs and cats, and liked being with people, talking with them, laughing at their jokes and making jokes himself. Most of all, he loved telling stories and listening to others tell stories. He was easy to live with, too. There was never a meal she made for him that he didn't like, a drink he couldn't drink, a child he couldn't charm. He needed her as well. He would sometimes have vivid dreams – he never called them nightmares -- and wake in a cold sweat. At times, he would look across a field or into the fire and start to cry softly. When she asked the cause of his trouble, he'd simply shake his head and say it was "So sad, so sad, they lost their youth. I mourn for them. All of them. The older I get, the sadder it all is." Then, the sadness would pass quickly and he'd spy a horse he thought beautiful, or laugh at the crows that haunted his backyard, bickered with each other and chased cats, or find something to do, something vigorous and useful.

Over the years of their marriage he had her cottage, where they lived, completely rebuilt inside and out, rewired and replumbed, fully insulated in the most efficient way, so that it was cool in the summer and warm in the winter, quiet inside with no drafts or leaks. He expanded it to add another bedroom, a study and a second full bath. What had been a dark, cramped little house was now airy and light, with stone walls and a slate roof that would last for centuries, skylights, a beautiful stained glass window that featured a vine of glass roses set in thick polished wood half a millennium old for the front door, and every modern convenience, yet the cottage remained true to the town and matched well the other houses and buildings.

After a brief illness, Patrick, at age 91, died softly. He coughed and sneezed and three days later expired. His heart slowed, lost its resiliency and left him exhausted and weak. His final words were, "Thank you, Darling. You gave me love." Then, panting for breath inside an oxygen tent, "I wanted to be an engineer, you know." He squeezed her hand, closed his eyes and expired.

His death left her feeling alone and friendless, an exotic stranger with no roots in the land, living in a small island country of hearty patriots.

As she was growing up her grandfather told her stories of China and tried to imbue her with a sense of her heritage, the grandeur and history of that magnificent, ancient country. The stories were fun, but they were a mix of legend, Confucian philosophy, family lore and her grandfather's fertile sense of dramatic construction. If it wasn't that way in reality, then it should have been and for him that was good enough. Her grandfather, you see, although of Chinese blood, had absorbed much of the spirit of story-telling from the Irish. This mixing of traditions could be seen in the fictions and legends he told of ancient emperors, of the Manchu and Mongols, of witches and demons, monks and scholars, wise men and mandarins, as he borrowed freely from Irish tales and moved the venue to Asia. Saint Patrick was confused with Confucius, Cromwell with the Mongol King.

She loved her grandfather and loved his tales, but she knew she was no student of Chinese history and had only the vaguest idea of the real history of that land. The legends and myths of her grandfather, some authentic folklore, some his own invention, told of the Han and Tang and Ming dynasties but she had no coherent concept of where they ruled, who they ruled and what they did. She didn't even know whether the history of China could be told just through them or whether there were other dynasties and families that mattered. Modern China was mysterious, too. She knew what she saw on television, but her knowledge of China's path through the 20th Century and into the 21st was too fragmented. This was all so sad because the only lessons she ever had in Chinese history came from the grandfather she loved and revered, but she knew his knowledge was incomplete and polluted with legends, myths, folklore and his own constructions. In short, as Chinese-Irish, she was as ignorant, perhaps a little less so, as Irish-Americans are of their true ancestral heritage. She felt neither Chinese nor Irish nor loved. Her daughters were scattered to America and elsewhere. None of them came to Patrick's funeral, and only one sent a sympathy card. She knew her grandchildren only through photos, e-mails and holiday cards. She was secure in her home, in her wealth, but alone.

Brendan McCarthy, postman and postmaster retired, friend to every person in town, an ancient and respected citizen invited to everyone's baptism, most marriages and all funerals, peddled by Mary Chin-O'Mara's cottage and glimpsed her inside, sitting at her fine dining table staring vacantly into space, piles of paper stacked before her. It was a fine day, much too fine for this time of year, a rare sunny gift of a day from the gods and he hated to see poor Mary waste it indoors. He didn't know what widows did to pass the time. His own sweet wife, Moira, died eight years before. He knew what he did when she died and he wasn't proud of it. He'd taken her death hard, gone to drink and spent a month mourning her in an alcohol haze. That phase of his mourning ended when, drunk one night, he passed out in the mud by the road out of town, nearly drowned in a rain puddle, woke up drenched in his own vomit and dragged himself home. He looked in the mirror, was shocked at what he saw and burst into tears. He hadn't touched a drop of spirits since, well, maybe a drop but not enough to matter. Mary was twice widowed now, old, without many friends, none of them close, and by herself. So was he, but he was welcome everywhere, had a kind word for everyone as everyone had a kind word for him, and he was content with that. He peddled on and said a prayer to St. Teresa for Mary as he passed St. Teresa's School for Girls.

He would have stopped and knocked on Mary's door, said "hello," given her a friendly "good day," but Mary Chin-O'Mara, as everyone knew, was not only a widow but a rich widow. He was afraid his motives for any sudden friendliness would be misunderstood. Besides, she kept to herself, and he hardly knew her to speak to her, except from what he'd heard, had seldom entered her first husband's restaurant, and although he was a gregarious and friendly fellow, he wouldn't know what to say to her. It's then the miracle struck. The sun's reflection in the windshield of a passing truck blinded him for an instant, he went into a ditch and found himself lying topsy-turvy in a meadow used for grazing Sullivan's cows. He could swear he heard a soft whisper, a saintly voice that murmured "go to her." It was like what happened to Paul on the road to Damascus, stuck by lightning, except in his case it was a lesser mission so God used the flash from a truck's windshield and didn't bother to leave him blind. Well it could be that, couldn't it? Or it could be an accident. He treated it like Pascal's wager and followed the notion that God and St. Teresa were cooperating on this.

He brushed himself off – easy to do since he was wearing a Scottish tweed suit which can look presentable even after most clothes are a mess – turned his bicycle around and headed back up the road. Past Sullivan's pasture, past the Burns house and there it was, Mary's pretty stone cottage with its rose bushes and vines. As he peddled onward, Mary herself came out of the house to check on her roses, and to get some air. He was relieved. He couldn't very well knock on her door, say "Hello, I saw you through the window as I passed and thought you looked depressed." Her appearance out front made it easy to stop and strike up a conversation.

He stopped in front of her house. She was inspecting her rose bushes. No flowers were in bloom this late in the year but she wanted to check on the health of the bushes and vines anyway. It was part of her daily routine. She was dressed in jeans, a blouse and cashmere sweater, and over that an expensive, tight-fitting leather jacket. She didn't look her age and she moved like young woman, strong and without hesitation.

"Halloo, Mrs. O'Mara," he called, "Good day to you."

"It's Brendan McCarthy, is it not? Hello to you Brendan."

"That is me, M'am. I confess to it. Now, it may not be me, of course,"

"What do mean, it may not be you? Sure, it's you. I've known you or of you for a very long time. You brought us our mail and sold us our stamps. My parents knew your parents. Ballintogher isn't Dublin or New York, you know. It's easy to know everyone, even the ones you wish you didn't know."

Brendan grinned and responded, "I heard of a strange case last year in which a man was called before a court, sworn in and asked his name. His attorney leapt to his feet and shouted 'I object, your honor.' The judged glared at the lawyer and said in his most fearsome voice, 'What was that?' 'Your honor, my client has been asked to repeat hearsay evidence. He only knows his name because he heard his parents say it, and they never showed him the proof.'"

She smiled, "Did it get the client off?"

"No, but it got the attorney a night in jail for contempt. As for me, I've seen my birth certificate so I know my parents didn't lie."

"Praise God and Saint Patrick for that," she said, grinning.

"You know, Mrs. O'Mara I've been retired now 5 years, and I don't know I am. I always awaken in the morning with the feeling that I'm hiding from my job and that I've a pile of things to do."

She responded, "I find myself working projects that I never thought I'd have. Although, I'll tell you, working a restaurant is no easy thing. I've been splendidly retired from that."

"I've always meant to tell you that your roses are gorgeous. I don't know much about roses myself, but I do know that different varieties have different names, some names are just pretty adornments, and some are named after people. Do you have one named after you?"

"I've got *Irish Elegance,* which of course grows well here, and another hybrid, *Touch of Class,* and several others, both bushes and vines, but none named after me, thank you."

"Well, you should have one named after you, *Mary of Ballintogher*." That made her smile and her smile looked very pretty to Brendan. "I've noticed there's a mix of colors in your roses. Is that why they call them 'hybrid?'"

"Well, the colors come from the cross breeding of strains, you know. There are hybrid roses that show the color mix, but for some roses the mixed colors don't hold. Over the years the bush or vine will turn to one color or the other and produce roses of solid hue. Soil can affect the colors as well, you know."

"I had no idea… I'm not much of a horticulturist."

"But Moira, your wife, bless her soul, cultivated beautiful flowers, and you still have panels of Zinnias, Amaryllis, Pansies, Mums, and many other kinds, some of which I couldn't name but know only for their beauty. They're all annuals, so you must be planting every year."

"I have a gardener do it to honor Moira's memory. The flowers lift the spirits of those who pass by the house. I like to feel that Moira is blessing all who see them. To think she died so badly of the cancer…" he sighed.

"Joey had no time or money for flowers," said Mary, "He worked so hard and was home so little. While he lived only I had an interest in the flowers, a few rose bushes, one vine. I got the cuttings for free from one of our customers at the restaurant. When Patrick came into my life, he was retired with a good pension and plenty of time on his hands, but he was no lazy man. In Patrick I found I married a demon for work in the home. He hired two men to dig the beds, then joined them and dug as much as the two of them combined. He loaded the beds with fine planting soil and scientifically mixed fertilizer and other ingredients to give the flowers the acidy bed they loved, mixed sand with the soil deep down so the local clay could be penetrated by the roots. I had to call him in at midnight to get him to stop, and he awoke at dawn the next…" Her face suddenly contorted, she began to sob, stammered "day," but could not continue. Her shoulders heaved, she fell on her knees and the tears that eluded her for weeks came.

Brendan was not a man who could ever tolerate a woman's tears. He did not know what to do when they did so much as sob a bit, and would normally evacuate any room that held a woman who cried or looked as if she would cry. Mary was not merely sobbing, however, this was a tornado of sorrow. She was heaving and panting and keening, her face contorted, her nose running and the tears were a flood. His first impulse was to panic, hop on his bike and flee. That's when the small voice seemed to come to him again, "Hold her. Comfort her." That voice – Was it St. Teresa, the Little Flower? -- was clear and remarkable. *Give me a hand, Teresa*, he said to himself in a desperate little prayer. As soon as he mouthed the words, his fear drained from him, and he knew instinctively what to do. He fell to his knees beside the hysterical woman, took her in his arms, kissed her on the forehead and pulled her to him. She hugged him in return and sobbed into his chest while he stroked her hair and said little, meaningless words. Short of any wisdom to offer he began to pray the only prayer he remembered from his childhood, the "Hail Mary."

"There… there, my Mary, my good, good Mary...Hail Mary,

full of grace the Lord is with thee…" he said the prayer softly in a sing-song way, as if crooning to a baby, then said it again. Ten, fifteen minutes passed as he padded her head and back and murmured meaningless words of comfort. Eventually the fit seemed to fade, her sobbing slowed and finally stopped, but they remained in each other's arms. He gave her his handkerchief, which was clean and spotless, and she wiped her nose, dabbed at her eyes, sniffed a little and smiled shyly at him. The tornado had passed and they had survived. He kissed her on the forehead once more, and smiled back at her.

"Forgive me this familiarity, Mrs. O'Mara, but the circumstances called for it," he said.

"Forgive my frailty, Mr. McCarthy. You have been superb. And call me 'Mary' now that we've grow close."

"That I will, Mary, if you'll call me Brendan."

"Oh Brendan," she said, hugging him, "What am I? I live here with no connection to anyone, a stranger all my life, always a foreigner."

"What are you? Why, Mary, you're Irish, an Irish woman of Ballintogher, County Sligo. Your family has lived here for over a century. You're as Irish as DeValera and more Irish than the Parish Priest who came here from Poland, may God bless him."

"But I'm Chinese!"

"And what am I? My father used to say that his great grandmother -- Or perhaps great-great grandmother; he would add an extra "great," sometimes two, every now and then. I lost count of the 'greats.' – anyway, he said the woman came from Zaragoza, Spain, where my great, great grandfather, a soldier in Wellington's army met her. It's from her we get our dark hair and eyes. Zaragoza was once a Roman city called 'Caesar Augustus' that over time and various occupations by Moors and Arabs who mispronounced the name, became Zaragoza, which must have been fine with the

Spanish who took it back in 1491 because they kept the name. God knows what a splendid mix of races blended in that town and made its way into my blood – Italians, Spanish, Goths, Moors, Arabs, Jews and Gypsies. On the other side of my family, my mother swore one of her ancestors came from Armenia, and my Uncle said there were both Jews and Turks in our line. The Mayor, Joseph Walsh, can trace his ancestry back to Wales, and God knows where the greatest living Irish patriot's ancestors were spawned, it's Robert Briscoe I mean, of course, who's Jewish. All Irish are descended from Irish who mixed with Swedes and Danes, from the old English who settled here under Henry II, from the new English who came after the old, from the Flemish in Henry's army, from the Welsh, from Scots, from Spaniards, from Norman Frenchmen, who themselves were a mix of Scandinavians, Franks and whatever, from Germans and probably from Eskimos and Hottentots as well. Your ancestors are from somewhere in China. So what? You were born here. That's all that matters."

"Sometimes I think that, but mostly I don't know who I am or where I belong," she said.

"Me, too, but it's easier for me because I look the part. Let me tell you this -- You, Mary, and your family are part of the fabric of Ballintogher. Your people came here from 10,000 miles away and brought us a wonderful gift, the exotic foods and dishes of the Far East. What a remarkable, miraculous thing it is that we were blessed by you all these years, that you gave us something we could never have known without your gift. There should be a monument to you in the town. In fact, I'll collar his Honor, Joe Walsh, tomorrow, and demand it should be done."

She smiled broadly and Brendan spied a twinkle in her eye. "Do it, Brendan, and I'll make you Moo Goo Gai Pan."

"The way I look at, Mary, maybe 50,000 years ago we were all in a group that left Mesopotamia for greener lands. Somewhere in what's now Turkey, we parted, families split, and half of us went

East while the other half went West. I'm sure we shook hands and hugged and cried and bid each other luck and success, promised to write, then went our way. Over many thousands of years, some descendants of that mob crossed over to England, which was not yet an island and still part of Europe, saw Ireland on the horizon, and somehow made the trip there. Those who went East entered what today is China, and some kept going to Mongolia to the Bearing land bridge, for it existed in those ancient times, and into the Americas. They became the Indians of the New World. All of us, whatever our pretentions to race are, came from the same stock, are the same people. We all belong." He kissed her chastely once more and let her go. They stood. She was recovered.

"Can I offer you a spot of tea?" she said, brushing the dirt off her knees.

"I could use one to bolster me on the ride home, but only if you're going to make it for yourself anyway. I wouldn't want to put you out."

"It's nothing, Brendan, I've got a tea-making machine that produces a perfect cup with no work on my part. Besides, I want to talk with someone about my Patrick's papers anyway. Do you know anyone who knows much about the military?"

"When I was a lad of 16, I signed onto a ship that made its way to Canada. I left the ship on my seventeenth birthday, crossed the border and went to Boston. I found work, but nothing much, and being an 'illegal,' as they call it in the States, had to look over my shoulder every minute. The Americans were fighting in Vietnam and the army needed men. I was out of work and out of money so I talked to a recruiter and found that I could enlist and if I served in Vietnam would be promised citizenship after two years of residency. I lied, told him I was 18 and that I'd been in the states for 15 months. They took me, trained me, fed me, paid me, and sent me to Vietnam. Three months into my time in Vietnam, I became a U.S. citizen."

"Hard way to do it," she said.

"Not very hard. I worked for the brigade supply Sergeant, an Irish-American named 'O'Connor,' whose ancestors were from County Mayo. I was stationed at China Beach, DaNang, one of the most beautiful spots you've ever seen. I had it better than most officers, and I never saw any combat. I did save all my money, though. I stayed in the U.S. Army for six years, most of the time after Vietnam at the Presidio, an Army base that was in San Francisco. I was a Staff Sergeant and I would have stayed in another 14 years until I could retire when my father and mother wrote to me and told me the sad news of my older brother's death. They needed me in the store, so I came back. I've never regretted it. I met my beautiful, sweet Moira at that store, married her and loved her for 30 years. My father's little store was also the postal center. When they opened a real post office here, my father retired and I became the first mailman and then the first Post Master, which is why I'm famous in Ballintogher."

With a mug of hot tea in each hand, she led him into the dining room.

"Welcome to my office. Here are the papers I read and understand" she pointed with one mug to a small pile in the corner, "Here are the ones I'm having trouble with," she pointed with another mug to a neat stack about one inch high, "And the rest are the great pile in the center. Can you help me with these?"

He shuffled a handful from the pile in the middle. "Army documents, some from my era, too, some from before then. Sure I could. I was a great Army clerk in my day."

A friendship began. Brendan read the documents and interpreted them for her, but it wasn't enough. Mary had a small computer and he used it to search historical records to reconstruct the time line and put the events in context that spawned the orders, letters, memos and the rest of the assorted papers in the pile.

The work seemed to give her a kind of courage, too. She was always shy, but she grew reclusive after her second husband died and she came into money. Her wealth allowed her to live virtually without leaving her cottage. Now, however, she began to make excursions into the village on a fine bicycle to buy her bread and other things. Everyone knew her or about her because she lived in Ballintogher her entire life and because her late husband Patrick used to invite people to the house to talk. He was a great raconteur. He would talk while she would welcome people, smile and serve drinks, but she said little herself on those occasions. In the village, she began to greet people by name and they would respond with gusto. She volunteered a few hours per week at the local clinic, helped with services for the housebound or handicapped, read stories to the children at the library and the school, and contributed substantially to local charities. Soon she was part of the scene, one of the elders and icons of Ballintogher, welcome in people's homes, respected for her wit and charm, her warmth and kindness. She found herself being invited to weddings and funerals, to baptisms, to recitals. She was asked her opinion on matters concerning the village, sat on village councils, conferred with and wrote to the mayor, who kindly replied to her suggestions, which were always creative and helpful if not always followed.

Brendan, meanwhile, helped her build in a cohesive way the story of Patrick O'Mara's life, and enjoyed doing it, enjoyed the time he spent with her, and felt whole and content. In her large collection of O'Mara's papers, there were military orders, memos and letters, citations, award documents, the transcript of two Military Board hearings, personal letters, and notes and comments written by O'Mara himself. One of those letters, apparently never mailed, caught Brendan's eye. He read it and silently passed it to Mary, who was reviewing some other papers.

"What's this?" she said, taking the paper from him.

"It's a letter from Patrick," he said, "Read it, Mary, and tell me what you think."

She took it from him, moved by seeing Patrick's precise

handwriting. Patrick had wanted to be an engineer after all and his script looked like the lettering of an old-fashioned blueprint.

From: Patrick O'Mara, Lt. Colonel, United States Army, retired

To: The Widow of Admiral Marion Butler, United States Navy

My Dear Mrs. Butler:

I knew your husband as the Commander of the USS *Sioux*, a destroyer that was part of the fleet that led our heroic invasion of the Inchon Peninsula, Korea. He was a good commander respected by all of us on board ship, and a good man. His death was an awful blow to everyone, and all who knew him mourned his passing, especially me. It was my plane that struck the bridge of the *Sioux* and killed him. I cannot tell you how much that has dwelt in my mind and how many times I have gone over that awful night recounting the facts that led to the fatal accident.

First, I am in the Army, not the Navy. The Navy needed pilots for its observation planes and I volunteered for assignment to the fleet. I flew a Curtis SOC-3 observation plane. It was made in 1941 but saw little service during the war. It was a good pontoon plane, made for catapulting from a ship and for being recovered from the open sea. It was made with care and it flew well but slowly. That gloomy September night, I catapulted off the deck of the *Sioux*. A catapult is a violent thing. You feel its kick like a punch in the back, and unless your wits are with you, you can lose control easily and crash into the ocean. I only practiced a catapult take off once before that night, and that practice was in daylight. When I was launched on that night, it was pitch dark. There was almost no visible horizon and what could be seen of the line between sky and sea drifted in and out of vision, the sea and the sky melting together. I had to rely on my instruments, which were not that good and my instincts, which were probably worse.

In a sweat I pulled back on the stick, pointed her up and hoped she would climb rapidly at a steep ascent without stalling. I made it up and headed east at 5,000 feet. As I approached land, I came down lower to see whatever I could see. My orders were to observe and report and that's all I could do. The aircraft had no armament, and that night I was the only one aboard. I came down near the water and could see the blue harbor lights that led ships in. The Communists were so confident that any invasion would take place at the southern end of the country, they didn't even bother to extinguish the harbor guide lights. I reported this and kept going. I knew I was over land when the string of blue lights was played out and as soon as they disappeared, I cruised slower, looking for any sign of movement towards the port. I was hoping to see truck lights, even muted ones, or a flash of some sort, even a fire, but I saw nothing. By this time my eyes were so used to the dark, I could just pick out a road below. The moon came out from behind the clouds and that helped. By moonlight I could see a few more details. I dropped lower, to just above treetop level and looked for anything that moved. I followed that one road until my fuel ran low and I was almost at the point of no return. Just as I was set to head back to the fleet, a column of men and trucks appeared on the horizon. I wanted to get an idea of the size of the column, of the equipment they had, so I flew straight at them, hoping they'd mistake me for a friendly in the dark, but they didn't. I flew right into a barrage of small arms fire, climbed and turned back.

Rounds penetrated the fuselage and knocked out my instrument panel, at least most of it. I flew back, following the road, found the harbor, and tried to radio the *Sioux,* but my radio was out as well. As the ships came into view beneath me, my engine sputtered and failed. I couldn't restart it and the plane fell, gliding in a steep path toward the ocean. I knew it would crash and sink. You need power to land a plane on the sea, and a sea crash would destroy the plane and probably kill me. I had no time to think. The controls were difficult to handle without power, but I managed to flatten the plane's trajectory a small amount and point it away from the fleet.

At the very last minute, thinking the plane would fall somewhere in the sea, I bailed out. The *Winslow*, a sister ship of the *Sioux*, saw my parachute. The crew shined their searchlight on me and picked me up. I was only in the water about one-half hour, chilled to the bone and soaking wet, but alive and safe.

My plane didn't stay on course. The wind was blowing in powerful gusts over the ocean. It pummeled the plane and pushed it around. After I bailed out, the plane, pushed by the wind, came round and dove into the line of ships. As I parachuted down the wind buffeted me, too, and I swung to and fro like a pendulum. Still in the air, I caught just a glimpse the plane falling in a sharp dive in the wrong direction. Later, I found out It came low and crashed head-on into the *Sioux's* bridge. It killed Captain Butler, the First Officer, Commander Guzman, and the Quartermaster, Chief Richardson. All were fine men.

There was a Board of Inquiry convened some time later. A Navy team inspected my plane. The fuselage was mostly intact – the nose and engine bore the brunt of the crash. They counted 14 hits from enemy rounds, mostly 50 caliber size from a large machine gun. The fuel tank was penetrated and the controls and radio destroyed. One round went right through the floor of the cockpit and exited out the side. By some miracle I wasn't hit. Had I not tried to overfly the enemy on my patrol, I would have returned with plenty of fuel, more than enough to put the plane down on its pontoons and be recovered. They exonerated me, however, said I did my duty and, since the crash happened because of enemy action, decorated the fatally wounded sailors with the Purple Heart.

This has always weighed heavily on me. I know Admiral Butler had not been married long and that he loved and cherished his wife. He spoke with me briefly about his marriage, showed me your wedding picture, and was extremely proud of you, of your wit and intelligence and beauty. He considered himself to be among the luckiest people alive. He died with that love for you in his heart. I've heard it said he called your name before he passed out and never awakened.

There is nothing I can do to change this event. I've questioned my motives and judgment a thousand times, kicked myself for my vain bravado. Things which seem courageous are often tainted with sins of vanity and pride, and I have begged God for his forgiveness for the sin I committed that night. Had I been less reckless and more of the soldier I thought myself, had I just flown higher or a bit to the side when I saw the enemy column, had I stayed with the plane and risked a sea crash, your husband and two other good men would have lived and you would have enjoyed happiness with him.

If it is any consolation, he was a superb officer. I respected and admired him as did all the officers and men on that ship. He deserves the accolades he received and more. It would have been better for the world had I died that night and he lived, but that wasn't to be.

Please accept my condolences and my prayers.

Sincerely,

Patrick James O'Mara, Lt. Colonel, USAR

There was a note clipped to the letter.

To whom it may concern:

If you're reading this, I'm probably dead or demented. I never had the courage to send it and so many years have passed, I don't imagine it would be easy to find the person I intended it for. If you can find her, please send it for me.

Patrick

Mary sighed deeply. It was so like Patrick to blame himself for an accident of wind and circumstance.

"You read it, Brendan, what do you think?"

"I think Patrick was too hard on himself. He was told to observe. Perhaps, in hindsight, he could have been more careful, flown higher over that column, turned back earlier, who knows? 'Could have' and 'should have' are the great enemies of contentment, aren't they? As a soldier it was his duty to see what he could see. If there was an enemy column approaching, it would have been his duty to overfly them and try to ascertain how large the column was and whether it had any tanks, self-propelled artillery, air defenses and whatever else he could discover. It was in the dark of night. He wanted to come in low to get a good look – what else could he do? -- and he risked his life in pursuit of his duty. He was doing his job. The eventual consequences were nothing he could know when he did it."

"Do you think we should try to find the widow?"

"Yes. That's what he wanted."

"How do we do that?"

"It shouldn't be too hard. If she's still collecting his pension, the Pentagon will know where she is and what her current name is, if she remarried."

"Will they tell us?"

"No, but Patrick held the Congressional Medal of Honor, and Butler was an Admiral. That'll peak their interest. We can send the letter to the Navy and ask them to forward it. The widow, if she's alive, can respond to us if she wants to, or she can remain silent. The same goes for her heirs. Either way, we've done our duty by Patrick."

"Good," said Mary. Let's do it today, Mr. Postmaster. We're not getting any younger." He kissed her nose and she smiled shyly. He was glad to see it.

By noon of that day, their letter to the Pentagon, along with a copy of Patrick's letter, was in the mail.

****

Chapter Seven – In the Attic

Penn expected Seth Williams to be a Vermont rustic, an "Ay-yuh" Yankee, old, brusque, laconic, mildly hostile, intolerant, and sarcastic. Seth was none of those things. He was from Colorado and educated at Auburn University in Alabama, which he attended on a partial athletic scholarship. Over winter vacation in his Senior year, he was invited to spend two weeks at a friend's chalet in Stowe Vermont. He fell in love with the place and moved there after graduating. His major was architecture and he hoped he could get a job with a local company designing chalets, cabins and resorts. He had limited success. The real estate market was in the doldrums, and new construction had slowed to a crawl. Building renovations and extensions were being handled by existing architects and there was nothing for a new graduate trying to find work in Vermont, especially one with mediocre grades from an Alabama school, even as good a school as Auburn. He did manage to snag a few clients, and his work was well-received, but the commissions were small and while he was still struggling, he needed a steady income. His father was a locksmith, a plumber and a general handyman, but he loved studying and picking locks and as Seth was growing up, showed Seth a number of things about them. Seth went to work for a local locksmith, got his license and when the local man retired took over the business. He was still doing some architectural work, but he earned his bread selling, installing, removing and opening locks of all kinds.

Seth was already above the garage in a dusty storage room that was cluttered with assorted old items – two large fans, a pile of tarpaulins, spare shingles for the roof, miscellaneous pieces of lumber and 2 old trunks, both triple locked.

Seth started to work right away as Penn stood by. Penn had already asked Seth to help him lower the trunk to the garage floor if anything of value were to be found inside. The first trunk was loaded with old clothing, old uniforms, a horrid linen suit, several pair of trousers, old cotton shirts, and several pair of men's shoes. There was also a box of shaving items, straight razors, safety razors, desiccated soap in an old shaving mug, and two badger fur brushes. It all had to be carefully removed, catalogued and the trunk searched for secret compartments, false bottoms, and other hiding places. Penn even went through all the clothes pockets, and felt the linings. Nothing. The items were returned exactly as they were removed.

Seth donned white gloves and helped with the project. The second trunk was much heavier than the first. Seth and Penn together hoisted it into the light by the window. The second trunk not only had its latch locks, hardware for a padlock was installed and a large key-operated *American Power Lock* kept the contents secure.

Seth shined a small mag light on the American Power Lock. "Funny," he said, "the hardware is at least seventy years old, maybe older, but this American Power Lock is fairly new."

He pointed the mag light at the lock. "See any oxidation? I don't. If you wipe off the dust, the finish returns to the original chromed shine."

He continued his inspection of the latch locks. "Someone's been at these latches, perhaps in the last couple of years. They've been opened."

Penn, looking over Seth's shoulder, said "How can you tell?"

"They're scratched. You can't see it from where you are, but someone very carefully worked these locks and in all likelihood opened this truck. You can't avoid leaving marks on an old piece like this, but you try to keep them hidden. Whoever opened this trunk probably wrapped his tools in a leather sleeve and moved the pick or master key very gently. You can just see where it touched the inside of the lock and scraped off some dirt and oxidation. He -- or she -- scratched the metal, too. Unavoidable."

"Do all locksmiths have tools like that?"

"No, they don't. Only a preservationist would buy and keep leather-sleeved picks. They're used for specialized work, not for modern locks."

"Do you have a set?" said Penn.

Seth smiled and looked up. "I do. Caleb Parsons, whose business I took over, left me a set. He used them when working on antiques or on something expensive and delicate. The antique market in Vermont is its major cottage industry. Every old family has an old barn loaded with junk they were too cautious to let go or too lazy to dump or too cheap to have hauled-away. It's amazing how much folks from Boston or New York will pay for an old scrub-board or a cracked leather suitcase."

"You think he worked on this trunk?"

"You know, I checked the records and saw two previous calls from Henrietta Butler, but both of them had to do with car locks, that is locking the keys in the car, which is a pretty common problem. Nothing on trunks. That doesn't mean much, though. Locksmithing is mostly a cash business and Caleb's records could have holes in them. He always felt that taxes were too high and that too much paperwork was a magnet for the IRS, not that he was ever audited."

Seth stood. "The American Power Lock can be picked, but it would take me a while. It's not an heirloom. Do you mind if I just snap it off with a cable cutter?"

"Is there any other way? Henrietta didn't have a key, did she?"

Seth shook his head. "Told me she didn't have a key and had no idea where to look for one." He paused for a moment. "Let's see, I could take my time and pick it, but even when I got it open it would be useless without the key. We could contact the company, give them the serial number and ask for the key, but there's no guarantee we would get it and that process might take a month or two."

"How old do you think it is?"

"My guess is less than 2 years old, maybe a few years older. I'm guessing by the lack of oxidation. I can call the company and ask."

"Go ahead."

American Power Lock was delighted to help and confirmed the production run that made the lock was in November, three years earlier.

"One thing more," said Seth, squatting down again, "I want to take a look at the hinges, see if the dirt and rust on them has been disturbed. Someone could have just added the lock without opening up the trunk." Out came the Mag light again. "Yep, this truck has been opened in the past couple of years. The rust spots are broken in a few places and the dust and dirt are a lot thinner here."

Penn handed him his digital camera. "Let's get pictures of all this before we break the lock and open it up."

Seth photographed the hinges several times, got close-ups of the scratching in the latch locks and took several pictures of the trunk from the outside, even a close-up of the unbroken American Power Lock. Once the record was complete, he went back to his truck and returned with a large pair of cable-cutters. The tool wasn't new, but Penn's practiced eye saw that it was well maintained, lightly oiled to keep the rust away, and probably stored in such a way that it didn't scratch other tools. Later, as they were leaving and Penn saw Seth put the tools into storage in the panel truck, he developed an appreciation for the care Seth took of everything he used. It's no definitive test of competence, but a workman or woman whose tools are maintained in order generally does work carefully and with the kind of passion that makes him or her attend to details and get it right.

Seth was careful, almost gentle in removing the lock. Although the cutters were large and clumsy, he handled them deftly and was able to pinch the steel of the lock's loop and cut it without scratching anything. *The man could have been a surgeon* thought Penn, as Seth deftly turned the broken loop and removed the lock without leaving a mark on the trunk. The latches picked easily, and Seth took care with them, too, not adding to the scratches previously made and of course not putting any marks on the exterior. Penn photographed every step. The weight of the trunk alone warned him that there was something substantial inside, although it could have just been filled with old books or something utterly worthless.

They opened the trunk and Penn found the load of documents he was looking for. There were orders, letters, notes, drawings, photos, that reached back to before the Spanish American War, into the 1890s. They were in good shape, too, some yellowed with age but the paper had held up. There were no mice or rat nibblings or droppings, always a problem with materials stored in this way, no evidence of water damage, either. The paper was frail. Paper is slightly acidic and begins to disintegrate over time, but this stuff was not in bad shape and before he was done, Penn would photograph every page, put every item in an acid-free envelope, and see that it all was stored in a properly constructed archival chamber.

Seth, who was careful not to touch any paper, whistled softly as Penn gingerly turned over a few sheets. "Was that a letter from Woodrow Wilson?"

"It might have been from Wilson or one of his aids or advisors," said Penn. He didn't want to say much more. Penn knew that Wilson suffered from problems of letter recognition all his life. Today, we'd call it "dyslexia." He didn't learn to read until he was 10 years old, and even then his reading was problematic. In his teenage years he compensated by learning shorthand and as an adult by using a typewriter, eventually becoming the first president to own one. His dyslexia didn't stop him from working hard at his studies, earning an undergraduate degree from Princeton, a law degree from the University of Virginia and a doctorate at Johns Hopkins. In Wilson's day, the White House staff was nothing like the army of lawyers, advisors, public relations people and general gophers and toadies that infest the modern White House. Wilson had, perhaps, four people on his personal staff at any time, relied heavily on the advice of a companion-advisor, Colonel House, and was pushed and advised by his second wife, Edith Galt. Apparently Admiral Pennington was in the small mix of advisors as well. Wilson also composed and typed his own correspondence. If this letter was from Wilson, the president might very well have typed it and signed it himself.

Penn hid his excitement and said simply, "We'll have to close the trunk, Seth, and get it safely taken to Annapolis. I can store the content there in a secure, humidity-controlled environment, start cataloging everything, and photograph every page for posterity."

Seth nodded. The trunk was closed, sealed with tape and a new padlock, and loaded into Penn's car. He was just able to close the car's trunk lid over it and lock it inside. Penn planned to leave that night for Annapolis. After that there was another drive to Atlanta to see Kate Hobson, as he promised Harriet, then reporting to Harriet on all the details worth knowing about the date. He really wanted to stay in Annapolis and begin organizing the contents of the trunk, but he made a promise to his auntie. It was part of the deal and he wouldn't break it.

Seth and Penn shook hands and Penn thanked him for his help and his care.

"Not at all, Penn," said Seth, "I enjoyed it. Come back someday and tell me what you found."

"I'll be sure to do that."

"One thing, I'm an architect by training and that's my real trade. If you ever know anyone who's thinking of building or remodeling in the Stowe area, hell, in any area between here and Siberia, let me know, will you?"

"I'll make a point of it," said Penn. Penn, always the gentleman, would eventually be true to his word.

Penn's cell phone rang just as he started his car.

"Hello, Auntie"

"How'd ya know it was me?"

"My cell phone tells me who's calling."

"How in hell does it do that?"

"It recognizes the number because I've added the number to cell phone's address book."

"I was going to get a cell phone back in '89, but they were too damn expensive."

"The phones are cheap now, Auntie."

"I suppose that's why everyone has them. Are you coming back to the house?"

"I've got a very busy week ahead of me, what's left of it, but I did plan on making some time for you."

"I don't believe you. Penn, but now that you've committed to coming over, I'll put on a pot of coffee, you can stay for a snack and then leave. I want you to make damn sure those records get to someplace safe before nightfall."

Harriet's short, thick hair was pulled back and gelled on the sides. She was dressed in mauve pants, a black top with three-quarter sleeves and turned-up collar, and slippers that looked like soft ballet shoes. It was 50s retro, and it suited her. The coffee was a dark blend of organically grown beans she bought from a company that imported only coffee grown by independent farmers. She gave Penn a brief lecture on social responsibility before she poured him a cup.

"People need a living wage, even if they are peasants and farmers working in third world countries out of our sight and mind. I don't mind paying a dollar more per pound for coffee that I know isn't being planted and picked by twenty-first century serfs working for substance wages and living in hovels," she said, her Yankee accent getting stronger as she emphasized the point.

"I didn't know you were so concerned about social justice, Auntie."

"Hell, yes. My generation cared about people. They didn't always act like it, but they cared. One of my heroines when I was growing up was Helen Keller."

"Helen Keller? The blind-deaf girl?"

"Keller may have been blind and deaf but she wasn't blind to the wrongs in this world, to the crimes of greed and selfishness and she sure as hell wasn't deaf to the cries for reform, for the fair treatment of people, for unions, for worker safety, for an end to child labor and for women's suffrage. Pushed her into socialism, though… She was a tough, strong, moral, righteous woman. Damned smart, too."

"Forgive me, Auntie, but most of the socialists I've met were well-healed people with time on their hands."

"Of course they were. They had the money and time to be socialists and they were all rich babies brought up in mink diapers who were embarrassed by a wealth they did nothing to earn, although, hell, I've known any number of Wall Street types who made lots of money with little effort yet never felt inclined towards socialism. I think that a just God would put the savable ones – the rich buggers with a conscience -- through a purgatory in which they'd have to prove their social worth. He'd have Mother Teresa manage it."

"You mean, like Jerry Brown did?"

"No, he was a dilettante having a vacation in hell. He knew he was going to emerge from that cocoon of misery a metaphorical butterfly ready to return to the politics of sunny California. I think he hoped it would both purify him of his sins and restart his political career. I don't know about his sins but his career went from V-8 to putt-putt. What is he now? Mayor of Oakland? Attorney general?

Somethin' like that. Stupid man should have married Linda Ronstadt when they were both young. Beautiful woman then. Looked like me when I was young. Shame she put on so much weight. Of course he did, too." She paused and took a drink of the coffee.

"What do you think of the coffee, Penn? Good stuff, huh?"

Penn thought of mentioning that Brown was once more Governor of the Golden State, but decided to let it be. Instead, he smiled and nodded.

"Good stuff, Auntie. I'll look for it when I get back."

"I'll order some for you… Look, you opened the trunks. Find anything of interest?"

"I think so, Auntie. One of the trunks was a dud, loaded with old clothes and nothing else. The other one, the one with the padlock, is full of letters, memos, and papers pertaining to the Admiral's life. I'm going to take the truck back to Annapolis, get everything in it photographed so that we have permanent digital images of every page, and put all the original documents in acid-free protection in a humidity controlled environment. Everything will be inventoried and cataloged. You'll be the owner, of course. The papers will be on loan to the Academy. It'll be a lot safer and a better environment than I found in that garage. I'll send you an inventory of everything."

"Could I get a tax deduction for donating them?"

"I don't know, Auntie," said Penn, "I'll ask one of the Academy lawyers. If we can put a value on the set and you want to donate it, we might be able to give you a substantial receipt. Of course, that depends upon whether the Academy wants to accept them. Emory, Harvard, some other school might want them as well. I'm sure some school or museum would accept them."

"Don't give a goddamn thing to Yale. Let the Bushes and Cheneys and Clintons do that."

Penn laughed. "My parents were Yalies, you know."

Harriett looked over her mug, a malevolent gleam in her eye. "Yes, I forgot. Well, Even Sodom had one good family."

Elizabeth, Harriet's younger sister, let herself in through the front door without knocking. Harriett feigned shock and surprise.

"Elizabeth! Good Lord you gave me a start!" said Harriet in mock complaint.

"No, I didn't Harriett. And what difference would it make if I surprised you anyway?"

"Lizzy, dear, you had no idea what I was doing in here with a gentleman. I could have been in a compromising position with some handsome young stud."

"Harriett, if you were, I'd applaud, but neither you nor I have been compromised in years, if not decades. Although I think if we had the chance… Oh! Penn is here. So sorry Penn. I hope you weren't shocked by any of the chatter."

"I'm sad to say that my life with sailors has prepared me for such talk, although I might blush any moment now."

"Don't waste your blush on us, Commander. Anything naughty you might hear is just wishful thinking. By the way, Harriett's been telling me you've been asking about the Admiral. You're going to write a book about him."

"I'm going *to try* to write a book about him. It's difficult finding sources and documents about his life and career, although I think the cache I found today will help enormously." Penn emphasized the word "try."

Harriet put down her coffee and said in a stage whisper, "Listen to the false modesty. He's going to *try* to write a book."

Elizabeth nodded. "Do you know much about him, Penn?"

"I know he had an exceptionally long career, was involved in Naval intelligence and died in occupied Japan in 1947. I also know he worked for a time on Woodrow Wilson's staff, and from what

Aunt Harriet has told me the family loved him. He was an exceptional man."

Elizabeth, pouring her own coffee, looked up, "Words like 'exceptional' and 'excellent' and 'wonderful' are over-used these days. I was taught they were superlatives that had to be reserved for those individuals and those actions that really did exceed all that everyone else did. The larger than life kind of thing. I can't speak for his career. You're the Navy officer and you're a better judge of that, but I can speak for the man I met and knew. He was exceptional, if being loved and respected by all is being exceptional. Despite everything, the family adored him, women and men, too."

Harriet narrowed her eyes and glowered at her younger sister for just a moment. The room seemed to fill with the dead weight of disapproval, as if Elizabeth had made some awful gaff and something had to be done to fix it before the floor collapsed.

"Despite everything?" said Penn looking from one Aunt to the other. Harriet was composing herself, controlling her temper and trying to appear calm and relaxed but her hand seemed to shake a little, of course that might have been just age. Penn wasn't sure how much he should read into that. Both the old girls were a bit eccentric, after all. Not that their eccentricity was tied to old age. They'd been eccentric -- if independent, intelligent and sharp-witted could be called "eccentric," -- all their lives. Elizabeth's smile had faded.

Elizabeth recovered first. "What I meant, Penn, is the Admiral was seldom with us and was very secretive about his work. Despite all that, the family loved him and respected him very much. We all wanted to be as fine as he could be, that is, as he was." She said this too sweetly and too deliberately, as if she were explaining some arbitrary restriction or limitation to a precociously intelligent child. Penn just smiled in response.

"Yes," said Harriett, now solid as a rock "I know exactly what Elizabeth means. I felt that way myself."

"I could see that," said Penn, with no conviction whatsoever.

"People are so complex, aren't they?" said Elizabeth.

Harriet raised an eyebrow and said to the room, "They're usually most complex when they've done something immoral, unnatural, or illegal…" She paused and said with a sly look "They're also more interesting."

Elizabeth giggled. "Harriett, I'm afraid, is *much* more interesting than me."

Harriet feigned astonishment and batted her eyes. "What in the world do you mean?"

"You've had many more years as a merry widow. I have a lot of catching up to do."

Harriet turned to Penn. "See what I have to put up with? Why is it you can change your address, your telephone number and with the right surgery your bra size, but not your relatives?"

No answer. Penn smiled politely.

Harriett continued, "Look, whether people are interesting or not, there are some things you'd just rather not know about them, if you know what I mean. I read Daneman's biography of Margot Fonteyn last year. I saw Margot Fonteyn dance, you know, several times. Got her autograph on a program somewhere. She was very gracious. As a dancer, Lord, she was incredible…" she paused, "I once studied ballet myself, you know."

"We both did, dear, remember?" said Elizabeth with mock sweetness.

"You lasted through one season. I kept up with it for four years before you joined in."

"Yes, dear," said Elizabeth, smiling slyly, "but I learned so much in that one season."

"You were sixteen, and you learned too much in *and out* of class. You cost the ballet master his job and got us both expelled.

Anyway, no one ever danced *Sleeping Beauty* like Margot Fonteyn. Hell, no one danced like Margot, *period.* That gossip Daneman reported information about poor Margot's love life, that, well, I didn't need to know, not that I'm in any way a prude, but it was so… personal and intimate it made even me blush. Some things should just be held back."

Elizabeth grinned slyly. "Blush? But Harriet, dear, you lent me that book, and I found you underlined the naughty passages you're referring to."

"You know that's not true, Elizabeth."

"Oh, then perhaps *I* underlined them," said Elizabeth giggling, "Of course I did. It was so that you won't have to look all through the book for them, dear, when I return it."

"Oh, posh, Elizabeth! You've had the damn book for a year. You never intend to return it."

"Poor Ms. Fonteyn had a long career and a complicated life. I want to savor her biography and read it slowly," said Elizabeth thoughtfully while holding her cup at her mouth, her dainty little finger raised just so.

Penn sipped his coffee. Harriet was right, It was very good stuff.

****

Chapter Eight – Brown Water

Penn kissed the Aunties goodbye and left them still bantering with one another. He had two long car trips ahead of him. First there was a run to Annapolis to deposit the trunk in the Library vault, then another long trip to Atlanta, this time to the Buckhead Hilton. His date on Thursday with Kate was set. They were going to the Fox Theatre to see the Mariinsky Ballet perform Tchaikovsky's *Swan Lake*. After that, a late supper, and then, Penn figured, his duty would be done. Harriett would be appeased. Besides, he liked Kate and wanted to see her again. Whatever happened, however, he didn't want anything to occur that would, well… move too quickly. For now, he wanted his independence. He didn't need or want the distraction of a love affair, even one conducted long distance between cities as far away as Atlanta and Annapolis, and especially an affair with the daughter of the next CNO.

The drive to Crabtown was uneventful. At the Academy he enlisted the help of a colleague and hauled the trunk into the library on a hand-truck. He had already called Captain Southerland and gotten the Library prepared to secure the trunk and its contents, so there were no delays caused by negotiating with library management. Penn was content to leave the trunk in the library vault for a day or two unattended. Once in the Annapolis vault, the trunk would be secure from thieves, but he still didn't want anyone to get curious, open it and remove anything, even if he or she did account for the removal with a note or a card. The contents were the property of his aunt, not a public dump of records. Seth padlocked it securely before it was packed away in the trunk of Penn's rented car. The padlock supplied by Seth had a U-shaped shackle made of especially hardened steal, and no ordinary cable cutter could dent it. If anyone wanted to gain entrance to the trunk without a key, they'd have to saw through the trunk itself. The trunk remained locked and was put in a corner of the vault behind a stack of ancient books, inconspicuous to the casual observer.

Penn didn't touch the files in the morning. Instead, he wrote a detailed preliminary report of his findings to Captain Southerland and developed a rigorous plan of examining, photographing and duplicating the documents. Southerland would need that to justify and authorize the expense. He also requested two days leave, which was granted immediately.

The trip to Atlanta was 12 hours long and exhausting. Traffic was miserable, his shoulder and back started to ache, and Tylenol didn't help much. He wouldn't take anything stronger because he didn't want to risk drowsiness and because he never did take anything stronger. Too much pain-killer could create a dependence on pain-killers and he didn't want to depend on any artificial remedies if he could avoid them.

Penn flopped into bed just past one AM, stuffed with a late dinner of salad, pita bread and hummus, had difficulty getting comfortable, but finally fell into a deep but troubled sleep. A new dream came to him. He was at the Annapolis library but a Marine told him there was an IED in the back, by the vault, just like in Iraq. He ran forward toward it, but, not finding it, stopped, his heart racing, and started yelling "Get out! Get out!" He yelled in his sleep and his own voice awakened him. He was so drenched in sweat, he had to get a towel from the bathroom, dry himself, and lay it on the bed. The room had twin beds, so he crawled into the unused one and slept there the remainder of the night. He awoke with a headache and backache, took some more Tylenol and let the shower run pulsating and hot on his back and neck for fifteen minutes. When he exited the shower to shave, he wiped the condensation from the mirror, looked at himself, didn't like what he saw, and muttered "PTSD sucks," his own form of self- administered therapy.

Freud claimed he cured himself of a sinus infection after several weeks of misery when he awoke one morning and was so tired of being sick he just willed it away, or at least that's what Penn's therapist told him. Penn preferred the self-cure to anything else. He got nothing from talking with the Navy psychiatrist, but at the psychiatrist's urging he attended a group therapy session out of uniform with others. The group was mostly lower-ranking enlisted Marines, who were suffering from or claiming to be suffering from post-traumatic stress. None of that particular group had physical problems of any sort; all of their afflictions were psychological. He listened to their complaints and stories, again got nothing from it, and dropped the sessions after attending three of them, each one more useless than the last. He thought most of the men and women in those sessions honestly felt some anxiety or problem, but the dialogue was so disjointed and incoherent, and seemed so shamelessly self-indulgent and self-pitying he just couldn't keep with it. But then it's hard to feel the sorrows of others, and he refrained from judging them, although he did stop attending the sessions.

Penn was troubled with occasional nightmares and was still recuperating from physical damage to his back and shoulder. He had burned the backs of his legs and his buttocks (which for some reason embarrassed him), but those burns had left their scars and healed. It was the deeper damage to tissue and bone that would take a long time to heal, if it ever would heal.

During the first decade of the Global War on Terror (GWOT) as the Bush Administration grandly called its adventures in Afghanistan and Iraq, Penn's duty stations were either in the Naval Academy as a Midshipman, or after graduation assigned to ships or to school. There were ships he sailed that ported at Rota Spain and cruised the Mediterranean. There was a posting in Bristol, England, with a ship that made several North Atlantic crossings visiting Philadelphia, Boston and other cities, along with ports in Germany and Belgium, and there was Brindisi with its American base and Lucia, his Italian sweetheart. All of this kept him out the GWOT for the most part. While his contemporaries in the Army, Marines and Air Force were enduring three, four or five tours to war zones, he was sailing to ports in Europe and North America. His work was still vital to the security of the United States, but he felt as if he were slacking-off in some way, cowering in a corner while other service members bore the brunt of America's latest fight.

The Navy units with the most direct involvement in Iraq were the "brown and green water" Swift Boats of the Riverine Group. They were soldiered by Marines, SEALS, and other Naval infantry forces of the Naval Expeditionary Combat Command but commanded and piloted by Navy officers. Penn was a late arrival to the Swift boats. Riverine Squadron 3 (RIVRON 3), the river patrol squadron, had deployed from Yorktown, Virginia, to Iraq a year before Penn's detail to the squadron. He came to them untrained and unprepared for the rigors of river patrol. His job wasn't to command a boat, but to observe and report.

Penn was part of a team assembled by the pentagon's Admiral Druning to get an independent assessment of the effectiveness of such operations. Druning was a deepwater sailor who was skeptical of the Navy's role in patrolling inland waterways. If Druning had his way, the Army and the Coast Guard would be doing it. He already had reports from the Riverine Group and from local commanders in Iraq. He even had classified IG findings, but he wanted to "triangulate" all this with the objective reports of experienced officers – deepwater sailors like himself -- sent to observe. Penn was one of three officers chosen for the role because of his sea experience, superb efficiency ratings, high standing at Annapolis, Master's degree, and detachment from any personal interest in the usefulness and efficiency of the Riverine Group.

Swift Boats, used by the RIVRON 3, were designed for work in inland waterways, shallow coastal waters, inlets. Swift boats can access the littoral areas and shallows and maneuver in narrow tributaries and swamps, yet are very fast, well-armed and extremely hardy and resilient. They're virtually unsinkable. They were first used in Vietnam, which is alive with rivers and streams, has an enormously long coast, and contains swamps and other wet areas that gave refuge to insurgents and enemy forces. There were over 500 Swift Boats deployed in Vietnam during the height of that war. By the time the Iraq War began, those Swift Boats were a vestige of another day. Two of the last Vietnam-era operational Swift Boats were given to the Island of Malta, where they remain in service. Two more are on static display at two different Naval installations in the U.S.

The occupation of Iraq gave rise to the resurrection of the Swift Boats for use on inland waterways. The ancient Tigris and Euphrates Rivers were the greatest of these waterways, but there are other rivers, swamps and tributaries as well. Penn was assigned to a boat that patrolled the Euphrates. The main role of the patrols was interdiction, just as the Navy intended, but, as he found, a secondary role, as a target and instigator of insurgent activity was just as important. If the boats could draw the insurgents out, the Marines and sailors could kill or capture them. The insurgents knew this, of course, but that didn't stop them from attacking and provoking a response from the Swift Boats.

Penn was relegated to riding along, taking notes when he could and generally observing how well the men maintained order, kept to their assigned positions, maintained the boats and their weapons and how effective they were in making any dent in insurgent activity. He started to form his opinions on his first patrol. The men were good, high-spirited, competent, professional in their approach to duty, obedient and seemed to have confidence in their Officers and Non-commissioned Officers. While relations were easy among everyone on the 32-foot vessel, officers were still addressed as "Sir," the Captain, whatever his or her rank, was respected as the Commander of the Boat, and the NCOs were respectfully called "Sarge" or "Chief." Weapons were clean, the boats were clean and the rigor of boat maintenance was observed. Nevertheless, every patrol began with a sense of expectation and excitement, and there was always some tension, a heightened awareness when they approached shore or ventured into a tributary.

Penn liked the river patrols. They started before dawn and as the first light trickled from the heavens the river would catch it, the waves would begin to sparkle and the first hours on the water were cool and pleasurable. He could see brilliant and colorful water birds, flocks of Egyptian vultures, and shore animals, water buffalo, antelope, cows. He even caught a glimpse of what looked like a lion off in the distance. As the day went on the heat could be oppressive, but he could always scoop up water and wash off his face or douse his head.

For the first weeks of his assignment to the lead boat in the small squadron, nothing much happened, save for some pot-shots taken at them. The boat was hit once, but by the time they put it on the sand and the Marines and sailors charged out, the enemy was long gone. The Captain, frustrated with the lack of action, began experimenting with different patrol techniques. He'd sometimes cut a patrol short and quickly backtrack to see if he could catch anyone running into tall grass or into a swamp. He then tried a different technique, patrolling in a routine and predictable manner to see if that would draw the enemy into attempting an ambush.

The Captain's last "trick," worked, if violating security measures to draw the enemy could be considered a "trick." They pulled into a tributary of the Euphrates and cruised for about a mile before turning back. They did this several days in a row, always turning at the same spot. On the fifth day, as they slowed and turned, automatic fire erupted on both banks, rockets came at them, even mortar rounds soared in. Before he could react, a round creased Penn's arm making him drop his clipboard and notepad. First Lt. McCormack, USMC, a wise-cracking New Yorker, said, jovially, "Watch it, Squid, or you'll lose a tentacle."

Their boat returned fire immediately. The boat's heavy rear machine gun tore up the reeds on both shores, firing alternately into the right and left banks. McCormack shouted orders for the Marines and sailors to return fire as well. The enemy seemed to disappear and the boat Captain ordered another turn and another reversal of direction. They sped back along the path of the ambush, and, finding the exact spot of their first turn, where the attack occurred, the Captain beached the boat and charged on shore. "There they are," he shouted, pointing ahead and to the left. "Follow me." He went after them with vigor, then there was an explosion and he was gone.

"Corpsman!" someone shouted, "Captain's down." Penn was in front by now, armed with an M-16, running as well as he could in the grass. McCormack was behind him, trying to pull back some Marines who had headed in the wrong direction, but he was coming up fast.

The enemy went to ground somewhere – it was hard to tell where exactly in the grass, reeds and palms – and began firing at them again. Time seemed to slow down. To Penn's eyes everything became perfectly sharp and vibrant. He could see the fine details in the grass, in the sky, in movement among the palms from a breeze and in movement in the grass from men hidden in ambush. He even noticed the grasshoppers and dragon flies. A Marine fell just in front of him. Another went down on his right. To his left, a Marine's face exploded with blood and the man fell backwards hard. Some Marines and sailors were shooting and running, others had halted and were trying to find targets in the tall grass and among the palms in the swampy ground. Someone was screaming. He saw an Egret rise slowly in the palms to his right and fly directly across the zone of fire unscathed.

Penn aimed, shot half a magazine in the general direction of the enemy hoping to hit something, then started running again, catching up with the men, getting ahead of them now, urging them on. He fired into the grass and reeds where he saw movement or thought he saw it, finished the clip, expelled it and rammed in another. The enemy – whether al Qaida or some other lunatics – was firing at them but backing away now, not aiming, trying to stay low in the bushes. Penn, pumped with adrenalin, ran even faster and was well ahead of the pack as they stated to cross over a low ridge and run toward the palms, where the enemy had gone and where they glimpsed running men trying to get away. A bullet tore through his trouser and grazed the outside of his thigh. He barely felt it.

He could see them running now, running low through the grass and reeds and into the palms. One of them turned and shot at him, but the shots went wild. Penn stopped and fired six shots at his assailant. He saw the man fall. Penn started running again. He wanted to catch them before they had a chance to scatter.

He looked around hard as he ran, looking for movement, details, anything that would betray the enemy. There was movement off to his right. He could just see in the reeds perhaps a hundred meters away, to the right of a copse of palms, something moving. He looked harder and it came into focus, an arm waving what looked like a cell phone, as if teasing them, provoking them. He shot uselessly at the arm, or where it was since it only appeared for a few seconds then disappeared from sight. He turned to look for Lieutenant McCormack to see if he was still whole and with him when he caught the glint of metal over to his left. A trap. The bastard with the cell phone was waving goodbye before he detonated it. Thought came first in images, not words, then it hit him *"McCormack,"* he thought, *"McCormack's right there, running directly at the IED."*

Penn didn't think further. He turned back and ran at them, "Down! Down! IED!"

He threw himself on top of the Lieutenant as the IED detonated. The force of the explosion lifted him and drove him forward. As he leapt, Penn was struck hard in the back and the shoulder by two lumps of jagged metal each the size of a clenched fist. The Lieutenant fell backward onto the Gunnery Sergeant and all three men went down, forming a low mound in the grass. Bullets whizzed over them and somewhere there was another explosion, then the pace of firing slowed. Penn's body armor saved his life, but the blow to his right shoulder both dislocated it and broke the bone. Two ribs were broken in the back where the other lump hit, and the muscle and nerves were damaged. His legs and buttocks were burned and hit with shards of shrapnel, the trousers literally burned off of them. There was no pain, at least at first. He tried to get up but fainted. He drifted on and off into unconsciousness. In a dream, he felt himself being dragged and lifted, heard a motor roar, felt the vibrations of a boat. He was in pain and groaning. A Corpsman injected him with something. He felt good and slept.

They got him to hospital, where they set his shoulder and taped his ribs. The doctors picked the debris and shards of metal from his buttocks and the back of his legs then slathered them with an antiseptic ointment. His left arm was bandaged where the bullet grazed it, and the surface wound on his thigh was stitched. He was stiff and in pain, but the pain was controlled and endurable. He braved it, joked with the corpsmen and nurses, and was generally in high spirits. At least he'd recover from this and be as good as new again or so he hoped at first.

Two days later, McCormack and Gunnery Sergeant Fernandez showed up at the hospital. Penn awoke from an afternoon nap to find them at the foot of his bed. Tall, lanky McCormack, with his freckled face looked like an eighteen-year-old. His nose was bandaged and that made him look even younger. Fernandez, a neat 5'3" of muscle and sinew, seemed none the worse for wear.

"I've got a bone to pick with you, Commander," said McCormack.

Penn was extraordinarily glad to see them. "I'm a Lieutenant. That's the same as a Captain in Marine-talk. What's your bone?"

"In all due respect, you've been listed for promotion to Lieutenant Commander, sir," said Fernandez, "That's a Major in

Marine-talk, sir, you know, *real* rank. We saw it in the orders."

"The promotion is probably a mistake or a joke, but anyway, you broke my nose," said McCormack.

"What?"

"During our picnic two days ago, in your unfortunate expression of affection for me, when you threw yourself on me in the high grass and hugged me, you broke my nose."

"Couldn't be helped. You were about to step on a perfectly good IED. Would have been a waste of explosive and metal. Besides, I wanted to save you in case I need domestic help or someone to carry my bags."

"That would never do. Squids are lousy tippers. Anyway, you've messed with my good looks and I'll thank you never to do it again."

"Good looks? Any change would be an improvement, but don't worry, I'll be sure never to make *that* mistake again."

"And thanks, Sir," said Fernandez, this time seriously, "If you hadn't thrown yourself at us, we would've walked right into it."

McCormack leaned over and in a stage whisper said, "For the rest of my life, I'll be able to tell the story of how a Squid Lieutenant took it in the ass for me and saved my life."

Penn groaned. "I should've leapt in the other direction."

McCormack stopped smiling. "Seriously, thanks, Penn. You would have made a hell of a Marine." It was the highest form of praise the man knew, and the accolade Penn treasured most.

Penn was recommended for several awards. He received the Purple Heart with two Oak Leaf clusters (three awards) for the wound in his arm, for the wound in his leg, and for the damage from the bomb blast. He was nominated for the Silver Star as well, but when the nomination reached the office of the Secretary of Navy an independent panel recommended an upgrade to the Navy Cross. A

Bronze Star was also recommended based on McCormack's report of Penn's initial assumption of leadership and continuation of the attack when the Captain went down. The Secretary agreed, and Penn became one of only two sailors – and the only officer -- to earn that combination of distinctions in Iraq.

Penn's career was doing well, but he wasn't. Recovery proved harder than expected. His shoulder ached, his back ached, and the places burned on his legs and buttocks stayed sore for months. Sleeping was difficult. He could only sleep on his back, which irritated his legs, and he couldn't roll over, not until his shoulder and back healed. It took almost three months before he could sit at a desk for any length of time and before the physical therapy wasn't pure misery. Gradually, the shoulder came around. Movement became less stiff, the pain subsided and he could anticipate some form of normal activity. The back was slower to heal but gradually improved as well. The burns healed well, and the effects were hardly noticeable on his skin. As he healed physically, though, the mental healing took longer. He suffered from nightmares. As time went on, they became less common, but the dreams of the Marine who was hit in the face, or of the IED and the explosion wouldn't stop. He figured he might be plagued by them all his life, and he often wondered how men who survived the Somme, Iwojima, Korea or Hamburger Hill lived with what they did and what they saw.

The medals were a problem for him as well. What had he done to deserve the Navy Cross? He had turned and thrown himself on another man when the explosion occurred. There was no plan, no fear to overcome; it was all just action and reaction, nothing more. No thought went into it. Was that courage? How was that like the courage shown by the men who sailed with John Paul Jones, by those who had endured the hell of Belleau Wood, by the Marines who invaded Formosa, by the men of the Army Air Corps who flew mission after mission into the fury of German air defenses, by the men and women of the French resistance, by quiet persistent courage of Helen Keller or Mother Teresa? He found nothing he did to be brave, just things done in an instant without thought that saved some lives, and that to him was phony, a diluted and pale image of all that was meant by courage and bravery.

The medals, however undeserved they were, would prove useful. They'd help him advance. It was a virtual guarantee he'd be on the fast track for promotion to Commander then to Captain. There was another thing they'd do. He wasn't scheduled to return to the Academy until a Medical Board could determine his fitness for sea duty. The final verdict on that might be years away since it would take that long for his shoulder and back to heal, if they ever did. Until then, if he taught at the Academy the medals by themselves would buy him the attention and respect of the cadets. Hearing a lecture from an unblooded officer with an academic background was one thing, having a professor who was a real sailor, with years of deepwater sailing was something else entirely. Add to that the Iraq Campaign Medal, the Navy Cross, a Bronze Star and 3 Purple Hearts, and he would command their unquestioned attention and respect. What he said to them would be remembered and held dear. He could affect and mold the thinking of a whole generation of Navy officers. The final adornment was academic respectability in the form of the Ph. D., which he had just earned.

Penn, however, while confident of the magic the experience, the medals and the Ph.D. would bring, was not confident that he should be the one so adorned with such symbols of accomplishment and courage. In his darkest moments he felt phony and Oz-like, a vacant vessel, made artificially wise by a paper degree, brave with decorations he didn't deserve and given an artificial heart that cleared his conscience, allowing him to be crass and vulgar enough to accept all these trophies and rewards, adorning himself with glory bought without guts or sacrifice.

He tried to come to peace with his conscience by telling himself that he asked for none of the medals, and his Ph.D. thesis was reviewed and accepted by a stiff academic committee not associated with the Navy in any way. Yet those felt like hollow arguments.

In his autobiography, Douglas MacArthur briefly refers to the seven Silver Stars he was awarded for gallantry in action during World War One, never quite admitting that he deserved such elaborate distinction, yet accepting them because they were awarded. He justified the awards simply by arguing that he must have earned them because they were awarded to him, not because he was the bravest and finest and best.

Penn was in that vein at present. He accepted the medals because they were awarded, and the Ph.D. because it, too, was awarded. There might be better or braver or more scholarly men who achieved much less recognition, but it came his way and he would use these glittering prizes to advance his own ideas, his own heart and cause. In the meantime he paid for it all with nightmares and cold sweats, with pain in his shoulder and back. The butcher's bill for his afternoon of glory was one sailor and three marines dead, four wounded, two wounded badly, and the death of the boat commander. Finally, there was the futility of the war. All his life, he would have to live with the gnawing sensation that the mangled and dead sailors and marines he'd led and urged into the jaws of the enemy suffered, bled and died in what may prove to be a fruitless and meaningless war. *That* would haunt him forever.

****

Chapter Nine – Two Women

Two women, 2,000 miles apart, who knew nothing of each other readied for their respective engagements.

In Santa Fe, New Mexico, in preparation for her performance that evening at the Santa Fe Opera House, Yoshiko Fujiyama was warming up her voice in her motel room. The cast of *Butterfly*, at least the ones not local, were housed at the nearby La Quinta Inn. It wasn't the Ritz, but at least it was clean.

She warmed up by singing some exercises, then a few Italian art songs, then all the lines from her role as Suzuki. With three hours before performance, her throat feeling warm and good, she tried the difficult aria *Un bel di*. This was the lead's aria, not hers, but she'd mastered it anyway, and she knew she sung it well. She'd made digital recordings of her voice on her cell phone and played them back, listening for flaws, mispronunciations, missed notes and flat notes. Time and again she sang *Un bel di* flawlessly, but she knew she needed more pathos, a deeper interpretation of the role.

Hye Young Rhee, the Diva who would be Cio-Cio San tonight, seemed to pull the music from her soul, as if she'd actually been abandoned with child by a lover herself. How she did this was a mystery to Yoshiko. Rhee was a proud virgin who had no intention of letting any man touch her until marriage, if that ever came. Hye Young took her lead from the magnificent Korean Diva, known to the West as Sumi Jo, who had put aside everything for her career. Singing meant more to Hye Young Rhee than all else.

Renata Scotto, a Diva of a foregone era, whose voice Yoshiko loved and for whom *Butterfly* was a signature role, left behind recordings that sounded less emotionally raw than Rhee's, but within the superficial sweetness of Scotto's singing Yoshiko could hear the bitter taint of desperation and hopelessness the role demanded. There were many other singers Yoshiko listened-to as well, since there are so many recordings of the opera and so many available on CD and DVD. Even Maria Callas made one, although Yoshiko didn't like her voice, thinking it too shrill and the vibrato too pronounced, thoughts she kept to herself since Callas fans seemed to be fanatical about the long-gone singer and would easily take offense.

If Yoshiko were to sing *Butterfly*'s Cio-Cio San, or *La Boheme's* Mimi, or *La Traviata's* Violetta or some other role that demands strong and effective acting as well as voice, she would create the character anew and put her own stamp and seal upon the role. She knew she was good enough to do this, and all she needed was a few years for her voice to take on the resonance and depth necessary. Cio-Cio is especially difficult because the character matures and changes as the opera plays-out. The feelings that propel a beautiful and high-born fifteen-year-old sold into marriage with a foreigner by a destitute family are much different than the pain and desperation felt in the final act of the opera, and the climax with its soaring pain and horrible end creates its own challenges.

She went back to the Italian art songs and continued singing, then to her role as Suzuki, sometimes singing both her lines and Cio-Cio's. As curtain time approached, her voice was warm and full.

In Buckhead, Georgia, on the edge of Atlanta, Kate Hobson flopped on her armchair and looked at the three gowns she'd pulled from her closet. The light blue was too old and too girly, and the pink was worse. It was an evening engagement and while no one really cared what you wore to the Fox anymore, she cared and she would dress properly for it. Penn was wearing a suit tonight, not his uniform, and she wished she knew a little more about his taste in clothes. She wasn't going to wear black again. She'd done that at the ballet, so that dress remained in the closet. The third gown hanging from her closet door remianed, a simple piece in blue almost the shade of her eyes. It wasn't new, and she might have gained a pound or two she bought it years ago, but it still fit, perhaps even better than before, since it clung to her nicely and showed off her figure without being tight or vulgar. She'd wear dark stockings with it and blue pumps that matched the gown. For jewelry, she would wear a necklace given to her by her father, Admiral Hobson, for her twenty-first birthday. On a gold chain, the necklace had a single large pearl set in gold within a collar of small diamonds. On her wrist was a matching watch she received from him for her twenty-second.

She was trying very hard not to expect much tonight. This was a polite invitation to a cultural event, not an intimate romantic evening. Penn's taste in entertainment was high-flung, first opera now the ballet. He was looking for a companionable escort, not a red hot lover. His real interest was in the event, not in her. He'd be picking her up this time, though, so it felt more like a real date, and why would he go to the trouble of traveling to Atlanta if not to see her? – Oh, she stopped herself, it was probably something at Emory, probably something to do with his degree. It's simple. He's in Atlanta, wants to see the Russians, what troop were they, the Mariinsky? Wants to see them do *Swan Lake*, the quintessential Russian ballet. She was just a handy friend he called upon to be with him. After all, going by yourself is such a bore… Yet maybe he did feel something more. No, don't think that. Don't think anything. Just go. Let whatever will happen, happen… yet, yet… Oh, hell, he probably has a girlfriend back in Maryland somewhere, maybe a couple of them. Don't expect anything. Don't wait for anything. Let it happen if it's going to happen.

She showered, brushed and comber her hair, brushed her teeth for a full three minutes then gargled with mouthwash, dressed carefully, and inspected herself in the mirror. She looked fine, like an actress she fancied, maybe Hilary Swank, no, *better* than her. Anyway she looked good, better at this point in her life than ever before. It was six pm; he said he'd be by between six thirty and six forty to pick her up. That would give them more than an hour to get to the Fox and park, which should be plenty of time on a Thursday night. She was dressed now, though, and she wouldn't sit and wrinkle anything until he showed-up.

The minutes crept by. She tried listening to music but didn't have the patience for it. She thought about brushing her teeth again, but she might get something on her gown and she certainly didn't want that. She paced back and forth in her sitting room, turning on and off the TV. She looked in the refrigerator rather vacantly and saw very little, although it was full. She picked up a magazine, adjusted her gown one more time. At six twenty, she dabbed some perfume behind her ears and little on her wrist, checked her makeup, inspected herself one more time, twirled in front of the mirror and liked herself. She almost didn't hear the doorbell, and when she realized it had rung was stunned for a few seconds. Her heart raced, she gulped, tried to calm herself, and, in a good mimicry of poise and confidence that masked everything she felt, opened the door.

Penn wore a Harris Tweed suit, an immaculate white shirt and a rep tie, tied in a four-in-hand knot and hung properly so no white showed above the knot. His shoes were highly polished brown brogues. The suit fit him well and looked newly cleaned and pressed. He could have been a prince of the royal blood dressed for an autumn outing, or a character from Masterpiece Theatre. Somehow, perhaps by instinct, his suit seemed to fit with her dress perfectly. They both could have just stepped off the television screen.

She opened her mouth and sighed.

"Ready to go?" said Penn, not hearing "hello" from her.

"Yes, yes, of course," she said, coming back to earth, "Let me get my purse."

Penn's rented car was no Rolls. It was a blue Chevy Malibu with black seats that smelt a little of ancient cigarette smoke and some sort of sweet car fragrance added by the rental company to cover the smell of smoke. The weather was nice, in the sixties, so he left the vent open as they drove down Peachtree, and the smells of the car soon dissipated in the cool air.

She found her tongue and chatted or chattered, depending on your tolerance for idle talk. She knew *Swan Lake*, and had danced in a student production at the Metropolitan Ballet Theatre.

"Odette or Odile?" asked Penn playfully.

"Neither. I danced in the background then as one of the four Swans, or Cygnets, in Act 2, and doubled as a Spanish Dancer in Act 3."

"You must have been busy."

"I was, but it was great fun. Miss Maniya, our teacher and coach, was so proud."

"Who was so proud?"

"Maniya Barredo, the founder and head of the school. She was the only Prima Ballerina ever to perform for Atlanta Ballet. She retired and formed the school up in Alpharetta. She's a wonderful person. The students adore her."

"Isn't 'Prima' some sort of honorific title? Don't you have to be named by another Prima?"

"Yes," said Kate, "Maniya was given the title by Margot Fonteyn, after Margot saw one of her performances."

Margot Fonteyn again. Penn whistled softly. "Couldn't do much better than that." The thought of Margot Fonteyn distracted him. He wondered what it was that Harriet and Elizabeth had found so salacious in her biography. "My aunt Harriet was a great fan of Margot Fonteyn. She told me she saw her in performance several times and has a program signed by her. She even has her biography."

"Oh, I've read that," said Kate, "I mean it was her autobiography I read. I read it then I purchased a signed copy from E-Bay. I also have an autographed photo of her hanging in my sitting room. Shame about her end. Fascinating person. She died of cancer, impoverished, you know."

"I didn't know. I figured she was buried in Westminster Abbey or wherever the British put great ballerinas."

"No, she danced well after most ballerinas would have retired, into her sixties. Still beautiful, still lithe. She was still dancing with Nureyev at sixty-one. All that work and it didn't matter. She wound up in a pauper's grave in Panama, the country where she spent her last years caring for her paralyzed husband who was unfaithful before he was injured and had wasted most of her money… I think they're trying to collect money for a monument to her now. I know they put her name on a plaque along with Frederick Ashton and the other founders of the Royal Ballet. *That* plaque is in Westminster Abbey. I saw it there myself and took a picture of it… I never saw her in live performance, of course, but I do have a DVD with her dancing *Sleeping Beauty*. Come over some rainy day and I'll show it to you."

Kate's last sentence didn't sound true. It was as if Kate were trying to be casual and light-hearted but was really eager, hoping for a response. The tension and anxiety were obvious. Penn chose to ignore that tension and took Kate's words at face value.

"I'll take you up on that next time I'm in Atlanta," he said.

"You're leaving soon?" Again, a subtext of tension and disappointment.

"I have to. I have to be back in Annapolis by Friday night. I've taken on some research work, and have a ton of documents to review over the weekend. I'm meeting with the Department Chair on Monday to outline an approach and try to get some money."

"Oh… I understand. Is this associated with your teaching?"

"Yes, in the sense that history professors have to research and publish or they soon find themselves looking for a job."

"What are you researching?"

Penn was used to the fastidiousness of military security

protocol. He wasn't a particularly secretive man by nature but had acquired the habit of evasiveness when asked specifics about his work. He answered as candidly as he would allow himself, "The Navy and Naval doctrine and strategy as the country matured from the 19th into the 20th Century, 1890 through the First World War."

"Sounds like a broad topic."

"It is. I'm starting with a piece of it, the years between 1890 and the end if the Russo-Japanese War. I may focus initially on the 1890s. It depends on what I find over the weekend and what my Chairman recommends. I'm planning on a book, or maybe a series of them."

Her heart sank. She had hoped, although she tried not to hope, that Penn would stay the weekend, that he'd sweep her off her feet -- *whatever that meant*, no one had ever swept her off her feet -- make passionate love to her (but in a nice way), and both of them, overcome with yearning and adoration, would pledge eternal love. Or something like that. She would have settled for a tennis date or a night at the movies, or, best of all, cuddling on the sofa watching her Margot Fonteyn DVD with him. Oh, well. She'd make the best of it, meaning it would be dismal for her. She felt deflated and less pretty now. A light rain began to fall. The weather matched her mood.

Yoshiko Fujiyama walked to the theater from the La Quinta Inn. It wasn't far and the evening was pleasant. She could have ridden in the hotel van but she was trying to avoid Manny Goldstein, who sang Pinkerton. He sang well enough and he certainly looked the part and he acted well, at least on stage. She acknowledged all that, but offstage he was an insufferable bore and bully. Although he was not much older the she, perhaps a year or two, he teased her and treated her as if she were an adolescent. Worse, he acted at times as she were some kind of pet or child, and he seemed to have a mean streak; he *could* be nasty.

At their rehearsal the previous day, the director, Lee Gross, was dissatisfied by Yoshiko's stage presence during some of the critical Arias in Acts II and III, especially Act III. "Don't look serene and serious, Yoshiko. Frown, look pained when Cio-Cio starts warbling about the first Robin of Spring. She's the dreamer, you – the good Suzuki-- you're the realist." They ran through it once, and he liked the effect.

The cast took a break and resumed the rehearsal, deciding to run through the scene they'd just completed one more time that day because Hye Young wanted to work on her phrasing. Lee Gross had gone somewhere, but following his advice, instead of sitting serenely by with a serious expression on her face, Yoshiko frowned and fretted, wringing her hands while Cio-Cio sang once more of the first robin of Spring.

Manny Goldstein, lurking in the wings, interrupted them, stopped everything, pointed at her and said "What *are* you doing?"

She had no answer. As the servant, Suzuki, her role was simple. She was supposed to linger on stage by her mistress looking worried as the bittersweet aria was sung. Wasn't that obvious?

"Stop the frowning and agony, will you? You look like a pixie with Cramps!" he said with a sneer.

Yoshiko was so embarrassed and hurt she didn't know what to say. She almost burst into tears.

Hye Young Rhee bristled, crossed her arms, locked eyes with Manny and snapped back, "You shut up and sit down, Manny! This is not your scene. You are not in it. You are not even near it. I *want* her to show concern and worry. So does Lee." Had Lee been there, he would have defended her as well and his language would have been much rougher.

Manny shook his head derisively and walked off.

Rhee could see Yoshiko's distress, and tried to comfort her by muttering "Don't pay attention. Goldstein is gay and those men don't like women," but it didn't help. Yoshiko knew plenty of gay men who did like women, who were kind and thoughtful and helpful. Manny was in a class by himself. She did respect Manny's ability as an actor and singer, and because of that his mean criticism of her acting cut her deeply. He had never done that before. He had been critical and nasty in other ways offstage, mocking her, belittling her, making her feel uncomfortable, commenting on everything from the way she dressed to the size of her hips. She feared and hated being around him outside the theatre, never knowing what he'd say. With this insult, he'd taken his meanness to the stage. It was too much.

Opening night in Santa Fe, a clear mild Thursday evening. Everyone was excited, nervous, and happy. The cast gathered backstage for makeup and costuming, while the grips, stagehands, sweepers, volunteers and lighting crew moved props and scenery and secured everything for the performance. The orchestra started to file in and tune their instruments. The Santa Fe *Butterfly* was about to go on but as the minutes ticked by and the preparations continued a sense of anxiety began to build. Something was wrong. It was less an hour before curtain time but the Director and the Stage Manager were missing. This never happened. Those two were always hyperactive on opening night, on the set long before the stagehands and singers arrived, running around making sure every detail was perfect. Backstage began buzzing with rumors. Someone said Lee and Harold, the Stage Manager, were in an auto accident, another that they contracted salmonella from eating bad oysters in the restaurant across the street and were in the hospital "sick as dogs". Hye Young Rhee wasn't in her dressing room, either; no one had seen her, and that spawned its own rumors.

Yoshiko ignored the rumors and started to prepare as usual, putting on makeup in the general dressing room with the others, preparing her costume and getting dressed. The costume, a kimono with all its accoutrements, wasn't too complicated. It was designed to appear authentic, at least on stage, but easy to get on and off. Thankfully, it was also much cooler than a real kimono of the period, which was a blessing because on stage under the lights she would have suffered from the heat and been soaked with perspiration had she worn a real kimono. Her hair was a problem. It had to be arranged to match the role, a fall added to make it look rich and full, and then gathered on the top of her head, in the style of a geisha's servant, almost in the style of a geisha. The hairdresser was practiced, though, and set the coiffure with little difficulty. Yoshiko once tried wearing a wig, but it didn't look right, and despite her role as a servant, she was determined to look good.

Lee Gross, the Director, finally arrived, charging onto the stage looking flushed, dour and upset. He summarily ordered the cast to assemble.

"Give us some light," he called. As the lights rose, he beckoned everyone into the middle of the stage, "People, people… please, gather round…" He pointed at the extras and the stage hands "Everyone, you too… Please be quiet we've got an announcement to make." They formed around him and he held up his hand for silence. They knew there was a problem, an issue, a situation, something not good at all. They grew quiet. No one moved.

"We lost Hye Young Rhee," he said. There was a collective gasp. He held up his hand again. "It's OK. She's OK, but she had an attack of appendicitis and was rushed to the hospital."

"When the hell did this happen, Lee?" said Goldstein. "I just talked to her a little while ago."

"It was about an hour ago," said Lee, "maybe a little longer. She started feeling pain in her abdomen. It got so bad she doubled over. The hotel called the ambulance and she was in the Emergency Room in five minutes… But don't worry, the doctors tell me she had an emergency appendectomy and she's going to be fine. There's no peritonitis, no abdominal infection of any kind."

"What about the show?" someone said. There was a general murmur among the group.

"We don't have a show, now," said Lee, "Not without Cio-Cio San. I thought there might be a local singer who could handle the role, but there isn't. Marie Robertson who could sing it, and who was supposed to be here to stand by, is in Dusseldorf."

Groans, murmurs, curses. Everyone knew there was no other understudy, no alternative. The company couldn't afford one.

This was Yoshiko's moment. It was fate, destiny, karma. She knew it in her heart, in her soul. Yoshiko hesitated for a moment, then gathered all her courage, for it took all the courage she had to make that first move. She stepped forward

"I know the part," she said with as much confidence and clarity as she could muster, "I can do it. You don't have to close the show." Her cheeks flushed and her heart raced. Confrontation wasn't in her nature, but she had summoned the will to overcome her fear and loathing of it, to seize the prize that dangled there, just within her grasp.

Lee shook his head, "You haven't rehearsed it, and I don't know if your voice can handle it," meaning he had no faith at all she could actually sing the role. Lee would rather cancel a performance than risk a bad review.

"My voice can handle anything! I can sing as well as any soprano in this company, and I know the role, every note, every word, every cue..." said Yoshiko, her heart into it now. She *knew* she could sing the role. Lee *had* to give it to her. She looked around the stage for support. Cast members were nodding, smiling at her; she could hear them murmur "right on," "go, Yoshiko."

Lee sighed in exasperation. *Another artist with an ego the size of Texas*, he thought. "I appreciate what you're trying to do, Yoshiko, but we have to be realistic. The show's gone." said Lee, and to emphasize the finality of his decision, he turned his back on her and started to walk away, "I'll let the theatre management know." Lee had spent all of his adult life dealing with singers. They always over-reached, always thought they were unappreciated or overlooked or undercast, always had an exaggerated opinion of themselves and their talent. He knew, or thought he knew, how to handle them.

Manny Goldstein, standing in the back, angrily elbowed his way up front and stood by Yoshiko.

"Lee, turn around!" he barked.

This was a command, not a request, it came out in volume. You could hear it clearly in the last row on the upper balcony. Manny was also big enough and fit enough to back it up physically if he had to.

Lee turned slowly and glowered at him.

Manny looked around, drawing everyone's attention.

"I think Yoshiko can do it, Lee. All of us do. Isn't that right?"

His voice and demeanor were unmistakably combative as he faced Lee. Behind him, there were murmurs of support, people could be heard saying "yeah," "right."

Manny continued, "I've hear Yoshiko practice Cio-Cio San's part during the day. Our rooms are right next to each other. She's good. She'll make it."

Lee started to answer, but never got to say what was on his mind. He'd lost control. The mob was behind Yoshiko and Manny.

"Eric!" shouted Manny. Eric was the troop's pianist. "Play *Bimba.*" He meant *Bimba, bimba non pangere*, (*My dearest, my dearest weep no more*) the Act One love duet between Pinkerton and Butterfly, "Give us some room – come on, everyone move back."

They cleared the stage and left Manny and Yoshiko together. The lighting technician put a spotlight on them. Eric played the introduction; the duet began.

Bimba, bimba non pangere, per gracciar de ranocchi – Manny sang, his arms around Yoshiko as if he truly loved her, voice rich and full. They were both in costume, and that helped the effect. Yoshiko responded in a voice warm, mature and anguished, *Urlando ancor.*

They sang the duet up to the point where Butterfly calls for Suzuki, her maid, to bring her garments. Neither Yoshiko nor Manny needed any prompting -- they knew the lines. They were good together, too, more than good. They looked their roles, acted well, sang superbly.

Lee heard enough. He clapped his hands, stopping the performance. The cast and crew burst into applause.

Lee stood for moment, thinking, his hand over his mouth pushing his lips back and forth. He was weighing the risk. If she sang consistently and well, the worst that would happen would be a mediocre review. If her voice was strong enough, the reviews would be good. A mediocre review was better than closing the show. Besides, critics were usually generous when an understudy took over. The hell with it. He decided the opera would be performed.

"Ok, you've made your point," said Lee, "We're going on. We've got our Cio-Cio San." Cheers, hoots, whistles and applause from the cast.

Lee waited until the noise died down and the cast and crew started returning to work. "Lisa!" Lee called. Lisa Reynolds, from Sacramento, was a small dark-haired singer, a member of the chorus who had years of experience and the right vocal range. "Can you do Suzuki?"

"Sure, Lee," she said. She'd sung Suzuki in amateur productions, for the Cleveland opera and in Houston. She knew the role inside and out.

They were set.

Penn and Kate arrived at the Fox one half hour early. The house was now sold out, but on Tuesday Penn managed to get one of the last available sets of tickets, two very good seats in the orchestra section, just 12 rows back from the pit. The tickets were waiting for him at the box office. Instead of going inside, Kate stood with him in line at the "would call" station, her arm around his, while he retrieved the tickets. It only took a few minutes, but Kate had chosen to stay with him rather than go inside the lobby to wait. He liked that

He'd never been to the Fox and knew nothing about the theater. He was stunned by what he saw, or, rather, surprised by it, and found himself in the lobby gawking at the walls, the decorations, the arches, everything.

"Never been here have you?" she said as he looked around.

"No. I expected something a lot different. Tell me about it."

Her mood brightened as she talked. "It was built in the 1920s as the national headquarters and gathering place for the Shriners. They called it the Yaarab Temple Shrine Mosque, and designed it as an elaborate monument to ersatz Moroccan design. It was built in the hey-day of American trompe l'oeil theater decoration, so almost everything you see is some sort of illusion. When we get to our seats, take a look at the ceiling. It's a blue dome and the clouds painted on it seem to move, or, rather, their images *do* move. The columns and arches all around us that seem to be of carved stone are actually plaster over wood. Everything is fake, but it's done well and the whole thing is kitschy and fun. Even the bathrooms are elaborate and palatial."

"I'm surprised the building lasted. Too many of these old, beautiful theaters have been torn down over the years to make way for parking lots or, worse, a Walmart."

"It almost was torn down, but my mother, Allyson, and her friends formed a committee to save the Fox and the committee succeeded. It's now a profitable, viable venue for performances of all sorts. Last week it was the Celtic Women, this week the Mariinsky Ballet, and two weeks after that a reprise of *Le Miserables*." It operates all year and does well, and it's now an historical landmark, so no developer can crush it and replace it with anything."

"Don't let Donald Trump hear you say that."

"Oh, don't worry about him," she said with a perkiness that seemed very natural, "La Donald has yet to confront La Allyson. My mother has men like him for lunch."

The lights dimmed and the performance began.

The Mariinsky Ballet of St. Petersburg was utterly superb. They were dancing Tchaikovsky and the national gift of the Russians for musical composition and ballet blended in a scintillating mix of dancing genius, gorgeous costuming, and exquisite precision. No art is as physically demanding as ballet and none as beautiful if performed well. This was beyond a good performance, however. It was at the very apex of ballet artistry, gorgeous bodies moving in geometric precision, beautiful men and women doing the impossible and for a brief time elevating everyone in the theatre to a plane of beauty and accomplishment they never had even hoped to witness, to a level they could not have imagined without being there, seeing it, being part of it.

This was Penn's first ballet and in some ways it was a shame he came to this performance naïve and inexperienced in the art. If he ever attended another ballet, it would almost have to be of some diminished quality, something less than he saw and heard this evening, a disappointment. The bar of his expectation would be set so high no future experience could rival it. Yet there it was, the indulgence of a lifetime. He was *swept away* into the art, into the excitement and deep satisfaction of seeing perfect artistry, impossible timing, angelic grace. Kate gripped his hand but he hardly felt it.

At the intermission he visited the palatial bathroom, relieved himself and washed his face in cold water. The theater was warm, although not oppressively so, but the ballet itself seemed to heat him. The excitement and delight raised his temperature and he could feel the perspiration on his brow, trickling down his back. His shirt clung to him. The cold water was a tremendous relief. He drank from the water fountain as well, took two Tylenol for his shoulder and back, and bought a bottle of chilled club soda at one the bars, which he drank while he waited for Kate. Women have longer waits and a harder time than men in theaters, although the Fox is quite accommodating to them. He didn't have to wait very long. The Fox rest facilities are set below the lobby down a broad set of velvety, carpeted stairs with stout brass handrails. She fairly ran up the stairs to him. She wanted nothing to drink, no souvenirs, so he gulped down the rest of his soda and they came back to their seats just as the lights began to flash. Both were eager for the second act more than they were eager for each other.

Before going to the ballet, he checked out a book from the Annapolis Library, *The Real Man's Guide to Ballet.* The Section on Swan Lake was especially enlightening:

> *Swan Lake* is a silly romantic story about a prince named Siegfried (obviously German) who, while out hunting swans (Do people actually hunt swans?) finds a flock of them landing in a secluded lake. As night falls, the swans turn into beautiful young women. He falls in love with one of them, Odette, and finds he can break the spell that condemns her into becoming a swan during the day if he loves her truly and promises her eternal love. He does so. Much music and dancing.
>
> The prince's parents, however, especially his mother, have a different idea. They want him to wed a suitably high-born bride. They decide to encourage

him and to give him some choice in the matter, which was quite liberal of them considering that most princely matches of the time were political in nature, arranged virtually at birth for the hapless royal. For his 21st birthday (in some versions, his 18th birthday) the doting parents hold a ball and invite all the eligible, and suitable, high born young women in the princedom. Meanwhile, Von Rothbart, an evil sorcerer who is also part of the prince's retinue (Von Rothbart's duties are not described but presumably they have to do with advising, not with evil specifically), and who, coincidentally, is the magician who created the flock of enchanted swan maidens, is determined both to get his swan princess back in the flock and to see his daughter, Odile, engaged to the prince. He casts a spell on the prince that makes him think Odile is Odette. The prince is delighted to find Odette at the party (actually Odile), dances furiously with her, pledges his eternal love and asks her to marry him.

Odette, incidentally, is always garbed in white feathers, while Odile is always garbed in black, making her obvious to the audience but, of course, not to Siegfried who is either not very observant or under Von Rothbart's spell or both.

Tricked by Von Rothbart into proposing marriage to Odile, Siegfried unwittingly brakes his promise of eternal love to Odette (One wonders about the nature of the contract and the matter of intent, but, then, this is a German state and not subject to English Common Law. Apparently intent is not considered in magical contracts anyway, form and action take precedence. Perhaps Harry Potter could explain.) and condemns her to a lifetime of Swaning during the day and dancing in the forest during the night. Siegfried discovers the treachery, runs from the ball, finds Odette in the forest and attempts to fix the situation by once more pledging his love for her.

There are different endings to *Swan Lake*. In one ending, Von Rothbart mocks and curses Odette with spells and flashes of magic. Odette, overwhelmed by the wizard, still in human form plunges into the lake from a high rock and drowns. Siegfried arrives too late to stop her. In another both Odette and Siegfried jump together into the lake. In yet another Von Rothbart interferes with the reunion of Siegfried and Odette, and either paralyzes her or makes her disappear, or paralyzes Siegfried or orders Odette to the lake while the swan maidens patrol the shore keeping Siegfried away. In another ending, Odette and Siegfried join hands and jump together from the high rock, but instead of dying outright, an apotheosis occurs and their pure souls glowing with love are drawn into heaven, or wherever pure souls in love go.

Joseph Stalin, sensitive soul that he was, ordered changes to the ending of the ballet that were, well, happier. In the Stalinist version, or at least one of the Stalinist versions, Von Rothbart is defeated by the magic of true love, the Swans are freed and Siegfried dances off in triumph with Odette. Stalin, it is alleged, loved the ballet, but once left a Bolshoi performance of *Swan Lake* at the first intermission, motored to Red Square's Lubyanka Prison, shot a few former friends in the head, and returned in time to take his seat and enjoy a happy ending. The lives of pathologically murderous dictators are a perpetual flurry of busyness and activity.

In some versions of the ballet, Odile is not supposed to be Von Rothbart's daughter, but Von Rothbart himself, in drag. Remember, he casts spells, in this case a spell making everyone think he is Odette. The audience gets to see a ballerina dance Odile, however, since having a ballerino dance the role might be distracting. Of course, there is the version of Swan Lake in which all the parts are danced by cavaliers. In that version, there has to be a tragic ending because the story takes place well before any state or country allowed same-sex marriage. Otherwise, it's just as plausible as the heretro one.

Despite the ridiculous plot and the assortment of happy and unhappy endings, the ballet is gorgeous in performance in any form. Tchaikovsky's music is, of course, marvelous and unforgettable, and Swan Lake is a platform for what may be the most difficult, demanding and intense dancing in the world of ballet. Sweet and troubled Odette's role is difficult, but Odile, as the Black Swan, must dance furiously with Siegfried, enticing him, seducing him, making him want no other. Sometimes the roles of Odette and Odile are split between two ballerinas (or ballerinos), but more often one ballerina, who must have incredible skill and unusual stamina, is chosen to dance both roles.

We never know what happens to Odile (not in any version except the one in which Von Rothbart disguises himself as Odile-Odette), who is easily the most enigmatic, sexy, spirited and interesting character in the ballet.

That evening at the Fox, the Mariinsky Ballet, knowing or, rather *thinking* they knew the tastes of a soft and sentimental American audience, employed a modified Stalinist ending. Von Rothbart got to throw a wizard's tantrum with flash-booms and smoke, Odette and Siegfried were bounced about the stage (bounced in the idiom of dance, not literally) as the wizard demonstrated his strength and fury and Odette, desperate to do something to stop the evil man and save Siegfried, nearly flings herself from the rock. Just as Odette is about to dive into the lake, a providential light from heaven, or at least from the light bar above the stage, shines down. Siegfried and Odette fall on their knees in thanks, and Von Rothbart falls dead. The lovers unite, presumably in endless bliss and dance a pas de deux. Oh, and the rest of the Swan-maidens are free to return home, after dancing in triumph. We never know what Siegfried's parents think about all this, but Odette, after all, is a queen, at least a queen of swans, and that should be high-born enough for a prince. Well, at least she's not a queen of ducks or turkeys.

Oksana Skoryk danced both Odette and Odile that night, and was breathtaking – beautiful, masterful, passionate, precise, a consummate artist. Both Penn and Kate were infatuated with her, but in different ways. Kate, trained over many years by a superb teacher, Prima Ballerina Maniya Barredo, could richly appreciate the technical difficulty and utter perfection of Skoryk's dancing. Penn knew the dancing was superb, but his appreciation was naïve. He also saw Skoryk as a strikingly beautiful young woman and as a consummate artist and athlete. *What is it they call ballet dancers?* Thought Penn, then it came to him, *the athletes of God.*

The performance ended with an explosion of applause, a standing ovation, many curtain calls, several bouquets of flowers and the ballet, in turn, endowed a satisfaction, an excitement, a sense of wonder and magic that infested every member of the audience. Penn was speechless. Kate, a sometime ballerina herself, hooted and clapped.

So far, it was a perfect evening, then, despite the Tylenol he'd taken, Penn's shoulder and back began to ache again.

10:45

Penn's tickets and reservations included a late dinner for two at the Georgian Terrace Hotel, just across Peachtree Street from the Fox. They didn't go straight to the restaurant. The rain stopped earlier in the evening and the street and sidewalk, washed clean, smelt of the rainwater and brisk November air. Penn and Kate walked down and around the block first, cooling down from the theater, stretching their legs and giving Penn's back and shoulder a break from the pressures of a high-backed chair. A 10-minute walk would go a long way towards relieving the ache and the tightness.

"I love to walk just after a rain," said Kate, breaking the silence. They'd barely said anything to each other since leaving the theater.

"I do too," said Penn, "I always have. The walk is good for me too. It takes the pressure off my shoulder and back and keeps them from getting sore from too much sitting. I need the stretching, the motion and the exercise."

"How did you hurt yourself?"

Penn never spoke about his experiences in Iraq. There was no deep-seated psychological fear of doing so, but if he told the truth of what happened in detail then it would seem as if he's singing his own praises. On the other hand, a partial truth seemed evasive and just begged questions.

"We were on river patrol. Someone shot at us. Don't know who. Insurgents, bandits, Al Qaida, maybe just locals with a bone to pick. We stopped, beached the boat, rushed to shore. A little inland an IED exploded. I was struck in the back and shoulder with some chunks of shrapnel, maybe with the bomb shell itself. I passed out, woke up in the hospital. I don't remember much about it."

"God. That must have been awful," said Kate looking up at him.

"Yeah, well, it could have a lot worse. I was wearing body armor and I wasn't hit in the worst place you can be hit. I still have my arms, legs and face. The boat Captain was killed that day by another IED. Some marines and sailors were wounded and killed."

She was quiet for a few seconds, wondering what to say. "Have you gotten any therapy for it?"

"Oh, sure. The Navy hospital folks have been great; they know what they're doing. Therapy began before the cast came off. At first it was every day, but I've healed considerably and now I have therapy sessions every week or so. Mostly I meet to confer with the therapist and make sure I'm doing the right things, the right exercises. It's been healing now for two years, gradually getting better. The soreness comes and goes. I think in another year or so I'll be completely healed. I did a lot of driving this week, though, and being frozen in one spot for long brings on the stiffness and soreness. I probably should have been more careful."

"Are you in pain now?"

"A little. The walking helps. The pain diminishes rapidly when I get up and move."

She took hold of his arm and leaned into him just a bit. "That doesn't hurt, does it?"

"No, not at all. I was hit on the other side."

"What did you think of the ballet?" She said.

"I had no idea. The only ballet I ever saw was part of a *Nutcracker* video I was forced to sit through in high school; ninth grade, I think. I thought it was dreadful. Tonight was a revelation. I've read about the balletomanes in Russia in the early 19th century. I thought it was a kind of fan obsession, their idolization of certain ballerinas, even a sexual obsession. Now I understand. A man could get obsessed with ballet. When it's done right, it's a beautiful, mind-bending thing. They should teach it at the Academy."

She laughed. "I'll tell my father."

"He just might do it. He's not an Academy man, is he?" said Penn, his mood improving as the pain diminished.

"No, Michigan."

"Well, see…" he paused.

"See what?" she said playfully.

"Ann Arbor and all, you know," he said, teasing her.

"I'm going to tell him what you said."

"I said? I didn't say anything."

"Yes, but you were thinking…"

They came to the corner of Ponce de Leon and Peachtree.

"Red light," said Penn, "Let's cross and head over to the Inn."

"And change the topic?" she said, sill playful.

"And change the topic," he said, still teasing.

The Georgian Terrace was crowded with people who had crossed over from the Fox, but Penn had reservations for 11:00 pm and they arrived at the minute. The table was ready, a waiter stood by, and wine was served. Penn ordered Prime rib; Kate had soup and salad. Service was fast and impeccable. The food wasn't memorable, but it was good.

Conversation revolved around ballet. Penn asked questions and let Kate talk. He had no idea that ballet training was divided into schools or theories – French, Russian, even German and British. Most schools taught a synthesis, or propagated their own methods. The Russians developed their dancers with classical ballet, but as the young dancers learned and grew brought them into neoclassical forms and the speed of modern dance. The French copied the Russians but added their own moves and techniques and Americans, bowing to Balanchine and all the great choreographers, developed versatile dancers whose styles were classical and modern. Even Hip-hop found its way into the repertoire.

"Do you dance at all? She asked him.

"No. I can dance in a way, of course. I can get on the floor and sort of move with the music, but if you mean waltz or fox-trot or tango I wouldn't know what to do."

"I thought all you New Englanders from those fancy prep schools were shoved into social finishing classes before your eighth birthday."

"My education was, unfortunately, impoverished in that respect. I was put into a Lacrosse uniform when I was still at a very tender age and dropped on the field. It was all muscular Christianity pounded into us by overeducated Augustinian monks who secretly wanted to be professional athletes and lived vicariously through their students. Masculine sport was to be the antidote to vice, the shield of sin."

"Did it work?" she said.

"Not particularly well. I was a barely competent player."

"The shield of sin," I mean.

"Please, Madam," he said in mock seriousness, "I would never kiss and tell."

"So it didn't work."

He sighed. "Like Joyce's Steven Daedalus, virtue had its place until puberty intervened. At that point, it became very inconvenient. The spirit is willing but the flesh.... But I'm sure someone with your high standards would know little of that."

She winked suggestively and with a cagy little smile agreed, "Uh huh," she said in a Cockney accent, "I'd know nothing at all, Ducky."

"I'll hold you to that."

Still in Cockney mode she answered "As long as youse 'old me

Ducks, it don't make no difference, no difference at all why."

Hold her? *Yes*, he thought, *I'd like to*." The ache quickly began to creep up his back and into his shoulder. He tried to will it away.

She could see the pain in his face, a kind of weariness. His eyes looked tired, even haggard.

"Is there anything wrong, Penn?" she asked.

"Nothing a good night's sleep on a firm mattress won't cure. It's late. I think we should be getting back. Don't you have to work tomorrow?"

"Yes," she said. Concealing her disappointment. She was hoping they'd go somewhere, to his hotel or even to her rooms. After that…

He dropped her off at her place a half-hour later. She invited him in, wanted him to come in, but he demurred politely. His back was hurting and all he wanted to do was to go back to the hotel, take some medication, and sleep. She could see that in him and forgave him for not coming in, and loved him even more.

"G'd night, Ducky," she said, Cockney again.

He kissed her on the lips and she melted into him.

"I'll call you," he said.

"If you don't, I'll join Odette in the lake."

He kissed her again, whispered "Good night," and got back into his car.

"Take care of yourself, Penn. Let it heal."

"See you later alligator," he winked.

"In a while crocodile," she responded.

He drove off. *What was it Freud said?* Penn thought, *Yes. "A man with a toothache can't fall in love." That goes for backaches as well.* All he wanted to do at this point was to get home, take some Tylenol, get under a hot shower, lay down on the extra-firm mattress the hotel had promised him and sleep.

DISTANCE

****

Chapter Ten – Butterfly in Santa Fe

Yoshiko celebrated with the cast for an hour after the show, but emotionally and physically exhausted, she left the cast party early, dragged herself to her hotel room, showered and slid into bed before midnight. She quickly fell into a deep, dreamless sleep.

At six, there was a knock at her door. It awakened her, but she lay in bed for just a minute before arising wondering if yesterday had been real or just an elaborate and vivid dream. No further knock. She rose, threw on her robe and opened the door. Her room opened to a long, open-air balcony that led to a central stairway. There, on the balcony paving, she found copies of the two local newspapers opened to the arts section and weekend preview, held down by a brick so they wouldn't blow away. The reviews were in. Her hands shook as she grabbed the newspapers and nervously slammed the door to her room. She stood there for several minutes with her eyes closed afraid of what she might see. These reviews might very well determine her fate as a singer and actress. Finally composing herself, steeling herself, she read them.

The Santa Fe Daily Sun

Madame Butterfly at the Santa Fe Opera House – It doesn't Get any Better than This

Rodney Perkins for the *Sun*

I want to hate Puccini's *Madame Butterfly*. I want to hate the opera because if I did hate it I could see it and not feel so emotionally overwhelmed by a good performance of that old saw. If I hated it, I could review it with a more jaundiced eye. Unfortunately, that‘s not the case. It was my first opera (Isn't that true of every opera fan?), and no matter how many times I've seen it, the old girl still has her charms.

I thought I'd seen every possible variation and interpretation of

Butterfly over the past 40 years, including some I'd rather forget, but last night I saw a *Butterfly* that was, to use a cliché that I can't avoid, *unforgettable*. National Lyric Opera, who is here in Santa Fe for only five days, gave us a performance of Puccini's sentimental old opera that is simply without parallel.

The young diva, Yoshiko Fujiyama, as Cio-Cio San, a last minute replacement for the remarkable Hye Young Rhee, who was hospitalized this afternoon, not only sang well, but she put a stamp on the part that is individual, profound and immensely moving. The beautiful Ms. Fujiyama may be young, and her voice may mature further in coming years, but last night her passion, the intensity of her singing, the depth, sensitivity and refinement she showed in her interpretation of the role, and the sheer beauty of her voice gave a vibrant new life and breath to an opera that I thought long ago was played-out and over-performed, and to which little more could be added or done. Her performance last night would bring any opera lover to his or her knees to thank whatever god he or she holds dear for the blessing of having heard it in their lifetime. Yes, she was *that good.*

Emmanuel Goldstein, as Pinkerton, a superb singer, added vigor, rakishness, and charm to a part that requires great plasticity in interpretation and a nuanced approach. Martin Broker as Sharpless, gave us an impeccable and compassionate interpretation that was subtle, nuanced and sophisticated. Tally Morris as Goro, played the role with a depth that went far beyond the usual interpretation and conveyed a character that was layered and conflicted rather than avaricious and crude. Suzuki, played by Lisa Reynolds, was an effective foil to the dreamy self-delusion of poor Cio-Cio San.

The singing was perfect. Just perfect. Fujiyama and Goldstein were the very embodiment of the tragic lovers. They exuded both the passion and tenderness that only two people in love can show and, too, that fatal emotional sear, the depthless pain of hope dashed by betrayal and incalculable loss. The acting was superb. The singing cherubic. After forty years of *Butterflys* I finally wept. Go, see it while you can. Just go. It's the performance of a lifetime.

The Santa Fe Bugle

The Perfect Madame Butterfly – National Lyric Theatre at the Santa Fe Opera House

Christian Howard of the *Bugle*

Madame Butterfly by an itinerant company in Santa Fe for a week? Yawn. I didn't want to go, but the demands of home and family for a paycheck pushed me on.

What a surprise! From the moment the curtain opened I sensed an electricity, an excitement that I'd never felt at any performance of a Puccini opera. Perhaps it was the perfect tempo of the orchestra, the sets, the costuming, the eagerness of the opening night audience. Whatever it was, from the first note I realized that something extraordinary was happening, something I could never have anticipated. I was right. My expectations, which admittedly weren't very high, were utterly exceeded. To put it in the vernacular, I was blown away.

Emmanuel Goldstein's Pinkerton was flawless. Not only was his singing perfect, his intonation, the subtlety and nuances of expression, the irreconcilable conflict of caddishness and nobility in a character who was continuously out of character was revealed in every note, every expression, every gesture.

At the very last minute, the marvelous Hye Young Rhee, whom we saw last year as a gorgeous Mimi in *La Boheme,* was taken ill and was replaced by a newcomer, Yoshiko Fujiyama. The brilliant, young Ms. Fujiyama (Cio-Cio San), ingénue turned Diva, was splendid. Fujiyama not only took the role, she transformed it and it made it hers in a deeply emotive way.

I've never been moved by a *Butterfly*. I always thought that

Puccini had gone too far in tempting and manipulating his audience and I bristled at what I thought was naked emotional pandering. Not last night. Fujiyama remade Butterfly and gave her both an innocence and a depth that was profound in beauty, love, pathos and suffering. Her interpretation and the excellence of her glorious singing defies description. Superlatives don't do it justice.

Perhaps inspired by Goldstein and Fujiyama, Martin Boker, a substantial artist in his own right, gave us a Sharpless that was profoundly compassionate and moral, and Tally Morris as Goro played the role with an intelligence and insight that transformed this shallow and avaricious character into a multi-layered and complex being striving to live in a rigid and uncompromising world. Suzuki was sung with sensitivity and passion by Lisa Reynolds.

This is a performance to eclipse all other *Butterflys.* At the Santa Fe Opera House until Sunday evening. Don't miss it.

Yoshiko, her face wet with tears, the newspapers in hand, pounded on the door of Manny Goldstein's motel room. No answer. She knew he was there. She could hear him snoring.

"Manny! I know you're in there. Open up!" She pounded on the door until her hand was sore.

"All right, all right, I'll be there in a minute," Manny responded, his voice weary and broken.

She waited and was just about to pound on the door again, when it opened a crack.

"Yoshiko. What do you want?"

"Here. The reviews," she said, thrusting the newspapers at him.

"Wha? Oh, yeah, the reviews. I don't need 'em. We blew the audience away. We were great. Now let me sleep." He started to close the door.

"I want to talk to you," she said as forcefully as she could.

"Yeah. Tomorrow. I've got a headache, I feel sick to my stomach and I need to sleep if I'm going to be any good tonight." He had a hangover, not a disease. If Lee found out his lead singer had a little too much to drink, there'd be hell to pay. He started to close the door again, but she grabbed the edge and pushed against him.

"Manny…"

"What?"

"Thank you."

"Nothing to thank. Go away." She let go and he shut the door in her face.

Hey Young Rhee was in good spirits. She'd be out of the hospital in another day and be back to work in a week or so. Of course, she missed *Butterfly* in Santa Fe, but if she had to be ill anywhere on tour, it was better to be ill in a town like Santa Fe than in Los Angeles, San Francisco, Chicago, or New York, some place that really counted.

Yoshiko poked her head into Hye Young's room, half expecting Hye Young to throw something at her. Yoshiko felt as if she'd stolen Hye Young's role, although she knew that wasn't the case. It was just circumstance, fate, that's all. She was timid nevertheless, worried about Hye Young's reaction to everything that had occurred. She admired and respected Hye Young so much she would never do anything to alienate her, hurt her or take from her. She just felt so *guilty* about all that happened and wanted so much to know how Hye Young felt, and if Hye Young was hurt to explain things to her and to try to get her forgiveness if she could.

"Yoshiko!" Hye Young exclaimed, beaming with excitement "Come in, come in. Don't linger there in the doorway. I'm OK, come see me."

Yoshiko walked gingerly to Hye Young's bedside, as if she

were afraid that Hye Young would pounce on her at any moment.

"Come *here*!" said Hye Young, holding out her arms, "Let me hug you, little sister."

Yoshiko bent over the bed, and hugged Hye Young gently, afraid of hurting her so soon after the operation, and started to cry. Hye Young was not so gentle. She pulled Yoshiko to her and hugged her firmly.

"Yoshiko, I read the reviews. You were wonderful. I am so proud of you!..." she stroked Yoshiko's hair, "Don't cry, don't cry, don't be silly. This is a win, a triumph. Be happy. Be proud."

She released Yoshiko, handed her a small box of Kleenex, and smiled broadly.

"You're not mad at me?" sniffed Yoshiko.

"Are you crazy? You've saved the company, made the season. Lee Gross was here. He told me what you did. What a brave, brave woman you are!... You know, I called Ms. Evelyn and told her all about you. I had Lee fax copies of the review to her. She's so excited, so happy! She's going to read them to the class and hang them on her bulletin board."

Dr. Evelyn Delrois (pronounced "dell-wah") was the senior voice professor at Curtis, famous both for the power of her teaching and coaching and the acidity of her tongue. She spared her students nothing but taught them discipline, concentration, and strength. She was the kind of teacher never forgotten, whose forceful coaching and consummate professionalism become embedded in her students. No one succeeds with her who isn't bent on a successful career in opera and is willing to do all the work, sacrifice and concentration that's needed to develop the voice, learn the roles and give themselves over to the art.

Yoshiko's eyes widened, "Ms. Evelyn? What did she say?"

"What I just told you, Yoshiko. She was ecstatic."

Yoshiko looked down at the bed. "I was so afraid you'd be hurt and angry."

"Yoshiko, you don't know how happy you've made me. If you hadn't stepped up the company would have lost the evening. If that local, Marie Robertson, had been here and taken the role, it would have been almost as bad, maybe worse."

"Why is that?"

"Have you ever seen her?" laughed Hye Young, "She's the size of a hippo, has kinky red hair, a large nose, and is so old she could be my mother, or maybe my grandmother's younger sister. She has a voice, but the package it comes in would have sent the audience home at intermission. Thank God you're here."

Yoshiko looked up and smiled. "You heard what Manny Goldstein did?"

"I heard," said Hye Young, "Lee told me. He was very vivid."

"Why would Manny do something like this? I thought he hated me," said Yoshiko.

"Hate and envy are strange creatures; sometimes they abide just on the other side of the curtain from love," said Hye Young, "I think Manny envies you and loves you in a way and he can't cope with that, so it comes out in nastiness and peculiarity. He's like a little boy who pulls a little girl's hair and the next day tries to kiss her. We had those in Korea; I'm sure you had them in Japan as well. I also think he would do anything for you and for me, too. There are times when he has been kind to me, although he would never admit that. I feel it, too, when we sing together. He likes to be my Pinkerton, yours too I'm sure. He likes to hold me and sing of his love, to have me in his arms, although he would never do anything about it. He's a man of too many internal contradictions and conflicts. His personality works well with opera since every hero and villain in opera is conflicted. Conflict and love are what all the great music and singing is about...." She paused and caught her breath. "Let Manny be. His unhappiness and confusion is his great asset -- they drive him -- and he has his own devils to fight."

Yoshiko nodded. Hye Young was right of course, very right. She was so wise.

"Thank you," said Yoshiko, "I understand more now, and I will try to do everything I can to wrap up this stay on a very high note."

Hye Young smiled and took Yoshiko's hand. "They will love you," she said, "They *do* love you. Remember that. Make them weep."

"Yes," said Yoshiko, "Yes..."

****

Chapter Eleven – In Buckhead

Kate overslept on Friday and called into work requesting 3 hours leave. No problem. After Penn left, she was unable to sleep. She lay in bed half the night, unusual for her, thinking, re-imagining the evening with Penn, going over every word, every sentence, every expression. Penn was an honest person; she was sure of that. He wasn't angling for a fast lay, that was for certain because he could have gotten his wish last night if that were the case. So what did he want, if anything?

He seemed to like her very much, yet there was something missing. It was as if he were holding back or holding out for something or for someone else. She couldn't quite put her finger on it but she knew that unless she could find what he wanted, what he needed, she would never have him. Of course she knew little or nothing about him. There was the "official" stuff – He was an Annapolis grad. He'd seen sea duty and service in Iraq. He was just awarded his Ph.D. from Emory, the university she attended for her MPH. Their parents were acquainted.

There was the personal stuff as well. She knew he had an interest in opera, or at least knew something about it. He was well-read and a good listener. Even if he wasn't particularly loquacious, when he did speak it was interesting and to effect. He had a gentle sense of humor and his speech was, since no other word fit, refined. Nothing coarse about him at all. Philosophically, he seemed to be a humanist and an idealist but one who could work comfortably within the constraints of the system not against them.

She did know one thing for certain, she felt so good when she was with him. As they walked down Peachtree together, she caught a glimpse of themselves, arm in arm, reflected in a storefront window. They were perfect together, like models posing for a catalog, like a movie poster. Yet, somehow, she felt she was failing with him, that she couldn't reach him, and that was a spike in her heart. It hurt. She couldn't say she loved him. She didn't know him well enough to love him, but she knew, *she just knew,* if she did get to know him, if they did spend enough time together that she would love him as she never loved anyone. And if she loved him, then he might love her in turn. The thought of losing that was painful, distressing, disconcerting. These were feelings she never had before and it was hard to cope with them, to concentrate on anything else.

There was a knock on her door. *Oh, God,* She thought as she looked through the viewer, *just what I need right now*. It was Allyson, her mother.

"Hi, Mom," she said, trying to sound perky as she opened the door.

Allyson saw right though the façade of Kate's superficial perkiness. "I saw your car here this morning and I wanted to check on you. Is everything OK?"

"It's fine, Mom. I had a late night and I just overslept, that's all."

"Not like you, Katie," said Allyson softly, "You had me worried."

"I'm a big girl, you know," said Kate.

"I know. You weren't out that late, though. Weren't you feeling well?"

"Uh, well in a way I couldn't sleep last night, that's all."

"I know he didn't stay and you were home a just little after midnight. I heard him drop you off then drive away. I saw his car flash by the window."

"Yeah, but it was really a great evening. We saw the Mariinsky Ballet at the Fox."

Allyson's mother raised an eyebrow. She studied ballet at one time and was a fan, too. She was also on the board of Atlanta Ballet. "You saw them do *Swan Lake*? They're marvelous, aren't they? I saw them last year in New York when Chip and I went to that business meeting in Manhattan."

"Oh, they were wonderful. They're at the very top and we had great seats."

"You and Penn Fuller?" said her mother.

"How did you know it was Penn?"

"He drove to the end of the drive, stopped and waited for a break in traffic. He was only there for a few seconds, but I could see him clearly in the light from the street lamp."

"Oh," said Kate, feeling as she were caught doing something wrong, but of course she was doing nothing wrong, and she was 27, not a teenager. It was silly to feel that way.

"You're falling for him, aren't you?"

"Oh, mother it's not like that. He was in town anyway and he just took me out to have some company while he went to the ballet. That's all. It's not like you think," She said.

"I never heard of a sailor buying tickets to the ballet so that *he* could see it," said Allyson.

"Yes, mother, and you never met an opera-loving sailor with a Ph.D. before, either."

Allyson smiled. "So you tossed and turned half the night because the two of you are just friends, ballet buddies, and that's the way you want it?"

"It wasn't half the night. I have some issues at work…" her voice trailed off.

Allyson put her arm around Kate. "You're stuck on him, Kate. I know the signs. Remember what I told you. No matter how nice, or charming or funny or caring he seems to be, the man's already married to the service. You'll always be second to that, and it won't be fun. Give your head half the chance you're giving your heart and you'll see what I mean." She said this softly, kindly.

Kate looked away. "He was hurt in Iraq. His back and shoulder were giving him trouble. He dropped me off and drove back to his hotel because he was in pain."

"That's a reason to respect him and honor what he's done, not to love him."

"I know," said Kate, "What do I do if I can't get him out of my mind?"

"Get busy. Work hard. To hell with him. Work cures almost anything," Allyson said, with kindness.

Kate knew Allyson was right. She'd known it all along. She sighed and hugged her mother.

"Thanks, Mom," she said.

"And don't call him. If he calls you be nice but don't let him think you want to see him again," said Allyson.

"I'll try, mom," said Kate.

"Kate, there are plenty of fish in the sea, but you know that. You're beautiful, intelligent and good company. Trust me. There are a million guys out there for you that will give you a good life, respect you, make you happy. Keep your eyes open and your knees together. Got me?"

"Got it, Mom."

They hugged. Kate got dressed for work feeling if not completely good, a lot better than she had felt.

****

Chapter Twelve – Flower Duet

Sunday, Santa Fe. *Madama Butterfly* at the Opera House. A matinee and a previously unscheduled evening performance at 7:30. After the reviews were published and as word spread, the theater filled to overflowing. For the first time in decades, every seat was occupied, even standing room was sold out. Tickets were actually being scalped, a thing theater management openly condemned but secretly delighted-in. They asked Lee Gross and the company to linger in town just long enough to add the unscheduled Sunday evening performance and were happily accommodated. Even that was sold out and scalped. Happy days.

Hye Young Rhee was back, but she was still weak and stayed in the wings watching the performance on Sunday, taking mental notes and planning to make suggestions. She was learning from Yoshiko's performance and seeing things that could be done just a little better, a little more effectively. Both of them would improve, making future performances even more memorable. She met with Lee Gross after the matinee and talked with him about the future. Hye Young wanted to retain Yoshiko as an equal who alternated with her in performing the role. Lee was happy with that. Cio-cio San is a demanding role. Neither one of them would sing out their voices and have to rest or turn in a tired and sloppy performance. The audiences would see a fresh Cio-Cio every night. Besides, it provided some insurance against another sudden illness or other disaster.

If he could have afforded a second Pinkerton he would have done that, too, but it was too much. Men are rarer than women in opera. A male singer who could take on Pinkerton's role would be expensive and demanding. Two ladies were enough, at least for now. Anyway, he could sit back and watch the company's share of the revenue build. They were going to finish the season well in the black this year -- a small miracle -- pay off some old debts and try to rebuild with new costumes and refurbished scenery. San Diego was next on the itinerary. No Los Angeles this year, but that was OK, LA was usually expensive and the audiences weren't always there. Then San Francisco, Portland, Seattle and Vancouver. After that, it was back to their home base in Pennsylvania for a rest, a change of opera, rehearsals, a trial in Philadelphia, more rehearsal and back to the circuit beginning next season with Montreal, then Providence and down the East Coast, Boston, Hartford, Brooklyn, Morristown, Washington, Charlotte, Atlanta, across to New Orleans, then Cleveland, St. Louis, and to Santa Fe, and up the West Coast ending in Vancouver. They tried to time their visits to each city so they didn't conflict with the local opera company or with any other traveling company. It was tricky, but worth it. The audience wouldn't be divided and the locals wouldn't be hostile.

The final Santa Fe performance was enormously successful. The audience interrupted several times with applause and at the end gave a standing ovation that went on and on. Lee didn't know it, but Yoshiko and Hey Young had a surprise planned. Hye Young and Yoshiko had previously gotten the orchestra to agree to an encore, unusual in opera and never done by the National Lyric company in the past. After the fourth curtain call, Yoshiko parted the curtain and took the stage by herself with a microphone in hand.

"My friends," she said. She had the remnants of an accent, just enough to sound cute to an English-speaker without distorting the words, "Our real Diva, Ms. Hye Young Rhee is back, and we'd like to offer you something very special. Please don't leave, take your seats."

The audience sat down and those who had exited their seats and were in the aisles stopped and turned round.

The lights dimmed, and Hey Young, in the spotlight as she crossed the stage, joined Yoshiko. Applause. She nodded to the conductor and the orchestra began the introduction to the lovely and haunting Flower Duet from Lakmé. Performed well, there is little in music, classical or contemporary that can equal it for sweetness and beauty.

Lee Gross, backstage, said to no one in particular, "What the hell do they think they're doing?"

"It's a special type of singing, Lee, called a duet," said Manny Goldstein.

"I know it's a goddamn duet, but who told them to do it?"

Manny just looked at him with contempt, crossed his arms, and muttered, "Lee, you're interrupting. Let me listen." There was a note of menace in his voice, so Lee, who had an answer in mind, kept it to himself and walked off. *Singers are all nuts*, he thought.

Yoshiko and Hey Young joined hands and sang together, a barely rehearsed, not exactly perfect but delightful performance. The charming duet normally finishes with a soft diminuendo and the exit of the singers from the stage, which is the way they ended it.

The audience exploded one more time. More curtain calls. The conductor came to the stage, took both the ladies' hands in his, kissed them and stood back applauding. Santa Fe had gotten its money's worth.

****

Chapter Thirteen – Commander and Admiral

Penn Fuller went straight to his hotel after leaving Kate, threw off his clothes, and stood under the shower, the water as hot as he could endure, letting it pour down his shoulder and back. He'd taken a dose of Ibuprofen and he could feel the soreness dissipate as the water warmed the area, brought in blood and relaxed the muscles. In ten minutes he was whole again. He slipped into bed on the rock-hard mattress provided by the hotel, and slept for nine hours.

By Friday morning he was restored. The shoulder and back felt normal, even loose, or looser than they were the day before. There was no pain and the night's rest cleared his head and made him both hungry and ambitious, eager to return to the Academy to begin reviewing and cataloging the papers he'd locked in the vault.

He finished dressing and the unmistakable marimba of his iPhone beat a cheery little tattoo that he'd grown to dislike. He once experimented by changing the ring tone only to find that every new tone was more annoying than the last, so he stayed with the marimba and endured it. The number was in his address book, so the phone identified the caller, Harriett Pennington Butler."

"Hello, Auntie," said Penn, "Good morning."

"How'd 'ya know it was me?" she said, her Yankee brogue thicker in the morning than at night.

"iPhone. It tells me who's calling if I have the number in its address book." He said.

"Humph! That's handy. I could cut off all these goddamn insurance peddlers, cemetery plot salesmen, hearing aid jackasses, money-grubbing preachers and phony charities that call me."

"You have to have them in your address book first," he said.

"I knew there was catch. How'd it go? She still in your room?"

"I'll ask her. Gertrude, roll over. My Grant Aunt Harriett wants to meet you."

"Don't be funny, Penn. This is serious."

"OK. She's not here. I dropped her off at her place last night and went home."

"Nothing else happened?"

"Auntie, as much as I love and cherish you, I wouldn't tell if it did."

"What'd you do last night?" she said, sounding a little deflated.

"I picked her up and we went to the ballet at an elaborate old Atlanta theater, the Fox. The Mariinsky troop from St. Petersburg was performing *Swan Lake*. It was superb."

"I've been to the Fox. Saw the premier of *Gone with the Wind* there. Liked the theater but thought the movie was a bore. I was only about 14 at the time and a Yankee, of course. The movie never set well with me… But that's all beside the point. Go anywhere afterward?"

"We went across the street to the Georgian Terrace Hotel," he said

"Is that where it happened?"

"We went there for a late supper, had spare ribs and wine, and I took her home. That's all we did."

"That's it?" she said.

"Pretty much."

"You kissed her goodnight?"

Penn weighed this question against his natural inclination for privacy both for himself and for Kate, and decided it would be all right to answer without evading it. "Yes, Auntie, I kissed her goodnight. She seemed very pleased by everything, as if she truly enjoyed the evening."

"Well, that's a start, at least," she said, "I know the girl is nuts about you. I'd be nuts about any straight man as good looking as you who took me both to the opera and the ballet. Hell, I'd be nuts about you if you took me to a rat fight and monkey wrestling."

"Thanks, Auntie," he said affectionately, wondering what "monkey wrestling" is but hesitant to ask the question and extend the conversation any further than necessary. If his curiosity persisted there was always Google, the last resource of meatball scholars.

"How's yer back, Penn? All this driving couldn't have helped." There was real concern in her voice.

"It was bothering me a little last night, but I'm shipshape this morning."

"All right. You kept your part of the deal, I suppose. I'll give you that much. Be careful driving back to Annapolis."

"You got it, Auntie, and thank you. I think there's really good material in that trunk."

She hung up without saying "Goodbye." She did that often. It was one of her quirks.

He wanted to drive straight through to the Academy, but he paced the trip and stopped several times to stretch his legs and back and give his shoulder a little exercise, keeping both the back and shoulder limber and pain-free. It took him longer to make the trip but he made it back comfortably, just before 10 PM, dropped off the rental car, and walked back to his apartment. He had his own car, but the Navy paid the freight for his trip to Vermont and the rental company gave him the extra mileage to and From Atlanta for free. He had only to pay for the extra day. It was all ethical and sanctioned by the law and regulation, the Navy was good with it, and so was he.

There was news for him back at the apartment. A manila envelope had been slipped under his door, Official United States Navy, addressed to him at his Academy Office. This was strange. No one ever bothered to hand deliver anything to his home before. It was only partially sealed, so he popped it open and pulled the contents. Good news. *Spectacular* news. Orders from the Office of the Secretary -- He was officially slated for promotion to Commander, USN January 1. Seven weeks away. By Navy tradition, he could wear the rank now. The official pinning-on (and raise in pay) would come the day after New Year. Good time to be promoted. Everyone would be on Christmas leave and he wouldn't be pushed into a celebratory party. He didn't like that sort of thing and he didn't want to waste the time.

There was a note from Captain Southerland, *Congratulations, Commander, no one deserved it more*. He was promoted well ahead of his class, the first one to make 05, full Commander. Unlike Southerland he had his misgivings about the promotion. He wondered if he deserved it. Some of his classmates had two or more tours in battle zones, Iraq and Afghanistan. One, he knew, had back-to-back tours in Iraq and Afghanistan then "wintered over" in the Antarctic. Three were dead that he knew of, one a carrier pilot who died in a training accident, another a Line Officer who died in an auto accident while visiting his folks in Cincinnati at Easter two years ago, and the third a Swift Boat officer who'd been shot through both lungs and drowned in his own blood before the doctors could save him. Several, all Marines, had been badly wounded, lost limbs or were partially paralyzed. There were others in his class who deserved the promotion more. *It's that way with any lottery*, he thought, *this time I'm the lucky one. Maybe next time I'll be the one on the cross.*

Morose thought. Better to work and forget everything else.

The next day, Penn took his uniforms to a tailor who specialized in military work, had the old top stripe removed and the Commander's stripe sewn on, picked up the collar pins and shoulder boards, and adorned himself with the new rank. He wore a Kaki uniform with the new silver oak leaves but no one seemed to notice his enhanced glory except Leroy the tailor who made his living noticing such things and who congratulated him heartily while overcharging him for the alterations. His uniforms settled, he then went to the Library, retrieved the trunk, put on his gloves and began to sort its contents on a long table in a secure room he reserved for his work.

He wanted a timeline, so he started putting everything in chronological order, which was better for now than trying to group them in some other way, and tediously typed all the metadata into the Naval Academy Academic Documents Database (NAADD), an automated records center designed especially for cataloging historical documents. His information would be uploaded to the Cloud and, with the right access codes be available anywhere. He would back-up the NAADD file initially with copies on two portable hard disks and when the complete set was done, put it all on a DVD. Meanwhile he was getting clerical assistance from the help pool and as he set up the record for each document had it scanned into an Adobe PDF which would be attached to the metadata file. If he worked at it constantly for a week – ten hours per day – and his clerical help wasn't taken away, he'd get it done before Thanksgiving.

Judging by the size of the piles he'd taken from the trunk, there were between two and three thousand individual documents, maybe less because some were reports that were tens if not dozens of pages long. Each one of the papers would be put into an acid free envelop and moved to a humidity controlled room as soon as possible. He wanted no damage to the originals and made that very clear to the help, who seemed interested in the project and promised to do everything they could to ensure the safety and preservation of the papers.

Penn liked cataloging and record keeping, at least as far as he did it to maintain his documentary evidence and create a trail other scholars could follow. Scientists and engineers – the good ones – are similarly scrupulous with their information and their records. Penn recently read a biography of Darwin and he was impressed by discovering that one of nature's greatest observers, Charles Darwin, loved collecting data so much he actually went so far as to keep the household records, watching every penny. He wasn't a skinflint, just a scientist who enjoyed empirical work and kept unimpeachable records of what occurred. Penn drew the line at financial records. He kept those simple and in his head. Academic work was something else.

Admiral Pennington didn't keep extensive diaries. No busy man has time for that. But as Penn saw, scattered among the official papers there were copies of the many letters he sent and letters he received, personal and professional, notes, and the professional journals he kept that supported the reports, research and advice that formed the Admiral's professional life. As Penn started to build the computer files he began to appreciate what a treasure he had. The gaps in his Great Grandfather's career started filling. He knew, for example, the Admiral served in Asia, but until now wasn't aware that it was a series of assignments, not just a single stint on a foreign shore. Penn summarized his preliminary findings in a narrative that served as the kernel upon which he'd build his knowledge of the Admiral and the Admiral's career.

The Admiral went to Japan for the first time in 1892. His duty station in Japan was at Hiroshima for all four-plus years of his initial assignment. The orders that sent him to Japan contained detailed specifications, several pages long, of a sort that no longer appear in military orders. He was to observe the shoreline, check the accuracy of Navy charts and maps, serve with the Japanese Navy on shore and at sea as an observer but in any capacity they required as long as it enabled him to fully understand and describe Japanese ships, their crews, their armor and armament, the seamanship exhibited by their crews, their NCOs and their Officers, their methods of ship-to-ship and ship-to-shore communication and the technical proficiency of their crews in manning the guns, torpedoes and any other weapons. He was to comment on the potential market for American made munitions and ships. He was to become as fluent as possible in the Japanese language, learn to converse with the officers and men, and report all observations and findings to the Naval Attaché for transmission to Navy Headquarters via diplomatic pouch.

After 4 years and some months in Japan Lieutenant Pennington was ordered back to the Pacific fleet, sailed home and served officially at Navy Headquarters in Washington, where he was promoted to the rank of Lt. Commander. Although assigned to Washington, he seems to have spent most of his time in Boston, New York and Philadelphia. He never purchased a home in Washington, D.C., and his permanent address was at the house he owned in Vermont. What he did during this time is obscure. There's little record of his duties or his assignments and nothing in the official file except his name on a roster of officers in the planning unit.

The Japanese Imperial Navy (JIN) was expanding and for both military and commercial reasons the President, Theodore Roosevelt, wanted to know more about the Japanese fleet. "By jingo," he exclaimed at a cabinet meeting, "if the British and French can sell ships to the JIN, then so could we!"

Lt. Commander John Pennington, the future Admiral, was reassigned indefinitely to Japan in 1898 to serve as an observer on the staff of Admiral Togo. During this time there were intermittent trips and details to the United States. While in Japan in 1905 he was promoted to the rank of Commander. After the Russo-Japanese War he lingered in Japan until 1907, then was ordered to join President Roosevelt's "Great White Fleet" when it visited Japan on its world tour. He served in the Great White Fleet as commander of an escort ship. Later, he was promoted to Captain temporarily and commanded a Battleship when its commander suffered a stroke and died unexpectedly. He finally returned to the States at the end of the tour and was reassigned to Naval Headquarters, Washington, D.C., where he was promoted permanently to the rank of Captain, not the first man in his Annapolis class to achieve that rank, but somewhere in the middle. The graduates who served in an active role during the Spanish American war fared better, at least initially. Between 1908 and 1914 he seems to have made several lengthy visits to Japan, to the Philippines and to China, but principally to Japan.

The advent of the First World War saw renewed Congressional interest in building the Navy. When the war began and as the fleet expanded, Captain Pennington worked with the famous Captain Sims and other Naval strategists to develop the doctrine of convoy protection for American and allied merchant vessels. He commanded three or five, the number's uncertain, North Atlantic convoys himself with the rank of Commodore. He was promoted Rear Admiral and was eventually assigned to the White House and became Naval Advisor to President Wilson's staff. The war ended on November 11, 1918. In 1919 at the specific request of Douglas MacArthur, he lectured on Asia at West Point, concentrating on Japan, China and Korea. He retired from the Navy in 1920 but lingered on as an official advisor to the Navy staff and returned on official business to Asia, where he resided principally in Japan, not returning to the states until the death of his wife, Catherine, in 1925. He returned to Japan in 1926 and resided there until the advent of World War Two. In 1939 he was recalled to service. Douglas MacArthur, who knew him, may have had a hand in instigating his recall.

The Admiral married Catherine Magdalene Fitzhugh in late Fall, 1897. She was an Irish Catholic, but from a wealthy, influential and politically connected family who claimed a long aristocratic ancestry that could be traced all the way to a particular baronage in Normandy, or so they said. They also claimed connections to the "old English" families who resided in Ireland for centuries and who remained Roman Catholic after Henry VIII's break with the church. To marry Catherine, he had to convert, which he did. The conversion cost him little. He was simply shifting from Episcopalian to Catholic. His religious views – if he had any -- were not central to his life, and the change, for him, was minor.

Whatever pretensions of ancestry the Fitzhughs had, James Strongbow Fitzhugh -- Catherine's father -- was a Tammy Hall politician who made his fortune from construction contracts let for New York City projects. Ten minutes of research in an academic library and Penn found him mentioned in a half-dozen histories of the era often alongside Fitzsimmons Connor, whose *New York Erectors* joined with Fitzhugh's *Manhattan Construction* on city buildings and projects, especially subway contracting. Their way of getting contracts may have been questionable, but they performed well and usually brought them in under budget. City administrations later in the 20th Century may have been cleaner but they weren't more efficient. Fitzhugh retired shortly after his 54th birthday and moved to Vermont. Connor followed him two years later. Their daughters, Catherine and Elizabeth, were very close and had a life-long friendship. Researching Fitzhugh and Connors was easy. There were books and articles that mentioned them, and even a half-dozen doctoral theses done on them and their companies by students at NYU, CUNY, Harvard and, curiously, one at McGill. All of these were available on inter-collegiate sharing sources.

Catherine Fitzhugh, the Admiral's wife, was what some would call a handsome woman. She wasn't soft, pudgy and cute, the ideal of beauty at the time. She had a good figure, lean but not skinny, solid and strong. Her face was strong as well, a fair complexion, high cheek bones, a split chin, dark blue eyes and black hair. She was photogenic and photographed beautifully, but in life her personality dominated her features, and her intelligence and strength, rather than her beauty, prevailed. She dressed well, but was never ostentatious, and she had her own money, a substantial trust fund untouchable by anyone except Catherine and her lawyer. Somehow the legal armor surrounding the fund even prevented her husband from dipping into it, not that the Admiral, who had his own money as well as his official salary ever tried or even wanted to.

Catherine remained at home during most of the Admiral's time abroad. It was her choice. She didn't like to travel, especially to Asia. She could have gone with the Admiral and stayed with him, but she preferred her home and knew well that his work was so demanding she would be alone most of the time anyway. Better to be at home in Vermont than to be in some noisome foreign port where she knew no one. She only made one voyage overseas to visit him, hated the place, and returned to the States on the next ship home. It was shortly after that trip her adopted son came into her life and the boy, to whom she devoted herself, firmly rooted her in Vermont.

Tall and hearty, she was a strong, active, independent woman. She played tennis and golf, swam in the Summer, hiked in the Spring and Fall, and skied or skated in the Winter. She was involved in various civic affairs and charities and was an active and vocal supporter of Women's Suffrage, though she drew the line at chaining herself to fences or going on hunger strikes.

Catherine loved her home in Vermont, her friends and the Admiral's somewhat eccentric family, who loved her as well. She had no children of her own, but was devoted to the sweet, intelligent boy she and the Admiral adopted, Asher. The boy's full legal name was Asher Pennington Fuller. The boy was one year and some months old when they adopted him. He bore the last name of a notable New England family who could trace their origins to the *Mayflower*, but like most adopted children his origins were cloudy. If asked, Catherine would just shake her head, or, if pressed, say she was honor-bound never to reveal his ancestry. "Pennington" was added by the Admiral to link the boy to his adopted father's family.

Catherine became deathly ill in her fifty-second year, September, 1925. The Admiral returned as quickly as he could to be with her, but the voyage across the Pacific took almost two months and the cross-country train was slow. By the time he arrived, she was on her death bed.

Her heart valves had ceased to function properly. The doctor explained that the probable cause was a bicuspid aortic valve, a congenital defect that can remain undetected for a very long time until the valve stops closing properly and the patient dies from lack of oxygenated arterial blood. Some patients live into their sixties before they have any symptoms at all. He assured the family there would be no pain, just shortness of breath, exhaustion, coma and heart failure. There was nothing the medical science of the time could do for her.

When the Admiral came into her room, she was still conscious, but gasping for breath. She smiled at him, and he kissed her. She lingered on, propped up with pillows because breathing was easier in a sitting position and with an oxygen tube held under her nose. Later, they installed a canvas oxygen tent with a glass window. Ten days after his arrival she died. She quietly started the final, terminal fall during the night. He found her comatose, gasping, her lips and fingers turning blue. He held her hand until she sighed, her breathing stopped altogether and she died. Betty Connor, Catherine's life-long special friend was staying at the house during Catherine's last days. She sat with the Admiral at Catherine's death bed, wept bitterly and was inconsolable for weeks afterward. She wrote four letters to the Admiral thanking him for his kindness and expressing her grief. His responses were short, gracious notes, offering his hope that time would assuage her sorrow. Many of these details were written in a long letter to Catherine's mother, who had moved to England years before. The draft was kept and retained with the Admiral's papers.

After Catherine's death, Betty asked to stay in the house and to help manage the property. The Admiral heartily agreed, contacted his lawyer and had a special trust fund created for the care of the boy and the remuneration of Betty.

The image of the Admiral was building. The blocks and pieces simply had to be assembled.

There was one other thing. Penn was intrigued by the forty or so letters in Japanese he found when excavating the trunk in the attic. Those letters were definitely part of the Admiral's papers, but for some reason were never put with all the other papers in the trunk above Harriett's garage. He now took them out and ordered that they, too, be scanned and labeled. He looked again at the address to which all of them were sent: *John Pennington, % Marbright, and Fuller, 221 First Street, Boston, Mass., USA.*

There were several things that puzzled him about these letters. First, there was the obvious question, what were they? From whom did they come? Why were they sent to the Admiral at all? The way they began, *My Dearest John*, unless Japanese correspondence was much different than English, this was a term of familiarity or endearment or even love. Further, they came not to his home, but to these lawyers in Boston, and look at the name of the firm, *Marbright and Fuller*. Was "Fuller" merely a coincidence? It could be. There were dozens of Fullers in New England, but then there could be some connection with Penn's own name. Penn's interest in these letters was personal rather than scholarly, but nevertheless if researching this could help flesh out some of the facts of the Admirals life, it would contribute to the history of the time.

Penn wanted those letters translated as well, but the nature of the letters was, well, sensitive, or at least it seemed that way, and he didn't want to ask anyone at the Academy to do it. Penn would keep family secrets secret. He would put nothing into print that wasn't significant in terms of its effect on the Admiral's career or the history of the Navy. The Admiral, even long gone, should not have his privacy ruptured or the dignity of his memory sullied, and family skeletons would stay in the closet.

Penn immersed himself in his work. Thanksgiving came and went. He spent the holiday at the Academy, still cataloging, compiling, researching, getting papers scanned, adding metadata, uploading to the Cloud, saving backups, making DVD files. He did little else. So much of the material he found related to events to which he was only vaguely familiar, the critical role of the Japanese Navy in the Sino-Japanese War fought over Korea, the Japanese Naval victories of the Russo-Japanese War, the expansion of the Japanese fleet during and after World War One and the consequent extension of Japanese power.

He had an enormous pile of esoteric historical literature to read and digest before he could put the Admiral's notes, letters and comments in context. He took joy in all this work, the pleasure and satisfaction a skilled artisan takes in puzzling his or her way through a difficult task, the joy of finishing a piece to a high sheen, a piece with invisible seams and quiet, efficient function. Scholars are like artisans, he thought. Much of the work is done with the hands, beautifully crafted sentences in a structured and researched paper or book are done with the same passion and quality that goes into a good vase, a well-joined cabinet, even a rebuilt car with a motor that roars, painted with a high sheen and body art. There's satisfaction in that. He bent to his work.

****

Chapter Fourteen – Everyone is Strange

One week before Christmas, Vancouver, Canada, the Queen Elizabeth Theater – Yoshiko stood in the wings watching and listening to Hye Young Rhee as Cio-Cio San in her exchange with Goro, the bride broker. She was so good, so charmingly naïve in adhering to her doomed love for Pinkerton, a young girl pretending confidence and sophistication while that cagey old swindler, Goro, saw right through her act and countered all her silly notions with the rude logic that dominated his life of scrabble, scrape and grab. Yoshiko had never heard *Butterfly* in depth, had never fully understood the role of Cio-Cio San, the profound love and the utter misery of Pinkerton's final treachery. She never understood it as deeply as she did now that she performed it, never realized its complexity, the nuances of the role, the depth of the characters. Hye Young taught her something new in every performance, a pause, a held note, a breath taken earlier or later, a subtle gesture that resonated with meaning and pathos, a change in facial expression or in posture. All of these things were tucked neatly into Yoshiko's mental file for practice and incorporation of her own interpretation of the role. Hye Young watched Yoshiko as well and, true colleagues and friends, they shared what they saw and what they knew with each other.

Manny Goldstein seemed to lose his mean streak after Yoshiko and he sang their first *Butterfly* together in Santa Fe, although he still was difficult, moody and combative when pushed. His voice was fine, though. He was maturing as a singer as they all were, and both his technique and his acting seemed to get better with each performance.

"You could make a career out of Pinkerton, you know," said Lee Gross. The last person Manny wanted career advice from was Lee Gross.

Manny sneered at him, "Didn't work so well with Frank

Hauptmann." Hauptmann sang nothing but Pinkerton for almost a decade than disappeared from the stage and eventually made his living as a bookkeeper.

"He got too fat to play Pinkerton. Christ, they put him on stage one night with Marie Spanelli. Remember her?" Lee didn't wait for an answer. "She was as big as a house. The two of them together looked like the Tons of Fun twins. Good voices, but God, how they filled the stage. He couldn't get his arms around her and she was the same with him. The only way to improve the performance was to put them both behind a brick wall. They sang well enough, though. I've a CD of them doing *La Rondine* if you ever want to borrow it."

"No. If I hear them sing that opera, I'll think about them every time I hear it," said Manny walking away.

"They had an affair together, you know," said Lee, grinning wickedly.

Manny didn't even bother to turn around. He already had the longest conversation he ever held with Lee. It wasn't productive.

Tomorrow would be the last *Butterfly* of the season. Yoshiko would sing and Hye Young would watch from the wings. There would be a cast party afterward. From Santa Fe onward the reviews were so good the company had already been requested to expand its tour next year to include Dallas, Denver and Minneapolis-St. Paul. "That's the way it is," said Lee, "Get a good review and suddenly you're golden everywhere." After Santa Fe, the reviewers were ecstatic and were lavish with their praise of Hye Young and Yoshiko, Manny Goldstein, the whole crew. There were rumors that contracts were being offered with the Met or New York City Opera or even Vancouver. They were only rumors, however, nothing materialized.

Even with all her success, Yoshiko felt unaccountably sad at the end of the season. Despite Manny's teasing early on, the tour turned out to be wonderful for her, for her voice, her technique, her career.

She was immensely happy with herself and with the company and wanted to the season to go on. It was over, though, and she couldn't escape the feeling that she was as close as she would ever get to stardom.

That night she lay in her bed wondering what the future would bring. She wanted to grow with her art. She especially wanted to perform in Europe, in Italy or France, England or Germany, somewhere that opera was loved and the audiences were sophisticated and difficult. That would be the real test, to take her voice and her skill to the places opera was born. She even thought about auditioning for the *Singer of the World Competition* in Cardiff, Wales. The competitors were good, but she thought, with reason, she might be better. There was Glindenberg, too, and the Scottish Opera, and contests in Ireland, Italy and elsewhere.

The minutes, then the hours dragged on. It was quiet in her room, and in the hallway outside. Her throat was dry. *Perhaps,* she thought, *I'll get some water*. Bottled water was offered by the vending machines down the hall. She slipped out of bed and started to open her door very softly and slowly – didn't want to disturb anyone – when, just as the door cracked open perhaps a half inch she saw someone standing there leaning into an open door on the opposite side of the hall. It was Manny Goldstein and he was standing at Hye Young's door. She saw him lean over, appear to kiss Hye Young and furtively step away from the room on tip-toe. He never looked back and didn't see the sliver of light coming from Yoshiko's door. She pulled her door closed and, at first shocked, began to giggle. Manny and Hye Young? He was supposed to be gay and she the virgin with the hymen of steel! It was too funny. She sat on her bed and laughed.

There was a knock at her door, three soft taps. Yoshiko sat perfectly still, not wanting to answer. A few seconds passed. Then she heard Hye Young's voice in a stage whisper, "Yoshiko, open up. I have to talk to you!"

Yoshiko didn't move. She held her breath, feeling awkward. Would they think her a voyeur, a nosy, prying person? She didn't want to confront Hye Young.

"Yoshiko, please!" Hye Young sounded desperate.

Yoshiko got up, reluctantly walked to the door and opened it. Hye Young slipped in and sat on the bed, looking tired and sheepish.

"I know you saw us, Yoshiko," said Hye Young.

"Saw what?" said Yoshiko trying to sound innocent and surprised.

"I could see the crack of light from the edge of your door. Manny didn't see it, but I did. I know you saw us."

"Hye Young, what you do is your business…" Yoshiko began.

Hye Young interrupted her, "Oh, shut up and let me explain. It was nothing, nothing. There is nothing between Manny and me."

Yoshiko grinned a shy little grin and looked down. A grin like that was worse than calling Hye Young a liar.

"You don't believe me, and that hurts me, Yoshiko. I don't know why, but I just want no one in this company to think I ever did anything with Manny Goldstein, ever."

"Then what *were* you doing?" said Yoshiko, "I saw him kiss you. I know it's none of my business, but if you don't want me to think…"

"He kissed me on the cheek, Yoshiko, like your father might kiss you" she pointed to her right cheek for emphasis, "He was thanking me tenderly and nicely. He comes over sometimes and asks me to hold him. That's all, just hold him and sometimes he holds me. I do it for him. He's like a little child. He gets scared, has bad dreams, and wants comfort. He came to me one night months ago, back when we were in Boston, and begged me to help him in this way. At first I was very angry. I wanted to throw him out of my room, to call the police but he looked so pathetic, so *small*, so needy, like a lost dog…I… I could not refuse. There is no sex of any kind. He prefers sex with men and only has sex with men, and I don't prefer sex at all, not now at least, maybe someday … but that's different. I want no sex with him, have no sex with him and will have no sex with him." There was a finality to this. She wasn't lying.

"But it sounds so strange," said Yoshiko.

"Everyone is strange. Normalcy is a conceit of the bigoted. All lovers have their quirks, fantasies and obsessions. Quirks are normal. Experimentation and variation in tastes is the only normalcy. All people have their eccentricities. Even the missionaries who preached the Missionary Position were themselves obsessed with something, doing sex in a certain way, or not doing it all. Manny is eccentric in many ways. He's like a child at times, and…" she paused, "I admit, I feel good when I comfort him, which I why I do it. If I ever left the company, I'm certain he would come to you and ask the same thing, and I'm certain, knowing you have a good heart, that you would do it."

Yoshiko shuttered at the thought. She still avoided Manny as much as possible off stage. "You told me once that he doesn't like women," said Yoshiko.

"He doesn't, except late at night when he wants to be with someone who'll hold him, sing a lullaby and treat him like a little boy."

"Oh…" said Yoshiko thinking *Hye Young is telling the truth.* Yoshiko was sure of that. Hye Young was so earnest, so candid, so unreserved.

"You won't tell anyone, will you?" said Hye Young.

"Never!" said Yoshiko, "I'll put it out of my mind and never think of it again."

Hye Young stood and embraced her. They hugged for a minute, and Hye Young, tears running down her face, said "When I marry someday I want to go to my husband a virgin. I want him to know I am a virgin. I want the man I will love forever to be the only one to ever have me. I want to give him that gift that can only be given once. Do you understand? I don't want anyone at any time to think that I did not give that gift to the man I love."

Yoshiko nodded. Hye Young's purpose in all this business with Manny now sounded noble, and kind and good. Yoshiko also shed a few tears. Hey Young kissed her on the cheek and left.

Afterward, Yoshiko hoped very much that no one saw Hye Young enter or leave her room in the middle of the night. She didn't want rumors and gossip to fly through the company about the two of them. Hye Young, back in her room, hoped the same thing. Relationships, even ones that were innocent or that haven't really happened but just appear to have happened can be so complicated.

Neither one of the women had anything to fear. The only witness to their late evening chat was a small spider whose web would be destroyed the next day by the maid and who would be forced to flee and hide. He'd be too fraught with his own problems to worry about either Yoshiko or Hye Young and of course he could never tell anyone. They were safe.

Two days later as she and Hye Young waited in Vancouver airport for their flight back to the East Coast, Yoshiko's cell phone rang, She go so few calls it startled her and it took her several attempts before she answered it properly. It was her mother. Her grandmother, whom she loved immensely, was very ill and had little time left. Always a vigorous woman, she was now 77, but had been in decline for the past two years.

Keiko, her grandmother, lost both her parents during the war, and her early years had been very hard. Had it not been for the kindness of the woman who took her in and protected her, a woman who had lost her own child years before, she would have died. She learned patience and kindness from that woman whose name was Ayumi, also called "Chou," and took that woman's name for her own, in her old age calling herself Keiko-Ayumi. Her greatest wish was to be buried next to her adopted mother and in fulfillment of that wish years before she purchased the plot and the stone monument. It awaited her now, near their home in Yokohama. The family feared there was little time was left. Yoshiko exchanged her ticket for a round trip to Tokyo. She figured on being in Japan for at least 3 months. She could return in time to rehearse for the next season, which would begin in mid-April. They were doing *La Boheme*, and she was cast both as Musetta and Mimi, alternating with Hye Young. She already knew the roles well and she would practice at home.

****

Chapter Fifteen – Dr. McGraw

"Brrrriiing, brrriiing!" Penn's desk phone startled him. The bell was set at maximum volume and there was nothing he could to reduce it, although he tried. He meant to replace it. He could pick up a phone for next to nothing in the hardware store, but every time he thought about doing that, he would get distracted, time would pass, the store would be closed and he'd forget until the next time the phone rang. Annoyed with his own negligence, he jerked the headset from the cradle, composed himself and answered.

"Congratulations, Commander! Why didn't ya' call me and tell me you were promoted." It was Henrietta.

"I figured you'd know about it before I did, Auntie," said Penn, smiling to himself. He couldn't help liking the brash old woman.

"Damn right I did. I knew about it before you came to see me in November. There was only one other sailor who got the Navy Cross in Iraq, you know, a Corpsman serving with a Marine platoon. No other Navy officer got your mix of bacon on their chest."

"I didn't know you knew about the Cross," said Penn almost to himself.

"You wore the ribbon when you saw me. I can read a sailor's chest, you know. Anyway, it got you the promotion at the head of your class. It'll get you Captain if you don't pee in the Admiral's beer. Might even do it even if you do pee in his beer."

"I might need a sea command, too."

"Hell with that. You have more deep water time right now than ninety percent of the namby-pamby officers in the Navy. There are people making Admiral who couldn't command a putt-putt in the park. You need to have a *wife* who can make your career. Obama will nominate Will Hobson for CNO in January, as early as January 10. The House and Senate will confirm him in fifteen minutes flat. For some reason all those grafting bastards in Congress like Hobson. Both parties. He must be one hell of slick Admiral. Ride his coattails while you can."

"We'll see what happens Auntie."

"You know what I don't like about Congress?" she didn't wait for an answer, "It's made up of Republicans and Democrats. Oh, I know we've got an independent from Vermont who claims to be a Socialist, but he's really nothing but a powder puff who can swing his vote any way he wants. Forget him. Democrats are schemers always pandering for votes willing to do anything to build their constituency. If they thought one-eyed green-skinned Martians would get them a half-dozen votes they'd try to find some way to give them money or privileges or both. Republicans are just loathsome grafters pandering to the worst in everyone and in thrall to a cohort of rich bastards who made their money swindling people."

"I'm not very much into politics," said Penn, which was true. He avoided contemporary politics as much as he could. Historical politics were part of his trade, however, as an historian.

"Best way to be. And don't retire twenty years from now and run for anything. You'll wind up like McCain, people callin' you Mr. McGoo and trying to get you to screw their pet pooch."

"I'll take your advice, Auntie, trust me on that."

"Why should I trust you? You haven't done anything yet with Kate Hobson."

"I've been cataloging records, you know, all the files you turned over to me."

"You should be done by now."

"Well, Auntie, you're right, and I am pretty much done with the cataloging. But this stuff has to be put into historical context. The Admiral was involved in a lot of activity. There's correspondence in here from Presidents Roosevelt and Wilson, from the Navy staff during World Wars One and Two, professional journals he kept, reports he wrote, observations and notes, and letters to and from family and friends. I could spend years on these documents and on trying to find related work."

"Years? Carpe diem, Penn, if you know what that means. I haven't got years. Get it on with Kate." She said this kindly, almost as a plea. It was out of character for her, but she sounded honest and truly concerned.

"If Kate and I can..." he hesitated trying to find the right words. He didn't want to hurt his aunt.

"Can what? Of course you can. If everyone else in the world can, you can."

"If Kate and I get to know each other and if we love each other, really love each other, then I'll propose to her, but I've only seen her twice and we haven't talked since then."

"And whose fault was that?"

Penn wanted the conversation to end. "I'll follow my heart on this one, Auntie."

"Follow your brain as well. That's what the Admiral would have done and that's what he did."

Penn wondered what she meant by this.

"Talk to me again when you're engaged." Harriett hung up. No "goodbye."

Dr. Philip Rhys McGraw, an exchange professor at the U.S. Naval Academy on loan from the Royal Military Academy, Sandhurst, politely waited outside Penn's office while Penn completed his telephone conversation. McGraw was an expert in forensic investigation. He had an undergraduate degree in chemistry from Cambridge and much later competed his doctorate in history at Oxford. In between, he served an officer in the British Army, fought in the Falklands War, led a Regiment back home, served with peacekeeping forces in Bosnia and was wounded in Afghanistan in 2003 while assigned as an observer with the American forces there.

McGraw retired from the active Army, finished his doctoral work and returned to Sandhurst to teach military history, strategy and tactics. His subsequent work in unearthing old files and reviewing documents and his knowledge of chemistry and physics led to a part time career as a forensic historian. He published a book on the investigation of files and file containers and was called to testify in court in modern cases involving embezzlement and fraud, usually as a government witness.

Penn asked McGraw to examine the records he'd gotten at his Grand Aunt's. He wanted McGraw's opinion of the condition of the trunk and the completeness of the files. Penn's careful review and cataloging of the contents convinced him – or at least made him strongly suspect --that documents had been selectively removed from the trunk. He couldn't prove it, of course, but he wanted another opinion, just to make sure his suspicions had some foundation. McGraw cheerfully agreed when Penn offered him to buy him a whiskey or two at the Officer's club after work in exchange for his opinion and advice.

He heard Penn hang up the phone and poked his head into the office. "Ready?"

"Sorry to keep you waiting, Phil. My Grand Aunt Harriett called. She tries to manage my career from Vermont." Said Penn.

McGraw laughed. "I had one of those, too. Was always trying to get me to marry someone. Never did, though, and I'm still a bachelor. Every military family has one or two of them."

"One is sometimes too many," said Penn, turning his computer monitor so that both he and McGraw could see it clearly, and starting a presentation that contained images he took of the trunk and its contents before removing them, "This is why I called you."

"Yes," McGraw said, staring closely at the images of the trunk, "This was opened, probably within the last year. The contents were disturbed as well."

"How can you tell about the contents?" said Penn.

"The pattern of wear and fading, the mismatch with the discolorations of the wood. It's subtle, but it's a strong indicator. Have you found gaps in the documentation?"

"Well, I didn't expect a complete day-by-day record of his activities. What I have are official documents that for the most part look secure and complete but personal records that seem to have been pulled apart and censored by removing whole blocks of them," said Penn.

"That can happen," said McGraw, "Queen Victoria kept extensive diaries. Apparently the ones of her early years of marriage with Albert were quite racy. Her daughters burned the first sixteen volumes of the diaries to hide the contents from the prying eyes of posterity. Historians of the period gnash their teeth and rend their garments when they think about the vandalism of those ignorant women. Families do that sort of thing all the time. I've seen it, and have, perhaps, been guilty of it myself."

"Really?" said Penn.

"It was a minor sin, and I was not yet an historian, so please don't report me to the Central Committee." He grinned.

"You have my word as an officer and a gentleman," said Penn.

"Nothing better than that, old man? Well, I suppose it will have to do...." He paused for just a moment, collecting his thoughts, "One of our Battalion Commanders, a very married man with a devoted wife, two grown sons and an adolescent daughter, died of a heart attack and I was given the sad task of supervising the removal of personal items from his office. Inside his desk we found several letters and other items from a woman curiously named 'Mrs. Loyal' --- I trust I can say her name in confidence here."

Penn nodded, his face a mask of mock solemnity.

"The Lieutenant Colonel, for that was his rank, conducted a torrid love affair with Mrs. Loyal for over a decade. The letters we found were not sweet and sentimental love notes. They were graphic to the point of being pornographic. There were Polaroid photos and, uh… certain under garments, as well. The clerk assisting me – actually doing all the work – was very fond and protective of his former Commander. He searched through everything in the office, even flipping the pages of the books and magazines, collected every remnant of the affair, every note and card, letter, picture and all the other flotsam and jetsam, placed them in a separate box and turned it over to me. I kept the Colonel's secret and had everything in that box incinerated rather than returned to the family."

"Understandable," said Penn, "Even commendable. I would have done the same thing myself."

"Yes, well I figured the damage to Regimental history was negligible compared to the damage the revelation of that affair would have done to the man's family."

"Did you know Mrs. Loyal, too?" asked Penn.

"Oh, yes, and not merely by reputation, but that's another story," McGraw looked wistful and sighed softly, "I did learn one valuable lesson, from all this," said McGraw, "Never keep your mistress's panties in your desk drawer."

"Confucian wisdom," said Penn.

"Many a famous man would be better for it," said McGraw, "Should be taught in the schools. Now, let's get to the task at hand…. I want to go through the documents on file myself. I'll need a few hours, because, of course I won't read everything, but I should be able to detect trends and probable omissions."

"Do you need anything?"

"I've brandy – I mean coffee – in my thermos and some biscuits in my case. I've a notebook and pen, too. Just leave me to it and we'll see I find."

"OK," said Penn, "The staff knows you're helping me, so if you do need something just ask Alice Blakely. She's at the desk in the reception area."

"The big woman with the..." McGraw didn't finish the thought.

"Yes, that's the one. She's really very good at what she does."

Penn left the man to his work and repaired to the library stacks to do some research on the Sino-Japanese Naval war.

Penn was deep into his notes when, almost four hours later, he felt a tap on his shoulder. It was Phil McGraw.

"When you concentrate, you do really concentrate don't you?" said McGraw.

Penn looked up, "I was trying to follow the fleet movements of the Naval actions during the Sino-Japanese war – 1890s. The detailed reports seem to be confused and to contradict one another."

"I think it's time for that whiskey," said McGraw.

They sat on bar stools in the "O" Club. McGraw nursed a large Bushmills, while Penn, who was still under low doses of anti-inflammatory medication and a steroid demurred and settled with Club soda and a twist.

"Ok, Penn," said McGraw, "Here's what I see. I find letters from a man who writes regularly to his wife three times per month, almost on the same schedule, the 1st of the month, 10th of the month, and the 20th of the month. She responds to most of them but not all. She's less regular, too, sometimes sends three letters, sometimes one or two, but all the letters I see from her are obviously in response to letters he wrote, so I think none of them are missing until – a block of five to six months and there are no letters. Then the letters begin again. A year is missing then four months of faithful correspondence then another year is gone. It looks as if someone pulled whole blocks of correspondence out of the file at various times."

"I thought the same, but I didn't go through the personal letters that thoroughly. I wanted another opinion," said Penn.

"Did you read any of them?" said McGraw.

"One or two. I felt almost as if I were eavesdropping."

"What did one of your presidents say about reading other people's mail?"

"It was Wilson, or at least it was attributed to Wilson, 'Gentlemen do not read each others mail.' Didn't stop him from reading the Zimmerman Telegram, though."

"Ah, that was one of our efforts, breaking the German code and getting the message to you Yanks."

"Good thing you did. If you hadn't, you'd be speaking German now," said Penn.

"Humph! Might not be such a bad thing, given their economy and their national health system.," said McGraw, "Anyway, I read the letters."

"All of them?"

"Enough to see something interesting. When a man goes overseas and writes home, the first letters are usually chatty, telling as much as he can about how things are, what the service is like, the place that's going to or has arrived-at. Then, as time goes on, the tone changes and they become more sentimental and shorter, telling how much he misses home and how much he loves everyone, and by the time he's ready to return most of the letters are less than 100 words, more like 50, and repeat a lot of the same things he's said 100 times before."

"And," said Penn.

"The early letters to his family from the Admiral's first journey to Japan in the mid-1890s follow that pattern to a "T," with a handful of exceptions when he had something particularly interesting to write. But later, after his marriage and during his second Japan station, your Great Grandfather wrote to his wife in a tone that I can only describe as 'friendly,' as if he were writing less to the love of his life than to a woman-friend. The tone never changes, either, and the content is remarkable. His observations of shipboard life, of living in Japan, of the officers and crews he worked with, of the streets of Hiroshima, and of the characters he met, both Western and Japanese, are wry, colorful and interesting, but there is something missing. There was nothing, or very little, in terms of sentiment or the normal endearments I would expect from a husband to a wife, not even an 'I love you and miss you' or some similar sentiment."

"Perhaps that was just his way," said Penn.

"Perhaps, but there was something else as well. The letters reveal that his wife, Catherine, bought a ticket and followed him to Japan on a commercial steamer, not an easy trip in the early 20th Century, nor an inexpensive one. The Panama Canal didn't become operational until 1914, so she had to cross the continental United States via rail first to catch the ship. That in itself was an exhausting journey. A voyage to Japan from that point could take 50 to 60 days, and this was in the era before stabilizers, weather forecasting that was worth a damn and GPS. Well, here's the interesting part, she arrived in Japan, apparently in the port of Hiroshima, stayed a fortnight, and went right back home on the ship that carried her to Japan two weeks earlier. All correspondence after that point is missing for a period of more than a year. It picks up again for a month or two, then nothing."

"I understand she didn't like to travel," said Penn.

"Yes, but if that's the case, then why spend almost three months getting there in the first place? I'm an historian and I base my judgments on facts supported by documents and objects. Fact: she went there and she returned. The ship, the departure and arrival dates, even the ticket number is mentioned in the letters she wrote to him. Fact: She left Japan after a stay of two weeks. Again, we know that from the letter she wrote aboard the ship when it docked in Yokohama for a day before venturing into the Pacific."

McGraw finished his whiskey then took a drink from his thermos. It may have been Penn's imagination but he thought he detected the aroma of coffee with a fortifier, probably brandy. "Ah!

Nothing like the stimulation of caffeine," said McGraw, smacking his lips, furrowing his brow and collecting his thoughts, "Let's see. How do I put this?... As a detective of sorts, in my forensic work, I use an underpinning of science but I don't completely harness my imagination. I try to create a plausible scenario for events for which there is no complete picture. Here's what I think, and this is completely speculative. I think the Admiral's wife, Catherine, went there with some specific purpose in mind, did what she had to do and then left. Seeing that the Admiral survived the visit, she didn't go there to strangle him, and I'm sure she wasn't after the grocery money or wanted a kimono. She had a damn serious purpose, did it and left. Whatever that purpose was, she had to do it herself. She had to go there and she had to come back. I would bet that the blocks of missing letters and missing documents are all related to that purpose…" He paused and drew breath through the gap in his incisors, "God, she could have been an Englishwoman."

"Her family, the Fitzhughs, were Irish Catholics, but well-heeled ones. They claimed to come from 'Old English' stock," said Penn. He knew McGraw was right about Catherine's trip to Japan, but he thought for now he'd keep his own speculations to himself. He didn't want to feed McGraw's imagination, and this could turn into some sensitive matter the family wanted to keep in the closet.

"From the name, they were of Norman stock. Enough of them settled in Ireland," said McGraw.

"They claimed that as well, at least according to my family's oral history. Her widowed mother took the family fortune, whatever *that* consisted of – it must have been substantial -- and moved to England after Catherine's death in 1925. We've lost track of them since." Said Penn.

"There, I knew it. An English woman. Damn stubborn, intelligent and willful… Why I never married. I like Japanese women. They're, I don't know, nicer, I suppose. Maybe I'll marry one."

“Do you know any?” said Penn.

“Only in my imagination,” said McGraw, finishing his whiskey, “You don’t know any do you?”

Penn smiled. The image of Yoshiko Fujiyama flashed in his mind. She looked so delightful as she sang Suzuki; he couldn’t forget her. He shook his head, “No, I don’t. But if I do meet someone…”

“Give me a ring, old boy, if you do.” McGraw pushed the guest check over to Penn, “Your tab. I’m going home to search the internet.”

“For what?” said Penn, thinking he might be able to repay McGraw’s favor in kind.

“Brides, old man,” said McGraw, “Sayonara!”

****

Chapter Sixteen – Kate, a cat and Marianna

Kate Hobson looked out the window of her office onto a parking lot. It rained that day on and off, the sun braking through for a few minutes promising to make the day more cheerful, only to be obscured by clouds as the gray skies returned and the showers began to fall again. There was a feral cat, a beautiful white and beige short hair that she'd seen day-after-day crossing the parking lot, taking refuge under cars from the rain, then going about its business. She'd seen it not only from the window but up close as well. One evening as she as prepared to leave for home the cat appeared from under her car, saw her, and bolted into the adjoining woods, its tail straight up in the air, its back bristling. The cat looked healthy and well-fed, probably feeding on rodents, insects and birds, and, strangely, it didn't look unhappy, not with the harried, dirty look that feral cats all seem to have. She'd surreptitiously and very quietly watched it preening and lying comfortably in the sun, rolling on its back in seeming contentment. She'd left food for the cat, and seen the food disappear, but not always. *Perhaps*, she thought, *I'm not the only who sees her, who cares a little for her. Others may be feeding her as well.* She looked from her window for the cat now – it was easy to see, a white fur ball against the black asphalt of the parking lot -- but wherever the cat was, she couldn't find it. She figured the cat had its own places of shelter, secret places it could go to be dry, to feel warm and secure.

Kate was assigned temporarily to the CDC's National Center for Chronic Disease Prevention and Health Promotion, which sports the awkward acronym NCCDPHP. The CDC insiders just call it "Chronic," and the old hands like her mentor, Marianna Littlebear, sometimes call it "Chip-dip." Chronic's offices were not at the CDC's main campus near Emory, where Kate worked until just 3 weeks ago. They were located in a business park near "Spaghetti Junction," the complicated intersection of the Atlanta bypass, Route

285, and the north-south interstate, Route 85. The business park abuts a wetland preserve on two sides and Mercer University's wooded campus on another. It was certainly a pretty place to work, convenient, with more than adequate parking, and a lovely place to walk during winter days or in the cool of the morning during the Georgia Summer.

Marianna Littlebear, grabbing the doorframe with one hand, leaned her head and half her small body into Kate's office. "Wake up! We've got that meeting at 10 AM. Have you finished with the presentation slides?"

Kate, a little embarrassed at being caught daydreaming, turned to her computer, "Five minutes, Marianna (no one ever called Ms. Littlebear "Mari" or "Mar")," and started rapid-fire touch-tying on the computer keys. The presentation, whose pieces and facts came mostly from Marianna and one or two others, was well-done. Kate put all the data and prose together into a slide deck with handsome illustrations, even a small bit of animation. Marianna practiced making the presentation with the draft Kate prepared two days before, and this final work just involved some tweaking to change one or two statistics and move a few slides into a different order.

Marianna was a pert, attractive woman, small and slim, about 50. She was an American citizen, of course, but originally of Philippine origin, ethnically part Japanese and part Filipino, but mostly Japanese, a fact hidden by her family until they moved to the United States. Educated at Ohio State and Emory as an epidemiologist, she was intelligent, persuasive, zealous, and knowledgeable. She managed to be pushy without seeming pushy, had the personality and capacity to turn adversaries into advocates, and was eternally optimistic and active. Nothing set her back and no obstacle was too great.

In addition to her academic credentials, Marianna's experience included years of work as a state epidemiologist out West, involved with everything from HIV and Venereal disease investigation, to

Hanta Virus and public health issues among the Indian Tribes. She met her estranged husband, Martin Littlebear, while working with the tribes, but the marriage didn't last. He abandoned her and his small daughter, Julie, for work in Alaska, where he divorced Marianna and surrendered to the charms of another nearer at hand, an Alaska native who gave him three children before he finally married her.

Marianna kept her married name because of her daughter and never mentioned nor hyphenated her maiden name, "Mercado." The family name was actually Miyamoto, but her grandparents changed it to Mercado to sound Filipino for business reasons and to avoid the prejudice against Japanese residents that endured in the Philippines after World War II. Marianna intended to change her name back to Miyamoto some day and to use only her maiden name. Her daughter was cool to the idea, though. She was brought up as Littlebear and liked the name. Besides, changing names is no simple process and would generate years of confusion among her associates, with credit cards, deeds, and all the legal entanglements one has in life. The thought of it discouraged her and she never acted on the intention.

Marianna's experience on the state level gave her the credibility of one who had been on the front line of Public Health work, so when she spoke people listened. This didn't mean she always got them to act. Bureaucracies are hard to move even by those at the very top of the heap, so Marianna, whose ideas and enthusiasms were tolerated, even enjoyed and honored, had little success in changing anything. This didn't stop her from trying, however. After a particularly frustrating day, one of her colleagues left a copy of the "Serenity Prayer" in her office. She read it, scowled with contempt and pushed in into the shredder. She'd be damned if she'd be serene when millions of people died needlessly every year from conditions and diseases that could easily and cheaply be prevented by adequate Public Health measures and by education if only the blockheads, toadies, and crooks in the bureaucracies of the worlds' governments would take some action.

Marianna met Kate back in October when they both attended a conference on the Hepatitis C epidemic, its causes, consequences and preventive measures. Marianna made a presentation advocating a massive public information campaign funded through the Affordable Care Act. There were huge amounts of money being spent on tobacco cessation, but she was convinced, and the data showed, that further spending in that area would only lead to ever diminishing returns. After a certain point, it was like throwing money down a well. Funding for the prevention of Hepatitis C, which was still on the epidemiological growth curve, was needed now and would be very effective. Divert some money from tobacco, or, if that's not possible, tag Hepatitis prevention information onto "no smoking" messages. She was applauded. No action was ever taken.

Kate came up to Marianna after the meeting, introduced herself and told her how impressed she was by Marianna's talk and by her paper, which she'd also read. They went to lunch together, and a friendship arose. When an opening for a "management development fellow" occurred in Marianna's Branch, she solicited Kate's application. In two weeks, Kate was reassigned and given the office she now inhabited. Officially, this "detail" was only to last six months, but people sometimes went on details like this and the assignments became permanent.

Today's presentation had to do with the inefficient organizations that plague state health departments and what the CDC could do to encourage reorganization along families of related public health issues. It was a beautifully illustrated presentation, well supported with statistics and facts, and probably doomed to the same oblivion as Marianna's other work. Kate liked Marianna's passion, her joy in trying to achieve something, the pleasure she took in whatever modest success she had, her generosity with her knowledge and her professionalism and optimism. She liked

Marianna, too, liked her as a friend as well as mentor, liked to be with her and to talk with her, even when they weren't talking about the endless segments and byways and complexities of public health work. Marianna liked Kate as well, found her to an intelligent, capable, and congenial assistant who absorbed everything she had to say and who agreed with her yet was not just some toady or "yes-person" who tried to please her simply because she was senior.

The slide deck complete and loaded into the server, Marianna paused at Kate's office and beckoned her to come along.

"Am I invited to this meeting?" said Kate, "I thought this was just for the bigwigs, the Director, Dr. Feldman, and his staff will be there."

"Bigwig, little wig, what does it matter?" said Marianna, "I don't care if Obama, Putin and the Pope are there together. You come with me and no one will say a word. Just look important. Sit next to me at the table, too. There should be plenty of room. They've set up the conference room u-shaped with enough seats for fifty people. I doubt 30 will be there. We'll get a place up front, near the projector… and, if they ask questions, take some notes. Later we can type up the Q&A and send it to everyone."

The conference went as planned. Marianna's presentation was well-received, no one seemed to care that Kate was there among the Olympians, and only a few questions were asked. Feldman was fulsome in his praise, cut the meeting short and left. The rest of his court evacuated as well, some muttering congratulations to Marianna. With fifteen minutes still to go in what was supposed to be an hour-long meeting, Marianna and Kate were left in an empty room, the last slide still projected on the screen behind them.

"Well, you and I, with our invisible companion, Sisyphus, have rolled the stone one more time to the top of the mountain, and down it goes," said Marianna. She illustrated the point with a downward-sweeping motion of her hand, "And, boom! We're up here at the top, alone, looking down at the rock. Nothing to do but to go down and try again."

"Don't you get frustrated?" said Kate.

"No. I can't afford the luxury of frustration. I just try again. The way I see it, every time I advocate for something, an idea, a concept, something will stick. I may not make a difference now but a year, two years, ten years from now that idea will come to the mind of someone who's heard it and be put into action, maybe by someone who forgot where he got it or by someone who heard someone else talk about it. None of this, not if they're good ideas will ever really die. At least that's what I hope," she said.

Kate nodded. Marianna was such an incurable optimist. They packed up and started to walk back to their offices.

"The Serenity Prayer is crap, by the way," said Marianna, a large loose-leaf binder filled with back-up data under her arm

"The Serenity Prayer?" said Kate.

"Maria Parks has a copy hanging in her office. It's all that nonsense about accepting the things we cannot change. I have my own version of it. Want to hear?"

"Sure" Kate said with a little laugh.

"It goes like this – Lord give me the skill to convince these jackasses of what they should do. If they cannot be convinced, then, Lord, replace them with jackasses who can be convinced. Let some of this stick and let the sneaky and dishonest ones steal my ideas and do good whether they mean to or not. And, Lord, get people who like to pray to you up and off their knees so they can do something useful with their time and money. Yours, Kate, amen."

"That should get His attention," said Kate.

"Hasn't yet," said Marianna, "but I'm used to that. Anyway, it's my Serenity Prayer and makes me serene, or at least gives me the energy to march on."

They reached Marianna's office. It was lunchtime, during

which Marianna usually shut her door and unplugged her phone so she could eat her fruit, read, and listen to soft chamber music. Not today, however. She waved Kate in and sat behind her desk.

"Sit down and close the door. I want to talk with you," she said.

Kate did as she was told, and tried to suppress a growing anxiety about what Marianna was going to say. She was sure it had to do with her performance.

"I know we've only worked together for a few months, and this is probably none of my business, but you don't seem yourself. You've been dreamy and you seem tired. Is something wrong?"

"I'm sorry, Marianna. I haven't slept as well as I should, and…, I don't know. If my work isn't up to par, I'll fix it," said Kate.

"Your work is superb. In fact, I'm putting you in for an award, but don't tell anyone I told you that."

"Then what is it?" said Kate.

"You just don't seem… uh… how do I put this? You don't seem happy. You do good work. I have no criticism of that, and that's all I should expect from you, I suppose, but you don't seem to take joy in it, to have pleasure in what you do, and that's a shame, because if you did you'd probably reach beyond any of us," said Marianna, "I'm saying this as your friend, not as your boss…" She paused, leaned forward and looked Kate in the eye, "What's wrong?"

At first Kate didn't know how to respond. She'd been feeling low ever since her last date with Penn, she knew that. He never called her, not once, never send a note of any sort. An e-mail would have been just as good, but he didn't have her e-mail address, and she didn't have his, so that method of communication was not possible. If he had wanted to reach her, however, he could have. It was easy enough -- just call. She wanted to put him out of her mind, but she kept thinking about him, wanting him to call, willing him to call.

Kate didn't want to answer, "Everything's fine," she said.

"No it's not," said Marianna.

"Really," said Kate, "It's nothing."

"Is anyone dying or pregnant? Are you facing an IRS audit, looking at prison time?" said Marianna.

Kate smiled, "No, no nothing like that."

"Oh, so it's a guy, is it?" said Marianna.

Kate squirmed, "Really, Marianna, I'd rather not talk…" she didn't get to finish.

"Kate, you want to talk about it. That's why you're sighing and mooning in your office. I can't imagine you having man trouble. You're pretty enough to be giving trouble to men, not taking it from them. There must be someone very special involved here."

Kate looked down, "There is someone very special, Marianna."

"What happened?"

"Nothing happened. That's just the problem. I went out with him twice. He was wonderful, a gentleman in every way, took me to the opera and a few weeks later to the ballet. He's handsome, intelligent, not talkative but when he says something, he really says something. He's strong, but gentle, brave but humble, everything you could imagine."

"Is he gay?" said Marianna.

"God, no," said Kate, "He's a Commander in the Navy with lots of ribbons and awards, and he's an Annapolis grad. He was wounded fighting in Iraq. He also teaches at the Naval Academy and just got his Ph.D. in history from Emory."

"Does he have a girlfriend or, worse, a wife?" said Marianna.

"Well, I know he doesn't have a wife and has never been married. I have no idea who else he dates or whether he has a girl anywhere," she said, "But right now I'm pretty sure he's unattached."

"He's Mr. Right, then?" said Marianna.

Kate lowered her head and nodded.

"No, he's not," said Marianna, "Not for you. He hasn't called or written. He has some other agenda and you're not on the top of the list."

"What do I do? I feel miserable," said Kate.

"Well, first, you could simply find another guy, but that's not so easy, is it. The farts you work with here are all at least fifty. Worse, they're scientists or public health officers in wrinkled pants and flannel shirts and they all have grandchildren. Of course, there's always the chance a handsome, young M.D. will come your way, but they're few and far in between. Even if that worked it would take time and be a long-run solution but nothing that will work right away. Second, you could continue to wait for him, hoping he'd get back to you. He might be tied up in some way right now, and when he has the time he'll remember to call. That happened to me once. Took him two years. Third, you could just right him off. Make up your mind not to think about him and just lead your life, expand it, meet new people, have fun. You're young and beautiful. The bee will come to you. –This sounds like the first choice, doesn't it? -- Anyway, If your special one wakes up and calls you then you've got the bee you wanted all along. If not, you look for someone better. Fourth, you could call him or contact him. An e-mail might be less intimidating than a call, and you can edit an e-mail so that you don't sound too eager and scare him away."

"But I don't have his e-mail address," said Kate.

"I'll get it," said Marianna, "If you give me his full name and if he teaches at the Naval Academy, I can contact the Commander's office, pretend to be on official business, and get the e-mail."

"You can?"

"Trust me," said Marianna, "Now let me have my lunch break, OK?"

"Sure, Marianna, and thanks for everything," said Kate,

handing her a slip of paper with Penn's name written on it.

Ten minutes later she received an e-mail from Marianna. All it said was pennington.fuller@UNSA.gov Office: 410-277-8929 -- Good luck.

****

Chapter Seventeen – Yoshiko & Grandmother Keiko

Yoshiko Fujiyama, dressed in a sober kimono, knelt in front of her grandmother's grave, and in obeisance to the mix of religious customs in her family said a Christian prayer for the dead while holding joss sticks in her folded hands, touching them to her forehead and bowing. She probably would have said the Kaddish, too, if she could remember the words. She had a beautiful recording of it at home sung by Sumi Jo, a Korean soprano she idolized, on an album simply called "Prayer." She played the entire disk over and over in her room on her iPod, sometimes weeping softly, sometimes singing along, hoping the prayers would reach the Divine and hasten the journey of her Grandmother's soul to heaven.

If anyone deserved Heavenly bliss it was Grandmother Keiko. Her early years were horrid. Miserably poor and alone, her parents dead, the mere fact she survived until rescued by Lady Ayumi in 1942 was a miracle. Grandmother Keiko told the story many times, and even wrote it in down in a little book that she read many times to her grandchildren and great-grandchildren. Yoshiko had practically memorized it.

Grandmother Keiko's Book

> I was named at birth Hamasaki Keiko, but I now call myself Takahashi Keiko-Ayumi for Dr. Takahashi Masato was my beloved husband, and I wish to honor the name of the woman who rescued me. I was born in 1935, in Hiroshima, Japan. My parents and I lived in the Naka Ward, not far from Nobori-cho where the *Cathedral of Peace* now stands. Both my parents died in 1942, when I was seven years old. First my father died in an accident at the shipyard, then my mother died from illness. My grandparents lived far away. They had nothing of their own and no way of knowing what happened to me. All they possessed was

destroyed by bombs. Some people helped me at first but they had little, too, and I was left to scrabble for myself in the city.

The Lady Ayumi found me on the streets of Hiroshima, filthy, skinny, begging for small coins or scraps of food, foraging in the garbage. The first time Lady Ayumi approached me, I was afraid and I ran, much like a feral cat runs even from the kind hand that helps it. Lady Ayumi persisted, however. She would go by the cathedral, then called *Cathedral of the Assumption*, and look for me every day, ask other children about me. From them she learned my name, and she kept vigilant.

Lady Ayumi, my rescuer, was a Christian but one whose religion was not exclusive. Buddha and the Shinto rituals were known to her as well, and she practiced them. She had to be flexible and accommodating in her beliefs because she dealt with many people and her life was one of hospitality and kindness. She owned a tea house, actually two of them served by a single kitchen. One catered to a higher sort of clientele. Geisha entertained the gentlemen, the atmosphere was serene, and the accommodations expensive. The other was more public, a busier place with all sorts of people coming and going. There was an active kitchen that supplied both Tea Houses, that served noodles, fish, and cakes when she could get them. Rice wine was always available but the good Saki was hard to find and reserved only for the most exclusive customers.

There was an horrendous rain one day, a thunderstorm that blackened the sky, rocked the city with thunder and lightning, and dumped a huge quantity of dense rain water, so much that all traffic, even the military traffic, stopped, umbrellas collapsed and were useless, awnings fell, the streets filled with water, and one could not see anything through the density of the downpour.

Lady Ayumi took refuge in the Cathedral and it was there she found me shivering from cold and fear in a corner, coughing and wild-eyed. Lady Ayumi, always on the look-out for the rare treat for her customers, had a cloth bag with a few fruits in it, things once abundant but now difficult to find -- an Asian pear, some dried persimmons, a half-dozen dried plums. She offered these one-by-one to me, a shivering little girl who grabbed them and devoured them ravenously, in the hideous manner of a starving animal. Lady Ayumi squatted beside me calmly and quietly listened to the rain beat down on the roof. As the rain slowed and the noise from it became more gentle, she leaned close to me and began to speak softly.

"Your name is Keiko, is it not?" she said in a soft and friendly tone.

I stared at her, but didn't answer. *Who is this person?*, I thought, *What does she want? How does she know my name?*

"My name is Ayumi, and I live near here. I own Tea Houses and serve food and comfort to people. Would you like to come home with me?"

My first impulse was to run. I looked from side to side and got ready to bolt.

"I know how frightened you are and you want to run," said Ayumi, "At one time I felt that way myself. But what will you run to? Run with me. If you don't

> like it, run away. At least you'll be fed and you can bathe and you'll get some clean clothes." She paused." I will leave you now and go over there," she said, pointing to a chapel in the corner of the Cathedral, "to say a prayer of thanks to the Blessed Virgin. If you want to come with me, join me there. If not, I will simply go home."
>
> Ayumi arose. I quickly weighed the prospects in my mind. I could run, but only to misery. I had nothing to lose by going with this Lady. Dead children were found in the street every day, and sickness or injury or starvation would soon destroy me. I knew that. Aside from all that, the Lady Ayumi smelled so fragrant, was so beautiful, even at an advanced age --Ayumi was 62 -- with such a kind voice, I could not fear her, and I felt instinctively that this chance was my only chance. I closed my eyes and worked up my courage. When I opened them, the Lady was rising, lighting some votive lights and getting ready to leave. I dashed to her side and grabbed her hand with both of my hands. Ayumi smiled down at me. Our love for one another began at that moment and lasted for the rest of our lives.

Yoshiko first heard that story when she was five years old, sitting at her Grandmother's side. Grandmother Keiko read that story over and over to Yoshiko, who never tired of it and often asked to hear it again. There were many other stories as well. Yoshiko bowed before Keiko's monument, her joss sticks to her forehead, and said the *Lord's Prayer*. She then moved to Ayumi's monument, right next to Grandmother Keiko's, and prayed as well, her eyes watering, a tear rolling down her cheek. There was no one close enough to hear her, so she even sang a few bars of the *Kaddish.*

****

Chapter Eighteen – Admiral Pennington and the JIN

Penn's investigation into the life and career of Admiral Pennington was split along two paths. There was the professional career, which could be fleshed-out partially from the official reports and the much more colorful letters to family and wife. Then there were the personal details, the motivations, happenings, and events that were personal and obscure.

The official record of the Admiral's first four-plus years in Japan consisted of his observations of the Japanese fleet, the conditions of their ports and the competence of the Japanese Imperial Navy (JIN). Typical of his work was a report he sent shortly after arriving at Japan in 1894

Excerpt from *Dispatch to the Office of the Secretary of the Navy.*

> The Honorable Mr. Herbert, Secretary of the Navy:
>
> BACKGROUND: The Japanese Imperial Navy (JIN) was established in 1869, a latecomer to the world of imperial Navies. It was an artifact of the Japanese social and industrial revolution led by Restoration of the Meiji Imperial House, and the Emperor's subsequent drive for the modernization of Japan. Japan was relatively poor, but Navies are critical to the independence and security of a nation, so although the funds available to build a modern Navy were limited, shipyards were constructed, ships were purchased or built and the groundwork was set for the development of a Navy.

All this was common knowledge, at least in the Department, What they didn't know – and what Lt. Penning discovered -- was how much the French did and how much money they made in designing and constructing shipyards and ports for Japanese. The work was done under contract of course, contracts that could have gone to Americans had we been savvy and nimble enough to pursue them, contracts that, ironically, would never have happened had Commodore Perry not opened Japan in the first place and triggered the Meiji Restoration. From the *Dispatch:*

> Both the French and British have been very active in contracting with the Japanese for the construction of ships and for the design and building of shipyards. The JIN began purchasing ships from the British in 1875, but the French, after years of selling their expertise to the Japanese were able to secure large lucrative contracts for shipyard design and construction. The Secretary's office is familiar with the work of the French engineer, Mr. L. Bertin, because he and his firm have proposed on contract solicitations from the U.S. Navy (unsuccessfully). His work at the Tokosuka Naval Yard here, however, is very good and rivals any I've seen in the States. Yard design and construction is an area of commerce we have not pursued with the Japanese and we do well. Japan's Navy is still growing and there may be ample opportunity to secure contracts now that the French have joined in an alliance with the Russians. If we do not step in, the British will.

Lt. Pennington's reports on the JIN's armament were neither dramatic nor sensational. Since the Japanese either purchased outright or attempted to imitate European weaponry and ships, the ships and armament of their growing fleet were familiar to our Naval experts. Japanese innovation in armament design was practically non-existent. The Lieutenant knew that Naval Headquarters in the United States understood perfectly the design of British and French ships and was not terribly impressed. American ship designers, it was thought – and Lt. Pennington shared the opinion -- had approaches that were superior, more resistant to hull damage, more capable of controlling on-board fires, and more capable of designing fast vessels well-equipped with every technologically advanced feature.

As the Lieutenant remarked in his first extensive report, Britain had the great fleet, a huge force much larger than any ever contemplated by the American Congress, and the French, along with their substantial fleet, had terrific engineers and designers, and were capable of building some very fine vessels. The United States, although capable of designing the best ships and shipyards in the world, was an underdog in the competition for the seas. After all, our empire was built on land. If we were to compete in the ship building business, we'd better advertise ourselves and push for the business.

The French were also very interested in building an empire in Asia to rival the British in India and Africa. The French pushed their products to Japan not only for commercial profit, but also to use Japan as an unwitting ally in the expansion of French Imperialism. They eventually subordinated their Japanese interests to other Imperial interests, however, and allied with the Russians in 1892 against the Japanese. Even so, the Japanese still bought ships and weapons from them.

At the time of Pennington's initial assignment, Harvey armor, an American innovation, the strongest armor in the world, was a new development. Harvey armor, used properly in war ship construction, could resist penetration from torpedoes and most artillery rounds, keeping a ship afloat and dangerous despite direct hits on its hull. It took four years for Germany's Krupp to develop a rival product and even then the engineers who created Harvey armor thought the Krupp product inferior. From Pennington's *Dispatch:*

> The U.S. Navy staff has been impressed with the quality and remarkable strength of compound armor. Harvey armor is known to be the best of these

> products and is an American invention that, it was thought, could be of use to the Japanese and for which there is no rival product. To our knowledge Harvey armor was not yet in Asia in any form. It therefore surprised us to discover the Japanese, with the help of British engineers employed at the shipyards, hard at work installing large plates of Harvey armor mid-ship, plates high and wide enough to go well below the water line and offer protection against torpedoes.

Lieutenant Pennington went to Japan determined to do his best to sell his JIN contacts on the efficacy of American's Harvey armor, only to find *they already used it*, and our Navy Department had no idea they did.

The official reports that went to the Navy Department are dry reading, but a letter he wrote home is more colorful.

> Dear Family:
>
> I spent the last two weeks aboard the Japanese Battleship *Yashima*. It was built by the Brits in Newcastle (London Iron Works) and delivered to the Japanese earlier this year. It's a huge thing, 432 feet long and 76 feet wide, with a steel hull and teak decks, double masted, with a crow's nest on top of each mast and with two huge smokestacks. I looked down the hull and what I saw didn't impress me. We make steel hulls cleaner and smoother in Bath, Maine. BUT it's got a band of specially hardened steel 9 inches thick from stem to stern, and – three cheers to our side -- they copied our design, with a hull-wide panel of the USA's Harvey armor mid-ship. Mid-ship is where you take most hits, not on the bow or stern.
>
> The officers and men of the JIN are good. I'd put them up against any American crew, and if enthusiasm

and intelligence could overcome lack of experience I don't think we'd win. They need more practice, though, and their officers need to rely less on pomposity and blind obedience to rank, and more on seamanship and equipment competency. I saw a Petty officer strike a seaman with what looked like a swagger stick for failing to follow an order. It was no tap, either, but several hard blows across the head and back. My Japanese is still raw, but from what I saw, the seaman turned the valve in the right direction. Although he acted in contravention to his orders, he did the correct thing. The Chief should have seen that and thanked him. That's no way to run things below decks.

The *Yashima* is a fine ship, but they didn't use it in the fight against the Chinese last August. Their *Fuji* class battleships were too big to maneuver properly against the Chinese and made easy targets for the Chinese guns. Instead, they brought out their cruisers and rained enfilading fire on the Chinese Battleships. I watched the whole thing through binoculars from the deck of the *Fuji*, sister ship to the *Yashima*. It was almost pretty, like watching fireworks, until you realized that men were on the receiving end of that rain from hell.

None of the Chinese ships suffered damage to their hulls – the Japanese guns weren't strong enough to pierce the steel – but their teak decks and whatever was beneath them caught fire and the Chinese ships had to withdraw. The Japanese bottled them up at a place called Wei-hai-wei, sunk one of the battleships with a torpedo, and the other surrendered. Later, we found the Chinese ships were each hit over 200 times. The JIN tells me they've developed a stronger explosive and propellant they call *Shimosa* (Sounds like a flower doesn't it?) to use in future fights that can penetrate Chinese and Russian armor.

I had a sit-down with Captain Hajime Sakamoto two days after the battle. He's the Commander of the *Yashima*. He's a short man by American standards, maybe 5 foot three or four, which might keep him out of our Naval Academy, but isn't too short for a Japanese officer. He's built like a block of oak and looks as tough as a badger. I think if he wanted to, he could put his head down and butt right through me, and probably right through the hull. He keeps his hair very short, Prussian style, cropped to his skull on the sides and brushed up on the top, and he wears a long mustache that he waxes and twists on the ends so they form two fine downward sloping points (I'd put the angle at about twenty degrees from the horizontal. Shame I didn't have a sextant with me to measure it.). In all he looks very military and commanding, a no-nonsense officer who expects orders to be followed without delay and certainly without question.

Captain Sakamoto speaks some English but not much and I sensed my Japanese was as painful to him as his English would be to me. Luckily, we had an interpreter. When the Captain shook my hand, he gripped it like a seaman grips an anchor rope. He wasn't big, but he was as strong as a great ape. There's something about a strong grip that immediately promotes respect among men in a very basic way. I respected him a lot.

The Captain asked me what I thought of his ship. I told him frankly that it was a fine ship, clean and well maintained, and the crew was among the best-trained, most enthusiastic and most competent I'd ever encountered. He was very pleased and agreed with me. (What did he expect? The question was loaded. He asked "Am I pretty," and I said "You're beautiful." I meant it, too).

He then asked the question that calls for a clever answer. "What do you think we need to do to improve?" I wanted to say "Take the d__n swagger sticks away from your Petty Officers," but I didn't. Instead I said, "Sir, the American Navy believes training and practice are the greatest assets to success. If the JIN trains and practices until your men do the right things automatically, when battle occurs they will perform at their stations both with the famous heroism of the JIN forces and with unparalleled speed and competence."

I asked him what he thought of Harvey armor, and he gave it the thumbs up with high praise. I suggested the Japanese Navy might solicit some American ship designs and he grunted something like "sure, someday," which didn't sound too encouraging.

He agreed heartily with my assessment of his ship and crew, however, and ordered Saki for us both. We toasted the Emperor and the President, Mr. Cleveland, whose name he couldn't pronounce although he tried several times, the JIN, the ship and the U.S. Navy. We also toasted his officers and crew. By that time I could hardly stand. Thankfully he dismissed me, so I tried to avoid another handshake by donning my hat and saluting smartly. He returned the salute, smiled broadly, stuck out his arm, and I had to shake his hand again anyway. Later I soaked the hand in cold water to bring down the swelling.

I hope we never have to fight these fellows. They're tough, disciplined, smart and resourceful. One of the things a junior officer on the *Fuji* told me was that 95% of the ship's crew was literate. That's a far sight better than we do. Oh, we've got men that claim to be literate because they can read and write their names, and that was all right in the era of sail. Today, however, ships are run by people who can read manuals, do math in their heads, and operate complex equipment. Literacy and education might well make the difference between victory and defeat in some coming war.

My warmest regards to everyone

John

Pen read the letter for the fifth time and smiled. His Great Grandfather was coming to life. There were so many questions, though. As McGraw pointed out, Catherine, the Admiral's wife, must have had a reason, a very good reason, for going to Japan then leaving. Even the Admiral's death was shrouded. The Admiral died in a plane crash. The landing gear on the B-29 he took from Osaka to Tokyo collapsed and the plane disintegrated in a fireball that killed everyone aboard. There was an official inquiry and the digest of their findings was sent to the family, specifically his adopted son, in a one page letter, but there seemed to be no copy of that official inquiry on file.

And there was the law firm, Marbright and Fuller of Boston. Marbright and Fuller dissolved long ago, but typically successful law firms don't just disappear. They merge with another firm and their records are transferred or their business is bought-out and the records transferred. Marbright and Fuller dissolved in 1951, but where their records went is anyone's guess, and if those records did go somewhere, were they kept? As far as Penn could determine, the legal requirements on records retention were lax to non-existent back in the 40s and 50s, so the files could have been thrown away more than half a century ago. Penn and his assistants had already called most of the law firms in Boston, asked the help of the Massachusetts Bar, and even searched newspaper files, but nothing turned up.

The marimba tone on his iPhone sounded and Penn looked

down. Grand Aunt Harriett's name appeared on the green oval announcing the call. He sighed. He neither wanted nor needed any more exhortations from Harriett regarding Kate, but just as he was about to decline the call, his instincts or his curiosity kicked in and he accepted it.

"Hello!" he said, "How is my favorite person?"

"Don't you know it's me?" said Harriet.

"The phone said Jennifer Lopez," said Penn, "That's why I answered."

"She's too old for you. Besides, she's used goods and temperamental as hell. Find a new one," she said.

"What can I do for you, Auntie?" said Penn.

"Marry Kate Hobson, but do that tomorrow. Now, I need your help."

"Of course," said Penn.

She sighed, "I got a letter today. I hate letters, especially letters that aren't junk mail. Junk mail goes right in the garbage and eventually returns to the earth, I hope. Don't have to read it. A real letter has to be read, and I almost never get a real letter, not since e-mail was invented at least. Furthermore, I've never gotten a real letter that conveyed good news. Know what I mean?"

"Yes," said Penn, "I know exactly what you mean."

"Anyway I got a letter today. This letter should have been posted in 1950, but it came today, and I'm not sure what to do about it."

"What's in it?" said Penn.

"I'm getting' to that. My husband, Admiral Butler died at Inchon, Korean War."

"Yes. I knew that. You told me the story," said Penn.

"Then you know he died when an observation plane his the bridge of his Ship, the *Sioux*."

"I knew it was something like that." Penn wondered where this was going.

"Damned planes. Plane killed him and a plane killed your Great Grandfather."

"War is a hostile environment," said Penn.

"Stop muttering goddamn clichés," said Henrietta, "Makes me feel like you're patronizing me. Anyway, your Great Grandfather didn't die during the war. He died after it. But it was another damn plane, which was the point. Now, here's why I called. Today I got a letter from the pilot of the plane that killed my husband."

"What?" said Penn in disbelief, "But that happened sixty-two years ago. He wrote to you now?"

"His widow sent it to me. Looks like he wrote it back in 1950 or so, but didn't have the guts to send it. He blames himself for the accident. He bailed out when the plane ran out of fuel – tried to get it pointed away from the fleet – but that didn't happen. Wind turned it and it crashed into my husband's ship."

"What does she want?" said Penn.

"Who?"

"The widow," said Penn.

"Nothing. Just to send me the letter. He left a note on it asking it to be sent to me." She paused for a few seconds, "I want to answer this and thank her, but I still get choked up thinking about Marion. I did love the man and I was quite young then, much younger than you are now. You love someone at that age and it goes deep, especially if they die or leave you. Did you know Estelle Harkins?"

"No," said Penn, "Wash she a friend?"

"She was in my tennis club back in '51. Her husband, Paul, shot one of the partners in the law firm where he worked. Boom! Deader than a door nail."

"He murdered him?" said Penn.

"Hell, yes. Paul was a lawyer, but no other lawyer in Vermont wanted to take the case. Sort of a reverse professional courtesy issue. He killed a lawyer, you see, and no one would defend him, even if he was a lawyer himself. This was way before *Gideon vs. Wainwright* 'ya know."

"Gideon what?" said Penn.

"I thought you were an historian."

"My field is American Naval History, not law," said Penn

"Well, you should get out of your field now and then and look at the rest of life. Hell, squirrels come down from the trees and even a woodchuck sticks his head above ground every now and then. *Gideon vs. Wainwright*. 1960s Supreme Court case. Established the right for every accused person to be represented by legal council. It's also known as the lawyer's full employment decision. Guaranteed you'd have some pettifogger or legal hack assuring you'd be sent to the slammer if you were too dumb or too poor to refuse a public attorney and defend yourself. I've been to court seven times. Defended myself every time. Won seven times out of seven. If I was a lawyer, I'd have to pay myself a fortune for all that."

"What happened to your friend, Estelle?"

"Wasn't Estelle. It was her husband, Paul. He defended himself, said Geoffrey Shingleton, Esq., the man he shot, was a tyrant and a bully and had it coming. Said Shingleton kept telling him to revise a brief that was perfectly OK and they argued. Said Shingleton, in fit of rage over some legal form or procedural issue, reached into his jacket as if he were going for a gun. That's when Paul pulled his gun and shot him. Said he thought he was defending himself, he wasn't sorry, and that the SOB had it coming."

"Did that defense work?" said Penn.

"What do you think? Paul was a real estate attorney, and not very good at it. Had to take the bar exam four times and then just barely passed it. Rumor was he had a ringer take it for him. Hell, most of the lawyers I've known probably had ringers take the exam for them. The only court he'd even been in was moot court in law school and I'm told he lost that case and damn near flunked out. If his father hadn't been an alumnus and a major contributor to the school he probably would have flunked. Prosecution argued that Paul was just trying to create a vacancy among the law firm's partners so he could advance. Said that Shingleton was an anti-gun Quaker who never carried a weapon, and didn't own a weapon and everyone knew that. Called on Shingleton's preacher to testify as to the man's devoutness. Shingleton, it seems, attended every meeting of the Friends for twenty years. Collected money as a lay preacher for the Conversion of Fallen Women and the Reform of Drunks. Jury sided with the prosecution and found Paul guilty of Murder in the First Degree. Vermont policy at the time was only to execute murderers if they'd murdered someone before, so he got life. The judge was hard on him, too. Said the crime was aggravated by Paul's status as a lawyer and it besmirched the entire profession. Little like one pig in the sty saying another pig is too fat and smelly and made the whole species look ugly." She laughed at her own joke, more a snort than a laugh, "Paul couldn't believe it. As they hauled him away from court he kept on yelling 'I object! I object!'"

Henrietta paused and sighed, "Poor Estelle, who was only 26, stuck by him. Brought him goodies on visiting days, and never missed a visiting day. Even brought him her famous fruit cake on Christmas. Heavy as a block of cement and about as hard and dry, but he reportedly loved it. He was finally paroled after 28 years, but it was too late for her. She died two years before he was released, but she did leave five years' worth of fruit cakes for him in the freezer she loved him so much. Bastard got out – he was only 59 – charmed some widow in Stowe and retired to wealth and luxury. The Lord took him down, though. He died in an avalanche while skiing. Of course he was over 80 when he died, 84 to be exact.

Sometimes the Lord is slow in these matters." She paused again and took a deep breath.

"Would you help me, and answer the letter from the man's widow for me?" said Harriett, "Tell her I'm demented, and it won't do any good to send me any more letters because all I do is watch reality TV and Fox News, make doilies, and talk bad about the government."

"Sure, Auntie," said Penn, "Just send me the letter and I'll answer it for you."

"Already sent. Had Elizabeth go with me to the library and get it scanned. They showed us how to attach it to an e-mail and send it. Should be in your in box, subject: *Letter from Harriet.* "

Penn checked Outlook and there it was. He clicked on the attached PDFs and two documents came up. The letter from the widow and the letter from the pilot.

"Got it Auntie! I'll answer it today," said Penn.

"Thanks. Now marry Kate." She hung up.

The letter contained the email address of Mary O'Mara, omara99@hotmail.ir.com.

Penn responded to her via e-mail, with a copy to his aunt. He also mailed her the letter in hard copy on official stationary with his signature in blue ink.

> Dear Mrs. O'Mara:
>
> The widow of Admiral Butler, Mrs. Harriet Butler, asked me to respond for her. I am her nephew and I am a career Navy officer as was her husband.
>
> It was very kind of you to contact us and send us Lieutenant Colonel O'Mara's letter. It clarifies some aspects of the incident that have been shrouded in mystery for 62 years and has allowed the voice of your brave husband to reach beyond the grave and touch us with his

remorse and condolences.

Your husband was a very valiant and selfless man who repeatedly faced tremendous odds and risked his life for the defense of freedom and the fight for liberty. I currently teach history at the Naval Academy. I thought I recognized his name and I took the opportunity to look at a list of the recipients of the very highest awards for valor. I found him there, Lieutenant Colonel Patrick O'Mara, an Army Aviator who was awarded the Congressional Medal of Honor for extreme temerity in leading an infantry action during the Vietnam War. In achieving that award, he was wounded multiple times, but still managed to carry two men to his plane and fly them to safety and recovery in field hospitals. Few men alive have the courage and selflessness to act with such remarkable bravery. He was a rare and precious soldier, the best of the best.

The night of the Inchon invasion, I am certain his actions and motives were of the very highest ethical and moral standards. The very fact that he would question his decisions when an accident occurred over which he had no control only serves to underscore his deep sense of integrity and loyalty.

Thank you very much for sending us his letter.

Please accept my salute, and my best wishes. May he rest with heroes.

Sincerely,

Commander Pennington Fuller, United States Navy

Twelve hours later, Mary O'Mara responded.

Dear Commander Fuller:

Thank you very much for your kind words. It does my heart good to hear the window of the brave Captain Butler is still alive and that she was able to read and accept my late husband's condolences. I will keep your response with his things and read it over his grave so that his spirit will know we've done as he asked and that you understand and accept his sentiments.

I could not help but notice a coincidence. Your first name Is Pennington. One of the documents we saved from my late husband's war records was the *Report of the Commission of Inquiry on the Crash of B-29 #779624*. My husband was a member of the commission and thus received a copy of the report. Among the people who perished in the crash was Vice Admiral John Pennington. Although you have different last names, I thought that your first name might reflect a relationship to Admiral Pennington and that you might have an interest in seeing this report.

Please let me know if you would like a copy, and let me know where to send it.

Very Truly Yours,

Mary O'Mara.

Penn couldn't believe his luck. He immediately fired back a response stating that he would, indeed, like to see a copy of that report and he would pay any and all expenses associated with copying and sending it.

Forty-eight hours later the report arrived via DHL express. Mary O'Mara charged him nothing. He had it scanned and copied then turned it over to his assistants.

"I doubt if any of the commission members are still alive," he said to the little team of people helping him, "but there's a list of witnesses. See if you can find addresses for any of them. If anyone is still alive who saw the crash, I want to speak with him."

He was right about the commission members. They were all gone. Most of the witnesses had disappeared over the years, but there was one they did manage to locate. In 1947 he was an Army airmen in Japan, but he'd gone into the Merchant Marine after being discharged. He was retired now, living in a retirement home in Florida for Merchant Seaman, *Sailor's Snug Harbor*. He even had a telephone number. His name was Taylor Michael Costello.

****

Chapter Nineteen – Kate, Marianna and Mike Costello

Kate, back in her office, saw the white fur ball of the feral cat trot out from under a car and head towards the woods. From here she seemed to glow in the sunlight and her step seemed sprightly and somehow happy and independent, not furtive or frightened. The cat, which she hadn't seen for days, cheered her, and she was smiling as she clipped away at her keyboard finishing a report on the status of Chronic disease prevention management among six exemplary state health departments.

Marianna Littlebear leaned into Kate's office. "Cats aren't so good for the environment, you know. They kill birds."

"You've seen her, too?" Kate smiled up at her and sighed. "Cats can sometimes be harmful, I know. It all depends, Marianna, on where they are and what they do. So many natural predators have been eliminated directly by hunting or poisoning, or by development and the elimination of natural areas, cats – if not too prevalent – can fill in. Without them, there is little to control rodents. Rats and mice, as you know, are major problems both in urban and rural areas."

Marianna smiled. Kate was preaching what Marianna already thought. "I like her, too, Kate. I've even left food for her."

"So have I. If we keep doing that, she may leave the birds alone. I'd think there's a lot of rodents out there for her anyway and birds aren't much on her menu. At least I hope so."

Marianna leaned in a little further, "Look, something's come up, something really exciting"… paused "Your know that presentation we made to el jefe and the College of Cardinals?" She meant the director and his staff.

"Yes??"

"Some of it stuck. Must be the Christmas spirit. We're going on a tour of the six exemplary HDs – Maine, Connecticut, Maryland,

North Carolina, Montana and Washington."

"At once?"

"No, it'll be spread out over the next year. I figure we'll visit one every other month, spend three to five days meeting with the health commissioner and his or her folks, collect our data and write a report on it. At the end of the year, we'll collect the findings in a single book with the six chapters, and present it to the Director. The important thing is that we got the funding for the trips, probably more than we need, but we won't tell them that."

"Who's going?"

"Just you and I. If the funding holds up I may add Paula, but for now I don't think we need her."

Paula Tilson, RN, MS, MPH, was a registered nurse-epidemiologist who sometimes supported Marianna's projects. Kate didn't like her. Paula was opinionated and direct, a poor listener, intolerant of the ideas of others, and rude. She was no team player and best left working projects on her own. "Marianna, you're the boss, but do you think Paula is the right person to bring along on a conference with a state Health Director?"

Marianna smiled, or half-smiled, something she did when she was thinking. "No, I don't. It'll be just you and I, but I may ask her opinion on some of our findings. We'll need an objective third look and she's not shy about saying what she thinks."

"When do we start?" said Kate.

"January. First stop is Maryland, *Annapolis* Maryland."

"You're kidding," said Kate.

"No," said Marianna, "When do I kid? We'll get there on the 8th, and fly home the morning of the 11th". I hear you have a friend in Annapolis."

Kate grinned, "Maybe I do."

The e-mail, sent from home, went out that night.

Penn:

How are you?

We haven't spoken for some time. When we last saw each other, you told me your back and shoulder were bothering you and I thought I'd write to see if you've gotten any better. I know as well you were – and are – working on a project at Annapolis that is taking up much of your time. Your mother talked to mine last week and mentioned that you didn't come home for Thanksgiving and might even be tied-up over Christmas.

I know how it's possible to be caught up in projects. My mentor, Marianna LIttlebear, and I have been on a two-woman crusade to help state and local Health Departments more efficiently and effectively use their funding. I'm currently working with Chronic diseases. Many Chronic conditions are closely related – Diabetes, Heart Disease, Obesity, Cancer – and connected with preventable unhealthy behaviors like smoking, diet and lack of exercise.

Health Departments at the state and local, however, seem to be stovepiped, with organizations and offices set up in their boxes that treat these problems as if they're separate and distinct and don't coordinate their prevention efforts. If that's the case, it's duplicative, wasteful and non-productive. Right now, with the dire fiscal condition of most states, every penny has to count and waste has to be eliminated. Better coordination of efforts would help with that.

Unfortunately most of our information is anecdotal. There never has been a national survey of how these departments operate at the state and local levels. So, with funding from the CDC, my mentor, Marianna, and I are going on a six state tour to look in depth at some exemplary states and make recommendations for proceeding further.

The very first state we're vising is Maryland. We'll be in Annapolis in January from the 8th to the morning of the 11th. Perhaps we can get together one evening. I'd like you to meet Marianna, and you can tell us about your project.

Anyway, that's one of my projects. If you have the chance, send me an e-mail or give me a call and tell something about the book you're planning and the progress you're making. I'd love to know more about it.

Keep in touch,

Kate

Oh, if you ever need to call me at work – 770-408-2717; work e-mail: KHobson88@cdc.gov.

Penn saw the e-mail and felt queasy. He was afraid of what it might contain, but he opened it anyway and was glad he did. Kate sounded upbeat and happy. He was going home for a few days during Christmas then returning to Annapolis to keep researching, working on his book. He'd be here on the week of January 7th, and he'd like to see Kate again, especially if she was in the company of someone else. It would take the pressure off them. They could get to know each other a little bit more, and it wouldn't seem like courting. His back and shoulder would behave, too, or at so he hoped.

He answered:

Kate:

I'm going to be in Annapolis that week and I

> think it would be fun if we got together. Regarding your mentor, If I remember correctly the night we went to the ballet you told me that she's fifty or so and unattached. If that's the case, do you mind if I bring along a friend? Suppose we get together on the evening of the 9th. Let me know where you're staying and I'll pick you up or we can meet at one of my favorite restaurants, *Emile's*. It's not far from the Academy.
>
> Penn

Kate's response was simple.

"Great idea, meet you at the restaurant, say between 7:30 and 8:00?

Penn –

"It's a date! See you then."

Penn sat back in his chair, wondering what he had done. He couldn't escape the feeling that he'd kicked the wheels of fate and they were slowly turning, grinding all the grist of false hope and foolish expectation exceedingly fine.

In Cocoa, Florida, in the small senior community of *Sailor's Snug Harbor*, Mike Costello at 84, chuckled at the thought of an envelope he'd gotten addressed to "Mr. Taylor Michael Costello, ABS." ABS meant Able Bodied Seaman, and he was anything but "Able Bodied" these days. On the other hand, he wasn't crippled or bed-ridden either and the pangs of arthritis and rheumatism that sometimes afflicted him were endurable. He looked out at the sea. He liked to rise early and see the sun come up over the ocean. The sun was up now for almost 3 hours, but the day was pleasant and bright, there was a good breeze and he could stay out here on the bench looking down on the beach and the ocean with its sparkling leaden blue water all day. He wished he could see the sun set over the ocean as well, but that vista was on the other side of Florida looking towards the Gulf. On board ship you saw it both ways if you were on deck. Most of Mike's sailing career was spent on deck during good weather, and a lot of time on deck during dirty weather as well.

He was alone in life, but not lonely. He had a few old friends he could talk with, but for most of his life he'd been his own best companion. Christ, was the life good back then! You'd hear the thrum of the engines, feel the deck vibrate gently, see and feel the prow ride up and down over the waves, and sense the power of the ship as it plowed its way through the sea carrying cargo from one port to another. There were the port towns, too, the sights and sounds and smells of every corner of the world, and the women, oh the women!, of every hue and shade and size and accent and language. He dreamed of them sometimes, and thought about them every day. He'd had a damn good life. It was a shame so little of it was left.

"Mr. Costello!" The voice called. It was Peter Hill, one of the mangers of the *Harbor,* trotting up the walk to him. *What the hell did he want?*

"Yeah?"

"You've got a call."

"I don't want no calls. It's always someone trying to sell me something."

"No, not this time. It's a gentleman from the Naval Academy. He wants to ask you about an accident you saw in Japan in 1947. A plane crash."

"You gotta' be shittin' me," said Mike, suddenly interested.

"No. That's what he said," said Hill

"Ok. Give me a minute to get there… I'll Take it," he said as he got up and walked as fast as he could to the office.

Mike Costello planted the headset against his ear and fairly shouted into the phone. "This is Mike Costello. Who are you?"

"Mr. Costello," said Penn," Is this Taylor Michael Costello?"

"Yeah, except I go by 'Mike,' been that way since I was a kid. And call me 'Mike,' this 'Mister' shit makes me sound like an officer. *I worked for a living.*"

"OK, Mike," said Penn, "I'm Penn Fuller. I'm in the Navy and I currently teach Naval History at the Naval Academy. I want to ask you about the crash of a B-29 you witnessed. It happened in 1947. By the way, you can call me 'Penn.'"

"Ha! I knew one other guy named Pen, although his was a nickname because he spent time in the penitentiary. Killed a guy in a bar fight. Damn good seaman, though...." He paused for a few seconds.

"You did see the crash, right?" said Penn.

"I seen the crash alright. What's it to you?" said Mike.

"My Great Grandfather, Admiral Pennington, was on that plane. I just want to ask you about what you saw."

"The Admiral was your Great Grandfather? Huh!... I guess he was old enough to be. He must have been in his seventies."

"He was seventy-eight."

"Yeah, I guess that's right," said Mike, "but he was ramrod straight and tough as steel. Not a bad guy for a Admiral, either. I was sorry to see him go."

"I've got the report of the commission that investigated the accident. Do you remember much about it?"

"Oh, hell yes. How could I forget?," said Mike.

"Can you tell me about it?"

"Well, it's like I told the investigator back in '47, the plane was comin' in for a landing. The field wasn't perfect. The surface wasn't asphalt or cement. The runway was built of Marsden Matting, metal landing strips, if you know what them things are, but it was in good shape, and was kept in good shape. It was dark, but the landing lights were on, and a pilot could see the runway well enough, probably better than in daylight. The plane came in normal, but as it landed, the gear collapsed on the left side, the plane wheeled left and then the right side went down, then it just fell apart, pieces flyin' everywhere. There was an explosion, not a loud one, just a sort of 'whoomp!,' and the whole damn plane went up in a fireball. The fire crew got there in two minutes, but they couldn't do nothing except let it burn out. The next day, the bodies were pulled from the wreckage and taken away. They identified the military personnel from their dog tags, watches and such, and there was also a manifest sent via radio from Osaka after the plane took off there."

"You were on duty that night?" said Penn.

"Oh, hell yeah. I was on duty all that week. I seen the same plane take off the day before on the trip to Osaka. It was a regular flight, as regular as anything was in them days."

"Any idea what caused the landing gear to fail?" said Penn.

"Yeah, crooked goddamn defense contractors. Them planes was all jerry-built pieces of shit, thrown together in some shitty factory in Georgia or at Long Beach, made by crappy workers who were badly trained and supervised worse. Landing gear failures happened all the time, especially on B-29s. One thing, though, the planes didn't fall apart. They might come in on their bellies, but this was the only one I saw that just broke into a million pieces. From what I remember, the subcontractor that made the pork-chop fittings was blamed, but he was already out of business by 1947, so they didn't do nothin' to him. He should have gone straight to the slammer."

"What was your job at the airfield?" said Penn.

"I had a jeep with a large, spot lit sign on the back that said in black letters on a yellow board, *Follow Me.* When a plane come in, I drove down the grass by the runway until it stopped, pulled in front of it and the plane would taxi behind me to the hanger or the deck where they'd unload the passengers and the cargo. Wid'out me, the pilot had no idea where to go. I loved the job. It was a great job and I did good. Got the Good Conduct Medal and was promoted to Tech Sergeant before my stint was over. Got some good stuff from the pilots, too. Scotch, brandy, nylons. The girls were nuts about nylons."

"You knew the Admiral was aboard?" said Penn, "How did you know? Did you see the manifest?"

"No, I didn't see no manifest. The Admiral's staff car and driver was there. I knew the guy who drove for him. We had a smoke together and we talked," said Mike.

"Did you talk about the Admiral?" said Penn.

"Yeah, a little," said Mike. "I asked the driver if he was going back to HQ in Tokyo, and he said no, he was goin' to Yokohama. The Admiral was takin' a few days leave to see his Mama-san."

"His what?" said Penn.

"The old man had a Mama-san down in Yokohama," said Mike, "You know, a girlfriend. Everybody had a girlfriend in Japan, or a half-dozen of them. Even the brass. Hell, MacArthur and the Japanese big shots encouraged it. Christ, Japan in them days was like heaven for a GI."

"You didn't get her name, did you?" said Penn.

"Names weren't important and most of the girls never gave you their real names, anyway. She was probably some Aiko or Hana or Karin, even Polly or Betty or Suzy. I even met one that called herself Maggie. Nobody knew what anybody's real name was and nobody cared."

"You have any idea where he stayed?"

"Ah… Let me think, oh, *hell* yes. He stayed at the Hana Hotel. I remember we laughed about it. "'Hana'" means 'flower' in Japanese. It's a common girl's name over there. The biggest whore house in Tokyo, five stories of willing women, was the 'Flowers

Club'. The driver laughed and said, '*The Flowers* must have a branch in Yokohama exclusive for the brass. If it's got only one flower, they must have to take turns a lot.'"

"You're sure of that, the Hana Hotel?" said Penn.

"Sure as shootin,' Penn," said Mike, "Christ I can smell that Chesterfield cigarette, and see the guy's face who made that crack like it was yesterday. Makes me want to go back there again, but you never can. You only get it once then it's gone and it don't come back," said Mike, "the past lives inside you and hurts sometimes because you know you can't redo it, and there's no future, not at my age."

"Is there anything else you can tell me, Mike?"

"Yeah, the Admiral was a pretty square guy, down to earth. He'd talk to you man-to-man, if you know what I mean. One night we was out here by the runway. His plane was late, but he took it OK, not huffy and mad like some of these guys get. He offered me a smoke and we talked a little baseball and a lot about home. He was from Vermont and I come from Nort' Jersey, from Bayonne. It was nighttime and dark, and you couldn't see no rank. It was just like two GIs talkin. He never lit a nail hisself. I didn't think much about it, but later I found out he didn't smoke. He carried 'em, though, and would offer a guy a smoke and have a talk. Hell, I heard from the some of the guys that he talked with presidents in his day, and with MacArthur and everyone that mattered. And he talked to me, too, like we was friends. Hell of an Admiral. I felt real bad when I saw the crash and found out he was in the plane…." He paused and took a breath, "Tell people I said that, will ya'?"

"Mike, I'm writing a book about him and I've been taking notes as you've talked. You'll be in the book and the book will be bought by people and be in libraries until the world crumbles. People will know. I promise you that, people will know."

"Thanks, Penn. You know, yer a lot like him," said Mike.

"I could never measure up," said Penn, "but thanks for the compliment."

"Will you send me a copy of the book when you finish?" said Mike.

"I'll dedicate it to you," said Penn.

"I gotta' go," said Mike, beginning to get emotional.

"Thanks for everything," said Penn.

"Don't forget about the book."

"Never," said Penn, "Good bye."

"So long," said Mike with a sigh. He hung up, his eyes red and watering although he couldn't figure why, "Can't get it back," he muttered.

"What was that, Mike?" said Peter Hill from his office.

"Nuttin'"said Mike,"Nuttin'…." He turned and walked back to his bench, still wishing he could see the sunset as well as the sunrise.

Penn typed up his notes immediately so that he'd be sure to get in everything that was said. If there really was, or still is, a Hana Hotel in Yokohama he was going to find it. He checked his calendar. January was taken up with meetings and activities he couldn't avoid, but he could get some time in February. His course load was light this semester, just one internet-based class with maybe 15 students he could handle from anywhere. He could block out the whole month, maybe six weeks, and get the time in Japan he wanted and needed to research the Admiral, especially the later years, when he was with MacArthur's administration. One of the old Japanese Battleships, the *Mikasa*, was extensively refurbished by the Japanese government and put on display as a floating museum at Yokosuka. The *Mikasa* was Admiral Togo's flag ship during the Russo-Japanese war, and in 1904 then Lt. Commander Pennington walked its decks and stood with its men during the Battle of Port Arthur. It was also the last battleship of its era still in existence. Penn wanted to get the feel of the ship, to stand where his Great-

Grandfather stood and to walk those decks himself.

Penn wanted a scholar, a real Japanese scholar, to look at the letters in Japanese he'd found in the attic trunk. Those letters might fill in the blanks, tie in the events and resolve some of the mysteries surrounding the trip made by the Admiral's wife, the law firm of Marbright and Fuller, and what Mike Costello just revealed about the Admiral's life in Yokohama after the war. Penn also felt protective of the information they might contain. He wanted to control the content of the letters, release what was necessary to the scholarship supporting his work, and keep private what should be kept private. If the translations were done in Japan by a Japanese scholar working privately for him, the quality of the work would be assured and he would feel more secure in trusting the discretion of the translator. Besides, in the States even if the translator were a serious scholar, he or she would want to publish the uncensored results of the work, and Penn would never agree to that.

There was another issue as well, the loose way colleges and universities in the states were managed, a graduate student might get access to the letters and do anything with them. The last thing Penn wanted was to have the memory of his Great Grandfather made the brunt of someone's coarse humor or to have excerpts from letters which were never intended to be shared posted on some internet site or in *Wikipedia*.

Meanwhile, in Japan, Yoshiko Fujiyama continued her daily trip to the cemetery to honor her grandmother. She would do this for 100 days then return to the States to rejoin the National Lyric Opera. Returning to the States would be no problem. She was an American citizen, actually a dual citizen of both the United States and Japan, and had been for three years. During the day she practiced the roles of both Mimi and Musette, listened to various recordings of *La Bohème*, studied the interpretations of singers and tried to find the spirit, the subtext of the opera, to bring into herself the soul of these people, their goodness, their hopes, their frailties, and their suffering. She once played the opera to her grandmother, explained it to her and sang excerpts from it. Grandmother Keiko loved the story and said it was beautiful for it was universal, a story that could have occurred in Japan or China, the States or Europe – anywhere people loved and struggled and suffered. Yoshiko always meant to tell her the story of *Butterfy*, too, but never did, and the thought of what her grandmother missed made her sad.

****

Chapter Twenty – Christmas in Vermont

Penn couldn't avoid Christmas in Vermont. He actually looked forward to seeing his mother, but his step-father and step-brother were always distant, always a little confused about Penn's life and rank.

Roger, Penn's step-father, knew finance and banking, or thought he did. At Yale his major was liberal studies in preparation for law school, but he found the *Law School Admission Test* to be too daunting and never applied to any law school. It didn't matter. His main occupation was managing his own trust fund, money he inherited that was earned by some ancestor in schemes that would be considered villainous today, although were probably cruder but no worse than the banking machinations that collapsed the market in 2008. He had a "job" with a company that invested money in huge mixed portfolios for several different mutual funds. His job consisted mostly of taking people to dinner or golfing -- not mutually exclusive events – drinking cocktails, being hearty and optimistic, letting people know he was "Skull and Bones" at Yale, making them feel good and listening to their dreams and gripes. He went to no office and did most of his work on the golf course, at tennis, at restaurants or even at Polo matches. They paid him $350,000.00 per year and allowed a generous expense account, mostly because he was closely related to three board members. He considered all this remuneration little more than a stipend -- After all, a man of his quality was worth much, much more -- and he thought his work tantamount to an act to of charity.

Penn's step-brother, Harald, was eight years Penn's junior. Harald idolized Penn but barely understood him. Penn, to Harald, was an heroic figure at the vanguard of Democracy and Harald was both fascinated and frightened by Penn's uniform, his Annapolis education and all he'd done. Harald thought about enrolling in Air Force ROTC when he was at Yale, but never did. He admired the military but didn't want to be part of it. He was also in danger of flunking out at Yale and wanted to put more time into his studies. He managed to pass his courses, however, earn a respectable 2.1 grade point average, and graduate, just as his father had. He was even admitted to Skull and Bones; they had to admit Harald since his grandfather's will left four hundred thousand dollars to the fraternity with the condition that his descendants would always have a place there.

Harald currently worked with his father, learning the ropes, so to speak, and earning a stipend of $140,000.00 per annum, with bonuses and an expense account. He would come into his own trust fund in a year, so he was content with his life and his prospects. Nevertheless, Penn was *the man* to him and he was always trying to impress Penn in one way or another, to show his camaraderie with his military step-brother and express his political views as a testament to his support for all things Penn did.

For Penn, Harald was a bore and annoyance. Harald's insecurity and attempts at conviviality put him on edge, and the fellow's incessant chatter about politics soured any attempt at conversation. Penn hoped his grand Aunts would come to dinner early and stay late. They intimidated Harald and he usually fled somewhere when they were around.

Penn drove to Vermont on Christmas day, taking care to rest his back along the way, with the intention of leaving on December 26. That meant two days away from work, but twenty-four hours in the corral with his family. He got there at 4:00 PM to find the living room empty of people save for his mother, Julie, who was gracious as always.

He was in civilian clothes and he looked fine. Julie hugged him and kissed his cheek, then stood back at arms' length, her hands on his shoulders and looked at him.

"You look great, Penn. Academy life seems to agree with you," she said.

"I didn't think I'd like it, but I do. I like teaching and writing, and I like immersing myself in research and projects. It's good work and if I do it well, it goes far beyond me because every midshipman I teach is affected, and eventually the whole Navy will be."

"Go, get some eggnog. We bought a whole gallon of Dick Master's special blend. It's virgin, but you can add your own rum if you'd like," she said, pointing to a sideboard in the dining room.

"Where is everyone?" The parlor-living room-dining room, with its large heavily-decorated Christmas tree was void of everyone save his mother.

"Downstairs. We had the basement remodeled again and Roger had them install a pin-ball machine, a candy machine, a pool table and a table-top shuffle board. He, Harald and Harald's girlfriend are down there now paying something, if you want to join them."

"Harald has a girlfriend?" said Penn. This was welcome news.

"Elspeth Coming," said Julie, "a very nice girl he met at a young Republicans' rally."

His little step-brother had found a soul-mate. Perhaps they'd just bill and coo the evening away and he'd be spared all the political chatter.

"I think I'd like to put my suitcase away and wash up a little," said Penn taking a cup of the virgin eggnog. He might start adding rum later if the evening turned out to be as dreary as he anticipated.

"Martin can do that for you," she said. Martin was her butler and he sometimes cooked as well. Today, however, she had Miriam in the kitchen. Miriam was a good cook who loved to prepare feasts. A Christmas dinner with turkey, ham and all the dressings was one of her specialties.

"That's OK, mom," said Penn, "I can do it myself."

Penn wasn't raised in this house. The year after Penn graduated from the Academy Roger sold his old home when he inherited his current house with its two acres of partially forested land from an uncle. *Its amazing*, Penn thought, *how good things come to those who neither need nor deserve them.* It was a fine old house, done in imitation of Wright's Prairie Style. Even the lamps and doorknobs were ersatz Prairie. The bedrooms, however, were more comfortable than anything Wright ever imagined, every one with its own en suite and its own co-joined parlor.

Cocktails were on at 5:30 and dinner was set for 6:30. Penn unpacked, took a long, hot shower to relax his back and shoulder, and checked his e-mails and phone messages. There was nothing of significance, not on Christmas Day. He laid down and rested for a half hour then girded himself for the confrontation with family. He already heard the talk and laughter building. Familial bliss was at hand. The living room was filling up. Penn went downstairs.

"Penn!" bellowed his step-father, extending his hand, "I hear congratulations are in order!"

Penn took the man's hand, tried not to squeeze it so heartily he hurt him, but heartily enough to seem enthusiastic.

"Thank you, Roger." said Penn. He was about to say something appropriate, like Merry Christmas or How's your Trust doing?, but Harald interfered.

"Congratulations, Penn," said Harald also thrusting out his hand. Shaking hands with Harald was a new experience. Penn and Harald never shook hands in the past.

"You're what now," said Roger," A Captain?"

"I'm now a full Commander," said Penn.

"Aren't Captains commanders?" said Roger. Harald looked puzzled as well.

"Some are and some aren't," said Penn, "Commander is just the title of the rank I hold. It sets my pay grade. A vessel may be under the command of a Captain, which is a higher rank. Some vessels, smaller ones, are under the command of lower ranking officers, Commanders, Lieutenant Commanders, Lieutenants."

"What were you before?" said Roger looking puzzled.

"Lieutenant Commander," said Penn.

"Well, congrats to you anyway, Penn. We're all very proud of you." Harald stood behind his father, nodding enthusiastically.

After a short pause, Harald stepped back and put his arm around Elspeth. "I want to introduce you to someone very special, Penn," said Harald, "Penn Fuller meet Elspeth Comming."

Elspeth was five foot six, quite a bit shorter than Harald, who was a lanky six feet. She was lithe and wore heels, so she and Harald seemed a good match. She was pretty in the way debutants are pretty, nervously pretty, insecurely pretty, as if maintaining her looks took tremendous care and a concerted act of will, as if any diversion from that concentration would cause the whole image to collapse. Elspeth smiled. She had one of those smiles that didn't go to the corners of her mouth. When she smiled and laughed, the center of her mouth opened, revealing her gorgeous and well-maintained incisors and wrinkling her nose, but the effect was such that it was hard to tell if she was smiling or smelling something objectionable or both.

Elspeth smiled with an expression that made Penn think she objected to his after shave and presented her hand, too. "I'm always happy to meet one of our fighting men," she said.

Elspeth's one great asset was her large, dark eyes. Penn looked deeply into them, took her hand in both of his and said "You have no idea how comforting your support is to a person in uniform."

Her grin, such as it was, widened, her nose wrinkled even more, and she blushed. The moment was precious and Penn was mesmerizing, at least to Elspeth.

"Penn, leave that girl alone!" The spell was broken. Grand Aunt Harriet was making a grand entrance, "Hello! hello! everyone, Merry Christmas!.

Penn left Elspeth suspended in a trance of sorts, and hugged his

Aunt. "Where's Elizabeth?" he said.

"She's a little under the weather," said Harriet, "Or maybe she's dying in agony. Who knows at our age? But don't let that spoil the fun." She grinned malevolently at Harald and turned to Roger.

"Roger! You get younger and better-looking every time I see you," she said, "What's that on your trousers?"

Roger looked down, "Oh, they're my Christmas pants," he said. He was wearing blue corduroy pants with little holly sprigs embroidered on them.

"I guess men wear that kind of thing today. The embroidery must keep some poor family in Bangladesh or Peru or New Jersey employed. It's a boon to mankind."

"You know," said Roger seriously, "I never thought about it that way, but you may be right."

"Maybe everybody should wear 'em" she said, "How about it, Penn. Maybe you could talk to the Navy...." She didn't finish.

Turning to Elspeth, Harriet squinted her eyes, stared at her and said, "I don't think we've met."

Harald screwed his courage to the sticking-place and stepped up to introduce Elspeth. "Grand Aunt Harriet, this is Elspeth Coming. Elspeth, this my Grand Aunt Harriet."

Harriet was about to make an orgasm joke at the expense of poor Elspeth but her nature's better angel intervened and she said, instead, "Very pleased to meet you, Elspeth. I've met you coming, let's hope I never see you going. You're a fine match for our Harald," meaning you're a good mate for the insipid little prick and you'll make him proud and happy

Harald fairly beamed as Elspeth and Harriet shook hands. Encouraged by Harriet's new kindness toward him, he started to say "Elspeth and I met at a..." but Harriet had already gone and was talking with Julie.

The chimes were heard and dinner was served. The Turkey was already carved, the ham sliced and the table was filled family-style with plates of beans and cranberry sauce, gravies for both the turkey and the ham, a small mountain of hot rolls, butter balls in a large pile, leafy salad, broiled sweet potato casserole, a soufflé, a quiche, pitchers of water and tea, and four bottles of wine. Everyone had a full goblet of water and a large glass of a very nice red wine to begin.

Roger muttered a toast of some sort, but there was no grace said. This was not a religious family. Harald squeezed Elspeth's hand, Harriet looked from one face to another, an unreadable smile on her face, and Penn pretended to be happy and interested. He was counting the hours until his escape.

They passed dishes and bowls around the table, "ooed" and "ahhhed" filled up and ate. The dinner was superb. Miriam had outdone herself, or so they kept saying. Actually, she did what she always did, but she did it well and that was more than good enough.

There was local chatter about Vermont and the town, but Harriet concentrated on the food as did Penn and they let it go by without joining in.

It took a while, but when they'd finally finished the main course, the table was cleared and set for dessert. They had a choice between three different home-baked pies, two cakes and several flavors of ice cream. Harald, filled with food and moral strength, took two different kinds of pie, plopped French-vanilla ice cream on them, and began the after-dinner conversation.

"Have I told you how we met, Penn? Elspeth and I? You'd be interested in this, too Aunt Harriet."

Harriet squinted at him but not in an entirely unfriendly way. "I'd be fascinated," said Harriet in a tone that was either malevolent or sarcastic depending on how you interpreted it. It was the very same thing she'd said when she was 14 to a local boy who offered to show her a two headed calf in his barn. No calf, but he tried to show her a one-eyed snake. She learned her lesson and never followed a boy or man to see a two-headed calf again. Now, however, she was doing it once more but on firmer ground, sure Harald's revelations about the discovery of his inamorata would be the real thing and just as startling as any two-headed calf or snake, for that matter.

"I was at the young Republicans rally last October, over in Montpellier," he said, "and we got into a really spirited discussion of the Tea Party and what it means, and then that's when I heard this beautiful young woman stand up and say, 'I'll tell you what the Tea Party means, it means we're going back to our American roots, that's what it means; it means we harking back to the days of Paul Revere and George Washington and the founding fathers.' Well, people just cheered, and I knew I had to get to know this woman, and here she is."

"Young Republicans," said Harriet, "Didn't know there were any. And as for the Tea Party, all the Teabaggers I see on TV are fat, old and stupid. But that's just TV. I'm sure they're charming in real life."

"Well," said Harald, I wouldn't say…

"I'm not a partisan, person, understand," said Harriet, "The Liberals all seem to have bad teeth and a maudlin sense of indiscriminate pity for people who don't deserve it, a self-righteousness they solemnly spread on everything they preach like rancid butter on moldy bread, and what's worse, a stunted sense of humor."

"The Liberals are the problem, as I see it," said Elspeth, finding her voice, "They're eroding the moral fiber of America."

"Couldn't be better said," said Harald.

"Oh, hell, you're telling me that conservatives like DeLay, Gingrich and that idiot Sanford who was just elected to congress are moral paragons? Politics and morality as concepts are about as convivial as turds and punch bowls. Here's the issue. Liberals try to do things they think are good, some of which are and some of which are just vote-pandering, half-assed money-wasting nonsense, and conservatives try to stop them mostly to satisfy their big donors who come from the high income brackets. Liberals are half-assed but conservatives are vapid, heartless and venal. Conservatives *need* Liberals to survive. Without Liberals they'd have no one to despise and no platform."

"But there's a great intellectual tradition of conservative thought going back to John Adams. Russell Kirk, Barry Goldwater, William Buckley, Newt Gingrich, Ann Coulter, many others contributed to the development of conservative philosophy." Said Elspeth, not without conviction.

"Don't confuse philosophers with propagandists. Every bastard who wants to rule your life, lift your wallet and take your property develops a philosophy that's really just a sink of propaganda. The more philosophical, the greater the crook. Marx and Lenin wrote millions of words. The Nazis only lasted 12 years but Hitler, Rosenberg, Goebbels and Christ knows how many others dumped millions of words and scores of books into the crap pit of Nazi thought. Hell, Goebbels was a Doctor of Philosophy – got it from Heidelberg University, too, not the internet. The more they write, the worse they are. I don't trust philosophers in politics. They wind up like Robespierre, chopping off heads to purify the country."

The table grew quiet.

Harriet looked around. "I always liked *The Student Prince*, though. A shame Heidelberg also produced Goebbels...Anyone know the Drinking Song? Mario Lanza sang it and all the tenor roles in the movie, although some Brit actor played the part and lip-synced through the songs. I knew a fella who looked like Lanza. Worked at the butcher shop in Stowe, but he was German, not Italian." she paused for a few seconds.

"Well, anyway" she said, "I almost married a congressman, you know."

Penn looked up, amused. "When was that Auntie?"

Harriet smiled, "It was 1944, before the D-Day invasion. I was seeing Peyton Selby then."

"Did he run for Congress?" said Harald.

"No. Peyton was too sane for that. It was his boss at the insurance company. Peyton introduced me to his boss, a Yankee named James Elijah Harrison, both President and Board Chairman of the Vermont Peoples Assurance company. Peyton and I went to the movies together to see "Misses Miniver" and we ran into the man at the movie theater. He was there with his estranged wife, Thelma. They divorced back in 1938, but he still accompanied her to the theater because she loved the movies but was afraid to go by herself."

Harriet took a swallow of wine then continued, "She left him, by the way; he didn't leave her. She ran off with a Methodist Minister who abandoned his wife and two children for her. Later the defrocked preacher went to Federal prison for counterfeiting quarters by pouring melted lead into a potato mold. Works pretty well until the potato cooks. Considering how far from grace the man fell it sure does show the thin line between righteousness and perdition. No one is immune from the devil's snares. Anyway, we met Jim Harrison, and he met me and he insisted on taking us to dinner after the show, only he really just wanted to be with me. He slipped a note into my purse, by that I mean my pocket book." She winked. "Said to meet him at the restaurant the next evening. I liked him, so I did meet him."

"Was he a Republican or a Democrat?" said Harald.

"I'm getting to that," said Harriet, "I saw him the next evening, and again and again. Harrison told his former wife he wasn't going to the movies with her anymore and started going with me. I fell for Jim. He was older but he was everything you'd want in a man –

handsome, intelligent, sensitive, kind, strong – everything. He even had money, not a lot but enough to be comfortable. When he decided to run for Congress, however, politics seemed to take over his soul. He couldn't decide whether he was a Republican or a Democrat. He hated the Democrats because he thought they were what today you'd call racist, and a lot were. He hated the Republicans because he thought they pandered to the wealthy without regard to the welfare of anyone else. Finally, he decided to make the best parts of both parties his political agenda and called himself a Democratic Republican, a Republican who nevertheless believed in Social Security and a Democrat who was all for civil rights and for getting rid of all forms of racial and religious discrimination."

"What happened to him?" said Elspeth.

"He confused people. Democrats wanted to hear New Deal but segregation forever, and Republicans wanted to hear to hell with the New Deal and let's get rid of Jim Crow. No one wanted him. He got almost no votes and lost to a mouth-breathing moron from somewhere in the north of the state. The disappointment was too much for him. He took to drink, ruined his liver and died on the barroom floor in 1949. I was no longer with him. I'd met Marion, who was to be my husband, and fallen in love. Thelma was OK, however. Her beau was released from prison when he volunteered to join the Army, came back from the war, and they opened a tobacco shop down in Bridgeport. His grandson is now a Congressman."

"Which one?" said Elspeth.

"Oh, I can't say. That would be giving away too much. But I'll give you a hint. He has a pointy head, and he plays the piano, and he's not from Vermont."

Pen looked down and tried not to laugh. Harald and Elspeth would probably spend half the night going through congressmen's web sites trying to find the one with the pointy head who plays piano.

****

Chapter Twenty-One – Sparing the Emperor

Penn Fuller awoke to his iPhone's jolly Marimba tone and checked the time. Six-thirty AM. The call was from Philip McGraw.

"Phil! Good morning. Is there a national emergency?" said Penn.

"No, old chap, but I do have some news for you."

"I hope it's good, coming this early in the morning" said Penn.

"Not that early in Berkshire, England. I took the liberty of sending an e-mail to one of my colleagues at Sandhurst. He ran your Great Grandfather's name through the library database. Initially, he got nothing more than you already have, a few references from common American sources. He then turned the search over to one of the more clever lads who manages the database and he was able to do a deeper scan of the books they've digitized. He found one that mentions the Admiral in a way that you probably haven't seen."

Penn was fully awake and alert now, "What way is that?"

"The fellow came up with some references to the Admiral in the privately printed memoires of a Royal Marine Officer, Colonel Nigel Clark-Hewitt. The book is titled "Thirty-eight Years as a Royal Marine." Hewitt, a Lieutenant Colonel at the British Occupation Headquarters in Japan was assigned to the staff of General MacArthur as a liaison and general staff officer. MacArthur seems to have liked him and brought him into meetings and conferences that no one else outside MacArthur's staff attended. There was one meeting in particular that occurred early-on in the occupation, but you should read the account of that meeting for yourself. I'm going to send the book to your office via e-mail. Would you like it sent to your private e-mail as well?"

"Yes, please," said Penn.

"Done," said McGraw, "Oh, and we're still on for the 8th, are we not?"

"Yes," said Penn, "And now I owe you one."

"Whiskey at the club," said McGraw.

"If this book is contains something really exciting, I'll pay for dinner on the eighth."

Five minutes later, an e-mail arrived from McGraw with an attached PDF:

Penn:

> The book is attached. Go to pages 122-25. That's where you'll find your Great Grandfather.

Philip

From *Thirty-Eight Years as a Royal Marine:*

> Sunday, September 9, 1945 – The Embassy of the United States, Tokyo
>
> General MacArthur called a meeting for 9:00 AM. Neither the subject nor any agenda was given. The day before, the American flag was unfurled over the Embassy with some ceremony, but afterward work began immediately on planning and administering the occupation and rehabilitation of Japan. I worked until late in the evening on the Saturday 8th and was then ordered to attend the Sunday 9 AM meeting, which I did. When I entered the conference room, I found two officers waiting. I knew Colonel Clarkson of MacArthur's staff. He managed somehow always to appear crisp, neat and unwrinkled, and he greeted me warmly. Across the table was an officer of the Navy. He was in Khaki uniform but not wearing rank, and he appeared to be much older than the rest of MacArthur's staff, as old as MacArthur himself. I was later to discover he was older even than MacArthur. He was introduced

simply as Mr. John Pennington.

The room filled with officers and at precisely 9 AM General MacArthur arrived. He was in good spirits, ebullient, full of energy and optimism. Before he formally began he reached over to John Pennington (I was later to discover he was Vice Admiral Pennington), shook his hand warmly, patted his shoulder and greeted him as if he were an old friend.

"We meet in Japan once more," he said, "Great to have you on my staff, John."

MacArthur then turned to the rest of us and said, "When this fellow speaks, pay attention. He knows more about Japan than all of us put together."

The subject of the meeting was war crimes. We were sworn to secrecy and no notes were permitted to be taken. I have since been released from that oath, so I will briefly relate what I remember.

MacArthur specifically wanted to know the opinion of the staff regarding the initiation of indictments against Emperor Hirohito and the Imperial family. Brigadier General Adams spoke first, firmly declaring that the "snake had struck from the head" and the only way to kill it and remake Japan was to eradicate the whole Imperial clan. He asserted that everyone in the family was corrupt and was involved in Japanese war crimes. His allegations were not without justification. There was general agreement to this, although some of the staff wanted the indictments and punishment, which would probably include execution, be limited only to Hirohito and various selected princes. Throughout the discussion, Admiral Pennington remained silent.

He was quite alert and seemed to pay close attention to everyone's comments, but he said nothing.

After 40 minutes, MacArthur stopped all discussion. "I think I know where you stand on this issue, gentlemen," he said. "This conference is adjourned."

We all arose to leave, but MacArthur asked me and Admiral Pennington to join him in his office. We followed him. He bid us come in, closed the door, and sat behind his disk. I report the conversation to the best of my memory.

"Sit, gentlemen," he said, "John, I've asked Colonel Hewitt to join us because he is the British liaison, and I want the British to know my reasons, in a general way, for making whatever decision I make. Colonel Hewitt, you will agree not to relate any of this until I give my clearance?"

I agreed.

MacArthur turned to Admiral Pennington, "What do you think, John?"

"I think you have the opportunity to create of Japan one of the greatest and most powerful democracies in the world. I think as well if you punish in any way the Japanese royal family you will hurt that purpose, perhaps fatally, and incur the unremitting enmity and resentment of the Japanese people. We have destroyed their great cities, humiliated their armed forces and civil government, and compelled them to surrender unconditionally. It is time to forget the past, bring them hope, enlighten them and raise them up, to become the benefactors and creators of a great and just nation, an ally and force for good. Graciously pardon the royals, especially the Emperor, and you will strengthen and accelerate the remaking of Japan. Punish them and you will impede it."

"You don't think they deserve punishment?" said MacArthur.

"I believe in democracy and I don't think any man deserves to be born king, but I can accommodate myself to kings if that is what I have to deal with. I think the best choice, pragmatically, for the creation of a new, democratic Japan, and for the way we Allies will be perceived by the Japanese, by all other peoples, and in the telescope of history, would be to pardon them," the Admiral looked about the room, collecting his thoughts.

Pennington then continued, "There is one other factor to consider as well, the fate of China. As it stands, The Nationalists and Communists are struggling for control of China, and the Nationalists are not winning. Stalin is firmly behind the Communist leader, Mao Tse Tung, and if Mao prevails we may face a Communist block that commences at Singapore and ends in Berlin. Even if Chiang Kai-shek prevails, there's no guarantee Stalin won't embrace him. Chiang was trained in Moscow, his son resides in Russia and is reportedly engaged to a Russian woman. Chiang might well decide that China is better served by friendship with the Soviets than with Americans. We need to counter the Communists. To do that we need Japan to be our strongest ally in the East, a rock of democracy and a home for our Naval and military bases. Sparing the Emperor would serve that purpose"

"Well said, John," said MacArthur, "I agree whole-heartedly. I had misgivings either way and I wanted to assure my thinking on this issue had considered every factor. There were powerful arguments against clemency and for justice, but your eloquent expression of why I should pardon Hirohito and his family convinces me. My mind is made-up on this matter. The Emperor and his family will be pardoned. Not so with some of the generals and other officers who will face war crime tribunals."

"Yes, sir," said John.

MacArthur stood and presented his hand to the Admiral one more time, "Old friend, it's good to have the council of one who's been here and truly understands this place and these people. I think you can put your stars on now. I wanted you incognito because I didn't want to rattle those Colonels. They're good, intelligent men and I needed them to speak freely. If I can, I'll get you a fourth star."

The Admiral smiled and shook MacArthur's hand warmly. I thought they might embrace, but they didn't. Admiral Pennington's influence in this matter was very strong. Had he leaned toward punishment, I have no doubt MacArthur would have agreed with his staff and gone through with it. I am firmly convinced that the Emperor's life and the life of many members of his Royal family were entirely in Pennington's hands, and it was Pennington who saved him.

Penn whistled. McGraw had just earned himself a free dinner.

****

Chapter Twenty-Two – Annapolis, Bangkok, and Tokyo

The drive from Vermont to Annapolis, about 560 miles, took Penn almost 11 hours. He stopped to exercise, stretch his back and shoulder, and refresh himself several times along the way. Driving, especially driving alone without distractions, gave him time to think and plan. He'd been invited to lecture at an O'Hare Club meeting in January, and he was assembling the material in his mind, organizing information to set the pacing of the talk. He'd already selected the topic and a tentative title, *A Vermont Yankee on the Staff of Admiral Togo, 1904-5, Commander Pennington at the Russo-Japanese War*, but that might change by the time he finished collecting the presentation material. The drive was uneventful. The day after Christmas traffic was light, the weather was clear, and the further south he went, the better the weather became. There were no storms, although a gentle rain fell in Southern New Jersey, but that passed when he crossed into Delaware.

While Penn drove south, Kate Hobson went to her office in the nearly deserted CDC building where she worked and spent most of the afternoon completing an application for a position in the Office of Global Health (OGH). Marianna Littlebear brought the job to her attention. Kate told of her interest in international work, and Marianna, although reluctant to lose Kate, was generous and thoughtful. When she discovered that OGH was looking for someone, she got a lead on the job, saw the description and told Kate to apply for it before they advertised. If they liked her, she might transfer over to OGH in June when the position officially vacated. The job was at the CDC South Asia Regional Headquarters in Bangkok, and, although it wasn't a promotion it would promise extensive travel opportunities throughout Thailand, Laos, Vietnam and China, and even to Europe and Africa. The tour of duty would be five years and the work would be intense and fascinating.

Kate assembled her information and worked assiduously at compiling everything they wanted. She also composed the first draft of a required essay about why she wanted the job and what she thought she could accomplish working in Global Health. OGH was fussy and specific regarding the essay. It was limited to 1,000 words and had to be submitted double-spaced on plain bond paper with 1 inch margins and courier 12 type. No exhibits or attachments were permitted. She wondered if the reviewers would measure the margins with a ruler and reject the essay if it was off by a quarter of an inch.

She did all the work, but she was half-hearted and dreamy as she compiled the information and typed the words. The application looked perfect and the essay was nicely composed, but her feelings regarding the job were divided. She still hoped that something would happen between Penn and herself, although even there her feelings were mixed, confused, contradictory. She liked him very much. She could love him; she knew that. But he was too cool, it seemed, almost intransigent. She knew he liked her. He was polite and attentive and even affectionate in a way, yet there was some connection missing, something that missed the mark. Perhaps he was still affected by his experiences in Iraq, more affected than even he realized, or perhaps he just couldn't love her, could never love her, yet liked her and wanted to spend some time with her, innocent time, time that would not ensnare them in a relationship that was emotional, restrictive, cloying, and ultimately hurtful, involved and messy.

In a way, Kate wished she'd never met Penn. Going to the other side of the earth for five years would cure her of him, remove him, make him vanish, or so she hoped. But did she really want to go away and have that happen? She sighed. Life was simpler in September, before the opera, before she saw him.

In Yokohama on the day after Christmas the air was brisk, but the sun shone brightly, the sky was blue with scattered white clouds, and a light breeze blew in from the sea. Yoshiko Fujiyama lit two Joss sticks and knelt before the black marble monument to her Grandmother Keiko-Ayumi. She took the sticks in her folded hands, waved them up and down, pressed them to her forehead, bowed and prayed the Lord's Prayer, then sang some bars of Caccini's *Ave Maria* softly to herself. She put the Joss sticks in a brass holder and sat back, turned on her iPad and read from her Grandmother's Book. She read a section of it every day, repeating them frequently, trying to hear her grandmother's voice as she read it, imagining her warmth, the feeling of her nearby, the gentleness of her touch, the kindness of her face.

****

Chapter Twenty-Three – At Dinner in Crabtown

January 8 began in Annapolis with threatening skies, a drop in temperature and light snow flurries, but by two PM the atmosphere cleared, the clouds moved on and the sun reappeared. The temperature rose to well above freezing and the afternoon was very comfortable with Spring-like temperatures and clear skies. The change from dark and lowering skies to sunshine and the relative warmth of temperature well above freezing lifted everyone's mood with the false promise of an early spring and put a gloss of unwarranted optimism on the day.

At the Double-Tree Kate Hobson and Marianna Littlebear each prepared for dinner in her own way. Kate brought two dresses with her. They'd been hanging in the closet now for 24 hours and the wrinkles had virtually vanished. She showered, prepped her face a little – she used very little makeup -- experimented with various lipsticks and finally chose the dress, a blue one he hadn't seen before, sleek, which displayed her figure well and felt comfortable.

Marianna, who hadn't thought much about the dinner "date" – if you want to call it that – flopped on her bed, read and answered e-mails, sipped diet coke, and waited until 45 minutes before they were to be at the restaurant, a five-minute walk from the hotel. She hung her wool suit in the bathroom while she showered, washed everything from her hair to her toes, frantically used the blow-drier until her hair, which was cut short, what used to be called a "pixie-cut," felt reasonably dry, threw on a little makeup and her suit, then looked at herself without pleasure. She *always* brought the wrong clothes. She completed the ablutions and was garbed and painted for dinner with two minutes to spare. Kate was waiting for her in the lobby.

"What do you know about this person Penn is bringing to dinner?" said Marianna trying to sound nonchalant while sounding anything but nonchalant.

"He's a colleague and friend of Penn's," said Kate, "and he teaches at the Academy,"

"Is he some sort of Navy officer?" Marianna was growing more nervous as they approached Emile's.

"Penn told me he was retired from the Royal Army," said Kate, "He's English."

"Is he old?"

"No," said Kate, "At least I don't think so. Some men retire from the military while still in their forties."

"That young?"

"I didn't ask his age," said Kate, "I have Penn's cell number if you want me to call him and ask." She was teasing.

"No, no," said Marianna, "Don't do that. I just thought… well. You know if our ages were too far apart…"

"Penn's too clever for that, Marianna. I think you'll probably like whoever he brings."

"Do you think this suit's a little…"

"You look great, Marianna, professional but attractive. I should own a suit like yours."

The clip-clop of their heels echoed down the street as they walked toward the restaurant. "God! Do you hear all the noise my heels are making on this sidewalk? I sound like a dray horse pulling a wagon," said Marianna.

"Both of us are making noise. Don't worry, you won't be walking down the pavement in the restaurant…. Look, there it is." Emil's lay just ahead.

Marianna felt herself belch nervously, and she took her purse in both her hands to keep them from shaking. *This is ridiculous*, she thought, *I'm an epidemiologist. I have 78 peer-reviewed articles to my credit and one published book. I've testified before Congress, and I've given presentations to professional meetings and seminars with hundreds of attendees. Why the hell am I nervous about meeting some obscure lecturer at the Naval Academy? Why? Just because I haven't had a date for 2 years? It makes no sense.* She calmed herself, mostly through sheer will power. Her hands stopped shaking and the nervous twitter left her voice. She entered the restaurant as a gladiator might have entered the coliseum, her trepidation smothered under the mound of superficial courage and confidence she displayed for the audience.

Penn Fuller and Philip McGraw, both in tweed, could have been brothers or, better, a youngish uncle with his grown nephew. Penn's suit was grayish while McGraw's was pure Harris tweed, the colors of heather and loam. McGraw had a vest as well, which added a touch of maturity and elegance. Both wore brilliant white shirts and rep ties tied four-in-hand. Kate and Marianna wouldn't know but Penn's tie, a Christmas gift from Aunt Harriet, bore the blue and gold of the U.S. Navy. McGraw's had the stripes and colors of the Royal Military Academy, Sandhurst, although he could have worn the colors of the Royal Engineers Regiment as well. He was entitled to wear both.

The two men looked as if they'd just arrived from central casting, especially McGraw. He was Penn's height, but his build was fuller, not fat by any means, but his chest looked larger and shoulders broader. His soft, wavy brown hair was brushed neatly into place and he sported a small military mustache he could have borrowed from David Niven. Combine all this with a ruddy complexion, lively eyes and a ready smile, and the effect was unmistakably British military, polished and clever, but with warmth and humor as well.

Penn embraced Kate and kissed her on the cheek. He introduced McGraw and Kate Introduced Marianna to both of them. Marianna shook Penn's hand, but as McGraw took her hand, he said in the perfect round tones of an Oxonian professor, "Littlebear... is that an American Indian name?"

"Yes," she said, "My estranged husband's name. We divorced over 20 years ago. My parents emigrated from the Philippines but are ethnically Japanese." she replied, a bit nervously.

McGraw's grin widened and his eyes seemed to dance. "Did you say *Japanese*?"

"Yes…I understand you're British," she said, in her eagerness adding unnecessarily, "from the United Kingdom."

McGraw peered down at her, smiled and said in his silkiest tones, as he raised her hand to his lips, "Madam, I might very well be from the state of ecstasy, for in meeting you I am ecstatic." He kissed her hand holding it in both of his, then lowered it gently, never losing contact with her eyes, "Enchanté," he said, and then as if one were not enough, another "Enchanté!"

Kate looked at Penn, rolled her eyes slightly, grinned and looked down. McGraw was too much for her. Not so with Marianna, who kept hold of his hand. Cupid was at play that night. McGraw was enchanted while Marianna was mesmerized. If love can blossom in a moment, it did with them. McGraw led the way into the restaurant, arm in arm with Marianna. *This,* he thought, *will indeed be a night to remember.* Penn and Kate followed, amused by the ready intimacy of Philip McGraw and Marianna Littlebear. McGraw, now his arm about her, was talking softly into Marianna's ear, almost nibbling it, while she covered her mouth and tittered, obviously enjoying all his attention, all his charm and every remark he made.

Dinner conversation was lively and with no one driving home, wine flowed easily, every glass emptied, every drop drunk and then refilled. They consumed over two bottles, and ate perhaps the most perfect meal of Penn's life, shrimp cocktail and fried squid for appetizers, a crisp green salad in a marvelous, tangy balsamic vinaigrette dressing, filet mignon, crab-stuffed snapper, and lobster tail cooked in seasoned butter, all with buttered corn, small, purple potatoes and the house coleslaw. Fresh baked loaves of bread were delivered in an endless stream, and by the time the dessert tray came round, they were so sated they almost passed-up the German chocolate cake and the superb flan, but they somehow found room and ate both. There was whiskey, at least for the men, but the ladies insisted upon Grand Marnier. The coffee was rich and dark and fragrant, and that, too, was endless.

Penn and Philip told stories about far-off places, the military services, all the funny and dangerous and remarkable things that occur when you're serving in some hostile backwater or out at sea. Marianna had her own stories about virus hunting and epidemiological work and Philip talked of his career as a forensic historian and what that meant. The more he conversed with Marianna, the more they had in common. He, after all, was a scientist at heart with a taste for investigation and discovery who followed his own speculations and formed theories to fit the facts and data. She was similarly an epidemiological investigator. The constraints of her science were not unfamiliar to Philip in his work and his problems in performing investigations were similar to hers. They both relied on material evidence and, when possible, living testimony, all of which could be misleading or contradictory or mistaken. The more they talked, the more they seemed to grow together. Whatever magic blossomed when they met just grew stronger and more vivid as the evening wore on.

Time passed, the last coffee was finished, Penn rose from the table and quietly paid the bill, leaving a 20% tip, and the party rose to leave.

The weather was still clement, almost no breeze with a Spring-like temperature in the mid-40s. Philip helped Marianna with her coat, and to her delight invited her to take a walk along the waterfront, just a few blocks away. Marianna felt warm and safe and *everything* with Philip, feelings she never had with a man, not even with her husband so many years ago. Penn and Kate were asked to come along, too, but they demurred, allowing the two incipient lovers, Philip and Marianna, time to themselves. Of course, that meant Kate and Philip would have their own private time together. They walked the other way, towards the hotel, Kate's arm around Penn's.

Neither Kate nor Penn spoke at first, both afraid of the beast that lingered between them. Penn liked Kate's company very much, but he was sure now he wanted to take things no further. Kate also felt it. She saw the way that Philip and Marianna had simply connected, the irresistible attraction and immediate pleasure in each other's company, and she envied them. With Penn, for her it was almost that way but something cooled and instead of love flourishing, there was something calmer, less intense, easier, kinder in a way.

"We'll never be like those two, will we?" she said, both saddened and relieved by having said it.

"If there such a thing as love at first sight, I think we've just seen it. Both of them careening into amorous bliss while saying 'hello' for the first time. It's never been like that for me," he said.

"Yes…" she sighed, sounding distant and resigned.

Conversation trailed off, but they continued to walk together.

"I may have a chance for an assignment to our regional Headquarters in Bangkok," said Kate.

"Really?" said Penn, "I've heard it's a fabulous place, at least for a sailor." He didn't explain what he meant by that. "When would you go?"

"Not until June at the earliest, if they accept me. There will probably be other applicants."

"How does Marianna feel about it?"

"She's a very kind, very generous person. She helped me find the job," said Kate.

"Is that what you want?" said Penn.

"Yes," she said, "In a way. I've always wanted an overseas assignment. If I get this one it would mean extensive travel throughout South Asia, everywhere from Malaya to China. It's the chance of a lifetime."

"I'd hate to see you go that far away, but as you say, it is the chance of a lifetime."

"I won't go if you want me to stay, Penn," she said, "If you ask me to stay."

"I know," said Penn, and then with as much kindness as possible, "I don't want you to go, but I won't ask you to stay. I'm sorry, Kate. You're perfect but I've got some demons to conquer and I need some solitude to conquer them."

"I could help," she said.

"And poison yourself with my problems," he said. "I need to be alone for a while. I don't know how long. Right now if I concentrate on one thing, bury myself in my work, I can lift the cloud and get through the day and the night. I don't know if I'll be able to that while being intensely involved with another…"

He paused and shook his head, "No, that's not right, either. I'm lying to you and you don't deserve a lie. I'm evading a murky truth I can't quite grasp. Let me tell you what I've avoided saying. There is something – I'm waiting for something or someone who will simply drive out all my fear and recrimination and emptiness and disgusting self-pity, overpower me and bulldoze it all away, someone who'll restore me to what I was before I lost those parts that kept me balanced and whole. It's as if I'm sitting in a bell jar waiting for someone to smash it open. . .Sometimes I'm seized with the cold fear that I'll be hopelessly waiting for that thing, that person for the rest of my life. How fair and kind and honorable would it be for me to lie to you and use you as a distraction while I looked for someone else? And you are so beautiful, so kind, so special that it is very, very tempting for me to do exactly that. I'm not trying to sweeten what I say. My feelings may be confused and unfathomable, but if there anything I know since I met you, you're exquisite, rare and precious. You should be with someone who can appreciate you, not someone like me who'll regularly be meandering off into a desert of pathetic, obsessive, self-indulgent introspection, a moody brooding bore who'd rather keep his nose in his books and avoid life than appreciate love, kindness and beauty."

She sighed. She envisioned this sort of thing when she lay at home thinking about him and in her imagination she practiced her anger and resentment at the rejection. She composed snappy retorts, smart put-downs. None of them came to her now. The practice helped her get through it, though; it blunted the pain, the disappointment, feelings strange to her that she never faced in her adult life. She was still angry but the rejection was no surprise.

"I understand, Penn," she said, saying the polite thing, hoping she really did understand, "or I want to understand." Mostly, Kate understood that Penn didn't want her. He'd spent the time with her and he seemed to like her, but there was something missing. She was hurt more deeply than she wanted to be hurt. She wanted to scream at him 'What the hell is the matter with you?' but she didn't. She kept a brave face.

He squeezed her hand and smiled. "I knew you'd understand," he said, not knowing if she understood. *How could she?* he thought, *What a stupid thing to say. I don't even understand myself.*

"You, sweet, sweet Kate, are incomparable." He meant what he said, but it still sounded flat, false, and empty.

"Now," she said, putting a bright face on it, "tell me how your book is going..." A cold rage contained itself in her for days afterward. It slowly faded, though, and within two weeks she was over it, perhaps not completely, but enough to stop thinking about him. She'd never forgive him, though.

****

Chapter Twenty-Four – A Presentation

The O'Hare Theater was two-thirds full that Thursday, January 17. Penn was surprised that so many had shown up for his lecture. There were a few Midshipmen, but most were Navy Association members, retired sailors or Navy veterans, or simply folks just attending the talk because it was free and open to the public. He'd titled the lecture "A Vermont Yankee on the Staff of Admiral Togo, 1902-1907, War, Baseball and Battleships."

Phil McGraw and his inamorata, Marianna LittleBear, were there, but Kate remained in Atlanta. Captain Southerland was in the audience as well. There was no introduction. Penn crossed the stage and mounted the podium at precisely seven PM. He was in uniform and polite applause greeted him.

He paused for a moment, waiting for quiet as the applause ended. His papers and notes were spread before him and he had access to a pointer. A power-point chart with the title of the lecture was projected on a large screen to his right. He'd kept the charts simple and used them mostly to project images that would help the audience visualize the events. An hour earlier he'd gone through all the apparatus with the audio-video technician, assured that everything worked and that he knew how to use the controls on the electronic podium, checked to make sure the entire slide deck was loaded and even tested the battery back-up. The acoustics in the hall weren't perfect, but the amplification and excellent speakers made up for the design of the space.

"Good evening, I'm Commander Pennington Fuller, associate professor of Naval History at the United States Naval Academy. Tonight's lecture is about a little-known, virtually unknown Naval officer, Vice Admiral John Pennington. Admiral Pennington's name doesn't appear in the history books – At least not yet. I'm hoping to remedy that omission. -- but he was, nevertheless, a pivotal figure in the evolution of the United States Navy as it emerged from the

19th Century to become, eventually, the most powerful Naval force ever mounted by any nation on earth. This lecture is confined to the Admiral's experiences in Japan just prior to the Russo-Japanese War, and is based largely, although not entirely, on a recently discovered cache of letters written home reflecting his private and professional view of events.

From 1902 through 1907 Lt. Commander John Pennington was stationed at Hiroshima Japan, an observer assigned to work with the Japanese Navy in virtually any capacity suitable to them. This wasn't his first experience in Japan. He spent over 4 years there during the 1890s, and was reassigned because of his knowledge of the Japanese language and culture and his interest in the development of their Navy. He was ordered to collect information on Japanese war ships and men, harbor and docking facilities, and look for opportunities for American trade, especially in ship building and port facilities. He'd served there during the Sino-Japanese war in the last decade of the 19th Century and witnessed the seminal Naval battle of that war at Wei-hai-wei from the deck of the *Fuji*, a British-built Japanese battleship.

As the Russians and the Japanese vied with each other for military dominance in East Asia, they built up their fleets and both nations prepared to seize ports or territory from the crumbling Machu Empire in China, and from weak and virtually powerless Korea. The U.S. Navy Department was interested in all that was developing in Northeast Asia and consequently returned their most experienced Japan hand, Commander Pennington, to stations in Hiroshima and Yokohama. Other officers, Commanders Wellington Broughm Montgomery and Westfield Temple Stanton, both classmates of Pennington's, were sent to observe with the Russians. Pennington did receive some letters and other communication from these observers via diplomatic means. It was slow and round-about but proved valuable in his later reconstruction of events for the Navy Department. As I refer to his private correspondence, you'll hear his two classmates referred-to as "Monty" and "West."

"From a letter of Pennington's to his wife, Catherine, September 3, 1903

My Dear Catherine:

I told you in one of my last letters that the United States Navy, while still present here in port at Nagasaki, Hiroshima and Yokohama, has lost some of its prestige and a great deal of its influence with the Japanese. The British, now allied with the Japanese (*Penn's comment: "Here Commander Pennington is referring to the Anglo-Japanese Alliance of 1902*) presumably against all other enemies (although how much the British would support the Japanese in an all-out war is questionable), are at the top of the heap among foreigners. I figured that would happen and for a while, at least, we'd be playing second fiddle to them. I wish we were playing second fiddle, at least the second fiddler gets to play now and then, and sometimes gets to play some very good music. If this were a band we'd be playing triangle or just polishing the tympani and mopping the floor.

The Brits are everywhere. The Japanese are sailing in British ships, and – please don't repeat this – British intelligence has been working closely with the Japanese, not only supplying information but training them in garnering data. Rumor has it that Japan planted Chinese-speaking Japanese and Chinese spies under hire all over Manchuria, especially in Port Arthur, right under Russian noses, the Russians seemingly unable to tell one East Asian from another. Spies are even employed on Russian ships and in the Officers' mess. I suppose a few of those spies can speak Russian as well as Chinese. Russian radio security is almost non-existent and the British in India and the Malay are said to be listening in and intercepting messages from the Russian military command. All this intelligence serves the Japanese well. They know Russian moves inland even before the Russians in port know them and they can guess Russian intentions and strategies.

In terms of commerce, there's nothing much we can offer the Japanese that they'll buy. We *could* offer them a great deal, but they'll only look at the British catalog for now. My progress with the Japanese Imperial Navy (JIN) has been slow. I've been waiting for months to meet with Admiral Togo and although meetings are politely promised, I've yet to get an invitation to his base and HQ at Sasebo, which is about 200 miles south of Hiroshima, my home port. I think that's about to change, however, at least I hope so."

Penn clicked on the computer's mouse and a new image appeared on the screen to his right, a map displaying Japan, Korea, the Liao-Tung peninsula just to the west (to the left on the map), and eastern portions of Manchuria and China.

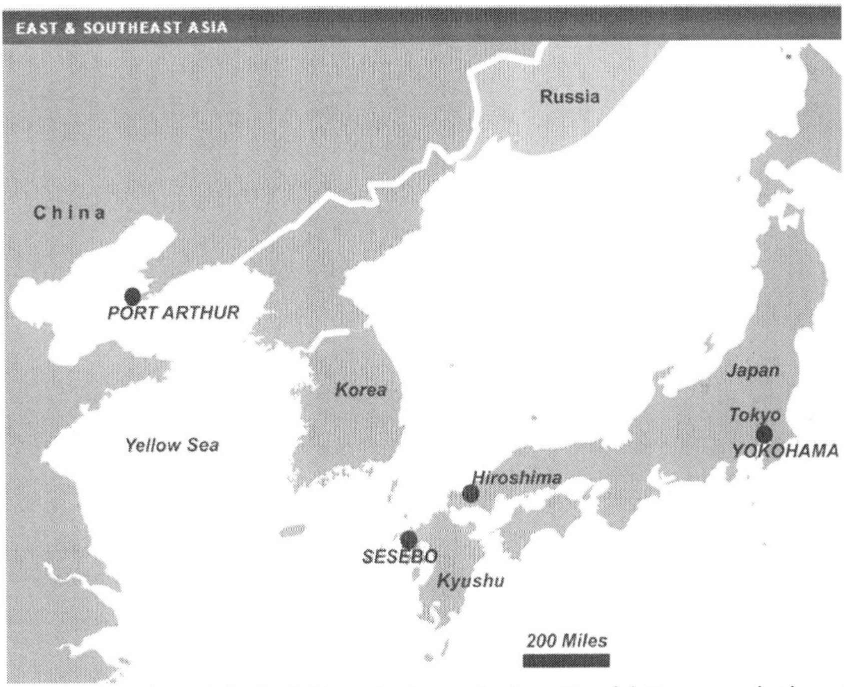

"Sasebo, Admiral Togo's base, is here" said Penn, pointing to a spot on the eastern tip of Kyushu, the large island at the southeastern end of the Japan archipelago. "Hiroshima is here," he said pointing to a spot about 200 miles north of Sasebo on Nippon, the largest Japanese island. "The major American base is here," he said pointing to a spot 700 miles north and east of Hiroshima, "at Yokohama, not far from Tokyo or from Yokusuka, a large Japanese naval installation." As he pointed the names appeared on the map.

The map dissolved and the image of a stern, bearded, short-haired, broad- shouldered Japanese Naval officer in full dress uniform, virtually covered with medals and decorations appeared. "This," said Penn, "is Admiral Togo. The image was made for the visit of Theodore Roosevelt's *Great White Fleet* in 1907, "

Admiral Togo of the Japanese Imperial Navy

The Admiral dissolved and the map reappeared.

"Now that you have your bearings, we'll leave the map in place and return to Admiral Togo in a few moments."

"Baseball is critical to the rest of the story, and some understanding of baseball and the importance of baseball to the Japanese is necessary at this point.

Although the term "baseball" can be found in British literature as far back as 1744, the game as it evolved in the United States wasn't known until the late 1830s, and the rules weren't codified until Alexander Cartwright published the rules of baseball for the NY Knickerbockers in 1844. There is considerable controversy as to who actually invented the game, but, since Congress recognized Cartwright as the inventor of baseball, I think it's safe to say that he did, at least officially.

Baseball was introduced to Japan just 28 years after the *Knickerbocker Rules* were published, so it's almost as old a sport in Japan as in the United States. Horace Wilson, an American teacher at the Kaisei School in Tokyo, taught his students to play baseball in 1872. Japan's first baseball team, the Shimbashi Athletic Club, was established in 1878. By 1903, baseball was as much a national sport in Japan as in the United States, widely played on amateur and professional levels, and played well. Japanese baseball players came at the game like Samurai preparing for battle. They stayed in superb shape by pursuing an exercise regime that would seem murderous to anyone else, and were fast, courageous and well-coordinated as individuals and as teams."

"Now let's continue with Commander Pennington's following letter sent 10 days later."

Letter to Catherine Pennington, Sunday, September 13, 1903, from Yokohama, Japan.

My Dear Catherine:

In my last letter I mentioned the difficulty I've faced in getting invited to Sasebo to meet with Admiral Togo. Well, the ice was finally broken! I not only met the man, I played baseball for him.

There's an American Athletic Club in Yokohama with its own baseball team. The club is almost all sailors and closed to Japanese, of course. I'm not a member; I never have been. For one thing I live in Hiroshima, several hundred miles away, and even if I lived in Yokohama I think I'd avoid those fellows. My job is to work with the Japanese, to try to learn as much as I can about them. The Yokohama boys are generally good sailors, but their superior attitudes toward the Japanese are not helpful to me. I've tried not to associate myself with them and I've been pretty successful in doing that, but nevertheless the Japanese, who are too reserved and polite to express much about it, naturally resent the way those sailors talk and act and some of that resentment rubs off on the way the Japanese view me.

Last week we had a breakthrough. Doug MacArthur, an Army Engineer Lieutenant on detail from the 3rd Engineer Battalion, arrived in Yokohama to look at the port facilities and to see the Yokusuka shipyards. Doug's father is Lieutenant General Arthur MacArthur, a soldier with the grandiose title "Commander of the Department of the Pacific." Doug is on his way to a permanent station in the Philippines, but in a year or two he's to be assigned as his father's aide-de-camp. The Army, to put it succinctly, is different from the Navy. I had to meet with him, but to be honest I had little confidence this general's son who had just graduated from West Point in June had the experience or competence to review the port facilities at Yokohama or anywhere else.

I was wrong. Doug knew ports well at least academically, had studied them, and had a good idea of what was right and wrong with the French design used by the Japanese. I liked him. After a day of touring the facilities, talking with Japanese engineers and generally enjoying the weather, we spied a Japanese baseball game in progress and stopped to watch. Doug played the game at West Point and was an aficionado of the sport. The Japanese impressed him and we lingered for almost an hour until the game ended. Afterward, we got to meet and talk with the Team Captain and some of the players. They were lean fellows, all of them, muscular, wiry and tough. The Team Captain said they were going to play the Americans from the Yokohama Athletic Club the following day and were practicing to hone their skills.

We repaired to the Yokohama Officer's Club for a drink and early dinner, where we met a few of the American ball players. Their arrogance and hostility towards the Japanese were evident and the comments they made about the Army aren't suitable for a woman's ears. For a moment I thought Doug was going to punch one of them in the nose. He contained himself, however. He had a different idea. He pulled me aside and said, "Let's go back and see if that ball club is still practicing." "Why?" I asked. "I may want to give them a little help tomorrow," he said.

We found the Japanese team and got them to throw us a few balls. I think the novelty of pitching to an American made them curious and they invited us right in. I got to bat first. I'm not much of a player and I think the pitcher went easy on me. The ball came at me fast but straight, I connected with it, drove it just short of the fielders and got a base hit. Then Doug stepped up. The pitcher didn't hold back this time. There was a fast pitch, Doug swung and missed. The pitcher figured he had Doug's number and did it again. But Doug had the pitcher's number. He hit the ball hard, in a high arc that took it right out of the park and across the railroad tracks on the far side. Cheers and laughter. They'd never seen anything like it.

That's when Doug asked me to offer his services for the game the following afternoon, which I did.

The Japanese Captain was surprised. "Why did the American want to play for the Japanese?" "Well, he's Army and they're Navy. They don't want him on their team." The Captain then asked me "What about you?" I nodded, and said "I can play for you, too. I'm not a member of that club." We played ball and practiced with the Japanese team that evening until it got too dark to continue. Baseball is baseball. There was no language barrier and we all got along well.

The following afternoon, Doug and I showed up on the Japanese side. The Yokohama Club boys thought it was a fine joke and jeered at us. We waved back good-naturedly. A few Japanese fans showed up, too, to watch the game and cheer their boys on. Among them was a fierce-looking older gentleman with a white beard and moustache well-dressed in a British tweed suit. The game commenced. I got in my licks, a few base hits, not much more. Doug drove in 6 home runs. The final score was 24-9. Yokohama Athletic lost. They were more sportsmanlike in losing than they were before the game. They shook hands and congratulated the Japanese, and everyone was happy.

As Doug and I were leaving, we were approached by a young Japanese man in civilian clothes who introduced himself as Commander Kiro Kunitomo of the JIN, assigned to Admiral Togo's staff. He spoke excellent English (I was later to discover he was a graduate of Annapolis, class of '77.). Kunitomo wanted to know who we were. I gave him my name and rank and Doug did likewise, then I asked why he wanted to know. "Admiral Togo watched the game and admired your skill." "He did? Which one was he?" I said. "Yes, he was the gentleman with the white beard and moustache." "Well, tell him I'm the observation officer from the US Navy and I've been waiting to get an invitation to meet with him at Sesebo for six months." "Yes," he said, "I am sure the Admiral will happily meet with you."

The invitation came this morning. I'm to meet with Admiral Togo next week. He's blocked off half the day for me. I'm sure it would never have happened if Doug MacArthur hadn't gotten us into that game.

Letter to Catherine Pennington, Tuesday, September 22, Hiroshima, Japan

Dearest Catherine:

I finally had my meeting with Admiral Heihachiro Togo. He gave me four hours on Friday the 18th, a generous allotment of time for man as busy as he. As I said in my last letter, I would never had gotten the opportunity to meet with him had it not been the baseball game Doug MacArthur got us into a few weeks ago. We met aboard his flagship, the *Mikasa*, a British build battleship girded with Krupp armor, launched in 1900.

I was given a short tour of the ship. The *Mikasa* is a British-made ship built at Elswick, not Newcastle like the *Fuji.* The shipyard can make a difference even if the design is similar. I think it's better built than the *Fuji.* The plating seems smoother, the joining more precise. (Remember how we walked through the port at Charleston and I pointed out some of the details of ship design and construction?) She's said to have a top speed of 18 knots. A knot is about 1.15 miles, so the top speed measured on land would be just shy of 21 miles per hour. Her range with a normal fuel load is 7,000 miles at 10 knots. It would be less than 4,000 at full speed. Like all Japanese ships, it's as clean as a place can be that houses over 800 men in a box that's 432 feet long by 76 feet wide, along with all their stores, boats, 42 guns and their bullets, propellant, shells and ammunition, and 4 torpedo tubes. *AND* spare parts, sanitary facilities, mess, engines, fuel, etc.

The Battleship Mikasa, JIN

(Penn's comment: The "Mikasa" later became familiar to Americans when an artist's rendering of the ship was featured on

the cover of "Scientific American," September, 1904. It survived the wars, was extensively refurbished in the 1950s, and is currently a floating museum in port at Yokosuka. Penn flashed an image of the Mikasa on the screen.)

I'm not important enough for the crew to go to any special work to spruce the place up, so what I saw is probably the way they live, which is clean, orderly and precise. This time I didn't see any NCO beat anyone with his swagger stick, but they still carried the d__n things.

The Japanese are buying battle ships made in Britain because they don't have a shipyard yet that can produce one, but they're learning. Doug MacArthur could see that as well, or so he told me before he left for the Philippines. The Yokosuka Naval arsenal has been expanding its facilities and we figure in a year or two they'll be able to produce battleships in Japan itself. Right now, they can repair or refurbish a ship as big as a battleship, and that makes them a Naval force to contend with in Northeast Asia.

From what West and Monty tell me the Russians can build a battleship at home with a lot of foreign help in terms of materials and equipment. But they are extended so far from home at Port Arthur, they're at a distinct disadvantage to the Japanese when it comes to maintenance and repair of their vessels. The famous Trans-Siberian railway is not as complete or reliable as they'd like the world to believe and they rely on supplies from the sea as much as they do over land. Port Arthur is a far and difficult stretch.

Both the Japanese and the Russians are preparing for a fight and if I were to place a bet, it would be on the Japanese. This is their home territory. They can expand their army almost indefinitely by using conscripts and with weapons and ammunition either produced domestically or purchased from foreign sources. They've got backing, too, in the form of international loans. The oppressiveness of the Tsarist government has pushed some members of the international community to support the Japanese. West had a lot to say about this in one of his dispatches and wants it kept confidential, but I don't think tens of millions of dollars loaned from the financial community in the United States can be kept quiet in any event, and in all probability most of the world already knows about it.

Penn's comment: *The loans he's referring-to were made by Kuhn, Loeb & Company of New York. Their head, Jacob Schiff – for both personal and professional reasons --was adamantly opposed to the oppressive Tsarist regime and he steadfastly supported the Japanese throughout the Russo-Japanese War, extending a series of loans totaling $200 million by 1905, an enormous sum for the time. In return, the Japanese awarded Schiff the "Japanese Order of the Rising Sun, Gold and Silver Star." It was presented personally by the Emperor. Schiff was the first foreigner ever to receive such an honor. The loans were eventually made good by the Japanese.* The map temporarily dissolves and Schiff's image appears.

Now, back to Commander Pennington's letter:

I ate lunch at 11 AM in the ship's officers' mess along with Commander Kunitomo Kiro (I put the given name last as they do in Japan) – the fellow we met after the baseball game -- and had a very congenial and leisurely time chatting with the Lieutenant and his fellow officers. These officers and the men of the crew seem very proud of the ship and their Navy and consider themselves fortunate to be members of the JIN. American seaman are proud of their ships, too, but they lack the enthusiasm displayed by the Japanese, a kind of religious fervor. When the Japanese talk about their ship their eyes light up in the way that some Christians do when they claim an infusion of grace and divine revelation. With most Christians, however, the divine affliction seems to vanish after a while, either by the passage of a small segment of time – spiritual enthusiasm being exhausting, after all -- or by the glittering allure and splendid delight of some new temptation and sin. With these fellows in the JIN, however, it never seems to abate.

I met with the Admiral at noon. I was ushered into his office without an interpreter and thought, if we had to rely on my Japanese, the day has just fallen through. I began with a salute and salutation in Japanese, but the Admiral, all smiles, jumped up, leaned over his desk and put out his hand.

"My good fellow," he said in English with a pronounced British accent, "Don't trouble yourself. I speak English fluently, you know. I'm a graduate of the Royal Naval College, Greenwich, and had three years at sea with the British before that."

Admiral Togo was another Japanese officer who was short by American standards, but burly and strong. Imagine a man the shape and size of a well-fed black bear and you'll get an idea of what I mean. He had a grip like a black bear as well and had I not gripped back with all my force, he would have put my hand out of joint. I've said before that men respect a strong grip. This was another man whose grip demanded a lot of respect.

"Sit down, please, Commander," he said, "and let me tell you how much I appreciated the help you gave us in that baseball game. I've wanted to smash the Yokohama Athletic Club for years, and you helped us do it! Your colleague was splendid, too, with his six home runs. What was his name?"

"He's Lieutenant Douglas MacArthur, a visitor on his way to our Army in the Philippines," I said.

"MacArthur? Wasn't there a MacArthur who was Military Governor of the Philippines?"

"Yes, sir, that is Lieutenant General Arthur MacArthur, The father of our visitor, the Lieutenant," I said.

"Well, we must invite him to Sasebo as well."

"I'm afraid the Lieutenant had to continue to his assignment in the Philippines. He left yesterday on the USS *New York*, but I believe he intends to visit Japan again within two years, along with his distinguished father. He was very impressed with your facilities at Yokusuka."

“Well, well,” said Togo, ”We may see him again when he returns. I will be sure to tell the government to inform me of the arrival of the Lieutenant and his admirable father. What do you think of our ship?”

“Splendid, sir,” I said in all sincerity, “No service in the world can rival the Japanese Imperial Navy for the quality and cleanliness of its ships and crew.”

“True, true,” he said, “but we’re still developing our seamanship and gunnery. Have you used the Barr & Stroud Rangefinder?”

“Fine implement.” I said, “I saw a demonstration of the prototype in Chesapeake Bay just before leaving for Japan. Even in prototype it was a formidable design, easy and fast to use, and accurate. I imagine it’s been perfected since that demonstration. Probably the best designed rangefinder at present. Edison had one in development, too, but he’s never been much for the military market. He prefers commercial business.”

“What do you think of the Liuzhol?”

(This was a loaded question. The Russians used the Liuzhol. I know because Monty mentioned it in one of his dispatches. The U.S. Navy preferred American inventions but was impressed by the Scottish – Barr, etc. I didn’t want to give away our intelligence but I had to answer in some way.)

“The U.S. Navy wouldn’t use it, Sir. It’s cumbersome and impossible to employ in a sea battle. The gunnery officer has to rely on seeing the splashes from missed shots. How do you do that when 40 guns are firing simultaneously at a target and splashes occur by the score?”

“The Russians are said to have equipped their ships with it,” said Togo.

(Penn interrupted here. *The Luizhol rangefinder was used on some Russian ships, but the newer ones used the Barr & Stroud, so the Japanese advantage in rangefinders wasn't perfect. Neither Admiral Togo nor Commander Pennington seemed to be aware of that.)*

"Sir, if I served in a ship using the Luizhol and had to go into battle against a similarly sized ship using the Barr and Stroud, I'd write my will and increase my insurance."

He laughed heartily at that. "One thing I like about Americans is their directness and candor. You have expressed my feelings exactly."

"I will say this much for the Russians. Their ships are well-armored both with Krupp and Harvey armor. Of course I would want a well-armored ship, too, if I had to rely on a crew that is mostly illiterate led by senior officers hand-picked by the Tsar from the aristocracy," I said, "They're going to miss the mark with those Luizhol rangefinders, if they can even get their crews to station competently, and they'll be taking lots of hits."

"Ah! So you would give us the advantage?" said Togo.

"Sir, I stood on the deck of the *Fuji* and saw the JIN in action against the Chinese in '94. The officers and men of the JIN were exemplary. If a battle is only ships and men, yes, I would give the advantage to the Japanese, but the Russians do have a bigger fleet and shore emplacements at Port Arthur. I think they would probably mine the harbor there, too, and they're known to be courageous if not always clever. It never pays to disparage the enemy. Contempt for a foe can lead to overconfidence and disaster."

Togo shook his head. "Bigger fleets don't always guarantee victory. Consider what happened to the Persians at Salamis, to the Turks at Lepanto, to the Spanish Armada, in a smaller way the victory of the American Captain Perry at Lake Erie, and the greatest Naval commander of all, Nelson, at the Nile and his monumental victory over the French and Spanish at Trafalgar. Nelson is at the very apogee of Naval brilliance, with undaunted courage, limitless resourcefulness, magnetic leadership, and the unquestioned devotion of every man in his command. He respected his enemies, but strove to understand them as well, and was able to exploit their weaknesses."

At this point the Admiral's eyes began to water. "I am simply amazed when I think of Trafalgar, Nelson's final battle, the impossible victory," said Togo, "and his words to his men, the simple eloquence of his exhortation 'Every man will do his duty,' as if the Navy were one body, one soul dedicated to a single purpose, and he could trust and rely on every man in every station."

Tears rolled down his cheek. I admire Nelson, too, but not enough to cry.

The Admiral's orderly interrupted by bringing in a tray laden with a bottle of Scotch Whiskey and two small glasses.

"A toast to Lord Nelson!" said Togo, and we both took a drink of the Scotch. Togo sipped at it, and I did as well. I was about to offer a toast to John Paul Jones but thought better of it, the Admiral being an Anglophile.

"Tell me," said Togo, "Do Americans believe in reincarnation?"

"Some do," I said. I didn't volunteer my own beliefs. Discussions of religion are usually pointless and nonproductive and they can become belligerent.

"So, the concept is not unknown to you?" he said.

"No, Sir, it is not," I said.

Togo tossed off the rest of his scotch, swallowing it in one gulp and poured himself another, downing most of that, too. He was preparing himself for something. I soon discovered what that was.

"Sometimes, when I think of Nelson and I look at the course of history," said the Admiral looking off towards the port window and nursing what was left of his second scotch, "I see a continual rebirth of great commanders. Themistocles, who devastated the Persians at

Salamis was no naval commander. He was a general, but inspiration came to him and he managed to devastate the massive Persian fleet by bottling them up and destroying them with a much inferior Greek force. Buckingham commanded the English fleet against the Spanish – of course he had the help of Frances Drake and others – but again here was a case of a man who was no sailor commanding a great fleet in a series of actions. Nelson was born for the sea, a sailor who earned every stripe and every accolade and whose command has never been rivaled. I think sometimes, that I, too, was born for the sea and for Naval command, that whatever spirit inhabited these men, I bear too, in my soul. Do you think that is possible?"

"Sir, I think birth and heritage play a part in every man's life. Perhaps souls do migrate and some insistent quality demands to come forward be it scientific genius, artistry, valor or Naval command. I have no idea of how this occurs, but to answer your question, it is as possible as the fate that put me here, half the world away from home, talking with you in this fine ship about reincarnation."

"Ha!" he said, slapping the desk," Good answer! Now, let's tour the ship."

The rest of the afternoon was taken up with touring every part of that ship. The Admiral knew every wheel and gage, every gun and how to operate it. He could talk with the engineer about the engine, with the gunnery officers about their guns, with ordinary crewman about everything from loading torpedoes to the quality of food in the mess. Food was a big issue with him. He told me he came near to starving on poor British rations of salt beef and sea biscuit when he sailed as a common seaman from England to Australia and back, and wouldn't let that happen to his men. I mentioned that I served as a common sailor, too, and sailed the North Atlantic before entering the Academy, and that pleased him very much.

He gave me the full four hours and an open pass to visit any

Japanese facility at any time. At 8 Bells precisely he bid me goodbye, shook my hand heartily, slapped me on the back, and took and returned my salute. We were friends at that point, as much as men can be friends when they're from different countries and they're separated by years and rank. Despite his theories of reincarnation, I liked him and I think he's a superb commander. The Russians have something to fear in him, that's for sure.

Now, the latest news. I've been scribbling this letter for two days, Caroline, and as I finished I was presented with a sealed document from the JIN. Admiral Togo has formally invited me to join his staff at my convenience as an observer. I have to confer with the military attaché about this, but it's something I've wanted all along. Depending upon permission, I'll be dividing my time between Sasebo and Hiroshima.

Penn pointed to the map of Northeast Asia. "This draws tonight's lecture to a close. Commander Pennington received only partial permission to sit with Admiral Togo's staff, and only as an occasional observer. Military and Diplomatic command thought it too indelicate for an American to be so close to Japanese Command. Observing was one thing, but joining in staff meetings and steadily serving on board ship would make it appear that the United States was taking an active role in advising and assisting the Japanese, obscuring our neutrality and disrupting our relations with Russia. The British, too, were active in impeding an American from gaining too close a relationship with a Japanese Admiral, since they'd formed the Anglo-Japanese Alliance against their traditional adversary, the Russians, and their commercial interests in the Japanese Imperial Navy, which were substantial, were at stake.

Admiral Togo did go on to command the Japanese fleet but the eventual victory of the Japanese and the destruction of the Russian fleet at the *Battle of the Yellow Sea* in August 1904 and the annihilation of the second Russian fleet at *The Battle of Tsushima* in

May 1905 was neither simple nor easy.

The adversaries fought well and bravely. Commander Pennington's warning of the dangers posed by shore batteries and mining proved accurate and the Russian defenses cost the Japanese heavily as the war progressed. Admiral Togo's destruction of the Russian fleet in 1904 was achieved partially through maneuver on the open sea, but the coup de grace came while the Russian fleet was contained within Port Arthur, and not without the loss of the battleship *Yashima* to mines. Port Arthur, however, did not fall to the Japanese easily. The Japanese Navy was held at bay until their land forces were able to seize the southwest tip of the peninsula, silence the shore batteries and help direct the fleet's fire into the port.

Although Port Arthur was taken, the battles of the Yellow Sea were not over. The Russians ordered their Baltic Fleet, every bit as formidable as the Japanese Navy, to the Far East. The sea war would continue.

Control of the Yellow sea was finally settled almost a year later. The Russian Baltic fleet, a powerful Naval force, arrived in May 1905, intent on recapturing Port Arthur and destroying the Japanese. What followed was the *Battle of Tsushima*, the seminal sea battle of the war, a protracted duel of gunnery and maneuver between two fleets that were more or less evenly matched. Here, Admiral Togo's strategy and leadership, the precision and speed of Japanese maneuver and the superior capabilities of the Japanese crews came into play. Luck was also with the Japanese. An early Russian ploy to sneak past the Japanese fleet at night in bad weather would have succeeded had not a Russian hospital ship at the very end of the convoy broken discipline by keeping its lights on and was seen by Japanese scouts.

Good intelligence on the part of the Japanese, the heavy Japanese rate of fire, the accuracy of their guns and the ability of their officers and crews gave them a powerful advantage. The Russians, too, exhibited extraordinary seamanship, courage and determination. After fierce fighting, the last Russian fleet was destroyed and the Japanese command of the north Pacific waters was without challenge.

We've gone a little over, so there won't be time for questions at this point. We have, however, set up a moderated blog at www.pennington1905.org. A copy of this presentation will be available there and your questions will be posted and answered. Thank you."

The applause was more than polite. As the audience drifted out, Captain Southerland appeared in the wings.

"Fantastic presentation, Penn" he said, "What a fascinating topic! When do you think you'll start working on the book?"

"I've still got research to do and questions to answer. I'm going to Japan next month to see what I can discover there. The Admiral spent a good portion of his adult life in Japan and I think I may find the clues to some fill some of the gaps there," said Penn.

"I haven't seen a travel request," said Southerland.

"I'm taking leave – I have a lot in the bank -- and going on my own nickel," said Penn, "The Admiral was an historical figure but he was also family. I have personal as well as professional reasons and I don't want to compromise the Academy in any way by spending money on a trip that may not add to the history while it does little more than satisfy my curiosity."

"Have it your way, Penn, but if you change your mind let me know. I'll get the funds even if there is a sequester."

****

Chapter Twenty-Five -- Yoshiko

Yoshiko Fujiyama was the youngest of three children in her family. Her father, Akihito, was, and is, a physician. For almost thirty years he practiced internal medicine three days per week at the Hanzomon Hospital in Tokyo, commuting by train from his home in Yokohama. The trip only takes 30 minutes. On Thursdays, Fridays, and Saturdays he could always be found at a small clinic not far from his home, where he maintained a private practice, not usual in Japan but done by some physicians. Many of his patients at the clinic were elderly, and many were poor. His work wasn't entirely charitable, since the complex Japanese health insurance system covered his patients, but by charging lower fees and making himself available locally, the services he provided and continues to provide were eagerly sought and the community thought of him with gratitude and admiration.

Akihito's eldest son, Hiro, also a physician, followed his father, and worked in the clinic as well as in Hanzomon Hospital. He spoke reasonably good English, some Mandarin, and some German. This was very helpful, since Hanzomon had a patient roster that included ex-patriots from several countries.

The younger son, Riku, attended the University of Tokyo where he studied law and international relations. He was accepted into the Japanese Foreign Service and spent years abroad in Peru, Canada, and Malaya. He was back in Tokyo now, working at the Ministry for Foreign Affairs.

Both sons were married, each with a son of his own, and both lived nearby. Akihito was proud of his sons and doted on them. He spent more time with them and with their families than he did at home. Yukio's mother, Hinata, also spent much time with her sons, caring for her grandsons, helping the daughters-in-law, cooking, and generally acting the benevolent grandmother.

Hinata, however, was no ordinary grandmother. She was a

graduate of the Toho Gakuen School of Music, where she majored in piano and keyboard. She could also sing, and while at music school studied vocal technique as well as piano. She often said that splitting her studies between keyboard and voice was a mistake. It left her a competent but not virtuosic pianist and a good but not exemplary singer.

Both her boys showed musical promise when children. They both studied piano and learned to play well, but as they matured their interests migrated elsewhere. HIro was fascinated by his father's work, and Riku's exposure to foreign languages and the music of Europe and the Americas filled him with the urge to travel, to meet people and to see first-hand all the things he saw in books or heard from his teachers.

Yoshiko was different. Her mother, Hinata, sang to her in the womb. As a toddler, she would follow her mother listening to her sing in the house, trying to imitate her. When she began studying music in her childhood, she sang the notes as she played them on piano. When she was very young, she started voice lessons, learning to control her breath, to phrase, to read and interpret music for the voice, to pronounce and enunciate lyrics in Japanese, English, Italian, French and German, listening to her mother sing and to recordings of the great sopranos, Sutherland, Moffo, Sills, Tebaldi, Scotto, Price, Caballé, and others, enjoying the coaching and lessons her mother gave her. She learned to play piano as well, but never harbored any ambition to develop as a virtuoso. Voice was her passion, and she worked incessantly at developing herself.

Following her mother, she attended the Toho Gakuen School of Music for vocal studies, but looked overseas for further development. Both Julliard and Curtis beckoned in the United States, but she chose Curtis because it was the first to accept her and because living in Philadelphia was so much cheaper and easier than in New York. The course of sturdy at Curtis was done in coordination with the University of Pennsylvania, and a degree from such a prestigious school would help as well.

She was required to have sponsors and the Feldsteins, a couple whose children had grown and moved away years before, stepped forward. They were music lovers, they lived within walking distance of Curtis, and both were graduates of the University of Pennsylvania Law School. She spent her holidays with them, learned Jewish traditions from them and even sang at a famous synagogue, Beth Sholom, in Elkins Park, just north of Philadelphia.

Of all in her family, Yoshiko was the closest to her grandmother, Keiko. As a child she would sing to her grandmother, whose voice, although untrained, was good as well. Sometimes they sang little duets together. Sometimes, too, if the weather permitted, her grandmother would take her by the hand and walk with her, pointing out each house and building and telling stories about them.

Her grandmother knew the area well because she lived for the rest of her life near to where she worked at Hana House, the small hotel and tea house owned and run by her guardian, Lady Ayumi, and she had attended Ayumi's school. Hana House had long since been replaced by a new office building, but the spirit lingered, or so her grandmother said. At Hana House her grandmother met her husband, Dr. Takahashi Masato, Yoshiko's grandfather.

The story of that meeting was also told in her Book.

Grandmother Keiko's Book

1953

> In 1953, my future husband, Dr. Takahashi Masato, was 42 years old. A veteran of the Army, he was wounded several times during the war. An injury to his leg left him with a slight limp; his right arm was scarred but not incapacitated, and he had a thin scar on his face, on the left side, from the edge of his eye to the edge of his lip. He had scars and wounds elsewhere as well. He attended medical school after

the war on a special program for returning veterans. He did well, graduated and went into practice in Yokohama, which was both recovering from the devastation of the war and growing since the Americans had their base at the port.

Before the war Masato was married with two children, but he lost his family in the bombing of Nagasaki. The heartbreak of that loss was so severe he swore never to marry again, but to work hard and make his medical career his life. In his medical practice, he partnered with two other doctors. Together, their clients and patients were spread about the city, and our Hana House was one of their clients. Masato's partner, Hideo, normally acted as the retained physician for the Hana House, and he was the doctor who usually came to help us when a guest or staff member was ill or injured.

Hideo was out of town one day when a cook burned himself badly and we called for the doctor's assistance. With Hideo absent, Masato agreed to come and help. The injury was painful but not too bad. Masato was able to apply a salve, provide medication to ward off infection, prescribe a pain-killer, and put a light dressing on the wound.

Before leaving, the doctor reported to me, the manager, to tell me his prognosis, to present the bill and to recommend a few days of rest and recovery for the cook. He expected to find Lady Ayumi, who was in her late sixties. Instead he found me, Keiko, behind the manager's desk. At the age of twenty, I was already the manager of Hana House since Lady Ayumi trusted me and thus felt free to spend much of her time trying to find contributors for her school and working in various charitable causes.

The doctor was very surprised to find me there, and he stood frozen for a few seconds in the doorway. He afterward said that he was immediately fascinated by me, for reasons I will explain later.

I was curious about him as well. The normal doctor, Hideo, was heavy-set, prone to wearing wrinkled, ill-fitting suits and shirts, generally red-faced as if exerting himself with everything he did, and always brusque and quick, as if his day was so full he couldn't spare a second. This new doctor, Masato, was deliberate and thoughtful. I had already been told by one of the kitchen help that he was kind and gentle in dealing with the cook he was treating and with others in the kitchen, a thoughtful man, humble more than proud, but confident, too, and with a strong personality that attracted respect without demanding it. Having just been told all that, I of course looked for it in him and found it.

The doctor wasn't especially young, but he wasn't old, either. He was handsome in a way, well-built, at five foot nine certainly tall enough. Although he wasn't short, he had small, beautiful hands and feet, and his clothes fit him very well. He smiled as he presented the bill and his smile was very nice, a friendly warm smile that revealed teeth unstained by tobacco, nor were his fingers with their clean and manicured nails stained with tobacco, either. I liked him immediately.

What did he think of me at that first meeting? After we married, he told me he found me beautiful, the perfect image of his departed wife, even in my facial expressions, the tilt of my head, in the colors I wore. In meeting me, what was dead in him before, the yearning for love and companionship, suddenly sprang up again and he felt a flood of emotions that had been lost to him for years.

Was I, his wife, shocked to hear him compare me to his first wife? Some people have told me that they would find it offensive. Not for me. He had no pictures of her. All of the photos they had were lost, yet he carried the image of her in his mind. He loved her for her beauty and for her goodness but his perception of her beauty was formed from the memory of how good and kind and loving she was. To me, a comparison with her was a wonderful compliment, perhaps more than I deserved.

After that first encounter, he persuaded Dr. Hideo to give up Hana House as a client and turn it over to him, which the partner was very willing to do, since he didn't like hotels or restaurants as clients.

Dr. Takahashi Masato, as I formally called him at first, was very attentive. He visited the cook several times to inspect the wound and change the dressing. He would come up to the office and report to me, but he told me all his expenses were already covered and he never charged us for this work. I thought it very generous and helpful of him and I grew to appreciate him very much. After his first call, if any of our staff felt ill, had a headache or some other problem, he would attend to it and never trouble us with the expense. This was very helpful and I always enjoyed seeing him at the hotel.

He and I became engaged through a deception planned by the Doctor and Lady Ayumi. In 1948

Lady Ayumi expanded her Tea House and purchased the building next door, which enabled her to have rooms for private parties. Geisha would visit and entertain the guests as they ate and drank. Lady Ayumi welcomed Geisha but never employed them herself; that was up to the client. She came to me on the day that marked the fifth anniversary of this extension and offered to take me to dinner to celebrate five successful years. Of course I agreed.

"This is a propitious occasion," she said, "so wear your best kimono and put up your hair. I will do the same and we can laugh and enjoy ourselves."

I did as she said. We walked together to the Tea House, where a room awaited us. When we entered the Tea House, we were surprised to find Dr. Takahashi Masato there. Lady Ayumi greeted him warmly. He was there to have dinner alone, but she would not hear of it.

"Doctor," she said, "You have been very good to us and I want you to join me and Keiko in our celebration of the fifth anniversary of our expanded Tea House."

He seemed very happy and agreed immediately. All three of us were taken to a very nice room, offered Saki, and our meals were prepared. Lady Ayumi had already ordered the cook to prepare a special dinner. A Geisha, hired from a local establishment, arrived to play the Koto and sing. The Saki was very good, and very warm. The food was excellent, and Lady Ayumi was in such a jubilant mood that soon we all were as well. As we finished the meal, one of the waitresses brought a folded note to Lady Ayumi.

"My heavens!" she said, "My friend, Fumiko, has lost the recipe for a dish she promised to a distinguished guest, and she asks my help. I know it very well, but I must be there immediately to show her some aspects of preparation. Please, please excuse me." Then she turned to the Doctor and said, "Everything is paid-for, so do not concern yourself with the bill, but, please, Doctor, can you stay with Keiko and walk her home, so we can be sure she is safe?"

"Yes," he said, "Of course. It would be my pleasure."

I was now alone with the Doctor. At first he seemed shy, but he and I began to talk. I told him my story, which he thought was very good and should be written down for others to see and to learn from. He told me his story as well, which was sad.

"My story was sad," he said, "but it may yet end happily. I am here, having dinner and conversation with you, and that is happy."

I reached over and touched his hand. He smiled and took my hand in both of his. No man had ever held my hand before. I was thrilled. His hand was strong but beautiful, and there was so much sadness and love in his eyes.

Before the night was over, I lay nestled in his arm, happy to be near him, neither of us talking, listening to the girl play the Koto and sing her songs, some sad, some lovely. When the Geisha's time was up, she took a small gift of money from him and graciously wished us good fortune. We walked back to the home I shared with Lady Ayumi, where he kissed my cheek and bid me goodnight. I was so in

> love at that moment I could barely breathe. I lay sleepless until very late and awakened thinking about him.
>
> Nine weeks later we were married in the Cathedral of the Sacred Heart. The next day we received Buddhist and Shinto blessings as well. The happiest phase of my life began. Our marriage lasted fifty years. We had only one child, a daughter, but we raised her well and she became our angel and our hope. She married a doctor, and from her, we saw born three beautiful grandchildren. We lived happily for 50 years, and I know he died happy and contented. He asked to be cremated. I have his ashes and his ashes will be mixed with mine and we will be buried together forever. This is his wish and mine as well.

The wishes of Keiko and her husband, Masato, were honored. She was cremated and the ashes of the husband and wife were mixed and sealed in the same monument. As Yoshiko honored her grandmother, and prayed for her, she prayed for her grandfather as well. Many people throughout Yokohama prayed for him because he had been kind and helped so many in his life, and had been such a splendid example to his son-in-law and his grandsons.

****

Chapter Twenty-Six -- Yokohama

Penn left for Japan from Baltimore at 11:30 AM, and after transferring at Atlanta arrived at Tokyo 5:30 PM, February 2. Groundhog Day. He left Baltimore in the rain and arrived at Tokyo in the rain. Despite ibuprofen, stretching, and several walks up and down the aisle, his back and shoulder ached, and he was exhausted from lack of sleep. He'd arranged to be picked up at the airport and driven to his hotel in Yokohama. The driver was there waiting, and the convenience was worth the cost. He checked into the Tokyo Inn Yokohama, a place with all the insipid ambience of older Holiday Inn but it had clean rooms, clean sheets and hot showers. He bought a sandwich from the refrigerated display in the lobby, and dragged himself up to his room. He didn't unpack. Instead, he threw his clothes on the bed then stood in a hot shower until his skin wrinkled, took one more ibuprofen, ate the sandwich, drank twelve ounces of bottled water, laid down and fell asleep. He awoke twelve hours later feeling good and ready for the day.

Winters in Tokyo aren't very different from winters in Atlanta, and much milder than in Annapolis. Penn's thick leather jacket, a pea-coat design he'd purchased in Hanover, Germany, his jeans and Doc Martin boots were comfortable and provided enough protection. He had an umbrella as well, a luxury for a Navy officer, since military regulations forbid a sailor in uniform to carry an umbrella. His cell phone was outfitted with a SIM that would work in Japan, so he could access GPS, his personal e-mail, and make calls. The cell service was expensive, but he would only use it for a month. His iPhone had a camera, of course, but he'd brought a high-resolution Nikon with him that fit comfortably in his pocket and would shoot fourteen megapixel images that could be blown up to four by five feet and still look sharp. He had a laptop and his iPad as well, so he could do some real work while at the hotel.

He had three current guidebooks to the cities of Yokohama and

Tokyo, and he'd carefully noted the train directions and stops. On Monday he was meeting with Professor Sato, an expert on post-war Japan, the American occupation, and reconstruction, but he wasn't going to waste the weekend playing tourist. He'd given himself a month, but hoped to finish in less time.

Penn's great-grandfather was entombed on a patch of land adjacent to the Yokohama Foreign General Cemetery, or so Penn had been informed. From the guidebooks Penn discovered that the cemetery had its origins with Perry's "opening" of Japan in 1854. A twenty-four-year-old marine, Robert Williams, died on board ship while docked in Yokohama, and Commodore Perry requested a plot of land to use for the burial of Americans. After some negotiation, the Japanese complied, allowing burial of the marine on the grounds of a temple overlooking the sea. The sea view was at Perry's request. As foreign concessions were opened in Yokohama, the need for a cemetery to hold foreigners grew and eventually the grounds of the current Foreign General Cemetery were established. The reasons were obscure, but Penn's great-grandfather was not buried in the Foreign General Cemetery itself but outside the fence in a plot of its own, although sources indicated that the cemetery had expanded over the years and if that were the case, the cemetery might well have absorbed his Great-grandfather's grave.

With the help of the concierge, who spoke English and was kind enough to tolerate Penn's rude attempts to speak Japanese, Penn found the right subway station and rode the Minato-Mirai Line to No. 6 Exit. His cell phone's GPS pointed the rest of the way to the cemetery. Finding the Admiral's tomb, however was not easy. He was early and the cemetery gate was locked, so he walked the perimeter of the place and found nothing, then, as soon as it opened at noon, he toured the cemetery itself, even visiting the British and French sections and monuments. His great-grandfather's grave wasn't mentioned in any guidebook and there were no photos of it that he could find. He began to think that the story of his great-grandfather's burial might just be a story or that the tomb was moved at some time. He took one more walk around the perimeter and found nothing. The temperature had dropped somewhere close to freezing, the day was gray and overcast and the skies were darkening. In Vermont, there would be snow on a day like this, but snow is rare in Yokohama and Penn expected rain instead, a day that matched his mood, which was darkening by the minute.

When the cemetery office opened, he went there looking for help. The office was dreary from the outside, but the inside, its institutional green and beige walls, lack of decoration and dusty, faded furniture radiated hopelessness and desperation. There was a young woman at the desk, incongruously bright and perky, who recognized him as an American, smiled revealing dimples and crooked teeth, which are sometimes thought to be cute by the Japanese, and greeted him in English. Altogether she was a pretty package, clothes, figure and attitude, as if she were a little sister of the *5,6,7,8s*, a Japanese girl's band. She wasn't busy. He was the only visitor so far today – traffic usually peaked about 3 PM – and she could help him without feeling pressed. He wrote-out his grandfather's name and rank, but she consulted her computer files and found nothing on him despite several different search attempts. Finally, she withdrew to an office in the back and Penn could hear a lively conversation between what sounded like a much older woman and the clerk who was helping him.

The older woman emerged from the back trailed by the pretty clerk. She was gray-haired, wore glasses, had a sweet, rosy-cheeked face, and bowed, greeting him formally in Japanese. He responded and she replied by extending her hand. A quick shake and introductions were accomplished.

"You are looking for the grave of Admiral Hennington *(she mispronounced the name)*?" she said in heavily accented English, "He was your grandfather?"

"He was my great-grandfather," said Penn.

"Ah!" she said, "You looked young to be his grandson. Admiral Henningten is not buried here."

Penn's heart fell. "He's not?" he asked, his anxiety undisguised. "Do you know where he's buried?"

She smiled kindly," His grave and monument is very nearby. He's in the American Yama Park, across the road and up the hill. Past the trees. You cannot see it from here, but you can as you walk past the trees in the park, on your left," she said, touching her left arm, "There is a narrow stone path that leads to it."

"It's an American park?" he asked.

"It used to be, but it became a Japanese park over sixty years ago. We kept the name, though, American Yama Park. His grave is with just two or three others, a small bit of land. Lady Ayumi, a savior of young people after the war, is buried next to him, and her assistant, Lady Keiko was recently buried there as well."

"Thank you," he said, all smiles now, taking her hand in both of his and squeezing it, "Thank you," and looking over the older woman's shoulder to the younger, "and you as well."

Penn fairly ran from the room, got his bearings at the gate, and headed to his left. He opened his small guide book and read the few paragraphs on the park. The American Yama Park was, at one time, a quarter for Americans of stature who lived in Yokohama. The old legation building is there as well as other elaborate nineteenth century homes and buildings, now turned into museums or shops. It's beautifully maintained and provides a pass-through for students attending the international schools, St. Maur's and the Yokohama International School.

He jogged through the entrance, walked quickly past some trees on his left and at the end of a narrow stone path that led off the main pathway, Penn could just see what appeared to be black and white marble monuments. He followed the stone path which twisted and finally took him up a slight hill to a small plot of land surrounded by a low decorative fence that contained an area just large enough for four or five graves. In the middle of the plot were three monuments, two older graves and one that seemed to be brand new. All were well kept. Flowers were planted and the grass maintained. They suited the park well, and they were so situated on the knoll you could just glimpse the sea, a fitting place of burial for an old sailor. His great-grandfather's grave was the furthest on the left, a black marble monument with a small tower engraved in both Japanese and English. The inscription was simple, Vice-Admiral John Pennington, USN, benefactor of the Japanese people, friend of the Imperial House. A seal and mark, centered under the inscription and carved into the stone, followed.

Penn's eyes watered and his hands fairly shook as stood before the grave. He hadn't prayed in years, not since his days at St. Augustine's and even then he was skeptical of religion, praying only to avoid to the wrath of the Augustinian monks. Now, however, the thought of prayer can readily to mind, but he restrained himself. Prayer seemed silly and somehow self-indulgent. He couldn't help thinking that an omniscient God, if there is one, knows his thoughts and feelings already and doesn't need to be conjured or cajoled with set formulations. Prayer at this point seemed redundant, even discordant. His heart told all, and that was enough.

The sky was still overcast and threatening rain. The soft, shadowless light was good for photos, though, and Penn started taking pictures. He covered every angle of the monument, even trying to find some way to shoot photos from the top looking down. As he photographed the foot and the base, however, he noticed something peculiar. The monument to its right, made of veined while marble, had protrusions that extended along the ground and touched the base of his of his great grandfather's monument, appearing almost to grip it. The protrusions were almost hidden by the marble chips and white gravel that filled the space between the tombs, but if you looked straight down, you could just see them.

Similar protrusions extended from the base of his great-grandfather's monument. From the front, the protrusions weren't noticeable unless you got very close to the ground. He photographed those protrusions, too.

While Penn studied his great-grandfather's grave, Yoshiko approached the park. She walked from her home; it wasn't very far, and she enjoyed walking. She thought about her grandmother as she walked, wondering what it would have been like to live in the streets during the war, how she must have felt when Lady Ayumi first took her hand and led her to safety. As she entered the gateway to the park she heard some loud talking and laughing in a language she didn't understand and couldn't recognize. Two days before three foreign women, apparently tourists, wandered up the path to the graves while she was praying and, laughing and talking loudly in a guttural language that sounded vaguely German, started taking pictures. They photographed each other posing by the graves and even photographed Yoshiko. She tolerated it until they tapped her on the shoulder, less of a tap than a prod, and through gestures asked her to take a picture of all three. She simply walked off that time, red-faced. Another time, some tourists tried to photograph the Shinto Priests who regularly visited the grave site, but the priests shooed them away. The thought of the insensitivity of these tourists angered her.

Yoshiko followed the winding narrow path to the grave site and found Penn on one knee taking a photo. Another annoying foreign tourist. By the look of him, he was European, at least dressed like a European, and was walking all over the white gravel upon which the monuments rested. Yoshiko, who hated confrontation, felt her anger snap. *What is the matter with these people*, she thought, *they're disrespectful, insensitive, ignorant brutes. Do they have any shame at all?* Her anger and indignation overrode everything. She couldn't contain herself.

Penn was on one knee taking a photo of the protrusions from

the monuments when he heard an excited barrage of angry words in Japanese. He looked up to see a pretty young woman, dressed in a plain, subdued kimono, pointing at his camera and firing a fusillade of angry imprecations. Penn tried to respond, but his accent was poor and his vocabulary so limited all he could muster was a weak smile and "Gomen nasai," pardon me.

She wouldn't be appeased. She pointed to him angrily, to his camera, and to the entrance to the park, fairly shouting. She obviously wanted him out and away. Even if there were no language barrier, it would be impossible to reason with a person as angry as she. Fine. He wanted no dispute with an irate Japanese citizen. He'd served enough time overseas to know that Americans always fared badly when dealing with hostile natives, and the last thing he wanted was to wind up in a Japanese jail trying to explain himself to the police. He had found the grave, had his photos, and could go for now. He could always come back later today if the weather held, or he could come back the next day if it rained. He had all month.

Something bothered him about the young woman. He felt as if he knew her from somewhere, although that was ridiculous. He'd never been to this part of the world before. He turned his back and walked away but toured the park instead of leaving, stopping at one concession after another, visiting the mechanical toy museum in one of the fine old houses, reading the plaques and generally acting the tourist. He found a snack bar and had a little to eat, toured the entire park one more time, then, an hour-and-one-half having passed, he went back to his great-grandfather's grave site. He could see the tops of the graves but little else from the main pathway, so he followed the narrow stone path again as it curved up and behind the grave site.

As he approached, he could hear someone softly singing what sounded like the Kaddish. He knew the prayer and the hymn. In past years he attended two memorial services for Jewish shipmates. One of the services featured a choir with rich voices who sang the doleful prayer powerfully; the other used a recording. As he came round the front of the grave, he stopped, stood very still and listened to the soft voice of the young woman, watched her as she knelt and bowed. He would have avoided any further confrontation, quietly turned and left for another hour or come back the next day, but she looked so familiar. *Lord, she looked like that young woman who sang Suzuki in Atlanta three months before.* The face was different but at the opera Suzuki was played by a singer whose stage makeup was troweled on. Any woman would look different with that all that makeup washed off her face. This young woman, however, seemed to move like the singer, to bow like her. She was the same size, she had a heart-shaped face, and her body, yes, her body was a perfect copy of that Suzuki.

Yoshiko finally noticed him, stopped singing and jumped up, startled. Hardly a second passed before her surprise turned to anger, her face contorted, and she was about to unleash another barrage of imprecations at him when he said,

"I know you." *Or at least I think I know you,* he thought.

She held her tongue, paused and said with virtually no accent but with an angry edge to it "What?"

"I know you."

"You *don't* know me," she said angrily in perfect English, "You're some tourist with a morbid desire to photograph graves. You probably want to photoshop the pictures and put them on your Facebook page. I despise the tourists who visit the cemeteries here. They have no respect for anyone. They walk around eating ice cream, taking pictures posing at the graves, acting as if the cemeteries are an amusement park…" she paused for a second, "Leave this place. Go away. We're still in mourning."

"I *do* know you," he insisted, "You sang Suzuki in *Madame Butterfly* last November in Atlanta. I saw you at the matinee performance at the Cobb Energy Center. You were amazing. Your name is Yukio something..,"

"My name is Yoshiko," she snapped, then thought better of telling this strange man her name and regretted her rashness, even if he had seen her on stage.

"Ok," he said softly, holding up the palms of his hands in a gesture of peace. "Yoshiko, please, you misunderstand me."

She glowered at him.

He pointed to the Admiral's grave, "This is the grave of my great-grandfather, Vice Admiral John Pennington."

She squinted at him suspiciously but seemed to soften a little.

"My name is Pennington Fuller. I was named for him," he said pointing at the grave, "Like him, I'm an officer in the United States Navy." He took out his wallet. "I can show you my military ID, if you don't believe me."

With that he removed the ID card, his driver's license, a and a business card, and handed them to her. She stared at them for a few seconds, compared the ID cards, then returned them to him, but she kept the business card. He wanted her to keep it.

"Now let me say I am sorry I disturbed you. I will leave you to your mourning and come back when I won't bother you," he said, "Good bye."

Penn left and headed toward the gate.

Yoshiko stood there for several seconds -- she wasn't sure how long -- trying to digest what the stranger had just said. Her anger evaporated and suddenly she felt horrible, suffused with shame and embarrassment for having treated him so rudely. She ran down the path after him, tears streaming down her face, got to the main walkway, looked to her left and didn't see him, then to her right. *Oh, God, he's gone!* She ran out the entrance and found him walking by himself toward the road. She chased after Penn, and caught his arm just as he turned round to look back. He'd heard the sound of someone running behind him.

"I am so, so sorry," she said, her face a flood of tears and regret, her hands pressed together as if praying, "Please forgive me…"

"There's nothing to forgive," said Penn, smiling, thinking how pathetic and how beautiful she looked at that moment, even with red eyes and a runny nose. "You protected my great-grandfather's grave as well. I'm happy there is such a tiger here to watch over the site."

"Please" she said, "Come back, come with me," she said pulling his arm. Then, her eyes widening, "Oh my God! I left my purse, my iPad, my cell phone, everything up there!"

She turned and began running up hill. Penn followed her, smiling now, caught up with her, took her hand and together they ran all the way back to the graves. Nothing was missing. They were probably the only two people to have visited the site that day.

Yoshiko sighed in relief, and flopped on a bench that faced the graves, panting, out of breath, her things gathered safely to her.

Penn sat beside her and leaned forward as if studying the monuments. "I know my great-grandfather's grave, of course," he said, "but who are the other two?"

"The grave to his right is that of Lady Ayumi, a revered figure in Yokohama whose work in helping orphaned and injured children after the war saved many lives from poverty and destitution. She was a very kind lady, but – from what mother has said – she was a smart woman, too, a shrewd businesswoman and a good leader and manager, tough when she needed to be. She built a school next to her hotel and a Tea House for children, and pressured the government into doing more," she said.

"Who's in the other grave?"

"My grandmother is buried there, at least her ashes are contained there. She called herself Keiko-Ayumi, in honor of her benefactor, but she is now referred-to as Lady Keiko. She was humble, you know, and would never have accepted the distinction of being called 'Lady' in her lifetime, although she earned it and was entitled to it. When she was still a small orphaned child, Ayumi took her literally off the streets and raised her. She worked with Ayumi for 30 years, and then continued the work after Ayumi's death. People loved her and, since it was in Lady Ayumi's will, allowed us to bury her here with the Admiral and Lady Ayumi. Actually the grave is not just the grave of my grandmother. According to the wishes of both my grandfather and grandmother, their ashes were mixed together and the monument houses both of them. My grandfather was a good man, too, a war veteran and doctor who often worked without payment. If there is a heaven, they must all be there."

"Why are they buried together in this group? Certainly Lady Ayumi and your grandmother and grandfather are connected, but how does my ancestor fit in? And, have you noticed this?" He rose, went to the spot where the extensions of the monuments reached from one to the other, knelt on one knee, and touched them.

"Here, do you see it?" He pointed with his hand. "The monuments touch. It's as if they're reaching out, holding one another."

The connection wasn't readily visible so he brushed the gravel back with his hand and about four inches of the connecting marble protrusions became obvious. He then pushed it all back into place, hiding the protrusions once again.

Yoshiko shook her head. She visited the grave sixty times since the death of her grandmother and never studied the base of the monuments.

"Why are you here?" she said, "Did you come all the way to Japan just to see your great-grandfather's grave?" She almost added *that's odd behavior for an American*, but held her tongue.

"I'm collecting information about the Admiral. I'm in the process of writing a book about him."

"A book?"

"I told you I'm a Commander in the US Navy. I'm a sailor, but

I also have a doctoral degree in history, and I currently teach history at the United States Naval Academy. I published a book last year, '*Brown Water Sailors, American Navy River Operations in Iraq*,' published by Dutton. You can find it on Amazon.com. There's even a Kindle Edition.'"

She looked at him, still skeptical.

"You have an iPad?" he said, "I'll show you the book."

"We don't have an internet connection."

"That's OK, I'll used my phone as a hotspot."

He set up her iPad, used his phone as a hotspot and invoked Amazon. "Here. See. Amazon.com. I'll type in my name and we'll see what comes up." He typed in his name, and the book appeared, *Brown Water Sailors, American Navy River Operations in Iraq* by Lieutenant Commander Pennington Fuller, USN." My rank is incorrect because I was just promoted last month to full Commander."

"You really are what you are, then," she said. "Sometimes you don't know what to believe with people...." She paused. "And you really did see me perform in Atlanta?"

"Of course. I not only saw you, I was utterly enchanted, and I was looking for some way to get to meet you, but your company left town and I was distracted with many other things..."

"You enjoyed the performance?"

"I thought the performance was marvelous, everyone in it, including you, *especially you.* I'm not terribly experienced in opera, but I'm not naïve either. I saw many operas in Italy, including *Traviata* with Gheorghiu and Vargas at *La Scala*. Your Suzuki was terrific, marvelous. I kept thinking about you for days afterward."

She responded as if the compliment to her went unheard or was of no interest. Yet, she savored his remarks and held them inside to think about and enjoy later, but not in front of him. He might think she was gloating if she did. Besides, it was always unlucky to take too much pleasure in the compliments of others.

"You've been to Italy?" she said, a wistful expression on her face "Seen Opera in Italy? Oh, how I've dreamed of doing that, of singing at *La Scala* or *La Fenice*."

"Keep at it," said Penn, "You may someday."

They sat quietly for a moment, then Penn broke the silence, "Look, I have a thousand questions about my great-grandfather and the many years he spent in Japan. I think you could help me, or you could point me to someone who could help."

"What kinds of questions?"

"To start with, what does the seal on his monument represent?"

"The seal?" she looked over," That's the seal of the Imperial House, of Emperor Hirohito. It is an honor, a very high honor and decoration almost never presented to anyone, especially a foreigner. There's a small inscription under it in Japanese that says 'For Unmatchable Service to the Imperial Family.' It's the kind of award you might get for a very high service, like saving their lives. Whatever he did, the Emperor was in his debt and recognized him for it. There is a temple of Shinto priests, you know, who pray for your great-grandfather. I've seen them visit, wash the monument, rake the gravel, burn incense and pray. One of the monks told me they would pray for him and honor him until the end of time."

"And no one knows why?" he asked, not expecting an answer.

"I could ask my mother," she said, "but it's unlikely she knows more than me. I do have my grandmother's Book, however, and there may be something in there."

"Please, let me know if you find anything. I gave you a business card. My cell number's on it." They were both quiet for a few moments. Penn figured he had burdened the young woman with enough questions. He stood and was about to leave Yoshiko to continue her veneration of Keiko when he said, on impulse, "One more thing, have you ever heard of the Hana, an Inn or Hotel?"

She smiled, "That was Lady Ayumi's place, the Hana Hotel and Tea House. My grandmother managed it for her. Why do you ask?"

"My great-grandfather was headed there the night he died," he said.

"Oh…" she said, her voice falling "I'm sorry."

"No, no," he said, "This is marvelous. I never thought I'd find a trace of it or anyone with a connection to it." He paused for a moment, thinking.

"There is something else, too," he said, "I have some forty letters written in Japanese to my great-grandfather. I have no idea what they contain. It's not Kanji. It's a florid 19th century script that's impossible for me to interpret, even with a dictionary. I'm hoping to find a scholar who can help me translate them. Do you know of anyone?"

"I could try, if you'd show them to me," she said, "I studied calligraphy when I was a child."

This could be the perfect solution. The translations would be completely private and the work would be under Penn's control. "If you would…it would be great if you could help me. I could pay you, of course. I wouldn't expect you to work for free. Is there someplace we could meet? A library or somewhere?"

Yoshiko thought about it for a minute. The man was a stranger, but he was no fraud. He'd not only proven who he was, he'd actually seen her in performance, and he was nice, a true gentleman, something rare these days. Normally cautious and reserved, she felt she could trust him and she liked him.

"You can come to my house tonight. I'll write down the address both in Japanese and English and you can have someone take you there." She took out a pen and began writing on a notebook she carried with her other things. She tore off the sheet and handed it to him when she was done.

"I wouldn't want to be a bother to you and your family."

"Be there at seven. Just knock at the door as you would in the states. My parents are gone to Kobe with my brother and I'm alone this week, actually the next three weeks, perhaps longer. My parents plan on traveling north after visiting Kobe to help at a clinic for victims of the 2011 tsunami. They were scheduled for one week, perhaps two, but the last time they did this, they stayed for two months. We'll have plenty of time and privacy, if you want. I will warn you, however, my uncle is deputy Commissioner of Police for Yokohama. He looks out for me."

"Yes," he said, smiling "I understand. Thank you. I'll see you then. Is there anything I can bring?"

"No, but eat before you come. I'm no good for anything except Ramen noodles.... And bring a laptop if you have one. You might want to take notes."

He looked at his watch. "It's after 4 already. We'd better leave, don't you think?"

"You go," she said, "I want to whisper to my grandparents some more. I live very nearby. See you at seven."

"Seven," he said.

"Seven."

****

Chapter Twenty-Seven – At Yoshiko's House

Penn was prompt. He came by taxi and arrived exactly at seven. Back at the hotel, he'd printed half the letters – he carried electronic copies of them in his laptop – in the clearest prints he could manage, and carefully put them into a manila envelope. He wasn't sure of the order. If the letters had dates on them, he couldn't find it, but then he couldn't read ninety-five percent of the ideographs anyway, even with a dictionary. As he approached the house, a police patrol car passed and the officer nodded to him. Penn nodded back. Apparently, she told her uncle he was coming. He knocked on the door. Yoshiko was right there, waiting. She was eager and opened it almost before he finished knocking.

The house had a living room, dining room, kitchen area, spare room, bathroom, and, on the second floor three bedrooms and another bathroom. This was large and luxurious for a Japanese house, but it was purchased back in the 1950s by Yoshiko's grandfather when property was still relatively cheap and passed down to his daughter when he died. It was fortunate that they retained it, because they could never afford a house of this size now, especially one with two bathrooms. The house even had a rear deck with a hot tub.

The temperature dropped down to a few degrees above freezing, but, typically Japanese, only one room in the house was warm. In this case, the dining room, where they would work. The furniture and seating were traditionally Japanese as well, a low table with cushions. Penn wasn't sure what this would do to his back and shoulder, but he had little choice. On the table, Yoshiko built a small pile of dictionaries and manuals. There was a pot of tea as well, steaming on a portable heater. She ushered him in and without any ceremony directed him to the work table, let him sit as comfortably as he could, which for him was cross-legged, then she gracefully folded her legs under and sat herself.

He set up his lap top and passed her the first of the letters.

"Perhaps you could read and interpret," he said, "And I'll try to transcribe what you say."

She studied the sheet for a few minutes and asked him to hand her the older dictionary with the faded blue binding. She flipped the pages of the book then turned to him.

"May I make notes on these copies of the letters?"

"Of course, please," said Penn, "Anything you need to do."

She studied the letter, consulted the dictionary several times and made notes, some in English, some in Japanese. She consulted a Japanese-English dictionary and several calligraphic manuals, too. She worked quickly and quietly for 30 minutes while Penn patiently stood by.

"Ok," she said, "Let me give this a try. See if it makes sense to you," and she read the letter as she translated it:

> "Hiroshima, January, 1897
>
> My Dearest John:
>
> I received your letter today, just an hour ago. I was shaking as I opened it, for my love of you made my hand tremble and my heart beat strongly. Let me answer you first so that you do not have to read this whole letter before knowing what you asked.
>
> Yes, everything you arranged with the bank is going well. There is enough for us, more than enough. Your generosity and kindness is so great, like a blessing, like an angel. Thank you my dear love.
>
> I am well. I am no longer sick at times and I eat very well now. Suzume…"

Yoshiko interrupted her translation to interject "That must be her servant," then continued,

"Suzume made a string and put evenly-spaced knots in it. Every day now she measures my belly and I am growing. I was between 3 and 4 knots at the end of the string and now I am past 4. Other parts are growing, too, and my face is rounder. I feel very well and the doctor told me everything is fine and the outlook for me and the baby is propitious. I pray every day to God for help and His blessing.

The house is good. The repairs made to the roof are very well done and not the least drop of rain enters the room.

I have everything I need, and I am saving for the baby. He will be a happy baby with love and all the milk I can give him. I hope he will meet his father one day and you and he will share your lives.

Mr. Springfield, your friend at the trading office, has been very good and very kind. He helped me with the bank and told to come to him if I need anything, but there is nothing I need.

I miss you terribly. I keep your pillow beside me and sometimes I sleep on it hoping it will bring me dreams of you. The things you left behind, your old shoes, the shaving mug, a cup. I keep these things near and touch them sometimes thinking of you. Speed back to me, my love.

I will love you forever,

Chou"

Penn typed as fast as he could, letting minor mistakes pass to be corrected later, and finished the transcription very quickly. He read it back to her, she nodded, and both of them were silent for a moment.

Penn broke the silence. "Beautiful translation, Yoshiko."

"I could feel the power of her love as I read the letter. She wrote it in love and in fear that her lover would abandon her. I could feel that very strongly. She was pregnant, alone save for her servant and a sometime friend of her lover. There is no mention of her family, perhaps because they abandoned her or perhaps she had none. Let me guess about this woman. She had good calligraphy. This letter was written not by a professional – it would have been better – but by a practiced amateur. Her use of ideographs, however, is not perfect, although the meaning is clear. This is typical of the kind of education given someone trained to serve men, a trained Geisha who could draw words prettily, but was not trained to write well. She seems very young, too. The hand is not yet mature, although she strives to be. One thing we do know, he was true to his word, at least at the time when this was written. You have, what? Forty more of these? I think we can hope he remained true to her."

Would you like to attempt another?

"Yes," she said, "Very much."

Now that the letters could be dated, they were put into order and translations followed that order. As they found, the first letter translated was the first in order, and the stack roughly flowed chronologically.

"You'd think I could have gotten the dates from the Post Marks, but it seems these letters were transferred to larger envelopes, probably heavier stock so they could survive the sea and trains. They were probably then delivered from the lawyers' office, which was in Boston, or perhaps they were picked up, or even repackaged and sent to Vermont. It looks like some effort was undertaken to conceal them," said Penn.

"I think there might have been a great deal of concealment, perhaps on both sides," said Yoshiko.

At just before ten, they stopped. Yoshiko told him how to find the subway, and which exit to take. It was very simple, really, and inexpensive. He didn't know how to say good bye to her. He would feel awkward embracing her, even it was only for a kiss on the cheek. Shaking hands seemed silly and awkward. Instead, he took both her hands in his, squeezed them, locked eyes with her, smiled and thanked her.

"Oh, no," she said, "This is very interesting, fascinating. It fills my time and I enjoy it. Please come tomorrow and we'll continue."

He noted the streets and landmarks as he walked to the train. The night was cold but bright, with moonlight and stars. His back felt good and there was not even a twinge in his shoulder.

Yoshiko watched him walk up the road from her bedroom window. She wanted to tell him that Lady Ayumi's nickname was "Chou," but didn't. She wanted to save that for later, when she could show him her grandmother's book and where that was written. So many things were coming together. The Admiral stayed at Hana House. Perhaps the young girl who wrote these sad, yearning letters was Ayumi, and the Admiral was the one who loved her and left her with child. And perhaps their love was true and deep and lasted a very long time. She would translate the rest of the letters and learn what she could.

Yoshiko sighed deeply. Her young life was devoted entirely to study and practice, to the development of her voice, her art. There was never time and never had been time for love or romance or much else. What would it be like to love someone with the intensity that she felt in these letters? To yearn for him and live for him, and he for her? She closed her eyes and lay down between the layers of her comforter. Sleep came quickly. There was a dream, a worrisome dream of loss or the fear of loss, but she couldn't recall it clearly in the morning. She awoke early, practiced on her keyboard and sang several arias from Boheme then listened to Scotto sing the same arias. Then Angela Gheorghiu. Then Natalie Dessay. Then she watched Dessay on Youtube. She experimented with all their techniques, then she prepared for her hour with her grandmother's tomb. And all this time she never thought once of Penn, yet she kept watching the clock. Time progressed so slowly. She took another of the letters and began to translate, and another. Eventually the story unfolded and she could see how the contemptible dilemmas of race and distance became more and more difficult and unresolvable. And how cleverly the lovers overcame all.

****

Chapter Twenty-Eight – Letters and Proof

The week passed. Penn and Yoshiko met every evening, and with each new day, Penn came earlier and stayed later. The letters translated by Yoshiko were poignant, sweet, and fairly breathed of the hopes, excitement and fears felt by "Chou," for that's how she signed the letters, and the love she felt for John. Yoshiko and Penn grew closer together, too, although it was gradual and they barely realized what was happening.

Penn summarized their findings in his notes.

In May, 1897, a boy was born, six pounds, 14 ounces, healthy, chubby, round-faced.

> Dearest John
>
> . . . The boy cried loudly at birth until he was washed, wrapped and placed in my arms. He soon found my breast, which has grown large, and has been sucking hungrily. I have named him Keitaro *(blessed)*, for he is a blessed child and a blessing to us both. He has your eyes, my love, dark blue. The little patch of hair he has is red-brown, almost like yours as well. The doctor tells me, however, that many babies are born with blue eyes, only to have them darken to deep brown, like mine, and the wispy hair babies bear at birth often changes, too, to black. We will see.
>
> He gains weight every day, and keeps Suzume and I busy keeping him clean, changing his diapers *(actually, "baby clothes")* holding him, singing to him. He cannot yet laugh but he knows us and loves it when we play with him. . .

Penn's comments:

The letters report that baby continues to do well, grows, is very strong and seldom sick. He's a good baby, too, who doesn't cry much, smiles happily almost all day and sleeps most of the night. Both Chou and Suzume adore the child. Their entire day revolves around him, playing with him, singing to him, making him laugh. The letters are light and fun. Apparently the money keeps coming because she is ever grateful for John's generosity. She misses him terribly, though.

Then, in July, the chatty, optimistic tone of the letters begins to change as Chou sees the child growing and changing.

> . . .The doctor visited today, weighed Keitaro, and measured him. He is growing very well, even a small bit faster than most babies. His health continues to be good and he eats very well. He has thrived on my milk and it gives me great pleasure to nurse him. He looks more and more like you, John, every day. Perhaps too much like you. There seems to almost nothing of me in him.
>
> His eyes have not become darker, as the doctor predicted. Instead they're even a little lighter and the hair that has come is light brown, like yours, and wavy. He is so very beautiful, rosy-cheeked with his wavy hair and his bright eyes. Oh! I love him so much! What will become of him, John? He's clearly sasshu *(a half-breed)*. When he is older, the other children will revile him. Schools will reject him. All his life he will live outside, separated by his origins, neither Japanese nor American.

Penn's comments:

Several more letters convey similar fears. As the child matures and approaches his first birthday, there appears to be nothing Japanese about him at all. The neighbors stare at him when she takes him for walks. Some people are just curious, one or two kind people will say how beautiful he is, but others will glare at them, call him "sasshu" and turn away. She's written to John about this and he's answered her. She responds:

Dearest John

My love, you have told me how it pains you to hear of the way people look upon little Keitaro. You have asked me what you can do. I love the child so much, every breath I take fills me with love, every thought I think is about my love for him. But I cannot let that love destroy his happiness, his future. Take him, John, adopt him. You've seen his picture. There is nothing of me in his face, in any of his features. It is you he reflects. He could live with you and grow up free and protected. . .

Penn's comments:

John develops a plan for adoption of the child. We don't see the plan directly but it's reflected in Chou's response:

Dearest John:

When I first read of your plan, I was frightened, but I understand now. The woman, your friend, will become your "little" wife *(she means false or phony wife)*. This is best for you and for her as well. She and you will adopt Keitaro, take him to your home and she will care for him. You will return to Japan to be with me and she will be free to be with her friend and to raise the boy. From what you have told me, it can be arranged through your lawyers. All the documents will show him to be American, the orphan or unwanted child of an old family. And, truly, that is not a lie. He is your son and is an American, and he should live in America. I fear losing him, but I fear for him if he stays here. I pray God we will be able to do this.

Penn's comments:

The pieces fall into place. Commander Pennington returned to Japan in April, 1898. His wife, Catherine, followed not long after. She stayed two weeks and returned home. A few months after her return – we're not sure of precisely how much time, but it wasn't longer than two or three months -- an adoption is arranged, most likely by John's law firm in Boston, Marbright and Fuller. Keitaro becomes Asher. "The blessed" (Keitaro) becomes "the blessed"(Asher).

"Fuller" as surname is awarded through the machinations of Marbright and Fuller and the conveniently manipulable adoption laws of Massachusetts and Vermont.

Why did Catherine agree to this? Chou alluded to the reason in the previous letter, Catherine "would be free to be with her friend": In a letter addressed to Catherine:

> Dearest Catherine:
>
> You have been our great benefactor. I pray that God will bless you as you have blessed us. I miss Keitaro so much, it is like a pain that cannot be relieved, but yet I am thankful that you helped us overcome the misery that would have diminished his life and you brought him to a world where he can live and prosper.
>
> John tells me that you are very happy now with your friends and your life, and you love the child as much as any mother could. You have kindly sent us word of him and I was so happy to see his picture with you in the Spring in your beautiful valley.
>
> You have given me something that only you could give, and I have given you the joy of my beautiful son. We must thank God for this and be happy. Please send more photos and tell us what he

does as he grows. You promised to be my sister and I yours. We will keep these promises and strive for mutual joy.

Penn's comments:

Catherine did not like travel and preferred the company of her friends, one friend in particular. Her life-long companion seems to have been Elizabeth Connor, the unmarried and never married daughter of Fitzsimmons Connor, a Tammany Hall politician who, among other accomplishments both sought contractors for and contracted to build large segments of the New York subways. "Conflict of interest" apparently wasn't an issue in those days. In 1900, Fitzsimmons Connor retired and moved to Vermont, for reasons of health, or so he said. Numbered among his life-long friends was Catherine's father, James Strongbow Fitzhugh, and Theodore Roosevelt.

I sent an e-mail to Cleveland James, research assistant, and asked him to search stacks for info on daughters of Connor and Fitzhugh. There's so much published on Tammany and New York the two women should be featured in someone's study of the era. He's working with a Doctoral student at NYU on it as well.

Penn and Yoshiko started their project at four every afternoon now. Penn brought dinner, usually noodles, which Yoshiko liked, some pickled vegetables, rice and dried fish. The concierge at the hotel showed him where to get everything. After two days, Penn was a regular at the market, and he didn't have to do any shopping. He bought a metal container and the noodle shop would fill it with everything he needed. Penn and Yoshiko would eat while they worked then he'd leave at eleven to catch the last regular train back. They worked hard together. Yoshiko was very thorough, consulting dictionaries in both languages, careful to catch the exact meaning of the words in the context of the time.

Professor Sato e-mailed Penn and asked him to delay their Monday meeting until Friday morning. Penn complied, of course. On Friday he made the trip to Tokyo University and after wandering about the campus, found Sato's office. Dr. Sato was younger than Penn expected, probably not more than forty, with a broad face, a ready smile, a mop of long black hair, tobacco-stained fingers, dressed in a dark suit but with a loosened tie and open collar. An open *Lucky Strike* pack was on his desk, his office window was open, presumably to disperse the smoke, and the whole atmosphere seemed very un-Japanese, with a clutter of books and papers stacked on his desk and on shelves around the room. There were books, too, in Japanese, English, Spanish, and French. Oddly, he seemed to enjoy reading Steinbeck in Spanish and Hugo in English. Whatever Penn's academic ambitious had done, they had not eradicated his military love for precision in timing. Penn arrived at Sato's office precisely at 10 AM. The Professor was in the midst of marking papers and hardly looked up.

"Please sit," he said, "I will be with you momentarily." The professor's accent was pure California, crystalline and clear. So were his manners. He could have been from Anaheim.

Penn moved a stack of files and papers from the one chair in the office to a vacant spot on a shelf, and sat, more amused than annoyed by the Professor's preoccupation with the exams he was grading.

"If you'd like a cigarette, help yourself," said Sato, still bearing down on exam papers, "they're *Luckies*."

"No, thank you."

"Bathroom's right down the hall if you need it. Has a universal bathroom sign on it as well as 'Men' in Japanese. You can't miss it."

Penn took the hint, got up and walked around the campus for twenty minutes before returning to Sato's office. This time, the Professor jumped up and shook his hand vigorously.

"Sorry about all that. We have only so many hours to grade the students' exams then post the grades. If I don't get it done the student union raises hell with the dean and provost and they come after me. In Japan, student unions are real unions, not just snack bars and television places like in the States."

"Where did you go to school?"

"Me? Tokyo – right here, then UC at Fullerton, Stanford, and USC. I taught Japanese history and culture at Stanford and USC as well. Published a text book there in English. They still use it. I spent ten years in California. I loved it. My doctoral work was done at Stanford then followed up with post-doctoral studies at USC and back here in Tokyo. I have a second Ph.D. from Tokyo. Because I have two Ph.D.s the students here nicknamed me *Dippudaburu*, 'double-dip,' but no one says it to my face. My wife, Reiko, thinks it's hilarious. She's Japanese, but I met her at Fullerton and she wound up adopting and blending the worst parts of American and Japanese culture. I rather like the worst parts, though, so she and I fit well together. You know, pizza, ice cream and coke if they go into the right places can turn any woman into a Kardashian, one fine aspect of American culture." He cupped his hands and made a wide semicircle in the air with them as if fondling a beach ball. He sighed in delight. "She draws figures and writes stories and captions for anime cartoons. The ones with the sexy heroines. Looks like one, too, or, rather they look like her. Lord, I'm a happy man…" He paused for a moment reflecting on his contentment. Not every man is so blessed that he lusts after his own wife. Not after eleven years of marriage. "How about you? I mean, where'd you go to school?"

"US Naval Academy, Maryland, then Emory."

"You're still in the Navy, right?"

"I'm A Naval officer. Right now I'm an Assistant Professor at the Academy. As you know, I'm working on a book about Vice Admiral Pennington."

"Yes, so you wrote me. Let me tell what I've found. Want a cigarette?" He pointed to the pack of *Luckies*.

"Thanks, no. But go ahead and smoke if you want. It doesn't bother me."

"I'll shake the habit some day. Smoking used to be *de rigueur* in Japan. Every man smoked. No longer. I'm a dinosaur in that respect, maybe in other things, too… Look, first let me explain that original copies of records in Hiroshima from before 1945 are practically non-existent. Truman did one hell of job destroying the place. Tokyo and Yokohama were fire-bombed to hell, too, and Nagasaki was obliterated. Lots of other places were destroyed, too. I'm sure you're aware of all that."

"Yes, of course."

"But some records were reconstructed. People kept papers in safe deposit boxes, in safes at home, under floorboards, behind bricks and in wall cavities, other places that survived. Property ownership could usually be established. Marriage licenses were found. Birth certificates, too, and those would indicate parentage and could be used as a proof of marriage, so gradually things came together. Plus, there was a concerted effort on the part of the occupational government and the Japanese government to help reconstruct official records. Here's what we found," he handed a Xeroxed sheet to Penn, "and here's the translation."

"What is it?"

"It's the official record, or piece of a record, of the witnesses to a marriage ceremony. We got these fragments – or, rather, digital images of the fragments -- from the ruins of the *Noboricho Church,* aka *Cathedral of the Assumption of Our Lady*, rebuilt and now the *Memorial for World Peace*, Hiroshima. It seems that two people, Tanaka Choko and Takahashi Hanako witnessed the marriage of Ayumi Yamada, 47, of Hiroshima and Admiral John 'Hen-nhe-tom,' as close as the Japanese language can get to "Pennington," 58, resident foreigner – sort of a permanent or permitted resident with no limitation on his stay – also of Hiroshima."

Penn sat up, excited, "When was that?"

"The date didn't survive, but we found it with other papers from 1926. Sure you won't have a cigarette?" He dumped the contents of his ash tray into a trash can and lit a *Lucky*.

"1926. Makes sense," said Penn more to himself than to Sato.

"Why's that?"

"His American wife died in '25. He was free to marry again."

"It's odd, though, him marrying her,"

"Why? Didn't foreigners marry Japanese at that time?"

"Oh, they did, certainly. Typically, however, it was some old fart attaching himself to a young babe. Japan was still a relatively poor country and women were virtually chattel. Parents sold their daughters off to older men all the time, Japanese, foreigners, it made no difference if they could pay. The American missionaries were the only ones who complained about it, and no one listened to them. If we're right about all this, this guy, Pennington – sorry, mean no disrespect – anyway *Admiral* Pennington, who was 58, married a 47-year-old-woman, an old woman by the standards of that day. He could have had a sixteen-year-old virgin if he'd wanted one, two or three if he could afford it."

"And her name was Ayumi?"

"Yes, Yamada Ayumi, not an uncommon name in this part of Japan." He put the name in the correct order this time, surname first.

"So are Tanaka and Takahashi. Isn't that like saying Jones and Smith?"

"More like Johnson and Thompson, but I get your point. I don't think they're aliases, though. Look, my name is Sato. It's *the* most common name, and trust me, it's no alias. I think the record's good, more than adequate proof. There's something else as well."

"Yes?"

"Lady Ayumi – she was awarded the honorific 'Lady' for her work with displaced children after the war – came into a considerable sum of money late in 1947, a trust handled by a law firm."

"Let me guess, Marbright and Fuller of Boston, Massachusetts?"

"Let me see. . .Yes, it's here in my notes. . ." He ruffled through the pages of a dog-eared, tea stained student notebook. "Here it is . . . No" He flipped more pages while he held his cigarette between his middle and index fingers. Ashes sprinkled his desk. . . "Ah! Here! Marbright and Fuller, Boston, Mass. How did you know?"

"They did other work for the family. I saw their name elsewhere." An image of the letters flashed in Penn's mind, followed by an image of Yoshiko. "Any mention of the Admiral in connection with the trust?"

"No. None. But the way she used the money is interesting. She expanded her business that year and founded a school for impoverished children. I would guess the trust enabled all that. The government stepped in later and funded the construction of a much larger school and home for displaced children. She ran it for seven years as administrator/head mistress, then she retired, or semi-retired. She still had her inn, Hana House, and its Tea House. She remained an advocate for the cause of poor or displaced children, not only in Japan but world-wide. She contributed to the peace memorial – her name is in one of the stained-glass windows – and stayed in the spotlight for a long time."

"How do you know all this?"

"I checked the newspapers. There was a long obituary in *Asahi shimbun.* Other papers, too. The Catholic press eulogized her as well. Bishop Luke Katsusaburo Arai of the Diocese of Yokohama, no youngster at the time, spoke vigorously and at length at her memorial service. St. Andrew's Cathedral in Yokohama was filled with people; even an emissary of Emperor Hirohito arrived. Buddhist and Shinto services and memorials were held, too. Everybody seems to have loved her. Aside from that, it appears that one of the kids she rescued grew up to become Takeuchi Akito, a media mogul, well, if not exactly a mogul he was CEO of *Asahi shimbun*. He did all he could to publicize her story, at least the parts of it that began after the war. Admiral Pennington's name is never mentioned, however, even though he'd been her husband since 1926."

"The Admiral had a knack for avoiding publicity. That's one of the things that makes him so hard to research. When he wasn't commanding ships, his job was to watch, report and advise, and to stay in the shadows. I even have a source that claims MacArthur's decision to spare the Emperor and his family was based on advice from the Admiral."

Sato whistled softly. "*Jeez!*…Is the source credible?"

"I think so. Once I review the entire document (he meant the book from Sandhurst) I'll cross-check it and look for holes, lies or exaggerations. Typically, a hoax isn't isolated in a book. The whole book will be based on lies and nonsense."

"Well, let me stuff all the copies I have for you into an envelope," he said, popping open an ancient messenger envelope, dropping ashes on his desk, and shoving the papers inside. "I've got three obituaries here, including the one from the Catholic press, and an article that appeared about Lady Ayumi's funeral. There are also the copies of the marriage witness papers and a few other items. You can keep all of these."

"I don't know what to say. Is there anything I can do for you? Any way I can repay you?"

"Can you get into the PX at Yokohama?"

"Sure. No problem."

"Here's my card. My home address is on the back. Get me a couple of bottles of Chivas. I'd really appreciate it."

"I'll do it today. Anything else?"

"Throw in a carton of Camels."

"I don't know if I can get them. Some PX outlets don't sell tobacco anymore."

"Do what you can."

Penn took the train directly to the American Naval Base and arranged for a case of Chivas to be sent to the Professor's home that afternoon. He could have sent him the cigarettes as well but it grated against his principles to do it, so he added a large box of expensive chocolates instead. If Sato's wife really had picked up American habits, she was probably a chocolate lover and there would be something in it for her and her hips as well.

Penn arrived at Yoshiko's house a little after 4 PM. She was waiting for him, tea steaming in its pot, the heat turned on in the dining room, all the papers readied for work. She saw him coming up the walk through the living room window and popped open the front door before he had a chance to knock. Two days before she called her uncle and told it the police patrols were no longer necessary or wanted. He was happy to comply.

Penn and Yoshiko set up bowls and plates and as they ate dinner, he told her about his meeting with Sato. She was excited. She grabbed the envelope and read through the copies of the papers, the obituaries, everything.

"This does it, Penn," she said, "It's proof of the marriage, and these obituaries are so wonderful. No wonder they buried her by the Admiral. She was his wife. They loved for over fifty years. In his will he must have left the trust fund to her, and she used it to rescue children and establish the school. Look, there's something I've been meaning to show you," she took out the folio that held her Grandmother Keiko's book. "This is a little book my grandmother wrote, an autobiography of sorts. It's really a testament of her love for and gratitude to Lady Ayumi. I translated this section. It's Called 1945."

Penn took the sheets and read them as Yoshiko set up dinner and heated it in the microwave.

Grandmother Keiko's Book

The Sorrow of 1945

> In that awful year, 1945, Lady Ayumi still retained her Tea Houses in Hiroshima, using every connection and favor she could to keep them supplied and open. Luckily, Hiroshima so far was spared the devastating bombing raids that hit Tokyo and other cities, despite the Naval headquarters there. Many of the citizens thought the city would be spared because there was the large Cathedral and so many people were Christians.
>
> In March, 1945, one of Lady Ayumi's oldest customers, Captain Hisakawa of the Japanese Imperial Navy, had a private dinner with her. He brought all the ingredients and the kitchen prepared them. Lady Ayumi and the Captain ate together, congenially, for they were old acquaintances. When the food was done, he leaned closely to her and talked with her in a very secretive manner about his fears. I, Keiko, know everything that was said because the walls were only of paper, and I was in the next room folding napkins and linen and despite their whispering I could hear them very well, and I remember everything they said.
>
> "Hiroshima," he said, "Is doomed. Japan will lose this war, has lost this war. We should have surrendered long ago, but the idiots in command, the fools who got

us into this war refused to do so and *still* refuse. If the Americans don't destroy us and occupy the land, the Soviets will. As soon as the war with Germany is over, and that will be very soon, Stalin will turn on us. Again, the fools in our government refuse to believe that. In all events there is no future unless we surrender and negotiate some terms. Even an unconditional surrender to the Americans would be better than to continue, much better, especially if it keeps the Soviets off our territory."

As I said, they spoke in whispers. They wanted no one to hear this conversation.

"Because we can no longer fight?" she said.

"Because we have yet – or our leaders have yet – to understand the enemy. The thirst for absolute victory among the Americans is insatiable. They won't negotiate. Their only term is unconditional surrender. The longer we hold out, the more we will be destroyed and humiliated. We have no defenses any more. Our Navy is powerless against their massive sea force, and we cannot defend our skies. Tokyo and other cities are a shambles. Nothing is too much for them in war; they want to end it on their terms and will stop at nothing. The reports of what happened in Dresden, Germany, last month are horrid, incredible. Have you heard?"

She shook her head, "No. I know nothing about it."

"Of course not. Our government would never share this dreadful thing with the people. Dresden is – or was – a beautiful city. I visited it when I went to Germany in 1934. It is ancient with well-kept stone buildings, a city for an artist or a story-book, and a cultural center as well. I was very impressed, fell in love with the place. The British and Americans bombed every target they could find in Germany, including the hospitals and schools in Berlin and elsewhere, but they spared Dresden. The city was beautiful and there was no strategic importance to it, no military targets. They spared it until last month, that is," the old Captain took a drink of tea and his eyes watered.

"On February 15, American and British bombers, 1,200 of them, attacked the city, and carpeted it with incendiary bombs, destroying everything. Can you imagine 1,200 bombers blackening the sky dropping fiery death on everyone? There was so much fire, it caused what is called a 'fire storm.' The air was sucked out of the city and fresh air rushed in, intensifying the heat like the bellows on a blacksmith's fire, causing a mushroom-shaped column of flame that reached to the skies. The Germans say that hundreds of thousands of people were killed, but of course the Americans and their allies deny that."

"How terrible!" said Ayumi," But what does that mean for us?"

"Despite devastating bombing in some of our cities and ports, others have been spared. One of those cities -- spared so far -- is Hiroshima. I am afraid if we do not surrender, Hiroshima will become their target, or one of their targets, just as Dresden was, and they will destroy us just as horribly. The Americans see no cruelty in this. They see it as justifiable because we initiated the war and this overwhelming violence will bring it to an end. We thought they were soft and that their real interests were in Europe, not Asia. We thought they'd negotiate a peace with us after we destroyed their fleet at Perl Harbor but they fought instead. Their resources are endless and their demands are unprecedented in modern warfare. We cannot underestimate their determination." he said.

"What do you recommend?" she said.

"The war will end within six months, I am sure of that," he said, "Leave Hiroshima. Go somewhere outside the city, someplace small and far from any targets, and wait for the end. Your business isn't very good anyway. You can close for a while and reopen when the war is over, if there is anything left here. This is my best advice. My only advice. Leave. Leave as soon as you can and wait for the end."

I could only see shadows, so I had to guess as to what they were doing. Here is what I think I saw. Ayumi agreed to depart Hiroshima, nodding her head. As the Captain stood to leave, she embraced him, and he hugged her, and I think he kissed her once, gently on the forehead, whispering "Sweet Chou," her nickname. There were tears in his eyes for her, for himself, for his country and people. I could hear him sobbing. See him rubbing his face. Ayumi pitied him; or so she told me later. She was at least free to go. He was trapped here by the iron constraints of duty. That was their last meeting; their last conversation. She never saw him again, nor he, her.

She found a place in the village of Hisaka, several miles outside Hiroshima, a little Tea House and restaurant whose owner was old and wanted to sell-out. She bought it. Both her Tea Houses in Hiroshima were sold cheaply to the owner of the neighboring buildings, but if the Captain was right, keeping them would make for a worse loss. I and some others chose to move with her, but most of the staff stayed behind, preferring their chances in the city to moving out to some rural location.

By May, we were fully at home in her little Tea House and noodle shop. Her cook in Hiroshima did not follow her, but the man who cooked for the previous owners of her new enterprise agreed to stay on. His work was not as brilliant as the culinary art she had in Hiroshima, but nevertheless very satisfactory, and she had plenty of help from me. Although still a child, I learned the business well, and was developing into a shrewd and capable manager. Clean, well-fed and dressed in proper clothing, I was said to be cute as well, and could be clever and funny. The customers liked me, and I liked them in return. Many said they came just to see me, forget the grim realities of life, and laugh with me. I say this because it was the truth, not to try to portray myself as anything more than I was.

In August, as the Captain predicted, Hiroshima was destroyed. We could hear the terrible boom of the bomb that fell on the city, and the sky darkened. The smell of smoke from the fires of Hiroshima infected the air of our small village for days. People wept openly when they heard the news of the utter devastation of Hiroshima, then Nagasaki, and again when Japan surrendered. Then, to aggravate the agony, a natural disaster struck. On September 17, 1945 Hiroshima was devastated by the Makurazaki Typhoon, killing 3,000 people. Gloom descended.

The peace that followed at first offered little hope. Lady Ayumi had assets, money and what was most important gold and jewelry, and some tracts of land – I know this because I was closest to her and she trusted me with everything regarding the business -- but she could not return to Hiroshima. No one could. Instead, as the weeks passed and the American occupation began in earnest, she looked to Yokohama. The Americans were planning a base there and so far they had proven not to be the devils portrayed in government propaganda. On the contrary, most were attractive young men, and people found them to be light-hearted and generous, even foolhardy with their money, and kind to children.

She made the trip to Yokohama, not easy to do at that time, and surveyed the situation. Yokohama was subjected to fire-bombing in May, 1945, just as Dresden was. Tens of thousands of people died and almost half the city was turned to rubble. But Yokohama is a city that survived destruction in the recent past through earthquake and fire and rose up again. It was rising now, as Lady Ayumi surveyed the possibilities. Land was already creeping up in value. She purchased a suitable building, still very cheap by pre-war standards, cleaned it, furnished it with used and repaired items, and set up business once again. She sold the Tea House in the village to the cook and started over. She was sixty-five and a whole new phase of her life began, the most wonderful phase.

"Look at this!" said Penn, taking the paper from Yoshiko, "This old friend, Captain Hisakawa, who came to warn Ayumi and probably saved her life, he called her 'Chou.' Keiko writes that 'Chou' was her nickname. No wonder she signed her letters 'Chou.' Of course. . . it all makes sense. She moved out of Hiroshima a few months before the bomb fell, then to Yokohama after Japan's surrender. Yokohama would be rebuilt and redeveloped by the occupation forces. It was the best chance she had for the type of business she ran, the best place to be. Admiral Pennington returned with MacArthur a month after the bomb fell. I wonder how long it took before they were reunited."

"Not long," said Yoshiko, setting the meal on the table. "Further on in her book Grandmother Keiko says that newspapers – small ones – started up in September and there was radio news as well. People even went to the movies where movie houses still stood or watched old movies projected on the sides of buildings. According to Lady Keiko, Ayumi saw a newspaper that mentioned the Admiral accompanying a Japanese municipal director on a port inspection. That was all she needed. She sent a letter to him at the embassy. He responded five days later and within two days after that visited her. He had a residency in Tokyo, but he spent as much time here as he possibly could."

Yoshiko and Penn began to eat. "There is something else I translated as well. It's in the stack to your left. It's another part of her Book."

Penn reached over and took the sheets.

Grandmother Keiko's Book

Picture Books

The picture books tell the story better than words do. There were many children like me in Japan at that sad time, many without parents or whose parents were so poor they could not keep them. As her business flourished, Lady Ayumi took in as many as she could. They worked in the kitchen, served the guests, helped with the cleaning, and did various tasks. She put me in charge and I enjoyed the work. Having been a street child I understood them and they trusted me. The Lady, however, would not just make them work, she created her own school. She bought the next building, outfitted it as well as she could with repaired furniture and some implements, and hired two teachers, an old man and his wife who were retired teachers but were happy to work for meals and a little money.

Lady Ayumi had a friend, and that is all I can say about him because she made me swear to secrecy about him. I can say that her friend sometimes came to visit and stayed with her because everyone saw him and knew him, and he talked with everyone. At first he frightened me, because his face seemed stern and very hard, like the stories one hears of the old Samurai, but then I saw him smile and laugh with the very small children. How gentle he was! And he smiled at me as well, and always spoke to me kindly in a soft voice. I could see kindness beneath the stone and what frightened me at first about him soon became warm and beautiful. Ayumi and her friend seemed to be very close. She told me he was an important man and had influence with the powerful people that would build the new Japanese government.

Ayumi's friend encouraged those powerful men to take an interest in her school, in the young women and boys she rescued from the streets. They, in turn, helped by getting the government to grant funds to the school. Eventually her small school seemed so successful the government in 1949 replaced it with the *Work, Live, and Learn Center for Displaced Youth*. Many hundreds of young people survived those days, were educated and given decent lives because of that school and home. Then, as time healed the wounds of war, there was less need for such a place and it gradually closed-down, but while it operated it saved many lives.

Lady Ayumi kept a picture book of the young women and boys she helped in the early days before the government money came and the school expanded. The book contains photos of them, and photos of their children and some grandchildren as well. It has their prayers, written on notes, newspaper articles about the school, and some articles about the accomplishments of the people she rescued. The "book" is very thick and is more than one book. It is in several volumes. She would say that to turn each page and look at the faces is to say a prayer for charity and goodness. Remember that, keep the books well, and honor her memory always.

"The friend of Lady Ayumi. That must have been the Admiral," said Yoshiko, "When I first read this, I thought the man must be Japanese. She writes of him having a face like a Samurai. I think she probably meant his face was weathered and strong, the face of sea Captain as well as a Samurai, or perhaps she was just trying to mislead the reader without directly lying since she was sworn not to reveal who he was. It seems clear to me that she meant the Admiral, though."

"I have to agree," said Penn, "All of this fits very well with what Sato told me and with the information we received today."

They were quiet for a few seconds.

"How many more letters are left?" said Penn.

"Only five." She sighed.

This was their seventh evening together. At first their evenings were spent on opposite sides of the table, but that changed. One evening they just sat together on the same side, then gradually slid closer. When something came up that was exciting or new or particularly touching, Keiko would touch his arm or knee or thigh.

They were so close now their legs were touching. It seemed natural and warm and comfortable. She picked up a small piece of pickled radish and put in his mouth. She giggled, which was unusual for her. She was usually so serious and concentrated so well. He smiled back and tried to do the same, but his dexterity with the chopsticks was no match for hers.

"You never told me about *Traviata* at *La Scala*," she said.

Penn told her story of Lucia begging for the chance to see the opera, his attempts at getting the tickets and the scalping done by Benedetti. He also told her how beautiful the performance was, the singing and acting of Angela Gheorghiu and Ramon Vargas, how exciting it was and how touching the final death scene. They looked up *La Scala* on the internet and he pointed out exactly where Lucia and he sat during the performance.

"What happened to Lucia?"

Penn laughed, "Lucia, Lucia. After all that, the minute I left for Iraq she moved in with Benedetti. He married her. I'm told they now have two children and live in Pisa."

"Do you ever miss her?"

"No, not in the least. We weren't really in love. We were convenient for each other, I suppose, and liked each other, but there was never real love, not like the love between Lady Ayumi and the Admiral. Nothing like that. . ." His voice trailed off.

"And that is what you want, you really want?"

He looked at her. She touched his arm and for a just a moment the sprightliness that animated her face all evening vanished and an eagerness overtook her, as if she were pleading for an answer.

Penn saw it, but was so afraid of saying or doing anything that would hurt her, he evaded the question. "Let's clean up and look at the letters you translated today."

She sighed and smiled, a small sad smile, "Yes. Ok. Ok." *No answer*, she thought, *he doesn't feel that way at all or maybe he does and doesn't want to say, or maybe he doesn't feel anything.*

****

Chapter Twenty-Nine – Breaking the Jar

Three more nights and the work was finished. They had spent ten days together. Penn wanted to take her out to dinner, but she demurred. "Just bring something special over. We'll celebrate here, by ourselves. It's simpler and cheaper and better that way."

He bought a bottle of Champagne, a cantaloupe – which is a luxury in Japan – a gold pen and pencil set as a gift for her, and had a special meal prepared by the restaurant."

He dressed in the one suit he'd taken with him, and showed up at her door at six, the time they'd set for that last evening.

It went well. They toasted one another repeatedly and got silly. She tried to get him to sing *Brindisi* the drinking song from *Traviata* with her while she played keyboard, but even with the music and libretto in front of him he fumbled through his parts of it and sang flat, while she sang gloriously. More champagne.

The evening passed too quickly. Eleven PM loomed. He thanked her profusely for all her help and she walked him to the door.

Her took her hands in his, as he usually did, and looked down at her. He was about to say goodbye when she jumped up and kissed him on the lips. He hugged her. She folded into him. The kiss went on and on. He missed the last train. It didn't matter. He was in love. They were in love. . .

The sun rose but they ignored it for four hours. Penn lay with her in his arm and gently sat up.

"What is it?"

"I have to go back to the hotel for a bit."

"Why?"

"I can't live in one set of clothes."

"Can I come?"

"I never want you out of my sight," said Penn, kissing her. "Please, come with me."

They washed and dressed and almost fell back into bed together but somehow had the strength to resist it.

By the time they arrived at the hotel, they had no resistance left and this time did fall into bed together, the sheets wrinkling, the plastic cover over the mattress making crinkling noises, the bed shushing and groaning as they hungrily feasted on the touch and taste of each other, making love, laughing, getting up and falling together again. The hotel had no room service but there were restaurants that would deliver, so they ordered food and never left the room.

The next morning she reluctantly returned home by herself because he said he had some unavoidable business on the Naval Base and would meet her at 2 PM. She spent the morning at Lady Keiko's tomb telling her all that had transpired.

Penn's "unavoidable business" was at the jewelers. Penn wasn't an impulsive man, but he was a man who could act swiftly and boldly when he saw the course of action he would take. He knew what he wanted and he wasn't going to lose it. He was on time as usual, precisely 2 PM at Yoshiko's house. She opened the door. He entered, fell to one knee, offered her a ring that cost him ¥1,777,859.95 ($18,000.00) paid-for with a cashier's check, and asked her to marry him. She fell to her knees gasping "yes" and thanked him on the tatami.

Yoshiko was the one he had hoped-for, the one who smashed the bell jar and brought him back to life. He was certain of that, of her. He would have married her that second if it were possible, but of course her family had to know and a proper wedding had to be planned.

Or did it?

She called her parents and told them the news. Her father had been through the weddings of his two sons, as had her mother. Her parents loved her, but they were people of service to others who saw little value in wasting time and money on elaborate wedding rituals. At one point in the past, her father told Yoshiko he wouldn't be offended if she eloped or ran to Vegas when she was in the states. He said that jokingly, but she knew that in his heart he wanted to avoid any more wedding nonsense and expense. He was older, semi-retired, and wanted to spend his years doing what he could to relieve the pain and misery of the world. He didn't have far to go; there was plenty to do in Japan since the tsunami.

When she told her parents that the man who proposed was the great-grandson of Admiral Pennington and Lady Ayumi, they were beside themselves with joy. She could hear her mother weeping. After the initial shock, her father asked her gently, "Are you married yet?"

"No, father" she said, "We were engaged today."

"Will you be married by the time we return?"

"Would you like us to be?"

"We wish for your happiness. If marriage today is what you wish, then, please, be happy. We'll tell your brothers."

Yoshiko smiled. She'd just been given permission to elope, but instead she'd go for a church wedding if she could. First, there was a civil ceremony, a license and contract really, which is required by law in Japan, then the marriage can be blessed by any sort of priest or minister you chose, or never blessed at all. It didn't matter; the civil ceremony bound you legally. After that, a simple church marriage could be arranged.

Father Scanlon, of the Society of Jesus, looked askance at Penn and Yoshiko.

"The church wants you to attend Cana Conferences for a year

before you marry. It also wants to announce banns for nine weeks," he said with a think Irish Brogue.

"We know, father," said Penn, "But we were already married officially at City Hall, and we really don't have much time before we return to the states. Yoshiko has to begin rehearsing and I have to return to my teaching."

Scanlon frowned and touched his coffee mug, thinking. The mug was emblazoned with a map of Ireland, one county in the northwest, Sligo, highlighted in green.

"You're from County Sligo, Father?" said Penn.

"You know the place? No Penningtons there, I'm afraid."

"Have you heard of Ballintogher?" said Penn.

"Oh, I've heard of it sure enough. I was brought up only a few kilometers from there in Drumrane."

"Ever hear of man named Patrick O'Mally, an American airman?" said Penn.

"Patrick O'Mally? You know of him?"

"Pilot. WWII, Korea, Vietnam. Won the Congressional Medal of Honor," said Penn.

"Oh, he was even more than that. He was a story-teller, a kind and generous fellow, too. He married Mary Chin and was one of the great, the legendary men of the town. I went to his funeral. If God loved him the way people did, he's sitting in heaven right now, probably teaching the angels to fly. How do you know him?"

"We helped his widow get into contact with the widow of a military colleague of his."

"Well, isn't it a small world?" Scanlon went back to studying his coffee mug for a moment.

"The church allows exceptions, son, or perhaps I should call you Commander," he looked at Yoshiko, and in flawless Japanese said "You've been very quiet Miss Yoshiko, what do you have to say?"

She answered in English. "Marry us quickly, Father. We can't wait, and it is urgent," and she added as an afterthought, "Would you like me to sing at Mass this Sunday?"

Penn leaned forward. "Yoshiko is a trained singer, Father. Opera. She sings professionally. She has a beautiful voice."

"Can you sing the Ave Maria?"

"Schubert's, Caccini's, whichever you want, or both if you'd like."

"Sing Schubert at the 9:30 Mass and I'll do the marriage at 11:00. Do you need witnesses?"

"My brother and his wife will be there."

"Good. That gives us two. You have the paperwork done?"

"Yes, father," she handed him an envelope with the certification of marriage from the city office.

"Good. You're bound by the law of man. Sunday we'll have God do it." His face turned stern and he waved his finger. "Be good until then." Then he smiled.

Before they left he blessed them both.

St. Ignatius Parish wasn't the largest in the area, but the church was comfortable, smallish, and warm inside. Yoshiko sang "Ave Maria" to a church full to standing room. Applause isn't usual during services, but this time the parishioners applauded. During Communion she sang, too, accompanied by the church pianist, and she sang for the recessional. Father Scanlon fairly beamed with pride as he greeted his parishioners after mass and they shook his hand or bowed and told him how beautiful the service was.

For the marriage ceremony Yoshiko dressed in a rented wedding Kimono, and Penn wore a tuxedo he purchased at the last minute at the Yokohama Sogo Department store. The store's reputation for customer service seemed well-earned. The Tux was good quality and they tailored it on the spot. Some Japanese brides will appear in both western and Japanese dress, usually wearing a rented wedding dress, but neither Yoshiko nor Penn wanted or needed that. They looked good together, natural, well-matched and happy.

To Yoshiko's surprise, her parents and both her brothers and their families arrived, so her entire family was there. Others came too, alerted when the word spread that the great-grandson of Admiral Pennington was marrying the granddaughter of Lady Keiko and the daughter of Dr. Fujiyama. The *Yokohama News* picked up the story and put a picture of the couple on their equivalent of the society page. The day after *Asahi shimbun* reported the story as well.

The service was simple; no nuptial mass. Many people congratulated the two, bowed or shook Penn's hand or slapped him on the back and shook the doctor's hand. There was a pile of gifts, completely unexpected, and someone sent a limousine to the church door. The family and happy couple, still in a daze, were taken to a local restaurant, feted and never presented a bill. There were many toasts and the food keep coming for hours.

Yoshiko moved her things into Penn's hotel room that evening, and they fell into bed never wanting to part. At 4 AM, however, Yoshiko awakened and started to cry. Penn held her and said nothing for a while.

"Darling, when I go on tour, I'll be away from you," she said.

"Not very far away, and we'll arrange to be with one another. I'll stay at Annapolis. Teaching offers lots of time to be away and to travel. And if we are apart, the time we're together will be that much more precious. Think of the love of the Admiral and Ayumi, and how that survived so many years. I'm his blood, darling, and I'll stay with you until we, too, are buried together."

"I know," she said, "but...." The sentence was unfinished. He kissed away the tears and they fell back to sleep in each other's arms. They were fools, of course, too in love to see how rash they were or to consider the consequences of what they'd done; too full of love to see one another realistically, to have any concept of the difficulty and sacrifices involved with sharing your life bound legally and emotionally with another. But if people did think of all that rationally, carefully considering the risks and disadvantages, would anyone ever marry?

At 10:00 AM their phone rang. Front desk had a package for them. Penn told them to send it up. The package was wrapped in heavy off-white paper closed with the ribbon and seal of Emperor Akihito. Penn opened it to discover a gorgeous gilt card, embossed with the seal of the Chrysanthemum Throne and a box. The card contained an inscription in Japanese with a signature. Yoshiko opened the box. It contained a brilliant gold bowl with the Emperor's seal stamped in the base.

"I don't believe this," said Yoshiko, "It's a congratulatory note from the Imperial house. Wishing us long life, happiness, prosperity, good health and many children. The Shinto Priests have been ordered to pray for our well-being. The Emperor can do that, you know, he's the titular head of the Shinto religion."

"Good. They'll keep the demons away." Penn hefted the bowl in one hand, raising and lowering it to get a feel for the weight. "The bowl appears to be solid gold, thick, heavy gold, probably 18 carat or higher." said Penn, "What's proper when you get a wedding gift from Emperor Akihito. Do you send him a thank-you card?"

"Yes, I suppose so. I'll ask mother."

The *Thank You* card went out that afternoon.

****

Chapter Thirty – The Lawyer

Skies the color of pig iron were lowering over San Francisco, a cold wind blew in from the bay and threatened rain the entire day, although no rain came until late that night. Penn and Yoshiko walked from the Hotel Nikko, where they were staying, all the way over to the law offices of Fuller, Ricardo, and Nguyen. They both liked walking, took their time and enjoyed the city. It was Penn's first time in the town, but not Yoshiko's. She chatted about her favorite restaurants and where National Lyric Opera performed when in town. She'd sung both at the Performing Arts Center on Van Ness, which is home to the San Francisco Opera, and at Symphony Hall. She preferred the Hall, but anyplace you can perform is a good place, and San Franciscans were a great audience, savvy and explosively enthusiastic. The critics in San Francisco always treated her well and she always enjoyed her visits here, even if they usually stayed at the ancient King George Hotel or someplace even older and mustier.

They were on time, but Fuller wasn't. They had to wait 30 minutes for him, and once he arrived they had to wait another ten minutes for him to do whatever he had to do in the morning. They were finally ushered into his office, a large, clean, modern-looking, obsessively neat desert of oversized stained teak veneer furniture, a built-in credenza that ran the width of the room under a large picture window that overlooked Jackson Square, the left wall lined with enough wooden vertical files to house all the records of a small nation. On the wall were two original oils by Thomas Calmann, *The Painter of the West*, large, expensive paintings of cowboys wrangling steers or driving them through an imaginary semi-desert somewhere in the vast reaches of the American western frontier.

Comstock Fremont Fuller's desk was clean, save for a black writing mat. His computer was mounted on a side return, and he was seated in a large black leather Eames chair, a five thousand dollar original, not a knock-off. His jacket hung on a coat-rack in a way to make to make the label visible. It was Oxxford. Both Bill Clinton and George Bush wore Oxxford suits while in the white house. The overall impression until you met the inhabitant, was one of understated wealth, neatness, confidence and order. His framed diplomas boasted of an undergrad degree from Stanford, Bachelor of Arts, and a Juris Doctor from Berkeley's Boalt Hall.

The lawyer's hair was obviously died dark blond to cover the gray. The roots were showing. His face had the seamless look of Botox paralysis coupled with a lift. His teeth were capped and bleached. His skin looked artificially tan, and he wore a gold Rolex on his left hand balanced with a glittering gold medic-alert bracelet on his right. He didn't wear a wedding band, but he sported a white gold pinky ring with a two-carat diamond set in it. He could be either a prosperous lawyer, a funds manager, a Carney owner, a well-to-do Mafioso, or a quiz show host. He had perfected in a most personal way that look of gilded tackiness that adheres to certain types of swindlers and hucksters.

"Penn Fuller, and this is my wife, Yoshiko." He liked the sound of "my wife." Yoshiko liked it as well.

"Comstock Fuller"

They shook hands, first Penn and Comstock then Yoshiko.

"You contacted us to ask about the files of Marbright and Fuller. How did you ever find us?"

"It wasn't easy," said Penn. "We were lucky enough to find some references to the termination of Marbright and Fuller in an article that mentioned Mr. Fuller's grandson was with the firm of Stern, Powers and Plimpton. That firm dissolved in the late 60s, but again there seemed to be a Fuller in legal practice in Massachusetts, this time for the city of Braintree. The Massachusetts Bar association helped with that; they went into their archives and provided some useful information. I gather the City Attorney was your father."

"Yes, that's right," he said flashing his fluorescent smile.

"Well, your father has passed on, but not your uncle. He told us you'd gone West. You were named for Comstock and Fremont anyway – apparently there's a family connection – and you wound up in San Francisco. The California Bar gave us your business affiliation."

"Some detective work, there," he said, sounding not too sure he liked any of this.

"I'm an historian, and I had some help from a colleague who does forensic document work."

"You want to know what happened to the records from Marbright and Fuller, specifically your grandfather's adoption files, right?"

"Yes," said Penn, "can you help us with that?"

"The files themselves weren't saved. We do have some old records on microfiche, though, another obsolete recording methodology."

"Do they go back to 1901?"

"1872, but they're not complete. There could be missing items. Over that much time – well, you're an historian, you know. Water, rats, fire, unintentional loss, intentional loss."

"Can I look at them?"

"We've done it for you. You wanted to know about the adoption of a male child in 1898, who was approximately 1 year old. There was only child of that description handled by the firm in 1898, a Babyboy Doe. We printed the records and have them on hand."

"If you do. . . I. . . We would be very grateful."

"There's the matter of the fee. Talk with June Little, our administrator, and she'll fill you in."

June Little had the pleasant appearance of a hungry carnivore, coyote-like, sly, sneaky and dripping with insincerity.

"Mr. and Mrs. Fuller, let's see, there were three hours of work done to retrieve these items, then there's the handling and printing fees, the copy fees, storage fees and tax for the records. That comes to eighteen hundred and seventy-two dollars and thirty-nine cents."

Yoshiko blanched and looked at Penn, who casually withdrew his credit card from his wallet.

"I'm sorry, sir, but we don't take American Express, only Visa and Master Charge."

"You will take a check?"

"If it's a cashier's check, yes, but a personal check, no."

Penn handed her a Visa card. She scanned it and the total bill came up on the computer, $2,380.54.

"Is there something wrong? You told me Eighteen hundred dollars and you've just rung up over twenty-three hundred."

"The attorney's fee, of course. Consultations are five hundred dollars per hour."

Yoshiko turned red. "He only gave us five minutes. That means he owes us fifty-five more."

Yoshiko picked up the file and marched into Fuller's office. "You owe us fifty-five minutes. "She dumped the file on his desk. "Tell us what's in here and explain what his is all about!"

Under normal circumstances, Fuller would have pushed a blue button just on the right side of his desk well which would signal Ms. Little to call building security, but the Bar association had been scrutinizing Fuller, Ricardo, and Nguyen due to a number of client complaints about their billing practices and had threatened to censor the firm. They were censored two years before and another problem now might get the firm on the Bar's "blue list" of lawyers to avoid. Instead of pushing the button, he smiled his most winning smile, which would probably scare some small children, and went through the papers quickly, separating them into two piles. As he did this, Penn joined his wife, the tiger.

"This is an adoption proceeding. Let me start by saying this would be highly irregular today, actually illegal, but in 1901 in New England and probably elsewhere they did it this way. Babyboy Doe is presented with a birth certificate based on the statements of two witnesses that will swear the boy is a native born citizen. They'll also swear to the date or approximate date of birth. A birth certificate will then be recorded with "parents unknown." The child will then be put under the legal custody of the law firm and the court will be informed. You have to understand, lots of babies were born outside hospitals in those days. Birthed by mid-wives or the family. Some people, many people, had no paperwork, so ginning up birth certificates years after birth took place was pretty common."

Fuller produced a bottle of Evian from somewhere under his desk, took a drink of water, then continued, "Court approval was perfunctory, given within minutes by the presiding clerk. The firm with custody would then adopt the child and make the child a ward of one of the partners. This time it was Fuller's turn. After some short period of time, another party would approach the child's guardian, Mr. Fuller, and request he abandon his claim to the child and allow for permanent adoption by Mr. and Mrs. X, again in this case Commander Pennington and his wife Catherine. The adoption occurs in Vermont and is handled by a Vermont "partner" firm. The child's natural parents are listed as Mr. and Mrs. Fuller, and the adopted parents Mr. and Mrs. Pennington. The record is then sealed in Vermont. The Penningtons, of course, may change the child's name and in this case they did from "Henry" – which was temporary – to "Asher." They could have changed the last name as well, but they chose to retain "Fuller," apparently because some family members feared that changing the last name would signal this child was the product of an illicit relationship by someone in the family."

"The process sounds convoluted," said Penn.

"They were good at it," said Fuller, his eyes watering with admiration, "Lawyers in those days would fearlessly manipulate the law for their clients. The way this was done, even if the adoption records were stolen or the seal broken, the trail would end without revealing the true parent. It sounds awkward, but some law firms were very adept at this. Some even churned the child through three or four temporary adoptions before delivering the baby whole, fat, goo-gooing and happy to the final custodians, usually the true grandparents." He sighed. "We'll never see that era again," he said, wistful and nostalgic.

"One last thing," said Penn, "Marbright and Fuller was the mail recipient for letters from Japan. Were you able to find anything in that regard?"

Fuller smiled," Marbright and Fuller had a lucrative business dealing with Japanese and Japanese-American clients, and with Americans trying to do business in Japan. The firm even had a Japanese-American partner, but his name wasn't on the letterhead, Victor Nakahara, Esq., Harvard Law grad, also Tokyo University grad. He dealt with Japanese legal issues – Ever see a Japanese contract? They still can't write a decent contract.—and had a small staff who translated documents for us and our clients. In all likelihood, they were translating the letters and then translating the responses. It was easy work, not like some 20-page contract, or some other legal document, and they charged a hefty fee for it. Good business, doing that," he sighed, "I was born at the wrong point in history, I think."

Fuller paused for a minute, put his hands behind his head and looked at the ceiling. "You're aware, of course, that laws were on the books that excluded or tightly controlled the emigration of people from Asia to the United States. They were strictest on the Chinese, but Japanese and Filipinos, the other large Asian immigration groups, were also affected. That's another area where Marbright and Fuller, along with Nakahara, excelled. They quietly bragged they could get anyone into the states for permanent residency with little fuss or bother. They knew just what levers to pull and palms to lubricate." He sighed, closed his eyes for a second and shook his head, touched with nostalgia for those halcyon days.

After a respectful second or two of contemplation, the lawyer sat up and continued, "State anti-miscegenation laws were something else, however. Although, I'll tell you, Vermont never had an anti-miscegenation law on the books and Massachusetts repealed its anti-miscegenation laws in the 1840s, although Massachusetts did recognize the anti-miscegenation laws of other states. In other words if you married outside your race, in, say, Virginia, where that would be illegal, then moved to Mass, you'd have to remarry. Marbright and Fuller and Nakahara made money from that business, too. Your grandfather, by the way, married in Vermont. I don't know if that was by accident or by design but he was part Japanese, although no one outside your family knew it, and he did marry a gal right out of the social register."

Penn thanked him, collected the file, shook the man's hand and left. Yoshiko scooted out of the office before him. She stopped at the door of Ms. Little's office.

"Excuse me, where is the rest room?"

"Out the door, past the elevators and on your left."

"Thank you. Is there a charge for using it?"

She frowned. "No, we can't do that. It's the property of the building owner." She said that with the tone a person might use who was frustrated with an intransigent and irrational bureaucracy.

Penn followed Yoshiko down the hall. "I want to wash my hands. I shook hands with that fellow twice and I feel slimy."

****

Chapter Thirty-One – Philadelphia, Vermont, Annapolis

Penn and Yoshiko were heading to Vermont so that Yoshiko could meet Penn's family before they traveled to Annapolis. They had a few weeks for a honeymoon. It was just Valentine's Day. Penn wasn't expected back to the classroom until the second week of March. Yoshiko wasn't needed for rehearsal until April. On the way to Vermont they planned a brief stop in Philadelphia. Yoshiko wanted to introduce Penn to the Feldsteins and Penn, whose trips to Philly had never included seeing the historical sites, was happy both to meet these good people who had sponsored her and to visit Independence Hall, Carpenter's Hall, Benjamin Franklin's grave and see the Liberty Bell. If they had the time, he wanted to see the Rodin Museum as well.

The Feldsteins were delighted to see Yoshiko and to meet Penn. Milton Feldstein, a self-made man whose fortune arose from commercial real estate, was a trained pianist. He'd come to the piano late in life, but he practiced assiduously and he played competently and joyfully. He accompanied Yoshiko on Puccini's touching aria *O Mio Babbino Caro*, so gorgeously sung that Penn almost fell to his knees and kissed the hem of Yoshiko's skirt. He would have done it if they were home. Instead he and Mrs. Feldstein applauded and cried *brava!* And *encore!* After an early lunch at *Bookbinder's*, they all toured Independence Hall, saw the tables and chairs that had once been filled with the delegates to the Constitutional Convention, then crossed over to Carpenter's Hall, a meeting place ostensibly for Carpenters, but at one time a hotbed of pre-revolutionary thought and activism. They visited Franklin's grave and spend almost an hour in the Rodin Museum. They would have visited the art museum, but the day was growing late. Penn and Yoshiko had to be back at the airport by 6 PM for their flight to Burlington, Vermont. Penn was expected "home," or rather where his mother and step-father lived by 9 PM. He figured they would just make it. Yoshiko hugged the Feldsteins and promised to return to sing at Beth Sholom, as she did periodically.

Penn tried to warn Yoshiko about his family, but she seemed sanguine and not the least nervous as they approached the house. If anything she was excited and happy. He was praying that no one said or did anything that hurt her or embarrassed her in any way. His family wasn't vicious or mean but they were all disconnected, people raised in a Petrie dish rather than *in vivo.*

They were greeted at the door by Martin, the Butler and general factotum of the family, who, not without warmth and a friendly, welcoming manner, brought them into the living then picked up their bags and took them to a guest suite.

Penn's Step-father, Roger, his mother, Julie, Harald, his stepbrother and Harald's inamorata, Elspeth, his uncle, Parker and his wife, Peyton, along with a half-dozen assorted cousins and people of undefined relationship awaited them. Missing were the Grand aunts Harriet and Elizabeth, but neither one was ever especially prompt.

Penn and Yoshiko seemed to take them by surprise. Everything stopped and everyone turned in their direction seemingly unable to know what to do. Roger broke the ice, and did it well.

"Penn! You've brought us your beautiful bride!" he exclaimed, pumping Penn's hand with both his then reaching over to give Yoshiko a hug. She was Japanese but she'd lived with Americans for many years and she knew enough to endure this sort of thing and pretend to enjoy it. She pretended rather well.

Roger having broken the ice, the rest of the clan fell into the pond as well, surrounding the two, shaking hands, slapping backs, hugging both Yoshiko and Penn, and generally acting warm and friendly. Then they backed away no one knowing exactly what to say. *At least,* thought Penn, *no one said You likee here?*

Yoshiko, who knew how to warm up an audience, took the lead. The "library" was adjacent to the living room. It had bookshelves but not very much in terms of books. There were some books there, of course. But for the most part the shelves were laden with knickknacks and curiosities, relatively expensive ones, with books decorating the space here and there. Roger actually purchased the *100 Great Books of the Western World* in beautiful leather-bound editions, and these were scattered about in no special order, Jane Austin lay upon Freud, Plato stacked on Shaw, Marx perched on Thomas á Kempis. There was a coffee table with the requisite amount of coffee table picture books – *Classic Automobiles, Paris at Night, Impressionism* and in the corner of the room a classic Steinway grand piano.

"Oh!" said Yoshiko with undisguised delight, "You have a Steinway! Do you play?"

"A little, and very poorly," said Julie. There was no false modesty in that. She did play very poorly and very rarely. The piano, like the rest of the "library" was a display. It was a beautifully finished 1893 Steinway Model B, stained a light reddish brown that highlighted the wood grain, its surface sealed with a highly polished polyurethane finish. Julie – who was canny with money, far more so than her husband -- picked up the piano at an estate sale for $15,000.00. It was easily worth twice that. The keys were perfect and the restoration had left it better than it ever was new. Julie kept it tuned and it played well. There were just no players in the house who played well.

"Yoshiko plays," said Penn not without obvious pride and love.

"Would you play something for us?"

"Yes, would you?"

"Play something, go ahead."

"Yes, we'd love to hear you play, dear." This last comment came from far back in the room. Grand Aunt Harriet had arrived.

There was acid in her tone.

Yoshiko smiled, nodded at Harriet and sat at the piano. "There is a Korean soprano whom I admire very much, Jo Su-gyeong. You may know her by her stage name, Sumi Jo. Ms. Jo has an interest in some older English pieces that are seldom sung today. One of them forms the melody for a well-known Japanese song, *Hanyū no Yado.* I've tried to learn her technique and in my poor way have attempted to sing as she does. Since we are at home, I'd like to play, and sing the English version of *Hanyū no Yado,* a song I think you'll all know.

She began playing the introduction to "Home Sweet Home" but with a complexity, a flourish, an emotional interpretation that went well beyond anything Payne and Bishop, the authors, ever wrote. She sang the old ballad, which normally sounds so sentimental and dreary, in a way that raised it above the original music, beyond Bishop's talent, to a polished and touching sentimentalism so intense it penetrated the heart of everyone in the room. The simple word "home" was filled with such heartache and yearning they all felt the loneliness and desperation of a soul in search of the warmth and love and security of home and family *be it ever so humble*. She sang the two English verses and a third verse in Japanese, then ended it in English with a repetition of the second verse.

Applause, exclamations. They loved it.

Yoshiko turned in the bench and smiled. "Penn tells me there are a lot of Yalies in this house. Raise your hand if you're a Yalie." Eight hands went up. "Good I went to the U of P, but Pennsylvania sometimes plays Yale. Here's a little song by Cole Porter, sing along if you'd like." She pounded out the introduction on the Steinway and started:

Bulldog, bulldog, bow wow wow, Eeeeliiii Yale!

She stopped and turned around again, "No one's singing, come on. Penn's told me you're *Skull and Bones* Sing!"

This time, by the second "Bulldog," they were roaring out the old, silly fight song.

Bulldog, bulldog, bow wow wow, Eeeeliiii Yale!
Bulldog, bulldog, bow-wow-wow, our team will never fail!
When the sons of Eli break through the line,
That is the sign we hail.
Bulldog, bulldog, bow-wow-wow, Eeeeliiii Yale!

They sang it twice with Yoshiko's bright soprano voice rising above the impromptu chorus, punctuating the sound of old Eli's name with a thrilling high flourish. They might not have stopped at two verses if the chimes weren't sounded for dinner.

Penn was so much in love with her, so proud of her, he was ready to burst. *God*, he thought, *what did I do to deserve her*? The most honest prayer of his life.

Roger took the head of the table and made some sort of speech. It was a collection of dreadful clichés cobbled together with good intent and gratefully received. He ended with a toast to the couple to a resounding chorus of "Hear! Hear!" from the guests. The wine was good, anyway, and the dinner was Miriam's usual hardy and tasty fare, ham, capon, steak, meatloaf various gravies, corn, vegetables, fresh-baked bread, and, in honor of Yoshiko, steamed Japanese rice. Penn could hardly eat, but Yoshiko seemed comfortable and confident. She ate well.

The conversation revolved about Penn's trip to Japan, Yoshiko's stage experience and training, a little on the Admiral, and a great deal of family gossip, most of which involved family members and events that were thoroughly foreign to both Penn and Yoshiko.

Aunt Harriet conspicuously said nothing.

When dinner ended and the guests were rising for after-dinner drinks, Harriet slipped behind Yoshiko and Penn and said in a stage whisper. "See me upstairs in a few minutes. I want to talk with you, both of you. Elizabeth will be there, too."

Penn pondered whether or not to ignore her, but he loved the old girl, so he said "OK, Auntie, but be nice."

"I'm always nice," she said, "Just not always good. Good's boring." She smiled crookedly, *like the executioner might smile when he sharpens the blade of the guillotine,* thought Penn. Harriet winked, however, smiled for real and Penn felt better immediately.

Five minutes later, Penn and Yoshiko found Harriet and her sister Elizabeth ensconced in the guest suite, Harriet curled into an arm chair, somehow managing to look both vulnerable and imperious at the same time, with Elizabeth standing behind, cupbearer and confident of the Pharaoh.

Harriet wasted no time on pleasantries, firing a look at Penn that could have downed an eagle, she said in a menacing tone "What have you done?"

Penn knew Harriet was eccentric and direct and he could generally handle her well. In the presence of his new wife, however, he was stunned but he quickly recovered, "Auntie, I married the most gorgeous, accomplished, intelligent woman I've ever met, excluding you and Aunt Elizabeth of course."

"Liar!" said Harriet sternly.

"What she means dear," said Elizabeth, "is . . ."

"I can say what I mean myself!"

"No you can't," Elizabeth persisted, "She and I both mean, there is no exception. Ms. Yoshiko – I have that right don't I?"

Yoshiko nodded.

"Ms. Yoshiko is much more accomplished than either one of us."

"Bleeding Christ, Elizabeth! You do pussyfoot. Come here, Mrs. Fuller," said Harriet, beckoning Yoshiko, "I'm old and I only have so many get ups and set downs in me in an evening."

Yoshiko went to her, and Harriet embraced her warmly then Elizabeth did, too.

"You did well, Penn," said Harriet at last," You may never be an Admiral, but, hell, with a wife like this you don't need to be." She sighed. "Now that I think of it, if you can teach her to play and sing *Anchors Away*, you might just get there."

"Did you save all the papers you removed from the trunk?" said Penn.

Harriet started to speak, but Elizabeth interrupted her, "We had Martin place them in the closet for you, dear."

"You know everything now, I suppose, or at least you think you do," said Harriet.

"Let me put it this way, Auntie, we've learned a lot, but there's a lot more I'd like to know." He put his arm about Yoshiko and she smiled up at him. Penn reached into his pocket and withdrew a folded sheet of paper, and as he handed it to Harriet said, "I received this e-mail last week from a friend that's been helping research the Admiral's life. Take a look and tell me if you think we're on the right track."

> *Catherine Pennington nee Fitzhugh and Elizabeth "Betty" Connor are linked in several sources. Their fathers formed joint ventures for large construction projects and their daughters are described as "fast friends" in one history of the Tammany Period, and "close friends" in another. A 1960s era coffee table book of old New York has a grainy picture of them walking arm-in-arm down Fifth Avenue. They're identified in the caption on the photo.*
>
> *Catherine met Betty while attending Barnard College. They were both in the class of 1894, and the two stayed friends for life. Catherine followed Betty*

to Vermont, and lived near her until her marriage to John Pennington in 1897. Apparently, during the long stretches of time that John Pennington was either abroad or at sea, Betty moved in with Catherine. Whatever their relationship, they seem to have meant a great deal to each other, were paired for life and spent all the time they could in each other's company.

Again, this is speculative, but the marriage of John and Catherine Pennington may have been a marriage of convenience. He could marry her, she could raise Keitaro/Asher, and both could have what they really wanted, to be with the people they truly loved but without this deception of theirs would be forbidden to have by prejudice, intolerance and stupidity.

Whatever John and Catherine had, it seems to have been a warm, loving and respectful relationship. He corresponded with her throughout his life, confided in her, trusted her and truly grieved when she died. In turn she responded with kindness, warmth and a fidelity of spirit if not of flesh. They'd be the envy of many, if not most, married couples.

Harriet put on her glasses, read the paper then handed it to Elizabeth.

"Oh, dear," said Elizabeth, "I suppose all those rumors and gossip were true."

"Of course they were true," said Harriet, "look, I never knew Catherine. I only know what my mother and aunts said after her death and they pussyfooted so much around the topic it was hard to know what they meant. It's a lot clearer these days."

"What Harriet means, dear, is that Catherine and Betty were

more than friends. If you know what I mean."

"It was the perfect match for the Admiral," said Harriet, "Damned good for Catherine and Betty, too, while it lasted."

"And for Ayumi and Keitaro," said Yoshiko.

"Who?" said Harriet.

"His Japanese wife, Ayumi, and their child. Catherine renamed him 'Asher.' It means 'blessed,' the same as Keitaro, which means 'Blessed' in Japanese," said Penn.

"Humph," said Harriet, "Always wondered where 'Asher' came from. We always called him 'Uncle Ash.' Sounded very masculine to me. He was a very masculine fellow, by the way. Played football and lacrosse at Harvard. Had to beat the Radcliff girls away when he was at Harvard, or so I've been told. Nice fellow, too. Was always kind to me, always had a present or some candy for us when we were kids. . ." she paused, "Who was Ayumi? I always heard the Admiral's wife called 'Chou.'"

"Chou was a nickname," said Penn, "You know more about this than I do Yoshiko."

"Actually it was more like a stage name," said Yoshiko, "Ayumi was a trained Geisha, and Geisha would often take false names that sound cute or pretty. 'Chou' means 'Butterfly.' Puccini used it in his opera, but he gave it the Italian spelling, Cio."

"Ha!" said Harriet, "Puccini, that sentimental old scoundrel. Superficial, smarmy, manipulative bastard of a genius. No one could invade your heart like that musical monster. I can't tell you what he's done to me, and for me – well, I could but I won't."

"Would it normally be repeated? Chou-Chou?"

"They might have repeated it just to make it sound cuter, dear," said Elizabeth.

"What *are* you babbling about Liz?" said Harriet.

"Remember little Jon?"

"The handyman's kid?"

"Remember how cute he was?" Elizabeth turned to Penn and Yoshiko, "He was the cutest little boy. Straw-colored hair, bright blue eyes, dimples," she turned back to Harriet, "Remember now? We called him Jon-Jon, just like Chou might be Chou-Chou."

"Yeees. I remember. He grew up, got hooked on methamphetamines, spent time in jail for trying to rob a gas station. Fool threatened the owner with a Yankee screwdriver. The owner, Eli Congrove, brute of a man, broke Sean's arm with a mallet. Didn't want to press charges against him, figured the broken arm was enough punishment, but apparently the police charged him anyway."

"Yes, Harriet, but there is a happy ending to that."

"If you want to call it a happy ending."

Elizabeth smiled and addressed Penn and Yoshiko, "Jon-Jon found Jesus in prison, entered an on-line seminary run by the Congregations of Christ and became a counselor and eventually a Minister. He earned a Doctor of Divinity degree in just four months!"

"Where's his church?" said Penn.

"Nowhere now," said Harriet, "He ran for Mayor of Mableton on something called the Republican Reformed ticket and won. Never thought much of Mableton."

"Isn't that wonderful?" said Elizabeth.

"Back to the point, Puccini got his inspiration from the play 'Madame Butterfly,' produced by David Belasco. Belasco based it in on a short story by that spavined ass, John Luther Long."

"That's not very nice," said Elizabeth.

"Oh? Alright that spavined poodle, John Luther Long. Is that better?"

"Much"

"Where was I? Yes, Long… Long's sister, Jennie -- I think her married name was Connell – Was it, Elizabeth?"

"Correll, dear," said Elizabeth.

"Jennie was married to the Reverend Correll, a minister who spent some years trying to drum up business for Jesus and morality in Japan. Reverend Correll spent time in Yokohama, Nagasaki, and finally in Hiroshima. He had little success with the Japanese so he went on a one-man crusade to purify the morals of sailors and soldiers and others stationed there. Buying temporary wives was common for Americans stuck for years 6,000 miles from home. In Japan they were quite reasonable in price, pretty and nice, or so it's said. Anyway, he visited Lt. Commander Pennington one fine day and complained about the Commander's living arrangements. It was 1896, and the future Admiral was already taken with Chou-Chou and living with her. Pennington invited him out of his house, told him to mind his own business and never to come back. Correll complained of course, but no one listened. All the sailors – even the Captains -- all had their "friends" – so to speak – and no one wanted to give that up. Correll's wife wrote to her brother, Luther Long, about it."

Harriet took a drink of wine, then continued "Ayumi became pregnant. Remember, she was married to John Pennington. At least they had a civil contract of marriage which could be voided at his whim, but they were married. John was ordered back to the states temporarily and he left her for a while, but he provided very well for her, and continued to support her throughout his life. She had the baby, and that was the problem."

"We read the letters," said Yoshiko, "the baby didn't look Japanese at all, and she begged him to take the child to the states."

"Yes, that's right," said Harriet, "but he needed a wife to adopt a child properly and to care for the child as a mother would. He had a friend, however, Catherine Fitzhugh. She lived nearby and they used to play tennis on the rare occasions when he was home. "

“I think it was a little more than that, dear,” said Elizabeth.

“What *are* you getting at , Lizzy?” said Harriet.

“John wasn’t home often, but, as Aunt Cordella told me, when he did come home it was for a month, sometimes two. He and Katie Fitzhugh – they called her ‘Katie Fitz,’ you know – He and Katie were very close. During that time in 1897, he was with her every day, all day and they seemed to be very involved with each other.”

“Of course they were involved,” said Harriet, “He was courting her, or, rather, pretending to court her. She liked the Admiral and trusted him – he was a very likeable fellow – and she confided in him. He, of course, confided in her and trusted her as well. He tucked that confidence away for a while, then returned to the states, went to Vermont, ‘courted her’ if you want to call it that, and offered her precisely what she wanted, a station as a respectable married woman whose husband, unfortunately, spent most of his time defending the ramparts of democracy on the high seas or in some foreign place, while she stayed home and maintained the house. A live-in female companion like her friend Betty would be the perfect thing to keep her chaste and relieve her loneliness for those long stretches of time without her man. She could also play mother to an adopted child. I think you know the rest.”

“We met lawyer Fuller,” said Yoshiko, wrinkling her nose in disgust.

“Yes, good. Glad to see you have a good nose for shifty lawyers – some lawyers are nice, though.”

“I remember a whole law firm, Baker, O’Connor, Katz and Baldi, and they were very nice, very nice, indeed . . .” said Elizabeth.

“We can reminisce later, Elizabeth.”

“You never did get to know Mr. Baldi, did you? Mario was such a lovely, generous man…”

“Poppa was very upset when his wife threw stones at our house and tried to shoot you.”

“He got over it.”

“You had a way with papa . . .To get back to John Luther Long, Jennie Correll and the Reverend were still haunting the American enclave at Hiroshima when Catherine came to pick up the child. You’ll see this in the letters, but Chou and Catherine loved each other from the start. Catherine spent two weeks with her “husband” – I put that in quotation marks – and Chou. During that time, Catherine played constantly with the child, even slept with him, and then took him to Vermont as agreed. Chou cried bitterly when the child left, but in her heart she knew it was best all-around. Chou and Pennington remained, and Chou corresponded with Catherine for decades, virtually until the point of Catherine’s death. Jennie either misinterpreted what occurred or simply was vicious enough to lie about it to her brother. My guess is that, being as she was, it was a little of both. Luther saw a commercial opportunity in the story, turned it into a florid melodrama of abandonment and callus betrayal, and ended his story with poor Butterfly gutting herself. He published this stupid tripe in a magazine called *The Century* in 1898. *The Century* was generally a classy publication, but it always contained some romantic pulp to attract the dolts. Long’s story of *Butterfly* was one of those dolt-catchers. ‘Pennington’ became ‘Pinkerton,’ ‘Sheffield’ became ‘Sharpless’ (what idiot would concoct such a name?), ‘Suzume’ became ‘Suzuki,’ ‘Gengo’ became ‘Goro.’ His imagination filled in the rest. On the positive side, your great-grandfather inspired one of the greatest operas ever written.”

“Always look for the bright side, dear,” said Elizabeth then, as an afterthought, “Mr. Katz proposed to you, didn’t he, Harriet?”

Harriet sighed deeply, “He did, but he was three inches shorter than me. If he’d just been a little taller…”

Yoshiko and Penn, seated on the bed at this point, looked at one another, “This is one sailor who loved his bride and took her home,” said Penn.

Yoshiko kissed him. “And she loves him.”

“One more thing,” said Harriet,” Just so you’ll understand what happened. Lieutenant Pennington, as he was then, never bought and paid-for a fifteen-year-old virgin as Luther Long insinuated. The girl, Chou, was indentured to Byron Sheffield, an ink-stained muck at the American legation, a low level Foreign Service Officer who had a taste for very young girls. Today the bastard would be thrown in the slammer for rape and child abuse, but in those days a young girl was chattel freely available for indenture or rent for any purpose.

Sheffield beat Chou regularly, and when she neared her sixteenth birthday he got drunk, beat her black and blue then dragged her into the backyard and started whipping her with his belt. Lieutenant Pennington heard her cries, vaulted over the fence, knocked Sheffield on his arse, tied him up with his own belt and left him squirming in his own puke, while he took the girl home and got her a doctor. Sheffield complained to the Military Attaché – the highest ranking officer at the legation – who told Pennington that Sheffield was a pain and a coward, but he was a sneak, too, and to watch out for him. A few days later there was an attempted break-in at Pennington’s house, but he chased the culprits away with his Navy revolver, vaulted the fence once more, kicked open Sheffield’s door, put the gun to the man’s head and let him know if it happened again he’d blow his brains out. No one would care and no one would investigate. He was right about that, too. Sheffield transferred to Nagasaki a week later.

Chou stayed with Pennington. She cooked for him, cared for him, bartered with the merchants for food and other items at a fair price, even sang to him. He tells the whole story to Catherine in one of the longer letters.

By the way, Elizabeth and I kept everything we had. All of Pennington’s letters to Catherine were gathered at her death and put into a chest. I left that chest in your closet, too. The copies I removed from the trunk are with them, too.

Anyway, Catherine wanted to know how they met, how they fell in love. Pennington said that one night he got home late, they ate together Japanese style, the August moon was high up, he went outside with her, held her hand, looked at the moon with her, and fell in love deeply, completely, and forever. She was sixteen, an age when many if not most girls would marry. He was twenty-seven. In the states at the time, that would have been considered a good match based on the ages. A young girl who could produce lots of children with a man mature enough to have a business, trade or profession. Hell, Will Durant, the historian and moralist married his wife, Ariel, when she was just fifteen and he was thirty, and that was in the 1920s. Anyway, that was how they came to be together, not anything like the story Luther Long told."

No one said a thing for a few seconds.

"Come on," said Harriet, breaking the silence "God knows what they're thinking down stairs."

"Oh, I don't think they think very much at all, dear," said Elizabeth.

Most of the family was milling around the living room and library. Some of the younger ones had gone downstairs to play snooker or shuffleboard. Penn's mother approached with a champagne flute in each hand for Penn and Yoshiko.

Roger saw them, slapped Penn on the back almost causing the wine to spill, and said in a stage voice loud enough to reach down the block to Yoshiko, "Mrs. Fuller, is there any way we can prevail upon you for one more song?"

There were cries of "Here, here!" "Yes!" "Please!"

Yoshiko was happy to comply. She took her seat at the piano, turned to the crowd, now all gathered in the library, and said, "I sang one song for the family, and one for all the Yalies here. Now, I want to sing one for my husband. The song was based on Bach's Minuet in G major, but the words were written in 1965. It's called *A Lover's*

Concerto." She played the introduction and sang:

How gentle is the rain
That falls softly on the meadow,
Birds high up in the trees
Serenade the flowers with their melodies

Penn knew the melody but never listened to the words before. Perhaps because it was sung for him or maybe it was just the champagne and all they had learned that night, but he came close to tears as he listened to her play and sing. Harald came up behind him and put his hand on Penn's shoulder, and Elspeth stood on his other side and took his hand in both of hers. Either they had changed or he had. He was starting to like them. Or maybe it was just Yoshiko and her peculiar magic. Penn hoped the spell would last until they left.

Yoshiko finished the recital for the evening with a rousing interpretation of *Italian Street Song* from *Naughty Marietta* by Victor Herbert. She got them all to clap along with the beat in the final stanza, and ended to cheers, whistles and applause.

At the end of the evening, as everyone was leaving, Harald and Elspeth hugged Penn and Yoshiko. Harald, with candor and sincerity put his hands on both their shoulders and said, "This has been the most fun evening of my life. Thank you."

Penn smiled and thought, *There may be hope for you yet, old man,* but merely said "Thank you, and all our best to you on your coming marriage to this beautiful lady," meaning Elspeth.

Yoshiko smiled sweetly. She liked them.

They drove to Annapolis the following day, got in late, and flopped into bed exhausted. Well, not too exhausted. They slept until 10 AM when Penn's cell phone woke them with its too jaunty marimba tune.

"Penn old boy!" It was McGraw, "What have you done? You

leave us for three weeks, go across the world and marry? Is it true?"

"Say 'Hello' to Colonel McGraw, Yoshiko"

She slid over leaned on Penn to get to the phone, and said "Hello Colonel McGraw."

"You do know this deluded fool thinks he actually married you."

"Oh, yes, and I think so too."

"Well in that case, my heartiest congratulations."

"Penn are you there?"

"Yes."

"Look, something's come up. We need you tonight at Barry Center. Formal affair from 7 to 10. Mess dress. Commandant's orders. You *must* bring the wife as well."

"What?"

"Some sort of military-diplomatic something. I'm not sure I understand too much myself, but certain officers were ordered by name to attend, if physically possible. I have a copy of the orders right here. They drafted me, too. I'm taking Marianna. We're engaged, you know."

"No. I didn't know. Congratulations to you, too, and my condolences to Marianna."

"I'll tell her… At 7 precisely. You'll be there?"

"If that's what the Commandant orders." McGraw hung up and Penn put his phone away.

"What's going on?"

"Some sort of official reception. This happens occasionally but you usually get warned a month or so in advance. Well, I've been gone. They probably would have told me weeks ago had I been here. You're coming, too. Commandant's orders. You need to get a gown."

They rushed to Nordstrom's, but Yoshiko thought the prices

were high and wanted to try Macys as well. She purchased a gown for a grossly reduced price, had a few minor alterations done while she bought some matching shoes, also on sale, and a few other things, and had the whole kit in hand by 4 PM. Penn had his mess-dress uniform pressed, his full medals attached, and his shoes shined to a high polish.

They dressed. He preferred blues or whites and always felt like a tin sailor in formal dress togs, but Yoshiko found him beautiful. She, in turn, looked gorgeous in the dark blue and white gown she chose.

Barry Center is divided into a lobby, much like a theater lobby, from which attendees can enter any of four double doors into a very large space that can be set for anything from banquets to lectures or subdivided with floor to ceiling partitions into smaller spaces. As they entered the lobby at ten minutes before seven, they saw no one. Penn expected people to be milling about. They stood there for a minute, Penn wondering whether or not McGraw had given him the right location, when the double doors in the middle burst open as Captain McCormack and First Sergeant Fernandez (both were promoted after Iraq) in full dress uniforms marched in perfect precision towards them.

They stopped. Captain McCormack stepped back a pace, unsheathed his sword, and formally saluted Penn. So did Fernandez. Penn, not sure of what was happening, but ingrained with military habit, snapped to attention and retuned the salute.

"Sir, M'am, We are to escort you to the official reception. He broke form, leaned over to Yoshiko and said in a loud whisper, "M'am, the Sergeant and I owe our lives to your husband. He is a very brave man, the best." Then back to formal brace and "Please follow us."

Penn relaxed, put his arm about Yoshiko's waist, smiled at her and said, "I think this is our party." She smiled back, sanguine and courageous as always.

As they passed through the door, they heard the command, "Sword arch!" They were led through a column of Navy and Marine officers, Marines on their left, Navy on their right, with swords raised in the traditional sword arch. As tradition demanded, the last two swords were lowered, barring the way for couple. Penn leaned toward Yoshiko and kissed her. The swords were lifted. In past years, the bride was given a gentle swat on the backside with the side of a sword, and a jaunty "Welcome to the Navy." Penn was happy that tradition was now obsolete and the sword bearers behaved themselves.

As Penn and Yoshiko kissed, the Academy band, or at least a segment of it, struck up *Anchors Away*. The room was filled with officers and their wives all of whom sang along with the band. Yoshiko joined in as well, her soprano rising above the mass. When the band stopped, they applauded the couple, gathered round to shake hands and offer their congratulations. McGraw and Marianna were among the well-wishers. McGraw, dressed in his regimental uniform looked splendid, and Marianna looked young and fresh in a light blue gown.

The rest of the evening was a blur. A few short speeches. A buffet table. Introduction after introduction. Several toasts. A large flat cake decorated with the image of a ship and the Navy Cross, inscribed in icing with a note of congratulations to Penn and Yoshiko. They stayed until the end. As the last couples left, McCormack, Fernandez and their dates (neither was married) came up to Penn. McCormack started to shake his hand, then, overcome, hugged Penn, his eyes watering, and kissed Yoshiko on the cheek. Fernandez did the same. They didn't say much. There was little to say.

Marriage is infectious. One week later McGraw and Marianna eloped, flew to Las Vegas and were married in the Elvis Chapel. McGraw wore his formal dress uniform there as well. Marianna wore white. McGraw's two-year stint at Annapolis was ending in four months, but he already had job with *Little, Montgomery and Blake*, a consulting firm that recently won a five-year contract with the CDC for forensic science services. The contract period would begin just a week after McGraw's time at the Academy ended. His residency was no problem. He had a work permit, a rare skill, an international reputation, a steady income, and the consulting company was expert in solving immigration issues quickly.

****

Chapter Thirty-Two – Stealth and Deception

Kate Hobson held Morrison and Steinberg's, *Principles of Organic Chemistry* in both hands and tried rotating it to the right and left. She made some notes and went back to the molecular diagram, scratched her head and tried to sketch a particular molecule.

"Didn't know you public health specialists went in for real science,"

She looked up. A tall, lanky, well-built man probably 30 or so was looking down at her. "Some do." She said, turning back to the book.

"Let me see," he said, coming into her office uninvited and looking over her shoulder, "You invert it with its mirror image. There's a trick to it. I'll show you."

He took her note pad, threw away her sketch and said very little. He drew, pointed with the pencil, muttered "See" every now and then, and solved the problem for her. She wasn't particularly happy about it. Although he wore his CDC badge, she didn't know who he was and couldn't read his name because the badge had turned leaving only the back visible. She knew only that he was brusque, pushy and rude.

She wasn't in the mood to see anyone at this moment anyway. Her application to the job in Thailand was rejected in favor of Lambert Lessing, Ph.D., who was considered more qualified and certainly more experienced. To aggravate her disappointment, her tour of public health departments was cut short by a reprogramming of sequestered funding. Neither she nor Marianna had any idea when funding would be available, but it looked as if years might pass, if, indeed, the project ever were to be renewed. She was stuck in Atlanta. If she was stuck here, then she might as well use her free time productively. She registered for classes at Mercer University, next door, to enhance her knowledge of biology and physical science. If she took enough courses, she'd qualify as an epidemiologist and that would bring her more interesting work, and work in the field rather than at the headquarters.

Marianna came by and rescued her from this annoying man. "Peter," she said, "Welcome. I've been looking forward to meeting with you."

Peter, whoever that was, smiled, said "Goodbye, and don't forget what I showed you," and left.

Don't forget what I showed you, she thought, mouthing the words sarcastically, *men are such turds.*

A week passed. Marianna and she were on their way to lunch when Marianna's new husband, Phil McGraw, greeted them in the lobby just as they were leaving.

"I had to come by and complete some paperwork for my new employer – they're right over at the McGill Building – and I thought I'd buzz by here and take you to lunch. What do you say to *Violette*?"

"You must be a mind reader," said Marianna, "That's where we were going."

Kate wasn't enthusiastic about being with a friend of Penn's, but McGraw was a genial fellow, funny and scrupulously polite. She couldn't blame him for Penn's intransigence, all that blather about needing to be alone then suddenly falling for someone in Japan and marrying her, all within two weeks. She'd never figure out men. They were all flighty, selfish, deceptive, cruel, mean bastards. And those were their good qualities.

Violette was crowded but there was a table waiting for them in the back, the only free table. They were studying the menus when Marianna jumped up.

"Look, Kate, it's Peter," she said waving to someone in the crowd, "You met him last week."

Kate groaned to herself, but tried not to show her displeasure.

"Let's invite him over. He'll never find a table by himself," said Marianna.

"Yes, let's," said McGraw, standing, smiling his good-natured, welcoming smile.

Peter approached, shook McGraw's hand while McGraw introduced himself, then he nodded to Kate and Marianna and sat.

"Can't believe my luck," said Peter, "Good thing I saw some of my CDC colleagues or I would have been standing around for the next forty-five minutes."

"Virtually everyone here is a CDC colleague" said Kate acidly, "or didn't you notice all the CDC badges."

"Have you two been introduced?" said Marianna, then without waiting for a reply, "Peter, this is Kate Hobson, she's our foremost public health specialist *par excellence,* and Kate, this is Peter Vandergraaf. He's an M.D. MPH with a specialty in epidemiology. Georgia Tech, too, I believe."

"That's right. Pre-med at Tech, then Emory medical school, and Emory for the MPH," he said.

"Well, what a small world. Kate went to Tech and Emory, too."

Kate looked up and smiled wanly, but Peter stood, leaned over and shook her hand. She hadn't noticed before but he was handsome in a way, with dark brown hair, brown eyes, full lips, a tanned complexion, and a bemused but friendly look to him.

They ordered, the food came, which was quite good, whatever it was. Kate didn't notice the food because she was talking with Peter at this point, laughing with him about the quirks of some professor at Emory, when McGraw pushed up his sleeve, looked at his watch, and exclaimed, "Oh, no! I didn't realize the time! If we don't bolt this instant we're going to miss our appointment at INS and, Lord knows, I might not get my green card."

Marianna looked earnestly at Peter, "Pete, we have to run right now. There's no time and this is very important. Would you mind taking Kate back?"

"Not at all. My pleasure."

McGraw dropped $60.00 on the table. "That should cover lunch with the tip. My treat."

Before Pete could object, Marianna and McGraw were gone. Pete returned to a spirited discussion he was having with Kate about the expansion of the malaria belt and the implication of recently discovered mutations in certain strains of *Plasmodium*. If there were just a way to prevent *Plasmodium* from penetrating the cytoplasm of a mosquito's midgut epithelial cells.... They stayed past their lunch hour and agreed to meet that evening, at the same table if they could, to continue the discussion.

Kate returned to her office revivified and excited, burst upon her work, burying herself in reports and e-mail to make time pass as quickly as possible; she was looking forward to dinner with Peter so much.

Benign deception is not limited to Japan and the Japanese.

****

Chapter Thirty-Three – Ballintogher Again

Yoshiko and Penn walked the road up the hill leading past Sullivan's pasture to Mary O'Mara's house. Penn had over 20 days leave remaining, so they'd taken a ten-day honeymoon tour of Italy and saw the opera both in Venice and in Milan. Yoshiko even took the opportunity to visit *La Scala* in the afternoon, introduce herself and sing a few bars of a Verdi aria, to the enthusiastic cheers and applause of the stage crew and the sweepers. Well, she'd sung at *La Scala*. No one could deny that.

On the way back, they stopped in Ireland for a few days, took a train to Ballintogher, *nearest town to the famed Lake Isle of Innisfree*, and called Mary O'Mara. She was delighted. She invited them right over, and it being an unusual day, which is to say there was no rain and no threat of rain, took the pretty walk along the road to her cottage.

"What a lovely place," said Yoshiko, "Like something from a child's book of stories. Look at it, brilliant white fence, stone walls covered with ivy, gorgeous roses just beginning to bloom, vibrantly green grass, slate roof, and a handcrafted door that must be three centuries old."

Penn knocked and the door swung open. Mary greeted them warmly while her latest husband, Brendan McCarthy, stood buy and shook their hands. Yoshiko could not help but stare. The last thing she expected was an Asian woman.

"I see you're a bit surprised," said Mary.

"I'm sorry. I didn't expect to see an Asian here. I don't why. There isn't any reason…"

"Ach, but I'm not Asian. I'm Irish. My family has been part of this community for three generations and I was born and bred here. I'm as Irish as any freckle-faced rosy-skinned child, or as Irish as this fellow," she pointed with her chin to her husband.

"That she is," said Brendan, "Maybe more Irish than me. She's even on the town council and I wouldn't be surprised if she's elected mayor next year when old Walsh retires."

"Go on with ya' Brendan," said Mary "Walsh is five years my junior, if a day. I won't run. I'll settle for the council unless I'm elected by a write in."

"They'll write you in, Mary. I know. Saint Teresa whispered it to me."

"He's a bit daft when he talks Saint Teresa. Pay him no mind. But come in, come in, don't stand out there."

Penn and Yoshiko entered the pleasant cottage and were surprised at how large and modern it was. The view from the road was deceptive. The hearth was original, or looked original, but the sitting room was large, furnished with a think carpet over polished rosewood floors, comfortable modern sofas, arm chairs, reading and sitting chairs, and a gorgeous multi-colored Danish coffee table large enough for a banquet. There was a TV, but it was built into a niche in the wall and concealed from view by a painting that would rise to the ceiling if the TV were used. There was also a concealed stereo and central heating and cooling. Even the hearth was modern with a gas burner and lava rocks, but disguised to look like a wood-burning fireplace. The cottage felt airy and bright, with skylights and French doors leading to an enclosed patio or sunroom.

Mary made tea while Brendan invited them to sit and chatted with them about their trip, the town, his recent marriage to Mary, and their happiness.

"When I proposed, she turned away," he said, looking at Mary "Didn't you?"

Mary just smiled and looked down at the tea and biscuits she was preparing.

"And she said to me, I've lost two husbands and can't stand the thought of losing another. I'll only marry you if you promise not to die on me."

"Oh, Brendan, it wasn't exactly like that."

"It was close... So, I said Mary, I won't die before you if you don't die before me. We shook hands on it." He looked at Mary, "don't deny it."

"He's right we shook hands on it." She smiled.

"And now we're here. And, as God is my witness, I love her more than I ever thought I could love anyone. We've a happy home and a good life."

"Brendan and I feel the same way. We're good here and with each other," said Mary.

Penn took Yoshiko's hand.

"How did you two meet?" said Mary.

"It's a long story," said Penn, "It would take some time to tell it."

"Well now, do you mind if I invite a few friends over? We love stories," said Brendan.

"I'll get the drinks and glasses," said Mary, "You will stay, won't you? We'll have a cold supper, light the fire and you can share your story with us and a few friends."

Yoshiko who liked them both immensely hugged Penn. "I'll even sing you a song or two," she said.

Brendan didn't wait for Penn's response. Why would the fellow say "no?" He sped off on his bicycle, heading to Mike Connor's house to invite him and to ask him to spread the word.

By seven PM, the fire was lit, the sitting room and kitchen were crowded, and small glasses of whiskey or wine (or larger ones with juice or tea for the teetotalers and children) were served by Mary, who kept refills on a small rolling cart, ready for anyone who wanted one. Yoshiko opened the evening accompanied by a girl named Teresa who played a small plastic keyboard quite well. Yoshiko sang *Amazing Grace* and *Danny Boy* with all the heart and poignant sentiment of a dozen Irish singers rolled into one. There was more than one wet face in the room when she was done, and Mary, not immune from tears herself, passed a box of tissues around.

Penn waited a minute, let the room quiet down, looked at the fire while gathering his thoughts, then, when the room was so quiet you could hear the fire crackling and the crickets in the meadow, he turned to the company and began his story. "This story is about love at a distance. Sometimes love can flourish and thrive even at great distances, distances of place, of culture, of time, if the lovers are true to one-another and if their devotion is deep and enduring. My Great-grandfather was a sailor…."

* * * * * * * * * *

Chapter Thirty-Four – Epilogue

In Atlanta. A condominium on Flowers Road.

A large white cat, with silky hair and beige markings, jumped down from the arm chair, caressed Kate Hobson's foot and licked her ankle.

"Well who is this?" Kate said sweetly, reaching down and scratching the cat behind the ears.

"I found her living wild in the parking lot and woods," said Peter.

"But I know this cat. I used to leave food for her. She was feral and high-strung. Can you train feral cats?"

"She was living on her own and was skittish with strangers, but she'd been raised as a pet and then either got lost or was abandoned. She's a pure bred Turkish Van."

"A what?"

"A Turkish Van. The breed comes from the Lake Van area in Turkey. They're also knows as 'the swimming cat,' because they like water and enjoy swimming. Their fur actually repels water. Notice how slick it is?"

"Yes, I see. She's beautiful."

"The cat's markings are distinctive. See the little white spot on the tan marking on her head. The Turks say that's where Allah in admiration of her beauty and sweetness touched her….I caught her, took her to a vet, had her examined, got her all her shots, rabies, feline Leukemia, everything, and had her blood work done. No worms but she was underweight. She'd already been spayed, so that confirmed she'd been a pet at some time. After that it was just a matter of bringing her home, getting her over her fear and suspicion, which didn't take too long, and making her my friend."

Kate sat down on the sofa, which was leather and wouldn't be a magnet for the cat's fur, and the cat joined her.

"Had to take her in, there's coyotes in the wetland now. I've heard them howl at night. They'd kill her and eat her."

"Does she have a name?" said Kate, petting the cat, who was now purring loudly.

"Princess."

"Good name. She looks like a princess."

Kate was awakened the next morning at six, when Princess licked her ear. Cats don't draw any distinction for weekends; they don't know what Saturday is. Their passion for regularity and routine is completely rigid. Kate didn't get up, however, she turned and embraced Peter, who took her hand and kissed it.

Princess turned with contempt from these two humans who could so wantonly disturb the routine she loved, moved to the end of the bed, and curled in a ball. She'd give them five or ten minutes then try again. She yawned. Life these days seemed very good to her, even with these irregularities.

Peter kissed Kate's hand again.

"Peter Rembrandt Vandergraaf, MD, MPH," she whispered.

He smiled and whispered in return, "the beautiful and remarkable Kate Porter Hobson."

*********The End**********

Afterword

Stories involving a military man stationed in some far off place and the fate of his "campaign wife" are as old as civilization. Homer's Iliad begins with Achilles sulking in his tent because his campaign wife, Briseis, is taken by King Agamemnon who had to surrender his own campaign wife, Chryseis, in order to lift Apollo's curse. Military men are mostly healthy young men and when they can they will consort with the local women. This happens in every duty station in every corner of the earth. There is nothing very special about a military member acquiring a local domestic or foreign girlfriend (or perhaps in today's military a boyfriend), and little can be done to stop it. Could there have been an American Navy Lieutenant who acquired, as his "campaign wife" a local woman in 19th century Japan? In all likelihood that kind of arrangement did occur at all levels of rank.

That doesn't make the tragic story of a despicably selfish and manipulative Navy Officer and an especially gullible geisha named "Butterfly," as told by John Luther Long, manifestly credible. At the time of its publication, Long received a raft of letters from Navy officers denying that any of their number would be as callous or dishonorable as Pinkerton, or that any such thing as Long described, especially the suicide of the deluded girl, ever occurred. Those complaints carry some weight. According to the Naval History and Heritage Command, there were only 1,399 officers in the Navy in 1897. The officer corps of the US Navy at the time was a small and close-knit group with high standards and a tendency to police its own. No officer with Pinkerton's cavalier disdain for human civility or decency would last long in the brotherhood and certainly wouldn't be promoted.

Long derisively dismissed those complaints. He claimed he was inspired by letters from his sister, Jennie Correll who spent years in Japan with her husband, a Methodist minister, and that *Madame*

Butterfly was fundamentally a true story. Jennie had been to Japan, but Long didn't have to rely on his sister for the story of a geisha and a Navy officer.

In 1887, 11 years before Long's fiction adorned *The Century* magazine, French author Pierre Loti's *Madame Chrysanthème* appeared. Loti's work contained the very similar storyline of a Japanese geisha who marries a naval officer. In Loti's novel, the officer, Pierre, despondent and heart-broken, on the hour of his departure returns to his Japanese love to bid her goodbye one last time only to find her enjoying herself, laughing with her servant, counting the silver dollars he left her, and planning for the next officer they'll snag. *Madame Chrysanthème* was a popular novel that underwent 25 printings and was translated into several languages, including English. It even inspired an 1893 opera by Charles Messager. It seems likely that Long borrowed Loti's plot, replaced the French with Americans and embellished it with the grim addition of the heroine's suicide.

Whatever the origins of the story, John Luther's Long's *Madame Butterfly* was very popular and inspired the play of that name by David Belasco and that, in turn, inspired Puccini's magnificent opera. It's the opera that has given immortality to the story, and indirectly to Long. There have been more performances of Puccini's *Madame Butterfly* on the American stage, and perhaps on the world stage, than any other opera. It's spawned other works, too, several movies, ballets by choreographers Frederick Ashton, David Nixon, and Stanton Welch, and Andrew Lloyd-Weber's *Miss Saigon*.

I've attacked the credibility of Long's story. The ending of his story is so ludicrous it hardly bears discussion. The thought that a serving Naval Officer at the turn of the 20th Century would return to his foreign posting, wife in toe somehow (Long never does explain how she got there.), introduce his American wife to his former sexual companion and then remove his half-American child leaving the poor local woman despondent and suicidal is so far beyond belief, it's stunning.

It is not beyond belief, however, that in 1897 a Japanese woman might beg a Euro-American father to take home a child who looks too Euro-American ever to pass for Japanese. The machinations necessary to do it are not impossible to imagine and much stranger things have occurred. Just ask anyone who ever served overseas for any period of time and you'll hear stories much stranger and more convoluted than the one I've concocted.

I started this afterward with a short discussion of campaign wives. Do campaign wives ever stay with their men and become real wives? Yes, of course that happens. Despite the legal barriers and distances they may have to cross, men and women will find a way to be together. For U.S. servicemen, similar things happened after the Civil War, the World Wars, Korea and Vietnam, and still happen where troops are stationed overseas. It's rare, but I've heard of it happening even in Iraq. Foreign officers stationed in the United States have also fallen in love and fathered children, and some have returned to marry their American consorts. Love can be so persistent and enduring that no distance will diminish it or eradicate it.

* * * *

Distance is in part historical fiction. I've taken very few liberties with the major historical events, which were as described here. Vice Admiral John Pennington is completely fictional, and not in any way based on anyone living or dead. The same goes for virtually every other character in the book, with a few prominent exceptions.

Douglas MacArthur was, of course, real, but he didn't visit Japan on his way to the Philippines. He *could* have but he didn't. He was a baseball player, however, and even as Major General Douglas MacArthur, Commandant of West Point, he stooped to hit a few balls with the cadet team. When Douglas was still a Lieutenant, he was made aide-de-camp to his father, Lt. General Arthur

MacArthur, and they did tour Japan in 1905 as military observers. Forty years later the decision to spare Emperor Hirohito was entirely that of Doulas MacArthur, and the logic behind that decision was as I depicted it.

Captain Hajime Sakamoto was Commander of the ill-fated Battleship *Yashima*. Unlike Admiral Togo, who trained with the British, Captain Sakamoto was a graduate of the Japanese Imperial Naval Academy.

Admiral Togo was real as well. He trained with the British Navy as an ordinary seaman, sailed to Australia and back, attended and graduated from the Royal Naval Academy and was an ardent admirer of Nelson. He did claim to be Nelson reincarnated. Whatever his claim, he defeated two Russian Navies who fought well and bravely, and annihilated the Russian naval presence in the Yellow Sea.

Kiro Kunitomo: I know of one Japanese Navy officer who attended the United States Naval Academy in the nineteenth century, Kiro Kunitomo. He graduated in 1877 and was subsequently commissioned in the fledgling Japanese Navy. He died in 1904, during the Russo-Japanese war.

Yokohama Athletic Club: The Yokohama Athletic Club's baseball team, mostly sailors, which for five years haughtily refused to play the Japanese, finally did agree to a game in 1896.The Japanese Ichiko team defeated the Yokohama Club 29-4.

Navy Cross: Only one sailor of the United States Navy received the Navy Cross for "conspicuous gallantry and intrepidity in action against the enemy" in Iraq. He was Luis E. Fonseca, Hospitalman Apprentice. I have the greatest respect and admiration for him. Fonseca's heroism is beyond anything I imagined and I certainly didn't mean to create a fictional character that would dull his unique glory in any way. Fifteen heroic U.S. Marines were also decorated with the Navy Cross for action in Iraq.

Turkish Van is a breed of domestic cat, an especially large and beautiful breed. If exposed to water while young, it learns to swim and loves it, and it does possess fur that sheds water. I know. I once had a gorgeous Turkish Van who lived a long time with me and was my affectionate companion until her death.

Maniya Barredo was adorned with the well-deserved title "Prima Ballerina" by Margot Fonteyn. She was the only Prima who ever danced with Atlanta Ballet. Upon her retirement as a dancer, she founded and manages the Metropolitan Ballet School and Theatre in Alpharetta, Georgia. She's a distinguished artist and marvelous teacher. Her students *do* adore her.

Sumi Jo is one of the world's greatest coloratura sopranos. Many of her CDs are available, including "Prayers," which I mentioned here. "Home Sweet Home" is on her album "Missing You," and can be downloaded from Amazon.com. All her albums are superbly done. Buy them all. I have.

* * * *

The Music: Let me preface this with a comment about opera aficionados. They are never satisfied. They'll find the flaws, real or imaginary, in any performance and carp on them while ignoring much else. Like other high-end connoisseurs, they're also prone to a clubbiness that haughtily excludes the observations of mortals less studied in the art of performance appreciation. So, a recording or performance that you find beautiful and satisfying might be the object of disdain or derision on the part of some "expert" who considers himself or herself infinitely more knowledgeable, but might be loved by some other "expert." Ignore the negative comments and look for the positives. There have been wonderfully moving recordings made of *Butterfly* by many remarkable artists. Among them are (in no particular order, and this is not a complete list) Victoria de Los Angeles, Renata Tebaldi, Renata Scotto, Anna Moffo, Mirella Freni. and Maria Callas. Of those, I prefer Moffo, Freni and Scotto, but your tastes may be different. There was a gorgeous and well-sung movie, available as DVD, made in 1995 directed by Frédéric Mitterrand, starring Ying Huang and Richard Troxell. I own the DVD, have made gifts of it and I can say only that the movie is beautifully done and well worth owning. An earlier movie, starring Mirella Freni and Placido Domingo can also be purchased. There is a recent Met Opera DVD available, with Patricia Racette singing the lead. There are several other DVDs as well. A stunning rendition of the aria "Un Bel Di" is contained on the EMI CD *Arias* by the gorgeous Chinese diva, Liping Zhang.

I don't usually refer people to Youtube, but there is a great clip from a movie based on the life of Cole Porter that features his Yale "Bulldog" song. The Yale *Bull Dog* can also be found on Thomas Hampton's CD *Night and Day*.

I've mentioned Sumi Jo's CDs. "Home Sweet Home" is on her CD *Missing You*. "Amazing Grace," the "Ave Marias" of both Schubert and Caccini, and the "Kaddish" are on her CD *Prayers*. "Lover's Concerto" can be found on her CD *Forever*. "Italian Street Song" is on her CD *Sumi Jo: Live At Carnegie Hall*. An aria from Messager's *Madame Chrysanthème,* "Le Jour Sous Le Soleil Beri," is on her disc *French Coloratura Arias*. All her CDs are wonderful, both the purely operatic and classical recordings, and the crossover recordings.

The "Flower Song" duet from *Lakme* is available on any complete recording of the opera. An EMI recording starring Natalie Dessay, Jose Van Dam and Patricia Petibon is considered one of the best, if not *the* best. The "Flower Song" can also be found on any number of very inexpensive compilations including *Most Famous Opera Duets* (1994). The gorgeous Opera Babes (soprano Rebecca Knight and mezzo Karen England) feature the duet on their CD *Beyond Imagination,* and a CD by Hei-Kyung Hong and Jennifer Larmore, *Bellezza Vocale, Beautiful Opera Duets*, also has the "Flower Song."

La Traviata has also been recorded many times. Sutherland,

Cotrubas, Gheorghiu, Netrebko, Callas and others have made recordings of it. The performance I mentioned in this book at La Scala with Gheorghiu and Vargas is on DVD. An earlier Gheorghiu DVD exists as well. Her acting is incomparable. There was also a gorgeous movie made of *Traviata* starring Placido Domingo and Teresa Stratas that is once again available on DVD. Anna Netrebko and Rolando Villazon made a MET DVD, and Australia Opera has recently released a performance as well. Among other DVDs is one starring Natalie Dessay.

* * * *

Sources of the images: All images used are from the public domain. The Map of Northeast Asia was based on an image provided by the *CIA World Fact-Book*, a U.S. Government Publication, the image of Admiral Togo and of the Battleship *Mikasa* were both taken from Japanese public sources. Both images were published before December 31st 1956, or photographed before 1946, under jurisdiction of the Government of Japan. Thus these photographic images are considered to be in the public domain according to *article 23 of the old Copyright Law of Japan* and *article 2 of Supplemental Provision of Copyright Law of Japan.*

Will Ryan 2013

ABOUT THE AUTHOR

Will Ryan lives in the Atlanta Suburbs. This is his second book and first novel. For five years he produced a weekly column for a local Atlanta newspaper, commenting on everything from constitutional law to the anniversary of Elvis's death. He served in the military and worked for the Department of Defense for 25 years, then for the Centers for Disease Control in Atlanta for another ten years.

31821372R00221

Made in the USA
Charleston, SC
29 July 2014